CONJURING THE DEMON

THE FINAL CHAPTER OF THE NEWPORT CURSE

JOHN DURGIN

Crystal Lake Publishing
Where Stories Come Alive!

www.crystallakepub.com

Join the Crystal Lake community today
on our newsletter and Patreon!
https://linktr.ee/CrystalLakePublishing

Download our latest catalog here:
https://geni.us/CLPCatalog

ISBN: 978-1-968532-41-3

Cover Art: Matt Seff Barnes
mattseffbarnes.com/digitalart

Cover Design: Ben Baldwin
benbaldwin.co.uk

Layout: Jacque Day
jacqueday.com

Follow us on Amazon:

BY JOHN DURGIN

The Cursed Among Us
(Book 1 of the Newport Curse Series)

Inside The Devil's Nest

Sleeping in the Fire: A Collection of 9 Horrifying Tales

Blank Space

Kosa

Consumed By Evil
(Book 2 of the Newport Curse Series)

What Swallows the Light: Suffocating Skies
(Dark Tide Book 19)

The Devil's In The Next Room

The Envelope

WELCOME
TO ANOTHER

CRYSTAL LAKE PUBLISHING
CREATION

To Todd and Kyle

I think you guys would have really dug this series...

"You can't run from your past. You will end up running in circles. Until you fall back down into the same hole you were trying to escape from, only the hole's grown deeper."
– Max Payne, *Max Payne*

"When there is no more room in hell, the dead will walk the Earth."
– Peter Washington, *Dawn of the Dead* (1978)

PROLOGUE

1999

Patrick Ellis sat in his recliner, sipping from his beer while thinking over how the last few weeks had gone. After relocating to Newport from Keene to fill the vacancy on the force with Mullin moved up to replace Chief Miller, who died during the Halloween Homecoming Massacre the month before, he never expected things to get worse. But they did. *Far* worse. Before coming to Newport, Ellis had only come across corpses at the hands of drugs or old age and fired his service weapon once. Never in a million years did he expect to find himself up to his ass in murders and demon-possessed coven members.

After helping Howie Burke and Bethany Carver survive the botched summoning at the hands of Felix Ruger—or Vorathor, if he was acknowledging the demon *inside* of the wealthy businessman—all he wanted to do was settle down. Let the residents mourn the losses of so many loved ones. Let Howie go back to his mom so they could plan the funeral of Bill Burke after the boy's father had sacrificed himself to allow his son to live. Let Bethany find a loving foster family that could take her in until she was old enough to decide the next step in her once promising life.

Yet Ellis wasn't satisfied. Something still ate away inside him, demanding he continue searching for answers. While the coven appeared to be dead and gone, they left a huge void in the town of Newport that most residents were happy to let die with Ruger. Ellis, however, couldn't let it die there.

One thing he knew to be abundantly clear was that nobody could ever discover the concrete slab that held the two demons and the bodies they possessed. Now that things had settled down around the scene at the factory, Ellis knew he had to do something with the slab. Before he could search for answers, he needed to know that the evil within the makeshift tomb could never get out.

After finishing his beer, he decided now was the time. Where would he hide the evil? He wasn't sure, but it wouldn't be anywhere in town; that was one thing he *was* sure of. He grunted, then pushed himself to his feet, peering out the window. A cold November night stared back at him, and the sight of the leafless branches swaying in the frigid breeze momentarily made him hesitant to leave. Nothing about this adventure appealed to him. *But it had to be done,* he thought.

At the moment, the concrete slab sat strapped in place on the back of a trailer inside the factory. Each day that passed with it sitting exposed to the world was a gamble that Ellis didn't want to take. Although the coven was gone—at least their power was—he knew Ruger's disciples would eventually come looking. Ellis tossed the empty beer bottle in the trash, threw his jacket on, and walked out into the cold night. The chilly air slapped him in the face, but he ignored it and hopped in his white Chevy Tahoe.

As he drove through Newport, he observed the ghost town—a shell of its former self. Even though he had only been around a few months, it was still jarring to see the community this way. Everyone was scared. Mourning. Attending more funerals than parties. When he filled the vacant spot on the force, he wasn't sure if it would be a permanent move or not. But now he had no intentions of leaving Newport. Ellis was determined to make sure the evil that haunted this town for the better part of three decades was gone for good.

Pulling into the concrete factory lot hit like a gut punch. He'd been here a dozen times since that fateful night and still, the dread was ever present. The crime scene had been cleared, but the remnants of it would never go away. The business had yet to reopen, forced to shut down for an extended period while the investigation was underway.

Which was why Ellis knew he needed to get this slab as far away from the murder scene as possible. He'd drive to fucking Maine if he had to. The challenges would be getting it out of the factory and transporting it without being noticed. He had at least been smart enough to have one of the workers move the slab to a trailer, explaining that it was evidence they would need to confiscate. If all went according to plan, he'd hitch the trailer to the back of his Tahoe and get out of town before anyone had a chance to question him.

Behind the windows, the building was dark—a warning for anyone dumb enough to consider coming inside. Ellis knew the demons were trapped within the concrete. But still...the moment he opened the door and stepped inside, the air thickened, suffocating any confidence he had mustered. As much as he wanted to turn the lights on, he didn't want to risk drawing attention. Instead, he grabbed his flashlight and clicked it on, then walked farther into the factory, reliving the horrifying events he had worked so hard to forget over the last few weeks.

Ellis aimed the beam straight ahead, spotting the trailer that was ready to tow. The concrete had thick straps holding it in place, tightened so much that they had no give. He walked up and did a lap around to make sure there were no surprises waiting for him. He knew the concrete had more than solidified over the past few weeks, yet he couldn't help but picture the two demon-possessed figures squirming around inside like an unborn child in the womb.

"You can stay right fucking there," he said to the slab.

After making sure his path was clear to drive in the police SUV, Ellis headed back toward the exit, scanning his surroundings on the way. Never shown in the movies are the bloodstains that remain after a crime scene is cleared. Here, in the dark, one could easily mistake the shapes on the floor as spilled oil, but the copper stench said otherwise.

Ellis opened the garage door and hopped in his vehicle, immediately feeling a sense of protection after being exposed to the makeshift tomb.

I knew I felt it. The closer I got to that slab, the more I felt...off. It leaks out of the concrete. It's floating through the factory.

He shook the thought and started the Tahoe.

When he looked in the rearview mirror, a towering figure stood in the shadows, watching him.

"What the fuck?!"

Ellis spun around, glanced through the back window, but the figure was gone. His heart pounded against his rib cage, and his breaths came in short, violent bursts.

It was hard to see through the partition, especially with the factory lights off, but Ellis knew what the hell he saw.

"Don't let the past get you worked up. Get in and get out," he told himself.

Easier said than done. I still have to get back out to connect the trailer.

He backed into the factory, inching closer to the hitch. Each time he pressed the brake pedal, the dark space lit up red, only adding to the sinister atmosphere. Something about seeing the slab elevated on the trailer like a king on his throne, doused in a blood red glow, nearly convinced him to put the vehicle back in drive and speed out of not only the factory, but right out of Newport and never look back.

If it wasn't for his promise to Howie and Bethany, telling them he would make sure nobody ever found the two monsters sealed in concrete, he might do just that. But those kids had been through too much to give up on them. He had given his word that he would take care of this.

The tow hitch bumped against the trailer, prompting him to shift into park. As Ellis stepped out to connect the two, he thought he heard something. A wet *crack*. A groan. Like shifting stone—or something deep inside it, stirring. Afraid to move, he stared at the slab, waiting to see if he had lost his damn mind.

You know someone was standing there. Waiting for you. Get out now while you still can.

Ellis ignored the thoughts and got to work hooking up the trailer. The slab loomed over him like a living entity, daring him to touch it. To rub it like some twisted genie's lamp. Would anything actually happen if he touched it? Howie had used a stick to carve in some ritualistic symbol Ellis had never seen before, but the boy assured him it would seal the demons inside. He didn't question how a high school kid knew something like that would work. Whether it succeeded or not, Ellis had no intention of making contact with the six-by-eight slab.

With the trailer secured in place, he scanned the factory one last time for any unwanted visitors, half expecting a hooded coven member to jump out at him, then got behind the wheel and pulled out of the building. He made sure the garage was shut and the door was locked, then coasted back onto the main road, periodically glancing in the rearview at his cargo.

Now that he was back on the street, he allowed himself to relax, just a little. He was one step closer to ridding Newport of its curse. One step closer to a normal life. His mind kept going back to what happened inside the factory. Ellis had lost countless hours of sleep thinking about it and what he could have done differently. He turned on the radio, hoping the music would distract him. Scanning through the stations filled with static, he finally found one that was mostly clear and turned up the volume.

"Of course it's fucking country. This damn town..."

As some Alan Jackson song played that he couldn't name, Ellis drove through the back roads of Newport, avoiding the center of town. They were dead to the world at this time of night, which he was both thankful for and a bit spooked by. It wasn't unusual in a small town like this to drive for miles without passing another vehicle, but Newport was especially quiet tonight. As if the town itself knew the weight of what he was about to do.

Up ahead, the town line came into view, letting him know he was entering the town of Goshen. As small as Newport was, Goshen was even smaller. Ellis had only passed through while traveling up from Keene. There was just one convenience store in the center of town, with two gas pumps that appeared straight out of the sixties. While Ellis liked privacy, he couldn't imagine being *this* secluded from the rest of the world.

Houses were few and far between, and those that he passed were completely dark. There weren't even streetlights to provide any extra visibility.

As Ellis drove, listening to the shitty country music, a flash of movement in the rearview caught his eye. It was quick, but he was certain something moved from the trailer. He pulled over in the breakdown lane and watched, keeping his eyes glued on the slab that sat there still as could be, bathed in the red glow of the brake lights. Nothing happened, but he planned to wait it out a bit longer just to be sure. Ellis knew he was on edge, but he'd always trusted his instincts, and he wasn't about to stop.

The song ended, and the DJ started rambling on about the possible Y2K bug coming. While the story fascinated Ellis on any other day of the week, he ignored the DJ, keeping his eyes locked on the concrete. He rolled down the window, breathing in the fresh air to clear his head, listening to the sound of the idling of the engine.

He rolled the window up and prepared to pull back onto the road when the DJ changed the subject.

"The New England Patriots come off their bye this week to face the Jets on Monday night. Let's hope they can improve on that 6-2 record! They've been killing it to start the season…" Static blocked out the DJ momentarily, but then he came back. "Will you die for them… *Patrick*?"

The man's voice dropped an octave, and Ellis stared at the radio, confused.

"Yes…keep going this way. You're almost there."

Ellis couldn't believe what he'd just heard. He swallowed down a dry gulp of fear.

"What the fuck?"

The station returned to static, producing a sound so obnoxious that he reached out and turned off the radio. His ears rang, so he forced a yawn to try and pop them, to no avail.

The sooner he got rid of this thing, the better.

He shifted into drive and pulled back onto the main thoroughfare, picking up speed. The trees flanked each side, leaving the narrow two-lane road suffocated by darkness.

SHZZZZ!

The radio came on spontaneously with the volume cranked, causing Ellis to jerk the wheel, sending the vehicle and trailer fishtailing across both lanes. He slammed on the brakes, coming to a complete stop in the middle of the road. His hands shook as he gripped the steering wheel tightly. He took a deep breath and shot his eyes to the rearview mirror, thankful to see the slab still firmly intact. The static buzzed on. Ellis reached for the dial, then the voice returned.

"You're almost there... Follow the blue signs."

He punched the power button, breaking the knob off the radio.

"Don't be scared, Patrick... Bring the tomb to us, and we will take care of it."

This time, it wasn't coming from the radio. Instead, it was whispered inches from his ear.

"W-who are you?"

As he asked the question, he found himself wanting to listen to the voice. It sounded so soothing. Like wrapping up in a warm blanket fresh out of the dryer on a cold winter day.

Follow the blue signs.

He had no idea what it meant, but he took his foot off the brake pedal and slowly drove forward, staring at the radio, waiting for instructions. Should anyone ask later on what led him to his destination, he wouldn't have an answer. But nobody would, because Patrick Ellis was the only person remaining in Newport who knew what was inside the concrete slab. He was the only one who knew where he was bringing it, even if he wasn't yet aware of the location.

After another few minutes of driving, a blue sign appeared in the headlights on the right side. Ellis squinted as he got closer, finally able to read the sign.

BIRD'S NEST CAMPGROUND
NEXT RIGHT

He made a turn on *Coon Brook Road*, according to the sign, finding it somehow darker than the main thoroughfare. He crossed a small bridge that sat over the Sugar River, continuing until he rounded a sharp turn, then spotted the second sign.

WELCOME TO BIRD'S NEST CAMPGROUND

The anticipation throttled him, and he had no idea why. In his heart, he knew this was the place. As he pulled into the entrance, he noted that the front gate was unlocked. Camping season was well past, so he hoped there wasn't anyone here to give him trouble.

The voice came again, unmistakable. *"No trouble. Only help. Drive to the pond in the back. We will take this problem off your hands."*

Ellis drove down a steep hill, past the home that doubled as the main office for the campground. *All the lights are off. That's a good sign,* he thought. He continued down the dirt road, passing a number of vacant campsites, until he came to the end of the path. The road veered right, but straight ahead through the trees, Ellis noticed a faint glow coming from something out of sight. Even before he knew what produced it, he understood this was where he was supposed to be.

He made a three-point turn, then slowly backed the trailer through the tall grass leading down to the trees. It was tough going, with many corrections along the way. When he reached the tree line, he cut the wheel and backed along the perimeter until he came to an opening. That's when he saw it.

The pond.

The glow pulsated from beneath the surface, giving the water a bright green hue. Carefully, Ellis inched closer until the rear wheels of the trailer sank in mud, then he turned off the ignition and exited the vehicle.

The cold breeze from earlier was replaced by a warm gust emanating from the low fog hanging over the pond. To anyone in a normal state of mind, the whole setting would send them running in the opposite direction. But Ellis wasn't in control of his own thoughts. He was there, inside his head, but he wasn't in charge.

The voice—the *presence*—was in full control.

"Yes. You don't need to do a thing. You don't need to think. Now, remove the straps, lift the trailer bed, and let the tomb sink to the bottom of the pond where nobody will ever see it again."

It all made so much sense. Of course this was the perfect location. Nobody would swim in such a disgusting body of water. And with zero visibility beneath, it would remain hidden.

Ellis got to work loosening the straps, still mindful enough to avoid touching the concrete. Then he moved to the front of the trailer and located the lift button. He held it down, watching as the trailer rose on hydraulics with a slight *buzz*. The slab held in place, and at first Ellis thought it might have melded to the trailer, the hell within molding it to the wood frame. But then it started to slide, slowly, as if the water was pulling it in.

The trailer locked in place, and the concrete tumbled down, smashing off the trailer as it fell into the water with a loud *SPLASH*.

Ellis stood in place, eyes glued to the pond. Shadows darkened beneath the surface, figures surrounding the slab. Multiple sets of algae-covered hands shot out of the water, grabbing hold of the concrete, pulling it below. The sinister form slowly sank until it was no longer visible, disappearing forever.

Vapor rose from the water, then the glow beneath churned brighter, throbbing with a life of its own. Ellis backed away, snapping out of his daze.

"What have I done?"

It was a pointless question. He knew exactly what he did, he just didn't know *why*.

None of that mattered now. It was too late.

The pond bubbled, as if it were the contents in a giant cauldron over a roaring fire.

Ellis had a brief thought that he'd just made a horrible mistake. That he'd been tricked by the demons trapped in the concrete. But it wasn't that. It was something in the water. Something that wanted Vorathor.

"You have done well...we will spare you. Now leave and forget this ever happened. Your life depends on it. If you ever return, you will die."

Ellis listened. After the trailer clicked into place, he got back in the vehicle and started it. Without another look behind him, he pulled out of the pond area, the tires kicking up algae-colored sludge, and left the property. With every foot that separated him from the campground, Ellis forgot bits of what just happened, only recalling flashes of the event like the last remnants of a dream after waking. And although he forgot the voice, forgot the road, forgot the glow, he never forgot one thought as it echoed in his bones. *I've made a huge mistake.*

CHAPTER 1

2024

Howie awoke to the *buzz* of his cell phone on the nightstand. He rolled over and looked at the clock, realizing he'd slept through his alarm. His boss would be pissed off, but he didn't care. While he had a great-paying job that he busted his ass for, he didn't exactly enjoy the work. He was in finance, and not a single day went by that he didn't fantasize about walking out and starting over somewhere else.

The only reason he had gone the safe route was just that. It was *safe*. After a childhood of constant fear, all he wanted was peace.

As kids, he and his buddies made a pact to break into the film industry together. They envisioned making the next epic horror franchise, standing side by side the whole way. That all changed when almost every single one of his friends died in 1999.

He was alone in every sense of the word. No friends. No family. Just a job he hated and a haunted past nobody understood. His dad was brutally killed by a powerful demon. So were two of his closest friends, Ryan Star and Todd Seymour. His best friend, Cory Stevens, was possessed by the very demon that killed his other friends before it was sealed in a concrete slab and never seen again. While they dreamed of making horror movies, the fact that he lived through a real-life nightmare stole the joy of chasing that dream.

He'd told his story once, writing a memoir. Not for fame, but to get it out. That decision cost him Bethany Carver, the last friend he had.

Her whole family had been murdered by the coven, and she blamed her father and his desire to tell the world their story.

Howie felt awful for doing the one thing Bethany worked so hard to prevent from happening. After the book was released, Howie never heard from her again. If he could go back and stop himself from making such a selfish decision, he'd do it in a heartbeat.

But Bethany had moved in with a wealthy foster family down in sunny Florida, away from the nightmare in Newport. She didn't have to worry about finances, her new family made sure of that. Howie had no such luck.

His phone buzzed again, snapping him from his daze.

"Who the hell's calling me this early?"

He grabbed the cell, surprised to see his mother's name pop up on the screen. After everything they had been through together, one would assume they shared an unbreakable bond. That would be the fairytale version. Living happily ever after.

It wasn't reality.

Howie let it go to voicemail. These days, his mom only called when she needed something, and he wasn't in the mood to deal with it right now. After his dad died, his mother got them out of Newport. Howie was grateful that she saw how serious it all was, packing their belongings and hitting the road as soon as the police cleared them to leave town.

They used his dad's life insurance payout to disappear from Newport without selling the house. The real estate market wasn't exactly booming in a town where a serial killer was only the beginning of their nightmare, eventually transitioning to a cannibalistic demon summoned by a sinister coven. While most of the truth remained buried, rumors found a way to spread. Nobody wanted anything to do with the town.

Howie's mom was forced to continue paying the mortgage on their Newport home even though they weren't living in it. As the life insurance money dwindled, Howie saw the writing on the wall and picked up a part-time job to help. He wasn't exactly rolling in money, and eventually, even with his additional income, the emergency fund ran dry.

Luckily for Howie, he was headed to college by the time that happened, racking up student loan debt. And while his mother was forced to move back to Newport, Howie swore he'd never step foot in that town again. He went to a tech college in Concord, living in the dorms even though the drive to Newport was only an hour away.

After he earned an associate's degree in business management—a far cry from film school—he applied for a job at a financial firm, where he'd been ever since. Almost twenty years working for a company that provided incredible benefits and a great income was what many would consider an aspiring career, yet Howie struggled to find the motivation to go to work each day.

It all felt so meaningless.

He had nobody to turn to. Nobody to care for him. He'd dated girls, even thought he'd marry a few of them. But when the dust settled, Howie Burke couldn't allow himself to get close to anyone else. Therapy helped to an extent, but anytime he felt himself growing any form of attachment for someone, he pushed them away.

The phone buzzed a third time. He sighed and picked it up, already regretting it. Nothing good ever came from Newport. He considered answering, but before he could, the call ended. He tossed the phone onto his bed and hopped in the shower, washing his hair quickly. After throwing a shirt on, he picked the phone up and saw that his mother had left a voicemail. He played the message on speakerphone, listening as he put the rest of his outfit on.

"Howie, hon...something's wrong with me. This isn't the flu, Howie,"—she paused, the phone muffled, but he heard her coughing in the background, and then—*"it's...something else. I know you swore you'd never come back. And I promised I'd never ask. But I'm scared. I need you."* She coughed again, and the call ended.

Howie stared at the phone, squeezing his fists so tightly his knuckles cracked. How could she do this to him? When she moved back to their house, she promised him she would never ask him to come back. She promised to always travel to him.

It was as if being alone brought out the worst in her. She started smoking again after years of giving it up. He had never seen her drink once during his entire childhood; now Howie often heard her slurred words when she talked on the phone with him. He couldn't blame her for picking up bad habits. Hell, he had vices of his own. But that didn't stop that perfect motherly image he had of her from changing. He wasn't sure when exactly the tables turned and *he* was the one caring for her, but it had happened in the last few years.

"Goddamnit, Mom."

Howie glanced at the time and knew if he ended up going into work today, he was going to be so late that he'd likely get written up. He made a call to the office and left a voicemail for his manager saying he was under the weather and wouldn't make it in. With that out of the way, he prepared himself to call his mom.

Why are you acting like a kid who just got locked up and is calling his mom to post bail? She's sick. Just call and ask how she's feeling. Make her realize that going to Newport isn't going to happen and that she'll be okay.

It was their deteriorating relationship that made him uncomfortable. He knew that. Because whenever they got on the phone or saw each other in person, both of them pretended like everything was fine. It was A-okay in the Burke family. One thing Howie inherited from both of his parents was the ability to pretend like nothing was wrong, just stay busy and keep his mind focused on other matters. That was another thing his therapist wanted him to work on. You can only plug so many leaks before they build up and burst through the dam somewhere else.

He sighed and dialed her, listening to the ringing until her voicemail picked up. Howie stared at the screen perplexed, ending the call before the beep. She always answered. Maybe a text would work better since she was sick. He opened his contacts and scrolled down to her name, noticing that the last time he texted was two months ago. Had it really been that long?

Howie: *Mom, I'm sorry you're sick. You know I can't come to Newport, though. I'm happy to talk over the phone. Or set up any doctor appointments you need help with. Hope you're doing ok.*

He waited to see if she responded, and just as he was about to give up and go about his day, she began to type.

Mom: …

But that's all that appeared, giving the impression that she was typing a very long message to him for the better part of five minutes.

And then nothing.

The three dots vanished, and no message followed.

"For fuck's sake. Just call me back."

After waiting for a response and getting none, Howie dialed her a second time. Again, it rang repeatedly and was headed toward another voicemail, but then the line picked up.

Instead of hearing his mother's voice, he only heard breathing. Wet. Raspy.

"Mom?"

Silence.

"Mom, are you there? Everything okay?"

Again, just breathing, like she was on the verge of crying.

"Jesus, Mom! Say something, you're scaring me."

"Howie..."

Her voice sounded painful. Just getting his name out was a struggle.

"What's happening? Please, Mom, just talk to me."

"Come home...pleeease."

CLICK.

The phone went dead.

Howie stood in the middle of his apartment, suddenly realizing just how quiet it was. He should have felt relieved when the call ended, yet all he felt was dread. Something was wrong with his mother. And this time, he knew there would be no avoiding Newport.

CHAPTER 2

Howie pulled out of his driveway knowing that he didn't pack enough, but he didn't care. It wasn't just the words his mom said, but the pain those words were drowning in. He thought of all the possibilities. Cancer from the years she'd resumed smoking. Depression. But one thing kept clawing its way to the front of the scenarios. The coven. It had been twenty-five years since Ruger's reign of terror came to an end in Newport, yet not a single day went by that Howie didn't think of the possibility that the possessed coven leader might come back.

It got to the point where his mother asked him to stop bringing it up. While he chose not to be in town, she said she had no choice but to be there, and she didn't want to go about her life waiting for something horrible to happen. It was partly why they stopped talking as much as they had before. Howie was pissed at her for moving back, and she didn't want to be pulled down into the depths of his PTSD.

Familiar landmarks among dead trees blurred past his window. With each mile, his chest tightened—like something unseen was waiting just around the next corner; as if the closer he got, the land knew what awaited him.

He worried that he'd wasted too much time getting ready to leave, unintentionally procrastinating to avoid the inevitable. Knowing it was pointless to try his mother on the phone again, Howie did it anyway, only to get her voicemail once more. He had never felt so helpless. The ninety-minute drive dragged by at a snail's pace.

Finally, the town line for Newport appeared. Howie wanted to vomit. He was pretty sure the sign hadn't been touched since he left, which wouldn't surprise him in the slightest. The town had all but given up after 1999. Overgrown weeds bled onto the edges of the road, the tall, dead grass almost blocking the sign.

Welcome to Newport: The Sunshine Town

"Sunshine, my ass," Howie muttered.

It was just past lunchtime, but the overcast sky could have tricked anyone into believing darkness was right around the corner. Maybe it was, just not the kind of darkness most might expect.

Stop thinking that way. Mom needs you. Just help her get her appointments set up, then leave before anyone even knows you were here, Howie thought.

Driving through the rural sections of town, something struck him. The unchanged parts were eerier than the ones trying to fake new life. Some buildings wore fresh paint like makeup on a corpse. Others had been left to rot with chipped siding, cracked windows, and mailboxes leaning like broken teeth.

Getting closer to downtown, Howie dreaded the landmarks that were fast approaching. Coming up around the corner, the home of his childhood best friend, Cory, would soon appear. Howie hadn't seen the house since he was fifteen years old. The last time he had stepped foot inside was the day he rode his bike there because Cory's mom turned Howie's life upside down by telling him her son was missing. That he was hiding somewhere because he thought he was a danger to the people he loved. And he wasn't wrong. Cory had been possessed by Atahsaia, the cannibal demon that once infested the mind of Jessica Black.

While many in town considered the boys heroes, Howie and his friends felt far from heroic. If they were the good guys, why the hell were their lives ruined for it? Maybe they should have just left the coven alone to run rampant on Newport, sacrificing whoever they deemed necessary. Maybe they should have told the parents and let them all figure out what to do instead of being a group of stupid teens thinking they were invincible because they had never faced a real threat before. Most of all, maybe they should have stayed out of those woods. They were told to never go there, but like most teens, that just made them want to do it even more. But it was all meant in good fun. Shooting a horror movie on forbidden land sounded like a thrill.

They just never expected to release a real horror in their town.

Up on the right, Howie spotted Cory's old house, worn down like the rest of Newport. He wondered if anyone bought the place after Cory and his mom died, but based on the appearance, he assumed it had sat unoccupied for the last twenty-five years. Howie stared at the house as he drove by, remembering all the fun they had in the yard. Jumping on the trampoline, filming backyard wrestling matches... And now it was just long, colorless grass swaying in the breeze.

He considered pulling into the driveway but thought better of it. He'd avoided his memories for so long, he didn't expect to feel anything, let alone nostalgia. And anytime he allowed himself to have a happy memory, it was quickly replaced by a horrible one that bullied its way into his head. As much as he wanted to give good memories the chance to win out, something his therapist insisted that he try to allow, he needed to get to his mother. He grabbed his phone and tried her again.

No ringing. Straight to voicemail. That wasn't normal, not for her. Not even when she was drunk. Or sick. Or pissed off.

Something's wrong.

As he drove past the town library, he noticed the flagpole was bare. Just a rusted hook tapping against the metal in the wind. A town in mourning. Or maybe just one that had stopped caring. It seemed to be a common theme so far. Howie picked up speed, knowing that one of the popular police traps in town was right around the corner. He didn't have time to slow down, so instead he just prayed there wouldn't be a cop sitting there. His car whipped around the corner, almost losing control.

"Careful, moron. You're no good to her dead."

The back roads offered more privacy, and he didn't need to worry about traffic lights, so Howie turned down Breakneck Road, careful to avoid the natural speed bumps that had formed after years of New England winters.

Finally, he reached his street. Not *his* street, not anymore. But in a strange way, it still felt like home. He turned down the road, forcing the awful thoughts away. It didn't take long for him to realize those thoughts were justified. As he pulled into his mother's driveway, he was greeted by flashing blue lights and two Newport police cruisers.

"No... Nononono."

Howie opened his door before the car came to a complete stop, heading straight for the front door. He was so focused on the house that he didn't see one of the officers approaching from the garage area until they almost ran into each other.

"I'm sorry, you can't go inside, sir."

Howie spun around, ready to throw down with whoever had the nerve to tell him he couldn't go in to check on his mom.

"You're not stopping me. That's my damn mother in there!"

"Howie? Howie Burke?"

With all the commotion, it took Howie a second to realize who he was talking to.

"Shawn Seymour... Why are you guys here? She called this morning, sick and scared. I haven't heard from her since."

"You shouldn't go in, Howie. I-I'm sorry. She—"

Howie's vision blurred. His chest tightened. Whatever Shawn had to say, Howie didn't want to hear it. He pushed past the cop and barged through the front door. If something horrible happened, he wanted to find out for himself, not secondhand.

A few EMTs moved about the house, oblivious to Howie, who walked numbly through the place of all his childhood memories. When he reached his mother's bedroom, he heard chatter inside. The *click* of a camera. More talking.

He pushed the door open.

Another cop and EMT blocked the bed, but not enough to hide the white sheet. Howie had seen enough dead bodies to know what that meant.

"No."

The two men turned around, shocked to find someone other than a colleague walking in.

"Oh, sir, you can't be in here," the EMT said.

"It's-it's my mom," Howie stuttered, forcing out the words.

"I'm so sorry. If you could please step outside, we'll come talk to you," the cop said.

"I'm not going anywhere. What the hell happened? I talked to her this morning. She sounded sick, but…"

He knew it before he even arrived. That call was her goodbye.

"We won't know for sure until autopsy results are in—"

"*Autopsy*? There must be some mistake. She can't be…"

Before anyone could respond, a hand landed on Howie's shoulder, and he turned to find Shawn Seymour staring back with genuine sadness.

"Hey man, I'm sorry you had to find out this way. Please, come outside and talk with me. I'll tell you everything I know. And you can tell me about your conversation with her so we can try to piece this all together, okay?"

Howie didn't want to move. Not until he ripped the white sheet off and looked for himself. But he knew that would be a terrible mistake. He hesitantly followed Shawn through the house and back to the driveway.

Shawn cleared his throat. "I haven't seen you in years, bud. Not since before Todd died."

Shawn was Todd Seymour's cousin. The two were close enough to be brothers growing up, and although he wasn't part of Howie's core group of friends, he and Shawn always got along. Now wasn't the time to reminisce, though. Howie needed answers.

"They told me she called 911. What did she say?"

Shawn looked over Howie's shoulder toward the house, as if he didn't want anyone to hear him, then said quietly, "She sounded scared, Howie. Sick, but also scared of something. Do you know if she had been diagnosed with anything? Or been into any drugs?"

"Fucking *drugs*? Are you serious? My mom never even drank a damn beer until she was a widow."

"Sorry. I don't mean to offend you. Please understand I'm just trying to piece this together. What about any diagnosis?"

"No. None that I'm aware of anyway. But whatever was wrong with her, it was bad enough for her to ask me to come home. She knew I'd never come back here. For her to ask... Fuck! I should've come sooner. When she first called me. Maybe I could've helped," Howie choked. Tears broke through the dam of shock, and he had to sit before he collapsed. Shawn let him cry without asking more questions, and Howie appreciated it. How could things have gone bad so quickly? Howie realized just how poor their relationship had been in the end. They went from talking on the phone almost daily and spending holidays together, to forgetting it was even the other's birthday. These past few years, Howie could count on one hand how many times they had been together.

So, maybe she was into something he didn't know about. He didn't want to put the blame on her, but the only time they really interacted was when Howie initiated contact. And she had seemed more...withdrawn. Was she depressed? After all they had been through, he wouldn't blame her. He had only been back in town for less than an hour and already felt the temptation to taste the metallic barrel of a pistol.

"Listen. I don't want to pressure you to think about stuff. You just found out your mom passed. Let the team handle everything in there. As much as you want answers, they won't come instantly. We will get them, and I'll be the first to let you know," Shawn assured, breaking Howie from his bleak musings.

Howie nodded but didn't say anything. He felt like he should be inside, helping move her body. She was his mother, not theirs. The thought of them putting their hands on her body, even as a corpse, left a sick feeling in the pit of his stomach. He had to remind himself they were there to help.

"I can't stop thinking about how we were just talking this morning. Fuck."

Talking. It was more like she was dying inside your phone. Begging for help, and you were too stubborn to come because you didn't want your feelings to get hurt, he thought.

"Where you staying while you're in town?"

"I haven't figured that out yet. I'll probably check in at the motel. Always used to joke that nobody would stay there but druggies and cheaters, yet here I am."

Shawn smirked, but didn't let out the full smile, which Howie assumed was the cop's attempt at remaining professional.

"If you stay there, just lock your damn doors."

"Will do. Thanks again, Shawn. I really appreciate it."

"Just doing my job. Wish we were catching up under different circumstances. I'm off at six tonight if you want to grab a beer. Salt Hill Pub is right in the center of town. I don't think it existed the last time you were here."

Howie shook his head. "A lot's changed, yet nothing has. The bowling alley bar and Plaza Pizza were the only places to get drinks last time I was here."

"Bowling alley shut down over ten years ago. Building was gutted and turned into a walk-in clinic."

"Damn. Well, I'll take you up on that drink tonight. It'll be good to get my mind off all this for a few hours. Until then, I need to take some time to let this all settle in. I'll talk to you later, Shawn. Good to see you."

With that, Howie hesitantly left his mother's house. Just like he had done since he was a child, he tried to keep himself busy, keep his mind off the real world. Instead of coping with the loss, he started thinking of funeral arrangements, who would need to be notified, and how much time he would need to take off from work. He drove through the back roads again, not yet ready to see downtown and the memories that would flood in with it. The motel was close to Cory's old house, but it would have to do. It was the only place of its kind within a three-town radius, and he absolutely would not sleep in his childhood home where his mother had just died.

She's dead. I'll never get to talk to her again. I'll never get to say I'm sorry for how the last few years have been. It wasn't her fault she had to come back here.

Howie shook the thoughts away as he pulled into the parking lot and stared at the sign.

NEWPORT MOTEL
VACANCY

"No shit. Who would stay here?" he muttered.

He sat in his car for the next thirty minutes, allowing himself to cry. When he was done, he double-checked his eyes in the mirror, cringing at the bloodshot webs branching out from his pupils. He opened the door to the lobby and walked in, expecting to see some old, toothless hillbilly about to warn him of the town's evil history. Instead, it was a boy barely old enough to have a job, likely still in high school. His face was covered in acne, and he wore a pair of reading glasses. He reminded Howie of someone who would fit in with his group of friends growing up.

"Hi, I need a room, please."

The boy stared at him with confused eyes, as if Howie was the first customer he'd ever interacted with.

"Sure. Okay. Um, just a second," he said as he turned on the computer. "How many nights?"

"I'm not sure yet. Can we start with three? I'm here...I'm here for my mother," Howie said, not feeling the need to divulge any more information.

"And your name?" The boy had a pen in hand, taking notes.

"Howie Burke. I can pay cash or card, whatever you prefer."

"Okay— Wait, Howie Burke? Holy shit! I read your book and loved it. You're a legend in this town."

Fucking lovely, Howie thought. *I go half my life without anyone recognizing me, and the day I just want privacy, I get a fanboy.*

"I don't know about that, kid. What's your name?"

"Zack. Zack King. I'm sorry, I just... I didn't expect it'd be you. Hope you don't mind me saying I loved your book. Would you mind signing it for me if I bring it in?"

He looked way too excited for Howie to say no.

"Sure, Zack. But do me a favor?"

"Anything!"

"Please don't go around town telling everyone I'm here. I'm sure they'll all see me eventually anyway, but I'm going through a lot right now and could use some privacy."

Zack zipped his lips with an invisible zipper. "Secret's safe with me! Plus, not many people talk to me."

"Thanks. How much do I owe you?"

"For three nights, that'll be one-fifty in total."

Damn. That's one good thing about a small town, I guess. That would be a single night down in Boston, on a weekday.

Howie pulled out his wallet. "Cash okay?"

"Yes, sir. Boss prefers it. Less he needs to give to the tax man, he says."

"Here you go." Howie handed him the cash and put his wallet back into his pocket.

Zack grabbed a room key, which had a red key chain with the number *6* on it.

"Room 6. Out this door, down to your left. If you need anything, let me or my gramp know."

"Thanks."

Zack handed him the key a bit too enthusiastically and smiled.

"Man, I knew you grew up here but never expected to meet you in person. I've always dreamed of making horror movies like you and your friends did."

Howie offered a smile that didn't reach his eyes. "Well, I'm flattered that you think I'm important enough to sign a book. I'll be seeing you around, kid."

Howie exited the lobby and grabbed his bag from the trunk. As he headed toward his room, he spotted a man hunched at the corner of the building. The guy looked sick, sweating through his clothes and mumbling to himself. Howie tried not to make eye contact on the way by, but the stranger raised his head and stared at him.

"We're all one thread. Are you connected too?" the man asked, his stained teeth chattering with each word.

"Sorry, pal. No idea what you're talking about."

He unlocked the door to Room 6, shaking his head, and stepped inside, greeted by stale air and the faint odor of cigarette smoke embedded in the curtains. He slammed the door shut and locked it, then peeked out the window at the weird druggie, wondering what the hell that was all about. Dropping his bag on the bed, he collapsed beside it, staring at the ceiling.

He didn't like how the room made him feel, like it was home to something horrible. As he observed the fading wallpaper and rickety dresser with an old tube TV on top, he was taken back to another time. A time when evil was still consuming the town. Had this room even been renovated since the murders? Doubtful.

He didn't have time to worry about his past. Instead, he had phone calls to make for his mother. But first, he needed rest. He closed his eyes and let exhaustion win out.

CHAPTER 3

1979

Jessica Black slid her fingers over the top of the dresser, pulling them away to find them covered in thick dust. She heard Henry sigh from the bed and turned to look at him.

"I know, it's not ideal. But it's only until the closing on the house, okay? After that, we can get out of this motel and never look back," Henry said.

It was as if he could read her mind. Was she really showing her disgust with the Newport Motel? She knew they only had to stay here for a few weeks while they waited on the house, so why did she find herself getting so agitated? She was being a snob, and she knew it.

"I'm sorry, honey. I know. I think I'm just letting the stress of the move get to me. I'll try harder."

"Girl, anyone in your situation would be stressed. Your parents disowned you. Left you for dead because you refused to follow the same ideology and religion. Told you if you left with me to never show your face again. So don't apologize to me. I get it. And I love you more every day for making that difficult decision."

"I knew they wouldn't take it well. But Henry, I couldn't live another day in that house. They forced it down my throat, the false beliefs that they swore by...made me sick. I want to believe as much as the next person, but they refused to listen to my questions."

"And they blamed me for it," Henry said with a smile.

He was right, but that was partly why Jessica ran off with him. She wouldn't admit it to his face. She loved him, but she was realistic. Had her parents not thrown a fit over her dating a non-Catholic, she very likely would have hung around her hometown longer. She wouldn't have gone for a guy like Henry, who, while cute, really didn't have much in common with her. Yet, he agreed to wait until marriage to have sex. Whether Jessica shared the same beliefs as her parents or not, they had beaten it into her to remain a virgin until marriage.

Henry was a good man. A loyal man. That was far more than she'd ever had before.

"What's the holdup on the house? I can't wait to start our life together," she said.

"Technically, it won't pass inspection yet. The seller is fixing a few minor things, then we should be good to go. Sorry for not keeping you in the loop, but I worried that if you knew of the holdup, you might hesitate to leave. And you needed to get out of there for your own sanity."

"Let's get out of here. I need to see something besides these walls."

Henry laughed and got up from the bed, then walked over and embraced her. He was a strong man—someone Jessica believed could protect her if need be. She let him pull her in, but the warmth of his chest awakened something she'd spent years suppressing. Lust. Guilt. Memories of the paddle in her mother's hand. She recalled her mother smacking her with it for staring at a few guys walking to the beach shirtless. Jessica swore they just walked by and she would have paid the same attention to anyone that crossed her line of sight, but her mother didn't believe her and took her to the basement. That was only one of many incidents that flashed through her mind every time she got the urge to do anything more than kiss Henry.

"Yes. Let's go for a drive, shall we? Check out our new hometown. Newport, New Hampshire. Has a great ring, doesn't it?"

"Sure, but the name doesn't make any sense. There isn't even a harbor or a dock for ships to come into. Seems a bit misleading, doesn't it?"

Henry laughed.

"Never really thought of it that way. Maybe we can find some water. Let me freshen up and then we can go for a ride."

He walked into the bathroom and shut the door, leaving Jessica with her thoughts. She sat on the edge of the bed and scanned the strange room. There wasn't anything in particular that made her feel uncomfortable here, it was more the sum of the parts. The walls were lined with ugly wallpaper that looked as if it had been thrown on in a hurry to hide what lay beneath. It peeled at the corners, and bubbles of air pockets spread across the wall like a rash. There was a door on the far wall that connected to the next room, and while the padlock offered some protection, she would be lying if she told Henry she slept comfortably the night before.

She got up from the bed, which let out a relieved groan as the rusty springs released her weight. It wasn't just the motel. From the moment they entered Newport, it felt like someone or something was watching. She couldn't admit that to Henry, not after how hard he had worked to get them out from under her parents' grasp.

Jessica slid her fingers across the dresser again, landing on a carved indentation. She turned the light on and wiped away the dust, revealing an intricate design. This wasn't just some stupid kid, bored because their parents were bringing them through a small town. Whoever carved it did it with intention. She shook the thought and opened the top drawer of the dresser, finding a Bible. It might as well have been a snake ready to pounce and latch its fangs into her. She slammed the drawer shut.

Mother would be smiling right now. She'd tell me no matter how hard I try to escape the Lord, he would be right there, waiting.

Something skittered behind her, and she whipped around, heart slamming in her chest.

There was nothing there, but she knew she had heard it. Like something tapping across the wall. Even with the lamp on, the room remained dim, the light shining only enough to display her surroundings with minimal detail.

She sensed movement, *behind* the wall. Hesitantly, Jessica approached the withered wallpaper, keeping her eyes locked on it. And then there was more movement, this time on the floor. She looked down as a small mouse scurried past her. Jessica screamed and jumped onto the bed.

"What's wrong?" Henry yelled, rushing out of the bathroom.

Jessica pointed to the mouse, which was reaching the far wall, squeezing into a small hole.

Henry chuckled.

"Babe, it's just a mouse. You've seen things far worse than that back home."

"I know, I'm sorry. This place just creeps me out. Something doesn't feel right here. Can't you feel it too?"

Henry furrowed his brow.

"Nah. You're traumatized, Jess. How could you *not* be? Everything will be just fine. I promise. Trust me?"

Jessica hesitated and slowly nodded. Henry again came over and hugged her. He was so patient with her. So understanding of her past and what she'd been through.

"Can we *please* get out of here?" Jessica asked.

"Yep. Let's go before the killer mouse comes back," he joked.

Jessica punched his arm and laughed.

They exited the motel, and Jessica glanced toward the lobby, hoping the owner wasn't in there. He creeped her out, holding stares a few seconds too long. She didn't feel the need to say anything to Henry, not yet at least.

As they got into Henry's black Oldsmobile Cutlass, Jessica glanced back toward their room once more. Room 6. The only comfort she got from it was that it wasn't close to the lobby. The thought of that man being right next door, between the walls like that little mouse, was an image she tried to force from her mind. She needed to remember that this was a good thing. They were homeowners and on their own for the first time in their lives. They were going to get married, have a family. So why didn't she feel happy? It wasn't just the PTSD of her family trauma.

It's this town. Something is wrong with this town.

CHAPTER 4

2024

Howie rinsed his face in the grimy sink. It didn't help. The nap was necessary, but he always found himself more exhausted after waking up. The bags beneath his sockets sank into his face, and his bloodshot eyes stung from crying. He was a grown man, yet the town brought out all his childhood insecurities.

The odds of someone recognizing him were high, considering so many residents of the small town never left. He helped end a curse, then proceeded to burn the town down with his memoir. No one cared why he wrote it, only about what it said.

He didn't just write about the events leading up to the Halloween Homecoming Massacre, he announced to the world that for over a hundred years, a coven hid in plain sight, controlling the town and its residents. He wrote about their influence, the sacrifices, the summoning. When Howie set out to write the book, he had intended to focus mostly on his friends; seeing it as a way to honor them and make sure they weren't forgotten. If he sold out, he wanted to make sure he did it for a good cause. While the royalties from the book helped him pay off his student loans, it still wasn't worth it. Not enough to ruin the only close relationship he had left—his friendship with Bethany.

There was a good chance some drunk yokels might decide to pick a fight with the former wonder child, and Howie wasn't quite sure he was ready for such interactions. A broken man would go to drastic measures, and he was as broken as one could get.

He grabbed his keys from the nightstand and gave the motel room a once-over, then went to the parking lot. He snuck by the lobby, making sure the kid didn't see him again—he'd experienced enough fanboying for one day—and hopped in his car. As he pulled out onto the main road, he drove toward downtown, feeling dread growing inside him with each passing mile.

While a child's memory differs from that of their older self, they don't know it in the moment. They live their lives one second at a time, taking it all for granted. And they should. Why would they think any other way when they have the rest of their days ahead of them? As Howie drove into the heart of Newport, this was what occupied his mind. The places he passed every day as a kid were still there—barely. Hollowed out, drained of life.

He wasn't sure what he expected to see, but this was somehow worse than anything he could have imagined. With the sun setting behind the town hall, it only added to the gloominess on display. Half the businesses he remembered from his childhood had shut down, vacant for years. Others were still there but on life support. And the only things new, to him at least, were some discount chain stores that every low-income town had these days.

As he passed the small plazas, he spotted the bowling alley—or what was left of the building—up on his right. Sure enough, it had been gutted, and instead of seeing the *Sunset Lanes* sign, there was a cheap-looking walk-in clinic sign in its place. Howie wasn't sure how he felt about it. On one hand, a place where so many memories transpired was erased from the town's history. The number of times he and the guys went there on a Saturday night to bowl, play some arcade games, and get a few hours of freedom was gone. On the other hand, the last time he stepped foot in there was the night his life changed forever. The night Cory became possessed and killed his first victim.

Two figures stood in front of the clinic, and Howie had flashbacks of coven members wearing all black robes, hiding in the shadows. Then one of them lit a cigarette, and instead of a black robe, the man was wearing a ragged hoodie and had sunken cheeks. He locked eyes on Howie's car passing by, holding his gaze for an uncomfortable moment. Howie didn't get a good look at the guy as he drove by, but had a fleeting thought: *Maybe it wasn't a cigarette, after all. The man appeared sick.*

Finally, Howie spotted a sign.

SALT HILL PUB

He turned into the parking lot, shocked to find it so full on a random weeknight.

"Nothing better to do in this town."

The pub was located in a three-story brick building, giving it an industrial look. Howie parked his car in the first available spot and headed for the private entrance, which was an exterior set of stairs that entered the second floor where the bar was located. The first floor was the main restaurant, where families could avoid the drunk patrons bitching about their boring lives and politics.

A middle-aged man and woman stood on the outside balcony smoking, and it sounded like they were arguing about something. As Howie climbed the stairs, they shushed one another and plastered on fake smiles. He nodded and walked inside, holding his breath through the nicotine haze. Loud music blared from a jukebox in the corner, some modern country song that Howie had been able to avoid. As expected, the place was full, and the tables spread across the room were mostly occupied. He scanned the bar and spotted Shawn signaling him over, already nursing a beer.

Howie moved through the crowd, avoiding eye contact with everyone.

"Saved you a spot! How's it going, bud?" Shawn yelled over the music.

"Damn, you didn't tell me it would be so busy here. Happy hour or something?"

"It's always happy hour here."

Howie smiled and sat on the stool next to him.

"Feels so weird being back. I saw the bowling alley. You weren't kidding, the place looks like a meth clinic."

Shawn side-eyed the bar before allowing himself to laugh.

"Gotta be careful of the company you say that in around here. Drugs are a real problem these days. A lot different from when we were kids."

"Sorry to hear that. Can't imagine that makes your job too easy."

"I signed up for it, I suppose." Shawn gave Howie a tight, sympathetic look. "Hey, I'm really sorry about your mom, man. She was a good lady."

Howie wasn't ready for the shift in conversation yet and was thankful that the bartender came over to break up the chat.

"What can I get you to drink, hon?" asked a middle-aged woman who looked like a three-packs-a-day kind of person.

"Um, I'll take a Sam Adams, please."

"Coming right up. You're getting yourself into trouble hanging around this one. Don't let the badge fool ya. Shawn can drink with the best of 'em," she said.

"Last I checked, drinking wasn't illegal, Val."

The bartender chuckled and headed to grab Howie's drink.

"So, what have you been up to all these years?" Shawn asked.

Howie shrugged. "After college I stayed down in the Concord area, got a job in finance. It's boring as hell, but it pays the bills and lets me live a simple life."

"Wife? Kids? Pets? You just a loner?"

"Just me and my thoughts. What can I say? I don't want to burden anyone with my broken ass. My therapist says I need to get over that and open up to people more. Blames it on survivor's guilt. She's probably right."

"Sounds like a boring life to me, but I get it. After all that shit, you've seen enough excitement for a lifetime."

"You can say that again," Howie muttered, taking a big gulp of his beer.

"But it wasn't all bad, right? Our childhood? I know we weren't as close in those high school years as we were in middle school, but we had a lot of fun back in the day. Todd sure made us laugh a shit ton."

"Yeah, he did. You remember that time in ninth grade when we slept in a tent out back of his house on his birthday, and snuck into his parents' alcohol supply?"

"How could I forget? He got drunk off his ass and pissed in the corner of the tent like it was a fucking urinal," Shawn said with a grin.

"Thought you were going to kill him. The rest of us thought it was funny as hell, though."

"Best part of it all was that when he pissed in the corner, he didn't see my shoes there. I woke up the next morning hungover as shit and slid them on, only to have his dank piss soak into my socks."

They both laughed, then sat in silence for a few moments just sipping their beers, before Shawn's expression hardened.

"You know, the main reason I became a cop was because I never felt we got the answers we deserved. About Todd's death, and all that stuff that happened with Jessica Black."

"Newport was as corrupt as they come," Howie said, instantly looking around to see if anyone was eavesdropping. Some habits never went away, no matter how long he'd been gone.

"*Was*? I'm sure you've looked around. This place is a shell of its former self. Sure, there aren't any witches or covens lurking around town, but they're still up here," Shawn said, tapping on his head. "They haunt this town. And because of that, I have a massive drug problem on my hands that literally nobody else seems to care about. Gone are the days when our holding cell was reserved for Tommy, the town drunk. I'm lucky if I don't have some junkie drooling and pissing themselves in there on a nightly basis."

While Howie noticed a few residents he'd come across looking pallid, he didn't realize how bad the problem was. It broke his heart to know this once quaint little town was nothing more than a product of depression and trauma that he was responsible for.

"You say you became a cop to get answers for Todd's death. What is it you're looking for?"

Shawn took a final swig from his beer, then slammed the empty glass mug onto the bar top. He flagged the bartender, Val, to grab him another before looking into Howie's eyes.

"After Jessica and the coven, you had to deal with Ruger, am I right?"

Howie nodded, glancing around again out of habit. Nobody seemed to be paying them any attention.

"After you left, things didn't end there, at least not entirely. The town went dark and just waited for the media to eventually latch on to the next story of the week. Obviously, I was just a kid still, couldn't really help. But I was up Patrick Ellis's ass looking for answers. He was a good cop. I know he helped you and Bethany escape. I don't think he was involved with the coven, but I do think he was hiding something from the town."

"What do you mean? And you said he *was* a good cop. Did he...did he die?"

Howie hadn't thought of Ellis in years. His mind took him back to the memory of Ellis fighting off the demon; bringing the corrupt police chief, Mullin, to justice; and helping make sure he and Bethany had all the help they needed after it was all said and done.

"No, no. Nothing like that. Ellis retired a few years ago. He put in his twenty years and called it a day. Stubborn bastard didn't want to, though. The department basically had to force him to retire. He took over as chief after you left. We threw a big retirement party for him here, and you would have thought we forced him to watch his parents have sex."

Howie chuckled.

"You're Todd's cousin all right."

"I miss that bastard every day."

"You and me both, man. I miss the whole crew. Cory, Ryan, Bethany."

"Have you talked to her at all?" Shawn asked.

"Not in years. We were pretty close for the first few years after she moved. My dumb ass thought maybe we'd end up getting married someday. A love out of shared trauma, you know? But then I went and wrote a book about everything, and she wouldn't talk to me for years. I tried to explain why I did it, but she couldn't differentiate me from what her dad tried forcing her to do. She blames him for the family dying because he saw dollar signs and wanted her to talk. I don't blame her. It was selfish of me. No matter how much I try to defend myself."

"Well, I know plenty in town weren't too happy about it. But I'm sure Todd was up in heaven fist pumping that he was a character in a book."

"I think that's safe to assume about him," Howie joked. "I have to say, one day back here and I don't miss it. No offense."

Shawn laughed.

"None taken. I wouldn't be here either if I wasn't trying to get my own form of therapy by cleaning up the town. Pretty obvious after one lap around the place that I'm doing a bang-up job, huh?"

Howie shook his head. "I don't think this place is fixable, Shawn. No matter how hard you try."

"It's not just this town. It's the whole fucking area. Your mom probably didn't say much about all of the incidents these past few years. Sure, Newport has been out of the limelight, but that doesn't mean weird shit isn't happening. Over in Sunapee this past year, a girl who'd been abducted as a baby by a nasty old lady, who was apparently a witch, escaped and told the local PD about all the kids she'd killed. And that wasn't the worst of it. The old bag fucking *ate* them. Can you believe that?"

"Jesus."

The word *witch* hit too close to home for Howie. Was this lady linked to the coven? He wasn't sure he wanted to know.

"Yep. And then over in Goshen, at Bird's Nest Campground, six people were brutally murdered, including most of the family that owned the place. Some real estate agent who got mixed up with the mob. At first, investigators assumed the murders were linked to the crime family. But cut-up body parts of the mob boss, along with two of his workers, were found chopped up in the back of a pickup truck that had caught fire. The real estate agent's wife and son survived, and she got him the hell out of Goshen the moment she was allowed to leave.

"She's been trying to get the pond drained that's at the back of the campground, saying something evil lived inside it and drove her husband to kill. As crazy as it all sounds, nobody local wants to step foot in that campground now. It was always rumored to be haunted anyway. You ever hear anyone call it 'Devil's Nest'?"

"Of course. I worked at Northstar Campground as a kid. Bird's Nest was our competition, but then some weird shit went down, and it went out of business."

"That's right, you've been gone so long, I forget you're a local," Shawn said. "Anyway, enough of that dark shit. You've got enough on your plate. Here's to your mom." Shawn lifted his glass to Howie's.

They continued to catch up, reminiscing about childhood memories and drinking late into the night. It wasn't until Shawn got up to use the restroom that Howie allowed himself to really scan the bar in detail. Maybe it was the buzz allowing him to relax for the first time since passing the Newport town line, but he found himself wanting to take it in. Most of the faces were unfamiliar to him, either new to the town since he left, or aged to the point they were now unrecognizable. But then he felt eyes on him. It took him a minute to find the culprit, but sure enough, someone sat in the far corner of the bar, watching him. It was a man, about the same age as Howie.

Did I go to school with him?

He didn't recognize him from this distance, but he didn't need to wait long to find out his identity. The man, who was mostly masked in the shadows of the bar, got to his feet and made his way toward Howie.

Here we fucking go. I knew this would happen.

As the man got closer, his features pieced together, and Howie realized he did know who it was. Twenty years hadn't been kind to everyone, far from kind to Derrick Patten. He was one of the star athletes when Howie was in school. One of the lucky people who wasn't slaughtered on the podium of Halloween Homecoming at the hands of Jessica Black.

"Howie fucking Burke. Whatever have we done to allow you to grace our presenccce?"

The former jock was shit-faced, and Howie thought he might fall over and pass out before he uttered whatever inevitable insult he came over to deliver.

"Hey, Derrick, how have you been?"

"Oooh, now he wants to be *friendly,* huh? This town was ruined cuz of you," Derrick said, placing his hand on the bar to steady himself.

Howie glanced at the clock, wondering where the hell Shawn went. Maybe if a cop from town showed up, Derrick wouldn't be flexing his beer muscles so much. Derrick took a step, getting close enough that Howie could smell his garlic and beer breath.

"Trying to keep some vampires away?" Howie asked sarcastically.

"What? What the fuck you talking about, author boy?"

"Nothing, never mind. Just leave me alone and I'll be on my way in a minute, okay? I don't want to be here any longer than I need to."

Derrick sloppily lashed out with his hand, grabbing Howie by the collar.

"That's right. And we don't want you around here anymore. Would hate to see you join your ma prematurely, *Howwwie*."

"What the fuck did you just say?"

Howie shoved Derrick, slamming him against the bar, sending a few empty glasses shattering to the floor. Patrons nearby scattered to avoid being caught in the cross fire between them. Derrick raised a fist to strike, then Shawn caught his forearm.

"Easy does it, Derrick. No need to spend a night in the think tank and wake up in your own piss."

"Get the fuck off me, pig!"

"I'll let that one slide. Now get the hell out of here before I escort you out in cuffs."

Derrick lifted his upper lip in a snarl, bouncing his eyes lazily between Shawn and Howie, then turned and stormed through the crowd of people to exit the bar.

"You good, man?" Shawn asked.

"Yeah...figured I had some of that coming to me when I came back."

"Jesus. I can't even take a piss without you starting a fight, huh?"

"Oh, please! Says the guy who was starting shit with kids every day in school. How'd they let you become a cop after all that anyway?"

"Small town. They were desperate," Shawn joked. "Now let's get the hell out of here before you pick a fight with someone else."

Howie wasn't going to argue with that. As they both exited the bar, Howie caught someone else staring at him from a table in the back. He knew he had never seen this man before because it was impossible to forget a face like that. The man didn't just stare at him, but *through* him with piercing green eyes that followed him all the way out, unblinking. His stare sent a chill down Howie's spine.

Who the fuck was that?

Howie shook the thought and followed Shawn to the parking lot, ready to leave this night behind. He couldn't ignore the feeling that those eyes weren't just watching, but waiting.

CHAPTER 5

Derrick Patten kicked a rock across the parking lot of Salt Hill as he stumbled toward his blue Ford F-150. Howie fucking Burke. The prick who unleashed the curse, then cashed in on the blood it spilled.

Part of him felt bad for making the jab about Howie's mother, but beer often led to loose lips for Derrick. He knew he had a drinking problem; the whole *town* knew he had a drinking problem. He heard the whispers about how he was well on his way to being the next Tommy, the town drunk. If he didn't smarten up, his remains might also be found ripped to shreds on the railroad tracks just like Tommy's. The trains didn't come through this way anymore like they did back in the nineties, but Derrick wasn't so sure it was really a train that left Tommy's body looking like roadkill.

Derrick climbed into his truck and turned the key so the radio came on. He knew he shouldn't drive, but he didn't feel like calling for a ride. He wasn't ready to go home yet anyway. Instead, he'd take a ride, try to cool off after Howie got his rage boiling.

Derrick pulled onto Main Street and headed in the opposite direction of home. He couldn't afford to lose his license again, so he'd take the back roads and drive carefully. That didn't mean he couldn't enjoy himself, though. He was a professional trained in the art of driving with a "road buddy" in hand. He leaned over, keeping his eyes on the lane, reaching blindly for his cooler. *Slow and steady,* Derrick thought. He cracked the top of his cooler and grabbed an ice-cold can of Natty Ice.

"There she is. Come to Daddy."

He popped the tab and took a long gulp, letting out a belch so deep it made his eyes water. The truck swerved, just slightly, but enough to make him look in the rearview mirror and make sure a cop wasn't tailing him. Luckily, it wasn't a cruiser behind him, just some old station wagon, black like a hearse. All good, it wasn't the po-po. That's all he cared about. Derrick thought back to the bar and the sarcastic remark Howie made about his garlic breath. He breathed into his palm, pulling his head away quickly.

"The fucker was right. Damn, that's bad."

As he rounded the wide turn that headed toward Sunapee, he noticed the headlights of the station wagon closing the distance behind him. Whoever it was decided to ride his ass. He sped up, trying to put some distance between them, only to have the black car match his speed.

"The fuck? That you, Howie, you prick?"

Up ahead, Derrick spotted the old "Make-out Mountain," a parking area that overlooked the Sugar River below. Back in high school, every-one used to drive up here to drink and make out with their girlfriends or boyfriends. Derrick had done a lot more than that here. More than one girl had given him road head in this very spot. He decided to pull in and see if this asshole followed. Maybe he'd get that fight in tonight, after all.

He turned his signal on and pulled into the dirt lot, careful not to bump the front of his truck on the rock wall against the edge of the drop-off. He'd scraped up the front bumper more than once during drunken joyrides, but avoided it this time. He turned his truck off and waited, and sure enough, the black station wagon pulled in as well. Only they didn't park in a spot next to Derrick. They parked directly *behind* him. The station wagon's headlights blasted through his back window, temporarily blinding him. He shielded his eyes, muttering under his breath. He considered taking one more sip of his beer before getting out, but he wanted to meet this asshole head-on before they got the upper hand.

Derrick whipped his door open so hard it almost bounced back against his kneecap as he went to climb out. Whoever was messing with him would regret it. He stood over six feet tall and while he'd lost the chiseled frame of his youth, that strength was still there, hiding behind a slowing metabolism and years of Natty Ice.

"You got a fucking problem? That you, Howie? Get the fuck out and let's do this!"

There were no streetlights to aid his failing eyes, but he realized the driver's side window was tinted, completely hiding the lone occupant from view. Derrick stood a few feet away from the station wagon, squeezing his fists together, ready for a fight. But nothing happened. The car just sat there, idling quietly.

He prepared to step up and open the driver's side door, yank the bastard out, and kick the shit out of them. But then the door slowly opened, revealing the faint outline of a tall figure sat behind the wheel. Derrick couldn't make out any of his features except a pair of green eyes. Eyes that had no business giving off such a glow, at least not human eyes. They reminded him of a cat staring into a flashlight beam.

"Mr. Patten, why the hostility? I come in peace," a deep yet oddly calming voice said.

"You're about to be in *pieces* is more like it. Step out and face me!"

Derrick hoped his aggressiveness intimidated the man, but instead, the shadowed figure laughed. It was a guttural bellow, rattling from deep within the man's chest.

"As I said, I'm not here to fight you. But if you continue threatening me, you'll quickly find out that I am far too much for a simpleton like you to handle."

"What the fuck did you call me?"

The anger was still there, but fear was starting to overwhelm his drunken bravado. This wasn't a normal man in front of him. It sure as hell wasn't Howie Burke. The man remained quiet for an uncomfortable minute. Every second that passed felt like another cinder block placed on his chest. Then the man stuck one leg out, revealing black dress pants and leather shoes, but that limb might as well have been a black mamba snake slithering toward Derrick. He slowly backed away, then froze in place as the green-eyed man stepped out of the car and rose to his full height. It was rare that Derrick Patten had to look up to meet anyone's eyes, but this guy was at least three inches taller than him.

Somehow, the man's facial features remained unclear, except those green eyes that produced a simmering glow. He was bald, with tattoos covering his scalp. Derrick knew he was drunk, but that didn't explain why some of the tattoos appeared to move along the base of the man's skull.

"Wh-what the fuck are you?" he whimpered.

"I'll ask the questions, Mr. Patten. You'll know what I allow. No more. No less. Do you understand?"

Derrick didn't respond. He couldn't if he wanted to. His eyes remained fixated on the man's scalp, avoiding eye contact. Something about those green eyes... Whenever he looked into them, he lost control of himself. It was like they hypnotized him, relaxing him when he knew damn well there was nothing to be relaxed about.

"I'll take that silence as an understanding. My first question to you, Mr. Patten, is really quite simple. Do you want to live, or do you want to die?"

Derrick was terrified. But he also grew up in a house where someone threatening you needed to be taught a lesson. He wasn't about to forget that, no matter how creepy this bastard was. He stepped forward, trying to catch the man off guard by throwing a right hook, expecting to connect with the jaw. Instead, he felt the sudden sensation of his fist swinging through a blank space, and he stumbled forward, his drunken state consuming any sense of coordination. His face smashed off the station wagon, sending a jolt of pain through the side of his head.

Did he really just dodge me that easy?

Derrick wobbled to his feet and turned back to face the man, who was no longer smiling. The eyes pulsed, latching on to him and not letting go. He couldn't move his body. Derrick tried to breathe, only to feel his airways tighten. How was this possible? The green-eyed man was doing this without laying a finger on him. Just when he thought he was going to suffocate to death, the invisible viselike grip on his throat vanished. He quickly took in lungfuls of air, impelling some last-ditch effort to fight.

Derrick lunged at him, but the man didn't just dodge him, it was as if he knew his next move before it even happened. Like he was inside Derrick's head. As Derrick landed face-first on the ground, something drilled into his head. A voice.

"I do know your next move. We still have use for you, but defiance needs to be punished."

"Impossible. Get out of my fucking head!"

He attempted to get to his feet, drunkenly wondering what the voice meant by having "use" for him.

Derrick turned, but he was too late. The man grabbed him by the throat with unnaturally long fingers that wrapped around his neck like a noose. Derrick clawed at the man's hand, but it was pointless. His strength was inhuman.

"Time to take your punishment, Mr. Patten. The pain will be intense, but the good news is you will pass out before I am done."

"N-no... please!"

The man lifted his free hand, raising it close to Derrick's face. The fingernails were disgustingly long, stained yellow. He thought he saw green algae caked beneath them. And then he tasted it. He tasted it because the man's fingers were entering his mouth.

What the fuck is he doing?

Those long nails slowly pressed into his tongue, one on the top, another beneath. Both tips forced into the meat.

Deeper.

Derrick faintly heard his tongue starting to separate from his body, but the sound was mostly blocked out by his own screams.

Blood poured from his mouth, covering the man's black shirt. He paid no mind to that. His smile had returned, revealing a set of crooked teeth behind narrow lips. Derrick felt himself losing consciousness, just like the man promised. But the pain did not let up.

"Look into my eyes, and this next part might not hurt as badly," said the voice in his head.

This time, Derrick obeyed. The glow relaxed him.

Then his tongue was torn free from his mouth, followed by a fountain of blood. The last thing Derrick saw was his own tongue writhing on the gravel like a dying worm.

Then everything went black.

CHAPTER 6

1979

Jessica wasn't sure where Henry was taking her, but he had stopped at a gas station in town and grabbed a twelve-pack of Budweiser, then said they were going somewhere relaxing. After cruising through Newport, he pulled into a parking area that overlooked the river. Henry had been told that the spot had a beautiful bird's-eye view overlooking the forest below, where the trees were plentiful until they ended at the flowing water.

"What is this place?" Jessica asked.

"Oh, just a hangout spot. One of the local kids told me about it when I asked about must-see locations in town. Apparently, all the high school kids come park here to drink and make out. Hence the name, 'Make-out Mountain.'"

"Henry Black! Did you think you could woo me into making out with you tonight?"

"I suppose I was hoping. More than anything, I just want you to feel safe and relaxed. I know none of this has been easy on you. I wanted you to see the good side of life." Henry gestured to the vast wilderness and clear night sky beyond the car windows. "Look how beautiful it is up here. Let's get out and explore."

Jessica opened her door and immediately felt the cool evening breeze. The sound of running water below was lulling, and the last of the summer crickets chirped a symphony. Henry was right. It was beautiful. He came around the front of the Oldsmobile and handed her a cold beer. Before she met him, Jessica had never even held a beer in her hand, let alone drank one. Her parents said it was a sin, and her father called it "the Devil's piss."

It took some real convincing from Henry for her to have her first drink. When she did, she spat it out, saying her dad's description was justified. Henry laughed, telling her it would grow on her and that it would help loosen her up a bit. She knew she could be uptight and boring, and until she met him, she didn't know any different. But Henry Black showed her how to enjoy life; to not take everything so seriously. And he was right; the taste had grown on her. Same with the feeling it gave her.

"This is our new home, Jess. A fresh start."

She listened to the flowing river and closed her eyes. It had been a long time since she felt this relaxed. When she opened them, Henry was on one knee, looking up at her with a ring in hand.

"Oh, my goodness, Henry!"

"Jessica, I want to spend the rest of my life with you. I know I did things a little backward, buying the house and moving you out here first, but I can't imagine a day without you. Will you marry me?"

"Yes! Yesyesyes!"

Tears welled up in her eyes, this time from joy. Henry jumped to his feet and grabbed her in a bear hug, lifting her off the ground and spinning. Her beer fell from her hand, slamming off the gravel and sending a fountain of Budweiser into Henry's face. They both laughed, then Jessica kissed him, tasting the beer dripping down her new fiancé's mouth.

Fiancé. I'm engaged!

They kissed under the moonlight for the next few minutes, until another set of headlights came around the bend. Jessica pulled away, her natural instinct in any intimate moment.

"Relax, babe. It's okay," Henry whispered soothingly.

Jessica watched the car, hoping it would keep driving, but she didn't get her wish. The vehicle's turn signal came on, and they pulled into another parking space.

"Talk about ruining the mood," she said.

"Are you kidding me? Nothing could ruin my mood right now. We're getting married!"

They hugged again, but Jessica found herself too distracted by the other vehicle to fully enjoy it. She didn't want to say anything to Henry, afraid to disappoint him. But he knew her. Her rigid posture gave it away.

"I'm sorry, Henry. Can we leave and be alone again?"

"Sure. Let's at least have a celebratory drink first. I'll grab you another."

He opened the back door of the Oldsmobile and pulled out two more cans. As he approached Jessica, he glanced at the other car, a red Ford Escort, and saw the driver's door opening. A man stepped out, rugged looking, and Jessica's first thought was that he was here to pick a fight. But then she saw a beautiful girl in the passenger seat, who spotted Jessica and waved enthusiastically. Jessica returned the gesture as Henry handed her a beer and eyed the other couple.

"Evening," the man said.

He wore a flannel shirt with suspenders, his jeans covered in dirt and wood shavings. A brown beard covered his face, but he looked young.

"Good evening!" Henry answered. "Beautiful place, huh?"

"Yessir. I take it you're not from around here. Everybody and their mama within a two-town radius knows about this place," the man joked.

Henry chuckled, but Jessica wasn't sure she trusted the guy yet. Could her mother have sent people from the church to look for her? She wouldn't put it past the devout woman.

"We're new in town. Name's Henry Black," he said, reaching out with his free hand to shake the stranger's.

"Bill Burke. I've lived in this shithole my whole life. What brings you folks to such a no-nothing town?"

"Fresh start, I suppose. As a matter of fact, I just proposed to Jessica here right before you pulled in!"

"And?"

Henry stared back at Bill confused, and Jessica wondered whether this man was being genuine or not.

"What did she say?" asked the girl from Bill's Escort.

"Oh! She said yes! We're getting married!" Henry exclaimed.

The girl clapped excitedly and got out of the car. She ran over and wrapped Jessica in a hug, which she wasn't prepared for. Physical contact of any kind made her uncomfortable, even from Henry. She had worked really hard to adjust to receiving hugs from him, but not from strangers. Still, she wasn't about to let that ruin this moment. The girl must have felt how uncomfortable Jessica was because she let go and backed away with a smile.

"I'm sorry! I didn't mean to be weird, you don't even know me. I'm just excited, is all. Bill and I are engaged too. And"—she rubbed her belly, which Jessica realized was bulging out—"we're expecting! The fact that I'm showing this much at only six months tells me this babe is going to be a tank like their daddy."

"Well congratulations to you, too, then!" Jessica said, trying to hide her judgment of this woman for being pregnant before marriage.

Remember, not everyone shares the same beliefs. That's why I'm here in the first place, she reminded herself.

"Thank you. And here I am spilling the beans before you even know me. My name's Sheila. Welcome to Newport."

Jessica noticed the men standing by the overlook, carrying on a conversation about something. They were laughing and joking, bonding over whatever guys liked to talk about. For the first time since arriving in town, Jessica started to feel welcomed.

"I'm Jessica. Nice to meet you."

"So, have you guys found a place to live yet?" Sheila asked.

"Yes. Henry bought a house as a surprise, but it's not quite ready. We're staying at the motel in town while we wait for it to pass inspection."

Sheila frowned. "Wait...you're staying in that grimy old place? How long until your new home is ready?"

"Supposedly real soon. I hope by tomorrow. I really don't want to spend another night there. It gives me the creeps."

"For good reason! I've heard too many stories about that motel. Strangers passing through going missing. Deals gone wrong. Just be careful there. The rest of the town ain't so bad once you get used to it. I'm not originally from here either. Bill was born and raised in Newport. He said there are certain people to steer clear of and everything will be okay."

"Like who? That sure would be nice to know!"

Sheila laughed, but Jessica saw it in her eyes. The first bit of concern. Sheila looked over at Bill, who was still chatting with Henry. Both men were drinking a beer and leaving the girls to themselves.

"Do you believe in witchcraft?"

"I'm sorry, what?" Jessica laughed. "I grew up in a really religious home, so that sort of thing would be considered blasphemy to my parents. Why do you ask?"

"Because, there's a coven in town. Both men and women members, and they practice witchcraft. Most of them are harmless and keep to themselves, but I still don't trust them."

"Are there any certain people I should know about?" Jessica asked. Curiosity stirred in her chest.

"How about this? You and your fiancé come over for dinner tomorrow night. Maybe even stay at our place if you're comfortable, so you don't have to sleep in that hellhole again. We'll tell you everything you need to know about this town. Bill might get mad at me for talking about it out in the open."

Jessica liked the sound of it, but she still wasn't sure. She didn't know these people yet. While she considered herself a good judge of character, the interaction was far too brief to make sure. Before she could answer, Henry and Bill approached them, both laughing hysterically at something.

"Sounds like you two hit it off." Sheila smiled.

"Well, we both love sports and hate the government, so that's a good start," Henry chuckled.

"I was just telling Jessica that they should come over for dinner tomorrow and maybe stay the night so they can get out of that shady motel, which is where they're staying at the moment. What do you think, Bill?"

The men looked at each other and shrugged their shoulders in unison.

"If it's an excuse for you to make your beef stew, I'd let the Son of Sam sleep over," Bill said.

"Oh, stop it! That's not funny, Bill! It's too soon for a joke like that."

"Relax, hon. It's been two years."

"That doesn't mean there aren't other sickos out there doing the same thing. Copycat killers. Hell, it was only a few states over," Sheila said.

"Fine, fine. Probably not the best thing to joke about with people we just met." He laughed.

Jessica didn't find the idea of making light of girls dying very funny. Again, she forced herself not to pass judgment on something she normally would have. Henry didn't seem to care about the tasteless joke and continued drinking his beer with a grin plastered on his face.

"Tomorrow night sounds great. We really appreciate the hospitality, guys." Henry beamed.

"Least we could do after crashing your proposal. Maybe these girls can start wedding planning together, because I sure as shit don't know what I'm doing," Bill said with a chuckle.

"He literally just proposed, Bill. Give them time to soak it in for a night, will ya?" Sheila rolled her eyes.

Bill waved her away jokingly. "We'll stop by the motel an hour before dinner and you can follow us to our place, sound good?" he asked.

"Absolutely. Thanks again," Henry said.

They shook hands, the girls hugged, then Bill and Sheila got in their car and left, returning the overlook to only the sound of running water.

The temperature had dropped a few degrees since they arrived, and Jessica wrapped her arms around herself to keep warm.

"Henry, do you really think it's a good idea to go stay with people we just met?"

"It can't be any worse than that motel, can it? Plus, the killer mouse can't get you there."

Jessica playfully pushed him on the chest. She wanted to let her guard down and make new friends. They both seemed nice. But Sheila's words about the coven made Jessica uneasy. There was more to it than that, though. Something Jessica hadn't even admitted to Henry yet. Nobody knew the real reason Jessica left the church. Nobody knew the things she studied in her own time that planted doubts about her faith deep inside her core.

Jessica told Sheila she wanted to know who to look out for with the coven. In truth, it wasn't fear that led her to say that. It was curiosity. She wanted to know more about the dark arts. While everyone at church praised God and worshiped the Scriptures that told his story, nobody in the congregation had experienced the things Jessica had, for she had studied witchcraft. Her mother found out and planned to shut her off from the rest of the world and get her help.

She couldn't bring herself to tell Henry the whole story. Not yet. She didn't want to ruin this amazing night. He must have read her mind because he walked up and kissed her passionately before pulling away.

"I have a fiancée. You hear that, Newport? I HAVE A FIANCÉE!" His voice echoed off the land below. Thankfully, the overlook wasn't near any residential areas.

"Yes, you do. And I'd rather not have my future husband arrested for public indecency. Let's get out of here, *fiancé*."

Henry hugged her again, then they both got in the car and left. As they drove through the dark, windy road, Jessica couldn't get the thought of the coven out of her head.

Maybe Newport wouldn't be so bad, after all.

CHAPTER 7

2024

People packed into the funeral home quietly, full of somber expressions and heavy hearts. Howie wasn't sure he was ready for the funeral. It felt like just yesterday that he got the call from his mother to come home, and now he was sitting in the front row, supposed to greet all these people he hadn't seen in years, if he'd even met them at all. Many familiar faces hadn't changed since his childhood, while others were unrecognizable.

With no other close family left alive, Howie sat alone. It was a painful punch to the gut, a reminder that this town had taken everything he cared about. It was all a blur. He didn't even remember the conversation with the funeral home director or discussing that her casket would be up on the stage behind the podium that the priest approached. Why was a priest even here? His mother wasn't the slightest bit religious. Howie wanted to get up and say there must be a mistake.

Yet, here he was, glued to his seat and unable to move. He hadn't expected to feel nothing, but his grief sat numb and silent, as if it had been shot full of novocaine and was as dead as his mother's corpse inside the casket.

Howie continued to zone out, ignoring the crowd filing in. He didn't snap out of it until the priest began to talk from the podium. Finally, he forced himself to focus on the words, just wanting it to be over. The priest looked familiar, but he couldn't put a name to the elderly man.

"We are gathered here today to remember and honor the life of Crystal Burke. A mother, a friend, a neighbor. Her story is written not in books or Scripture, but in the memories of those who knew her; in quiet moments, in acts of kindness, in the love she gave freely and often."

Why does this man look so familiar? Howie thought.

"Loss is never easy. It comes to all of us, and we each carry it in our own way. Today is not just about saying goodbye. It's about holding on to the pieces of her that still live in each of you. In her son, Howie. In her community. In the simple, everyday things she touched."

I can't do this. Something isn't right. This doesn't feel right!

"As we say farewell, let us remember: our grief is a reflection of love. And that love doesn't end here—"

A muffled thumping sound behind the priest cut his sentence short.

The crowd murmured, the volume picking up as everyone tried to figure out where the sound was coming from.

THUMP!

Howie felt sick to his stomach. Behind the priest, the casket jolted a few inches, almost falling off the display. Something was moving *inside* the casket.

The crowd erupted in screams, yet Howie remained planted in his seat, watching it all unfold.

"Look at me, Howie!" the priest yelled.

Howie stared into the holy man's eyes, and that's when he realized who he was looking at.

Father Grimes. The priest who died in 1999 while helping him in his battle against the powerful demon named Vorathor. But Father Grimes was dead. He shouldn't be here.

"Howie... love doesn't end here... but neither does death!"

The casket lid flew open, leading to more screams behind Howie. He turned to the crowd, seeing them for the first time with any clarity. Mixed in among the crowd, he spotted his friends. His *dead* friends. Todd, Ryan, and Cory all sat together, their bodies in different stages of decomposition. Cory smiled, revealing blackened gums, and gave Howie an exaggerated wave.

"Turn around, Howie. You don't want to miss the show!"

Howie whirled around, refocusing on the casket. A figure draped in a white sheet slowly rose to a sitting position. He recognized the sheet as the one covering his mother's corpse when he had entered her bedroom. The figure slowly stood, completely covered on the top half, but once the legs appeared, Howie had to fight down the gorge. Pale limbs covered in saggy flesh. Thick green veins branched across her skin, wrapping around and traveling up beneath the sheet. The figure turned to face the crowd.

A sticky, algae-like substance dripped from beneath the cloth, and Howie didn't want to know where it was leaking from. While he couldn't see the top half of the body, he could see the sheet moving back and forth as it forced raspy, labored breaths. And then a hand appeared, slithering out like a predatory snake. It was also covered in protruding green veins. The hand gripped the sheet.

The sheet was torn off, revealing the top half of Howie's mother. Her eyes were hazy orbs filled with a gray cloudiness resembling a poisonous gas. Her hair clung to her cheeks, as if the body was absorbing it. She raised her bony finger and pointed at Howie.

"You brought the curse back into this world, Howie. And now we all rot for it!"

Howie wanted to say something. Anything. But he couldn't speak. He sat, paralyzed, eyes locked on this monstrous version of the woman who gave birth to him. Who raised him and tried her best to protect him when his dad abused him. This wasn't her.

He noticed that the screams of the crowd had stopped, but they weren't silent. They were all talking in unison. Chanting.

"It comes from within. It comes from within. It comes from within."

He knew he shouldn't take his eyes off his mother, but he had to see if his friends were still there. As soon as he looked, he wished he hadn't. He *wished* he could claw out his own eyes—anything to unsee what was now burned into his brain.

They were all still there, but their eyes now matched his mother's. This time, it wasn't just his friends still in childhood form, but all of the victims from the Halloween Homecoming Massacre. Mr. Carl, the old football coach, chanted with the right side of his head caved in, brain matter leaking out and down the side of his face. Next to him stood Bethany's dad, full of countless knife wounds decorating his white dress shirt.

"It comes from within. It comes from within. It comes from within."

As the chanting increased in volume, Howie sensed movement from the stage and turned just in time to see his dead mother in a crouching position. She leaped from the stage, gliding like a shadow with wings. She landed on the pew in front of him, leaning in only a few inches from his face. Something squirmed beneath her skin, burrowing deeper.

"It comes from within! Everyone will die!" She pounded on the pew, splintering the wood with her gnarled hands.

Howie screamed, long and loud.

He jumped up in bed, panting and drenched in sweat. Someone was pounding on the door to his motel room.

Daylight crept in through the crack of the curtain. Somehow, he had slept through the night. His head throbbed as the pounding at the door returned, louder this time.

Howie rubbed his eyes, his pulse still racing. He sat on the edge of the bed, trying to steady his breath as the pounding continued, sending a throbbing jab into his temples each time.

KNOCK! KNOCK! KNOCK!

He thought he might throw up, the bile inching closer to his throat.

"All right, all right!" he shouted, wincing at the sound of his own voice. It scraped at his throat like shards of glass.

He crossed the room and yanked the door open. A blast of sunlight hit him like a slap to the face, and standing just outside was the lanky kid from the front desk, Zack King, holding something tight to his chest as if it might shield him.

It was a book.

His book.

"Hey, um, sorry to bother you," Zack said, his voice cracking. "You were screaming. I thought maybe something happened."

Howie sighed. "Just a nightmare."

Zack nodded, but he didn't leave. Howie wanted him to get lost. "Right. I can't imagine going through what you did. I'm sorry, I didn't mean to bother you. But since I'm here, I brought my copy of your book."

He held it out with a pen like a peace offering, the worn paperback bent at the corners, multiple sticky notes poking out through the pages. Howie stared at it a second too long before reluctantly taking it.

"I've read it three times. I know some people in town hate what you did, but...it kind of makes me feel like I'm not crazy. Like some of the stuff happening around here isn't just in my head."

Howie sighed, uncapping the pen. "What's your name again?"

"Zack. With a *K*."

"To Zack," Howie muttered, as he scribbled a quick message and signed his name. He handed it back, trying to force a smile. "Stay out of trouble, kid."

Zack gaped in awe at the signature as though it was something sacred, before carefully closing the book. "Can I ask you something?"

"Sure."

"Do you think the coven's really gone?"

Howie looked down at the book in Zack's hand for a long moment. He wanted to say yes. He wanted to believe it. But after the dream he'd just had, the answer stuck to his throat like wet tar.

"I hope so."

Zack nodded slowly, his smile fading. "Yeah, I guess that's better than a no." He hesitated, then added, "Some of the kids I went to school with, they're dead now too. Not from demons or witches or anything. Just...drugs. They're everywhere. Feels like something's still wrong here, even though it's different."

Howie leaned against the doorframe, hit with another bout of nausea. He needed to take a cold shower. "Everyone has their own way of dealing with trauma, I suppose. That's what my therapist constantly tells me anyway. But something's always been wrong with this town."

Zack swallowed hard and took a step back, hugging the book to his chest.

"Well, thanks for signing my book. And, uh...I hope the nightmare wasn't about the coven."

Howie didn't answer. He just nodded and gently closed the door. As much as he tried to forget about this town and everything it stood for, there was one thing still clear as day. The nightmares were no coincidence.

CHAPTER 8

After showering, Howie still felt like shit, but at least a little better. He dreaded what he had to do today. Not only did he have a meeting scheduled with the funeral home, but he had to go to his mother's house to clear out some things, and in doing so, he knew those fresh wounds wouldn't be healing anytime soon.

He hoped he didn't come off as too much of a dick to Zack. The kid was nice, and even though the memoir had brought nothing but misery to Howie over the years, he'd be lying if he said there wasn't a part of him that appreciated the positive attention. Over the years, he'd received countless threats—anonymously, of course—but never had he received any sort of positive fan mail from anyone in Newport. The rest of the country ate the story up, assuming it was fictitious and a hoax, receiving a number of comparisons to *The Blair Witch Project*, one of the movies that inspired him and his friends the most when they were teens.

If they only knew.

All for a quick buck too.

You did it to stay out of Newport, not to get rich and famous.

And look where that got me. It got me a ruined relationship with Bethany, a distant relationship with my mother, and right back here anyway.

He tossed his towel on the bed and stared at his reflection in the dust-covered mirror. Same tired eyes. Same invisible scars that nobody could see. It didn't matter how many showers he took, he'd never be able to wash this town off him.

After throwing some clothes on, Howie exited Room 6 and headed to his car. He glanced into the lobby, wondering if Zack was still working. The kid deserved an apology for the way Howie treated him. But instead of the scrawny kid sitting behind the front desk, Howie spotted the back of a bald head. A large man, by the looks of it. He assumed it must be Zack's gramp that he had mentioned. Not that he could judge a personality by the back of someone's dome, but the air seemed to be thicker just at the sight of this guy, with his hunched posture and lack of movement. Howie decided he'd wait to go to the lobby. He got in his car and pulled away.

He dreaded stepping foot inside his mother's home. There would likely be some fond nostalgia, but he knew there would be just as much heartbreak. There were certain things he never wanted to see again. Unlike the previous drive through town, Howie didn't pay any attention to his surroundings, focused only on what awaited him. It wasn't just his mother's things, but the entire family's.

Why am I doing this to myself? Just hire a damn company to clear it out.

He knew the answer to that, though. He wasn't just going to pack up her things. Howie wanted answers. His mother had been a healthy, aging woman. And while he knew it wasn't uncommon for something to come on quickly and devour someone's body from the inside, this didn't feel that simple. She sounded terrified on the phone.

Before he knew it, Howie was pulling into the driveway, and the grief hit full force. Something as simple as seeing her car parked in its usual spot outside the garage, waiting for her to come out and drive into town, nearly overwhelmed him with grief. She'd never drive this car again. It was just another example of how the world moved on, going about its business.

He took a deep breath and grabbed the spare key to the house, then headed for the front door. He was immediately hit with the familiar homey scent that he had taken for granted his entire life, but it was mixed with an unpleasant smell—decay. Even though they had taken her body soon after she passed, it didn't prevent death from leaving its mark.

Thankfully, his mother kept the house pretty clean, so there wasn't much of a mess. He went from room to room, packing belongings into boxes, avoiding the bedrooms as long as he could. Not just his mom's but also his. He decided to save his mother's for last and went into his childhood room.

It was a time capsule, completely unchanged from 1999.

Howie scanned the room, moving his eyes left to right. Movie posters that the old video store in town used to give away when they took them down covered the walls: *Austin Powers, Scream 2, I Know What You Did Last Summer.* He couldn't help but smile, remembering how excited he and the guys were to see each of them. Sitting in the theater, laughing so hard at Dr. Evil that they were all crying.

He moved to his dresser, finding a framed picture of himself, Cory, Todd, and Ryan sitting on his bedroom floor playing a round of *GoldenEye* as his mom snuck a candid shot. Before he knew it, tears escaped, sliding down his cheeks. He expected to cry once he reached his mother's room, but he hadn't expected the pain of losing his best friends to resurface. He had spent countless years in therapy to help get over that trauma.

Howie grabbed the photo and raised it to get a better view. They were all so innocent. So happy. He could picture the conversation while they were playing, like it was yesterday. He realized he didn't have any photos of his friends back at his apartment and decided he'd take this one with him. If there was one part of Newport he wanted to remember, it was when he and his friends were at their happiest.

He would come back to his room later. It was time to go where his mother had died. He needed answers. Her door remained shut, and part of Howie hoped to open it and find his mom relaxing, watching *Jeopardy* after dinner and telling him to come watch it with her. But he knew that wasn't what awaited him. The bed would still be there, but it would be empty. All that remained were messy sheets where she took her last breath before the EMTs rolled her out.

Howie sighed and opened the door, revealing a dark room that matched his mood. He turned the light on and immediately something felt off. He couldn't explain why, whether it was a smell, an item out of place, or just the possibility that there was still something in there. He hadn't noticed it the night he rushed in to find her body covered by the white sheet.

The same sheet she wore in my nightmare.

He tried to shake the thought, but all that did was remind him of the repeated chant in that dream.

It comes from within.

What the hell did they even mean by that? Maybe it was foolish, but it felt like a warning. Remove all the theatrics and nightmare-inducing imagery, and they were telling him something. It was all the people he cared about, chanting the same thing over and over. If it *was* a warning, was the other stuff his mom said also true? Did she really blame him for her death? He hoped not.

Focus on why you're here, he thought. He had already been in the house for hours, and the day was getting away from him. He checked his watch, realized it was past lunchtime. His stomach had no problem reminding him of that fact. Before he went to grab a bite to eat, though, he wanted to go through the bedroom. He forced himself to focus, burying the feelings deep inside.

For the next twenty minutes, Howie shoved anything he could into boxes, only briefly taking the time to see what the contents were. He crammed all her clothes from the closet that he planned to donate into trash bags. It wasn't until he had the task completed that he picked up on another smell, unfamiliar and foreign. Whatever it was, it stung his nostrils, making his eyes water.

"What the hell is that?"

Howie pulled his shirt over his nose, crouching in front of the closet. His first thought was that she had left something to rot, but beyond the odor, there was a sweeter tang to finish it off. The light from the room didn't reach the closet, so he couldn't see much inside. He got on his knees and crawled inside, then pulled out his cell phone and turned the flashlight on. In the far corner, he spotted a jewelry box and immediately knew the smell was coming from within.

"What were you hiding in here, Mom?"

He grabbed the box, afraid to open it but knowing he had no choice. Turning it over in his hand, he found a latch and popped it open. The lid lifted a few inches, and the smell intensified. Howie jerked his head back.

"Oh, shit!" he said, turning his face to the side.

Howie got to his feet and brought the box to his mother's bed. He wasn't sure what to expect when he opened it, but what he discovered inside was the last thing he would have guessed.

A syringe, a rubber strip, and a vial half-full of some thick, green substance. He stared at it, confused. He wasn't an expert on drugs—he hadn't done anything worse than smoke weed in college, so he wouldn't have known if he was staring at heroin or infected snot. But it didn't take a druggie to realize that odor was deadly.

For some strange reason, Howie lifted the vial close to his nose. A single inhale forced the bile straight up his throat and into his mouth. He ran to the bathroom and threw up in the toilet, then rinsed his mouth in the sink. His appetite was completely lost.

"What the fuck is that stuff?"

"Inject it. You'll never feel stronger."

The voice came from nowhere, as though it was just floating in the air around him. He spun around, half expecting someone to appear in the closet. Perhaps a coven member hidden in the shadows, covered by their black hood.

The room was empty. Could just smelling this shit make him delusional? Howie went back to the bed where he'd left the strange substance. Whatever it was, he knew it had to be connected to his mother's death. The chief medical examiner had deemed there was "no foul play," and maybe that was technically right. Still, Howie would put money on this stuff having something to do with it. Before he knew what was happening, he was popping the cover off the vial.

"Drink it. We will numb your pain."

"I'm losing my damn mind. It's not real."

Howie brought the vial into the bathroom and dumped it in the sink. He watched as the tacky substance slowly slid down the white porcelain toward the drain. Before it all disappeared, Howie grabbed his mom's toothbrush and stuck the end of it in the goo. When he pulled it away, a string of green stuck to it, stretching like thick mucus that reminded Howie of the Gak slime he had as a child.

None of it made sense. His mother didn't do drugs, and sure as hell wouldn't put something like this in her body. And what was that voice? He needed to talk with Shawn, let him know what he had discovered. And while the last thing he wanted was food right now, he knew if he didn't eat soon, he'd pass out.

Howie grabbed his phone and texted Shawn.

> **Howie:** *Need to talk. Free for lunch?*

> **Shawn:** *Hey man. I was just about to grab a bite myself. Meet at Plaza Pizza in an hour?*

> **Howie:** *Sounds good. See you then.*

With that out of the way, Howie went to turn off the bathroom light, and as he did, he watched the last bit of slime disappear down the drain.

CHAPTER 9

1979

Henry and Jessica pulled into the driveway behind Bill. Henry wasn't sure what he expected, but it wasn't a mobile home. The front yard was full of logging equipment, wood chips scattered across the driveway at the side of the house where Bill's tractor-trailer sat.

Nightfall had come early this late fall evening. He slowed the car, tires crunching over the packed-gravel driveway.

"Here we are. You sure you're up for this?" he asked Jessica.

"Yes. Nice and quiet too. That's one thing I can definitely get used to in this town. There's something quainter about New England. It was quiet down south, too, but it was different in the Bible Belt. Even though it wasn't busy, it was like God was always looking over your shoulder, hearing your thoughts, making you ashamed of every wrong move. You know what I mean?"

"You don't need to worry about that stuff here. It'll take time, but I promise you'll eventually feel free of it all," Henry said, reaching over and rubbing her thigh. "Let's get in there before they think we're creeping on them."

Henry led the way, and before they even made it to the front door, Sheila opened it and greeted them with a warm smile.

"Hi, guys! So glad you took us up on our offer. I never get to cook for anyone besides Bill. Come in, come in," she said, stepping aside so they could enter.

Henry was grateful to be out of the cold night. It was an added bonus that the food smelled wonderful. His stomach growled loudly.

"Smells amazing, Sheila." And by the growl of his stomach, it agreed with him.

"Hope you like beef stew! It was my mom's specialty dish, and she passed the recipe down to me."

"Sounds wonderful right now," Jessica said.

Bill came into the living room from the hallway.

"Care for a beer?" he asked.

"Yes, please," Henry answered.

Bill waved him toward the kitchen while the girls sat on the couch. The aroma in the house made Henry's mouth water. He sat at the table while Bill grabbed a few beers from the fridge and handed him one before sitting across from him.

"How you guys adjusting? I'm sure it's a culture shock coming from the South," Bill said.

"Getting there. We'll be better once we can move into our house. Right now, it still feels like we're just traveling. Meeting you guys was a blessing, though. Jessica felt so alone leaving her home."

"Still can't believe you landed on Newport, New Hampshire, as your new stomping ground." Bill laughed.

"The farther away we got from her family, the better. We don't have to worry about them here."

"That bad, huh? My dad was a mean prick who beat the shit outta me. I was stuck here, though. No money, no real job besides working with him out in the woods. It's all I knew. Best thing that ever happened to me was that asshole croaking," Bill said.

"Damn. Her parents were more mentally abusive than physical, but her mother wasn't afraid to raise her hand. They just tried to push, push, push with religious crap. I'm all for someone having faith, but nobody should be forced into it."

"Amen to that." Bill held out his bottle to cheers with Henry. "Well, I'm glad you got away from all that. I gotta say, though, this place has plenty of its own problems. Sheila mentioned she told Jessica about the coven..." He ended the sentence early, and Henry realized he was waiting for his reaction before deciding which direction to move the conversation.

"Yeah... I don't know what to make of that. Is it just some peaceful group with their own beliefs? Are they dangerous?"

"Well, it depends on who you ask. Anyone that's lived here their whole life is tied to them one way or another. I had a grandmother who was a member. She was as mean as my daddy. They are known to many locals as The Withered Tongues. Rumor is that years ago, they used to cut out the tongues of their members. They trained in witchcraft and could communicate with each other using their minds. I don't know how true that is. My gram had her tongue, and she used it to say some nasty shit. Supposedly, they softened a bit through the years. Who knows what to believe? Either way, most try to stay clear of them."

"That sounds insane. Do you believe in that stuff?"

"Logic would say not to, right? Problem is, you grow up your entire life where people believe in it, and it kind of burrows itself into your brain. Like the legend of a local boogeyman but instead, it's an entire group. They call themselves a coven but seem more like a cult, if you ask me."

"Lovely. Anyone to watch out for in particular?"

"We have our suspicions, but they remain very private. Could be anyone in town. And they have connections from the top of the food chain all the way to the bottom. Cops, teachers, business owners, you name it. There are a few people you need to be careful around. Brian White, the principal at the high school. Joshua Miller, one of the new cops in town. They're both obvious. Anyone that is in either of their circles of trust, *I* don't trust."

Henry stared at his new friend, mouth agape. This group wasn't just full of backwoods crazies. These were people with power.

"The goddamn principal? How's that even allowed? Why would anyone want their kids led by a lunatic?"

"They don't. But the coven is powerful, Henry. Just keep that in the back of your mind and you should be okay."

It's not me I'm worried about, Henry thought, recalling a memory of Jessica reading a book by candlelight, whispering some chant under her breath.

He knew that although Jessica didn't dedicate her life to religion anymore, she wanted something to believe in. The reason Henry didn't find Bill's story entirely crazy was because he'd seen the books Jessica read. She was the perfect target for these people to brainwash. He had to be extremely careful allowing her around them. It wasn't something she could help—the need to know there was a greater power, whoever or *whatever* that was. If she didn't find *something* to believe in, she would spiral into feelings of depression and loss, unanchored and drifting. Henry found himself stuck in the middle of it all. Should he allow her to explore everything and choose what worked for her? Or should he try to influence which direction she headed in? If he did that, he was no better than her parents.

"Look like your dog just died, man. I didn't mean to make you uncomfortable. Let's drop this shit and talk about something more enjoyable, huh?"

Henry nodded, but before they could change the subject, Sheila and Jessica entered the kitchen, giggling about something. Bill used the interruption to shift the tone in the room.

"What's so funny in there? Sheila telling you my darkest secrets?"

"Please, Bill. No need to make our new friends think different of you," Sheila teased. "We were just sharing life stories. Can you believe Jessica is waiting until marriage to do anything sexual with Henry? She's an innocent virgin girl!"

Jessica playfully punched Sheila on the arm.

"Hey! I told you that in private. I see who I can trust to keep my secrets."

Henry felt his cheeks go hot as he squirmed in his chair. He wasn't one to discuss his sex life, or lack thereof, with anyone. Especially people he had just met.

"We don't judge, honey. I just don't want us corrupting you! As you can see, I've had a bun in the oven for months, and we aren't married yet," Sheila said.

"Okay, I'd be grateful if we could change the subject now." Jessica smiled.

After an uncomfortable laugh, the group continued to get familiar with one another, realizing that the relationship was more than just a convenient one. They actually enjoyed being around each other. And the food was amazing. Henry wished he could take the win after a week of losses, but in the back of his mind, he kept thinking about the coven. About Jessica and her need to find something to believe in. He saw the spark in her eyes when the topic came up. She played it off as just morbid curiosity, but he knew otherwise. He couldn't tell Bill and Sheila about Jessica's obsession with the occult, or that she had jumped in with both feet and was busy trying to learn more.

It was mostly innocent, but Henry knew she wasn't getting the fulfill-ment she needed. There was also the creeping feeling that maybe New-port wasn't an accident, after all. Maybe something called them here, a greater power that Henry couldn't sense, given his lack of belief. Bill must have sensed Henry's unease, clearing his throat to get everyone's attention.

"To new friends. Who would have thought a group of adults would meet at Make-out Mountain like a bunch of horny teens? We're happy to have you guys here."

"And we're happy to be here," Jessica said.

They toasted, continuing to drink well into the night. Sheila con-sumed nothing but water and mocktails, but the rest of the group was buzzed up nicely. While Sheila was the only one who wasn't drunk, it was her filter that evaporated first. Henry had hoped Jessica's past would remain buried, knowing it would likely come up sometime, but not the first time they all hung out.

"So, Jessica, my little mystery girl. We know enough to put some of the pieces together, but not enough of the details. What made you abandon religion? Was it an isolated event that made you want to run away?" Sheila asked.

"Sheila, come on. It's none of our damn business," Bill said.

Jessica waved a hand. "No, it's okay. Really. I haven't talked about it with anyone other than Henry."

Henry felt an uneasy pain in the pit of his stomach. The last thing he wanted right now was to bring down the night by digging up unnecessary evil. Jessica was lucky to be normal after what her parents did to her. He could tell Jessica wanted to talk about it, though. Maybe it was a sign that she was trying to move past it all. Henry decided to bite his tongue and see where it went.

Jessica pushed some of her food around her plate. "I think I started having doubts pretty early in life. I'd question a lot of what was discussed in church. Just to my parents at first, but that ended horribly. When I was six, I was forced to sleep outside on the lawn with only a thin sheet and no pillow because I told my mother something didn't make sense during Sunday services. Instead of having a normal conversation about it, she said I was questioning God and that He needed to keep a close eye on me. That meant being out in the open, surviving the night when it was cold enough to bring a frost."

Sheila rubbed Jessica's hand on the table, then squeezed it.

"That worked for a while. The problem was that I couldn't fake my belief. I had to talk to someone about it, so I went to my friends from school. I still don't know to this day if one of them told their parents what I said, or if my parents overheard the conversation. Either way, they found out. I got plenty of physical punishment—the switch was a go-to for my dad—but they wanted to break me mentally." A haze overtook Jessica's eyes, as if lost in the memory—or revisiting a nightmare. "They wanted me to give in and believe. So, they pulled me from school, shut me off from the outside world, and homeschooled me."

Bill shook his head in anger and sympathy. "Belt for my dad. People like that...there's a special place in Hell for them."

Jessica flinched at the mention of her parents and Hell in the same sentence. She composed herself though, forcing herself to finish speaking.

"I never got to see my friends again. My mom and dad told me my doubt was killing their souls and that God was punishing the whole family because of it."

"You poor girl," Sheila said, a tear slipping down her cheek.

Jessica's returning smile was bitter, but appreciative. "I wish that was the worst of it. They went on to say I had a demon influencing me, that to have so much doubt meant I was consumed by evil. They were too ashamed to go to the church and ask for an exorcism, so they thought they could beat it out of me. My mom tried to shout in my face and tie me down, demanding that the demon leave my body. My dad beat me until I was unrecognizable, and I almost caved and lied to them. But that's the funny thing about all of this. I feared that if I lied, then God truly *would* punish me and my family." Her chuckle was anything but mirthful. Dark and resentful, and there was pain laced in the tone. "Imagine that, being beaten for not believing, yet believing *just* enough to keep telling them I had doubts. When they thought none of that worked, they went to close friends who were even more extreme than they were."

"Shit, how's that even possible?" Bill asked.

Henry sat in silence, wanting the conversation to end, but knowing Jessica had to get it out. It was therapeutic for her, and the fact that she felt comfortable enough to tell Bill and Sheila was proof that his own opinion of their new friends must be correct. They were trustworthy.

"Well, they brought me to a dark basement and tied me up like I was some monster. My parents and their friends would read Scripture to me for hours on end, only feeding me if I recited it with them, *and* if they believed I meant what I recited."

"That's no way to live. I'm so glad you got out of that nightmare," Sheila said, her voice tight with anger on Jessica's behalf.

Jessica nodded. "I am too. My parents wanted me to break up with Henry, but I refused. The beatings got worse. Eventually, Henry feared for my life, so we snuck out of town late one night and got as far away as possible."

"And here we are now," Henry added with a forced smile. Jessica smiled back, equally forced, but there was clear fondness and affection.

"Thank you so much for sharing your story, honey," Sheila said, then got up from the table and hugged Jessica. They both cried together.

"Oh!" Jessica suddenly exclaimed, pulling away from Sheila and looking down at her pregnant belly.

"The baby just kicked!" Sheila exclaimed.

Bill jumped up from the table and went to his soon-to-be wife, placing his hand on her stomach. Jessica felt a twinge of longing, but also hope. She couldn't wait to start a family with Henry.

"Well I'll be damned! That's the first time I've felt the little shit! You must be good luck for the baby, Jessica," Bill said with a proud grin.

She glowed, running her hand back over Sheila's belly one last time before sitting back down. For a moment, Henry let himself believe everything would be okay. That maybe they really had found the fresh start they were looking for. But as he reached for his beer, a strange chill slid down his spine, tightening around him like a snake strangling its prey. Because the way Jessica beamed at feeling the baby kick was the same as when they were discussing the coven. And the deep-seated fear that something brought them here returned. He felt like they were being watched. Observed.

Henry glanced toward the window, half expecting to see someone staring back.

Nobody was there.

Just the empty night.

CHAPTER 10

2024

Andy Hixon parked outside the gate, reading the worn sign with its chipped, blue paint.

WELCOME TO BIRD'S NEST CAMPGROUND

Except **BIRD'S** was crossed out and defaced with the word **DEVIL'S**. He shook his head, hoping his employee, Joe Wise, a.k.a. "Wise Man," didn't see the graffiti before he drove through the open gate. He looked over at Joe and was relieved to see him still scrolling aimlessly through his phone.

Andy drove through the opening and down a steep driveway as a large house came into view, its appearance a reminder that disaster had struck recently. The porch had collapsed, leaving a pile of debris strewn across the driveway. But they weren't here for the home, they were here for the pond. Andy passed the house and continued down a dirt path until he came to the end of the road, then carefully turned the truck around. He kept his eyes on the rearview mirror, backing the hydrovac toward the tree line and the green pond. In the passenger seat, Joe continued to scroll through his cell phone. He swiped left and right on some dating app, randomly letting out a snort when a girl showed too much skin. Andy couldn't help feeling like he was supervising a teenage tool bag half the time.

"How long we thinking this job will take?" Joe asked, still mindlessly swiping on his phone.

Andy looked over at him, noticing his Batman bobblehead jittering around on the dashboard with every pothole they backed over. Behind it, a picture of his wife and two kids stared back at him, their beautiful smiles warming his heart.

"About six, seven hours, I s'pose. We need to drain it all the way down to the fucking mire. The lady said she wants to make sure there's no more water in that pond by the time we leave."

"Why you think they hired us from out of state for such a pissant job? Seems they coulda saved a ton of money to hire someone close by," Joe said.

"Fuck if I know. But I'm not about to turn down fifteen grand to do a quick job like this." Andy parked the truck at the edge of the trail, unable to get too close to the water due to the number of trees blocking the path, but they came prepared for this. "Jerry should already be here with the sump pump. We'll get it set up, then we'll head out for lunch. Guy at the gas station said Plaza Pizza over in Newport is the place to go around here. Then we'll come back and clean up."

After giving an estimate much higher than a job this size would normally cost, Andy expected the customer to balk at the price and move on. It's what he always did with jobs he didn't want. When she accepted without hesitation, he got his crew together and pushed back the jobs already scheduled ahead of it.

They climbed out of the truck and got to work, connecting the hose to the tank, then led it down toward the water. Andy's other employee, Jerry, had already parked his pickup truck at the edge of the tree line and carried the sump pump over to the dock. The hardest part of the job would be getting the pump into the deepest part of the water, but they brought rope to help guide it down. Luckily, the dock went far out enough that it reached close to the center of the pond.

"About time you peckerheads showed up. I've been sitting here the last half hour breathing in this dead fish smell. If I wanted to inhale that, I'd spend another night with Andy's mom." Jerry sniggered.

"Hey, fuck off. I told you what time to get to the jobsite. Not my fault you can't tell time without your Mickey Mouse watch," Andy said.

Joe shook his head and laughed as he hooked the naked end of the hose to the pump.

"If Andy's mom really smells like this, why the hell would you spend the night with her in the first place, you sick fuck?" Joe snidely asked Jerry.

"Sometimes, easy's better than pretty."

Andy gave Jerry a shove, causing his employee to almost fall off the dock into the murky water. Jerry grabbed hold of the support beam connected to the railing and caught his balance as Joe and Andy burst out laughing.

"Real fucking funny! Didn't you guys hear about what happened here? Why they want us draining this place? I'd prefer not to go swimming with that fucking lore spreading around town."

Andy looked nervously at Joe. Of course, Andy knew—he was the boss. He did his research before agreeing to any job. But he continued to play it off like he had no idea because Joe believed in all that voodoo ghost shit. Andy chalked it up to a crazy family man going on a killing spree, not some supernatural cult living beneath the water. Besides, fifteen grand was worth a little unease, right?

"What's he talking about, Andy? You said you didn't know why they hired us," Joe said.

"Wise Man, just do your damn job. If I turned down every offer that had a shady past, I'd be out of business."

Joe shook his head and continued the setup. Andy scanned the water, curious why the green had a slight glow to it. Like pea soup mixed with antifreeze. He couldn't see more than a few inches beneath the surface, which made him a bit nervous to lower the pump to the pond floor. If there were any rocks or uneven terrain down there, it could damage the equipment. Still, he was being paid enough that he didn't have to worry about minor damage.

After everything was set up, Andy did one last pass on all the equipment to make sure it was connected securely, then he and Joe lowered the sump pump to the bottom of the pond using the pulley rope. When they felt it reach the bottom, Andy wiped the sweat from his brow and turned to head back to the shore. He froze mid-step when he spotted Jerry standing rigid in the center of the dock, staring at the water. Andy couldn't see his face, but he noticed Jerry's fingers were curled into his palms, digging at the skin.

"Jer? Ya good, man?"

Jerry didn't acknowledge him, continuing to look straight out at the water. Joe came up and stood next to Andy to see what was wrong. He swore under his breath and sped past Andy, grabbing Jerry by the shoulder and turning him. Andy almost screamed. Jerry's eyes were rolling in the back of his head, only the whites showing as he whispered something to himself.

"What the fuck, man, cut that shit!" Joe snapped, shaking Jerry.

Andy hoped Jerry was messing with Joe, but either way, it made the hair on the back of his neck stand on end. Jerry blinked and his eyes went back to normal as his posture relaxed.

"What the hell…" he mumbled.

"You two need to tell me what the fuck's going on right now! If this is some attempt to get in my head, congrat-u-fucking-lations, it worked!" Joe snapped.

"I don't know what just happened, man. Stop shouting, my damn head hurts. What was I doing?" Jerry asked in clear confusion.

Andy and Joe exchanged worried glances, unsure what to say.

"You didn't smoke some pot while you waited for us to get here, did you?" Andy asked.

"You're an asshole, you know that? Of course I didn't." Jerry pushed past his boss and left the dock.

Andy sighed and looked up at the overcast sky.

"Sorry, man. Just trying to figure out what the hell's happening. Let's start the sump pump before the storm comes, then go get some grub. We'll come back in a couple hours, and this should be moving right along. Hope you don't mind us squeezing in your truck since we need to leave the hydrovac here while the pump goes," Andy said.

"As long as you sit in the middle and go skiing," Jerry muttered dryly.

"You're sick, you know that?" Andy asked.

They all laughed and packed into the truck, leaving the pond behind. Andy couldn't help but glance at Jerry on the ride into town. If he wasn't fucking with them, what the hell just happened? When Andy signed on to do the job, he forced the rumors of the camp into the back of his mind. It was too much money to pass up, and if he was being honest, he needed it to keep the business alive. With a family to provide for, being picky about clients wasn't an option.

The closer they got to Newport, the more homes and businesses began to look as if they were on life support. Andy knew the town had a dark past of its own, but he never expected it to look like it was home to the undead. Many of the building exteriors were warped or had chipped paint. Andy spotted a few junkies slipping between the homes, either making a deal or finding a place to shoot up.

"You sure you wanna eat in this town, boss? Can't imagine why anyone would recommend coming here," Joe said.

"Well, we gotta eat somewhere. And we ain't got time to go to the next town. It's pizza. Pretty hard to mess that up."

After driving through the center of town, they eventually saw the sign for the pizza place and pulled in. Only two other vehicles sat in the lot, one of them a police cruiser.

"Okay, fellas, let's be quick. The sooner we get this job done, the sooner we can put this place in the rearview," Andy said.

It had been a strange day, and he suddenly wanted only to be back home, hugging his wife and kids.

CHAPTER 11

Howie was shot back to 1999, sitting inside Plaza Pizza for the first time in twenty-five years. The interior layout hadn't changed, identical to when he had his fifteenth birthday here. Even the *Addams Family* pinball machine and *Cruis'n USA* arcade game in the far corner were the same. He had spent countless hours playing those games with the guys, trying to beat the high scores; bringing up dollar bills to the front counter, where the owner, Aba, would exchange them for a bunch of quarters.

The carpets were the same but now worn with age and the stains of past families, from a time when going to a pizza place on a Friday night before settling in to watch whatever movies they decided to rent from VideoSmith was the norm. The wood-paneled walls remained intact, showing two decades' worth of cracks and scratches.

"Weird being here after all these years," he said to Shawn, who sat across from him in a small booth.

"I can only imagine. Place hasn't changed at all, yet it's so different from when we were kids."

They were waiting for their food after each placing an order for a cheeseburger plate—a staple of Plaza Pizza. The bell above the door jingled as three men walked in, chatting and laughing with one another.

Howie didn't recognize them, but they seemed innocent enough. There was nobody else in the restaurant. Aba worked alone behind the counter prepping food, only stopping to take the new customers' orders.

"So, tell me more about this stuff. What did it look like, smell like?" Shawn asked.

Howie tried to recall in detail to give the best description. Aba brought their food over, so Howie waited for him to leave before answering, "I was cleaning out her place. After I got most of her bedroom packed, I noticed a nasty smell coming from the closet. I found it was coming from a small jewelry box of all places. But man, that shit was really weird. There was a syringe, a rubber strip, and a vial of some thick, green substance. It smelled like dead fish, but somehow sweeter."

As he explained it, he noticed Shawn's face had hardened. He couldn't tell whether it was because Shawn didn't believe him or that he knew *exactly* what Howie was describing and was terrified.

"That's not the strangest part, though. When I opened the box, I swear it was like the stuff *talked* to me. Got in my head. Something was telling me to inject it into myself. I thought I was losing my damn mind. I dumped it down the drain and...it was like it was alive. What the fuck was it? Please tell me you know."

As he explained, Shawn stiffened, his hand freezing with a french fry halfway to his mouth before he set it back on his plate. He stared down at the table, suddenly unable to make eye contact, then cleared his throat. Before he spoke, he stared toward the counter, as if checking to make sure nobody could overhear them.

"I've seen it around. I don't know exactly what it is or where it comes from, but it's a powerful drug being distributed in Newport. I—"

"My mom didn't do drugs. That wouldn't even make sense. Why would she have it hidden in her closet?"

"Listen, Howie. I knew your mom well when we were kids, but it's not like we stayed in touch after you moved away. If anything, she shut herself off from anyone and anything in town that reminded her of *you*."

That last sentence hit Howie like a hammer to the skull, but Shawn continued.

"The point I'm trying to make is, please don't take it personal, like I'm accusing her of doing anything wrong. I didn't know her well enough to question what you're saying. But I can promise you that I've seen that stuff break the strongest of people. It's a borderline epidemic in Newport but nobody else wants to admit it. I feel like I'm fighting an uphill battle to even have the stuff looked into. When I mentioned the drug problem in town, this is what I was referring to."

"If it's such a problem, why the hell won't anyone take it seriously? I know this place has its secrets, but even when shit was *really* bad when we were kids, it wasn't like this whole town was falling apart. When I was driving into Newport, it seemed like I saw a junkie on every corner. Half the houses and businesses looked like they hadn't been maintained in years." It was sad, seeing his childhood home become a hollow, diseased husk. As much as he hated Newport, as much as he wanted to stay away, it was still his home. "I know enough about this place to realize there's likely something deeper than what we see on the surface, so what is it, Shawn? What's the new big secret this hellhole is hiding from the rest of the world this time?"

Shawn shook his head and took a long gulp from his water.

"I'm trying to figure that out, Howie. You have to trust me. I want answers. For Todd. For all of you guys that stood up to that evil cult shit." Shawn's expression was a combination of weary and pleading to Howie. "Let me handle this, okay? You're here for your mother. Don't get caught up in this place's bullshit while you're in town."

Howie slammed his fist on the table.

"Yeah, I'm here for my mother! My *dead* mother. Dead because of some mysterious drug that only this fucking town could be responsible for. Is it the coven? Are they fucking back?"

The three men who came in after them stared in confusion at the commotion. Shawn gave them a polite nod and leaned in closer to Howie, whispering urgently.

"Please, don't bring that shit up. They're long gone and never coming back. This...this is something different, man. It might all be connected, but it's not them. I've been making progress on finding the source. Hell, I've even gone undercover to try and buy some so I could work my way up to the dealers' bosses."

Howie couldn't help the disbelieving snort. "Seriously? Undercover? How could you possibly go UC in a town with like five thousand people? They all know you."

"I have my ways. Please, let me do my job, Howie."

"Do your job? If you fucking did it, my mom wouldn't be dead right now. You're not moving fast enough."

Shawn flinched at Howie's comment, but in that moment, he didn't give a shit. Howie felt like he could shout at the top of his lungs. The rage he had been able to control for years thanks to countless therapy and meditation sessions was boiling back to the surface, and it was all thanks to this fucking cursed dumpster fire of a town.

Shawn's tone lost its edge, voice softened with remorse. "You're right. And I'm sorry. I know those words won't bring her back, but I'm going to do everything I can to get her justice."

Howie closed his eyes and took a deep breath, letting the air out on a shaky sigh.

"I'm sorry too. I shouldn't have snapped. But if you think I'm going to sit back and ignore the fact that my mom had this drug in her closet and *ignore* that it was responsible for her death, you don't know me like you thought you did. I won't leave until I have answers–not until whoever or *whatever* is responsible is stopped."

This time, it was Shawn who sighed.

"I'm not going to stop you, Howie. But you got your mother's funeral coming up. Focus on that first, then we can try to figure this out together. Okay?"

With all the distractions, Howie forgot that he had scheduled her funeral two days from now. It felt as if he couldn't lay her to rest until he learned more. But he knew Shawn was right. He had to focus on her funeral and give her the celebration of life that she deserved. After they finished their meal in silence, Howie grabbed his empty tray and set it on the counter.

"Thanks, Aba. As good as always."

Aba glanced at him and nodded, but Howie thought he saw disgust on the old restaurant owner's face. It wasn't the best feeling in the world to have someone who was part of your entire childhood view you with such disdain, but he couldn't blame the guy. While his book didn't say a bad thing about the pizza place—and in fact, talked about the magical nostalgia of it—anyone who owned a business before and after the massacre saw a substantial dip in sales that never returned. It was Aba's livelihood he messed with, not just the town.

Shawn started up a conversation with one of the kitchen staff who'd just arrived for their shift, leaving Howie hanging. The group of three men who entered after them were talking about something that had them all loud and enthusiastic. Howie planned to just walk out to the parking lot and wait for Shawn, but then he overheard what they were discussing. At the same time, he spotted their truck advertising sump pump and hydrovac services, and he realized who they were. They were in town to drain the Bird's Nest pond. He hesitated for a second, but felt he had to say something. As he walked toward their table, the man sitting in the middle, who appeared to be the boss, mentioned the water doing something to a guy named Jerry. Their conversation paused when they saw Howie approaching.

"Sorry to interrupt, guys. I couldn't help but overhear you talking about Bird's Nest. What in the world brings you to that place? I see you're from out of state."

The boss narrowed his eyes but kept his tone friendly.

"Same thing that brings us anywhere that isn't home. Just a job. What's it to you?"

"Well...I'm sure you've heard some of the stories about the place. You might want to think twice about going near that water. Some things in this area are better left undisturbed. Trust me."

"I appreciate the warning...I'm sorry, what's your name?" the boss asked.

"Howie Burke. I grew up here. Just be careful—"
The man held up a hand to stop Howie mid-sentence.

"Howie, name's Andy Hixon. Like I said, I appreciate your concern. But you see, my *real* concern is finishing a job that I've been paid to do. I'm not about to let some small-town campfire story prevent us from making a lot of cash. We all got bills to pay, am I right?"

The two crew members on each side of Andy laughed, but one of them was clearly more concerned than the other. Howie wondered if the man had already seen something at the pond that he wasn't comfortable talking about. As much as he wanted to try and convince them to leave the place before something bad happened, he didn't have the time to get mixed up in strangers' business, given all he had on his plate already.

"Well, just something to think about, is all. You fellas have a nice day," Howie said as Shawn finished up his chat at the counter.

"You ready?" Shawn asked.

Howie hesitated, staring at the crew a second longer.

"Yeah. Let's go."

Shawn gave a polite nod to the men before exiting Plaza Pizza. As Howie followed, an uneasy feeling overcame him. Something was brewing in the area, and he felt like his mother's death was just the start of it.

CHAPTER 12

A few hours later, the crew pulled back into the jobsite with Jerry at the wheel and their bellies full with a nice afternoon buzz. They hadn't planned on drinking as much as they did, but Andy wanted to celebrate after landing such a high-paying job. The pizza was top-notch, as advertised. Their buzz was almost ruined by the local named Howie. Andy didn't want to admit it to his men, but after what they had been through earlier with Jerry having some type of seizure in front of the water, hearing the concern in Howie's voice unsettled him, to say the least. As if Joe needed another reason to be freaked out. He was ready to skip town. But then Andy calmed him down and they went back to their pizza and beer.

"Let's go see how much progress we made while we were gone," Jerry said. His sentence was met with a *crack* of thunder, reminding them a severe storm was closing in. Light sprinkles had begun to fall—a warning before what was likely to be a torrential downpour.

The three of them hopped out of the truck and followed the trail through the tall grass down to the dock. Andy was elated to see that the water had almost completely drained already, and they were able to walk out to the middle of the pond where it was only ankle-deep. The three of them trudged through the thick gunk as their rubber boots stuck to the ground like suction cups, making squishy fart sounds with each step.

"Hey, what the hell's that over there?" Jerry asked, pointing towards the center of the pond.

"I'm not falling for it. You assholes can try and scare me all you want," Joe said.

"No, I'm serious. It dips in the middle, like there's a drain sucking some of the water down."

Andy squinted ahead. Jerry was right. The pond had drained too fast, and the tank wasn't even full. Was there a drain or possibly a sinkhole in the center? But that didn't make any sense; why would a hole open up just as the pond was being drained? Perhaps even more confusing was the large concrete slab firmly planted in the sludge. It looked like some type of support block for a dam, yet it reminded Andy of an ancient tomb. Just staring at it sent a chill down his spine.

"This makes no fucking sense. If there was a drain in the center, man-made or not, the water should've never been this full to begin with," Andy said.

They approached the center of the pond, the water still ankle-deep and the color of a blended avocado. Andy kneeled at the dip, feeling beneath the surface for the culprit. All he felt was an empty space, like there was a void below that led to complete nothingness. Jerry stepped around him, getting too close for Andy's liking.

"Be careful, Jer. Might be a sink—"

Jerry dropped beneath the surface, disappearing completely, as if he'd fallen in the deep end of a pool instead of six inches of pond water. There was a brief scream before he vanished, the water swirling around his body like a flushed toilet.

"Jer!" Joe yelled, charging toward the now empty space.

Andy's heart obliterated his chest muscles, but he remained focused enough to put a hand up and stop Joe's advance.

"Wait! It's not safe. We can't help him if we fall down there with him. We need to wait for the rest of the water to drain so we can see what we're dealing with."

"He's gonna fucking drown, man! We need to do something *now*!"

Andy felt panic take the driver's seat, unsure of what to do. He couldn't exactly go under and try to find Jerry, not when the water was as thick as stew. They both stood over the spot, neither making a move. And then Jerry's head shot above the surface, his eyes wide with terror.

"'Elllp me!" he gurgled, then went back under.

Was that blood on his face? Andy wondered in horror.

When Jerry sank below again, the water went with him, draining into the open space. A small puddle remained, bubbling until it also vanished, leaving only a long, zigzagging split in the ground.

"Jerry!" Andy shouted.

Both men dropped to their knees next to the sump pump, peering into the hole. The crack had to be at least ten feet long, starting narrow on each end, then getting wider as it got closer to the center.

Just wide enough for a body to fall through.

"I can't see shit down there. You got your phone?" Andy asked.

"Fuck, I left it in the truck. I can run and grab it!" Joe cursed himself and Andy.

It was company policy—Andy's policy—to leave phones in the work trucks, not just to prevent them from falling in water, but to make sure employees did their damn job without distractions. Andy regretted that rule as he continued to look through the crack, mindful not to get too close.

Something shifted a few feet below in the darkness.

Before Andy could get a second look, Joe shouted behind him. Andy turned to see what had Joe worked up, and his mouth dropped open in awe. Wise Man had stopped short, his face draining of color.

Scattered bones and skeletons poked up out of the muck decorating the pond floor. There was no possible way they were there before because the guys would have felt them crunch beneath their feet as they walked to the pump.

"What the hell…" Andy whispered. He turned to Joe and snapped, "Get the goddamn phone!"

Joe jumped and made a beeline for the pond's shore while Andy scanned the graveyard of the cult, or the cult's victims. He quickly lost count of how many bodies were scattered around them.

The sound of something digging beneath the ground brought Andy's attention back to the hole, just as a hand shot out of the crack, grabbing hold of his ankle.

"Help me out! HEEELP!"

Andy shouted an unnatural cry and looked down to see Jerry's face peering up from the hole, his eyes full of terror.

"They're coming back!" Jerry yelled.

Without hesitation, Andy reached down and grabbed hold of his hand, almost losing his grip as the algae and sludge lathered Jerry's skin. Then there was more movement behind Jerry. Multiple sets of white eyes dotted the inky black space beneath his friend.

"Jerry! Watch out!"

Before he could act, they pulled on Jerry, ripping his hand back into the hole, breaking free of Andy's grasp. Whispers buzzed beneath the ground, but Andy couldn't hear what they were saying. Jerry screamed over them as the figures surrounded him, suffocating him, ripping him apart. A green hand covered in worms and algae wrapped around Jerry's face, one of its long fingers poking into his mouth and pulling. Andy heard the tear of Jerry's cheek being ripped open as his employee continued to bellow in agony. The figures swarmed him like a horde of angry wasps. Andy had a fleeting thought: *That was just what these things were. Angry wasps whose nest had been disturbed, and they are vicious and determined to protect their home at all costs.* Except that wasn't entirely true; these monsters *wanted* them here. They *wanted* the prey to come to them.

Jerry's cries cut off, then his body disappeared into the darkness. Andy remained crouched, too shocked to do anything else, until he realized the figures behind Jerry had stopped moving or making noise. He brought his attention back to the hole to find all of them staring directly at him, their hazy orbs burning into his soul.

"Oh, fuck!"

He slowly backed up, keeping his eyes glued to the opening as the intensity of the rain picked up. Had he been paying attention to where he was going, he would have seen the large femur of a past victim behind him. Instead, he tripped over it and fell on his ass, landing hard in the muck. The crack in the ground began to branch out, weaving toward him as if it were hot on his trail. A dozen or more hands dug through the sludge, forcing their way above ground like flowers after a rainstorm. Jagged, caked fingernails clawed at the ground to gain traction. Andy tried to get up and run, but a hand clamped around his wrist, squeezing until bone cracked. Unable to hold himself up, Andy fell onto his back with a pained shout.

Another thundercrack launched his heart into his throat as the pain pulsated through his broken wrist. He tried to break free, but the hand holding him had inhuman strength, refusing to let go. Instead, it continued squeezing, pulling Andy toward the newly formed section of the crack in the ground. Rain pelted his face as he tried to break free. The figure pulled his hand into the hole, disappearing below. Andy dropped face down, unable to stand his ground.

A white eye peered up at him through the crack.

"Join us. Be one with Vodyanoy."

Suddenly, the fear that had consumed Andy a moment ago was replaced by a blissful calmness. That voice, it was in his head. It called to him.

The white eye remained locked on him, and he found himself transfixed by its haze. He wanted to join them. He belonged with them.

"Okay," he said numbly.

Joe came running across the empty pond, losing one of his boots to the sludge along the way.

"Andy! Boss! You okay? I got my phone—"

Andy stood up from the ground, his broken wrist dangling limply. Joe noticed it and ran to him.

"What the fuck happened?"

"I'm fine," Andy said blankly.

"Fine? Your goddamn hand is falling off! I'm calling 911!"

Joe lifted the phone to dial, and Andy struck him in the face, dropping his unsuspecting employee to the ground. Andy stood over him, dead set on making sure the phone never got used again.

"There's no need to call anyone."

"Andy, what the fuck?! Have you lost your damn mind? Jerry's stuck down there! We need to get help!"

"Jerry's with us now. And so are you," Andy said, his mouth forming a sinister smile.

Joe squinted in confusion, then multiple moon-white hands with green veins branching out across the skin rose from the muck around him, grabbing hold of his limbs. He looked down and screamed, unable to break free of their grasp as they squeezed, holding him in a crucifix position. A sharp *snap* echoed when each shoulder dislocated, stretched taut by the pale arms.

"Andy! Help me! What the fuck!"

The hands pulled him lower, half his body beginning to submerge into the muddy ground. The crack beneath him widened, allowing the entirety of his body to be swallowed by the nest. His screams were silenced as his mouth sank below and filled with the swampy substance. His eyes bulged, begging his boss to help one last time. Instead, Andy smiled again, then lowered himself into the ground as well. He allowed the nest to take him, to make him one with Vodyanoy. He could no longer see Joe, but he didn't care. He stared up at the gray sky, the rain lashing his face as he sank lower and lower. As his body disappeared, the pond began to slowly refill, covering the multitude of bones strewn about its floor. All that remained visible was the concrete slab in the center of the pond giving off a green glow.

It was time for Vorathor to return.

CHAPTER 13

1979

Henry pulled into the motel parking lot, taking note of how empty it was. There was only one other vehicle in the lot. Not that it surprised him much, the place was a dump and it was nice to get away from it for a night. He thought back to the lovely evening with Bill and Sheila and their warm hospitality.

"Those two really seem like good people, huh?"

"Hmm?" Jessica mumbled, dazed and staring out the window. Henry wondered where her mind was right now. He had an idea but hoped he was wrong.

"Bill and Sheila. That was very kind of them to do that for us. Made us feel right at home here."

"Oh....yeah. I really like them."

Henry parked the car and opened the driver's side door. He hoped the realtor left a message with the front desk that their home was ready to move into. When he had done a tour and put in the offer, it sounded like only minor repairs the seller needed to make before handing the keys over. But they had already been at the motel longer than expected. Thank God the real estate company put them up for free, having included it in the closing costs.

"I just need to pop in the lobby to see if we have any messages about the house, okay? You want to wait out here?"

"Sure."

Henry hesitated, taking a long look at his new fiancée.

"Jess, where's your mind at right now? You seem withdrawn this morning. You okay?"

"I'm fine. Really. Just a lot on my mind, is all." Finally, she took her gaze off the window and locked eyes with him. Those same eyes didn't flinch, but her lips lifted in a smile.

"Actually, I'll come in with you. If you get good news about the house, I'd hate to miss it."

Though he wasn't entirely convinced, Henry smiled and nodded. With that, they both got out of the car and approached the lobby. When they walked in, Henry noticed the same bald man working the desk.

The man lifted his face from the newspaper he was reading, his eyes magnified behind thick lenses.

"Oh, good morning. We were worried you'd left us early! Where'd you guys sneak off to last night?"

Jessica squeezed Henry's hand.

"Oh, you know. Out meeting some locals. It's a lovely town... I'm sorry, what's your name?" Henry asked, trying not to let the clerk's phrasing rattle him. *We? Who else is 'We'?*

"Tim Ripple. You picked a fine evening to explore. The stars were something else, weren't they?" He smiled too wide, his thick glasses catching the light. "Nothing quite like the night air to stir up what's sleeping inside."

Jessica's grip loosened.

Henry continued. "We just dropped by to see if we had any messages from the realtor while we were out."

"Let me check for you," the clerk said, as if he wasn't the only one working all day. Tim flipped through a notebook, then frowned. "I'm sorry, doesn't appear any messages came in for you. Would you like me to ring your room as soon as I get a call?"

"Yeah, that would be great. Thanks." Henry turned to Jessica. "Looks like we got more sightseeing to do after all, hon." He tried to hide the impatience festering inside.

"I think I know just the place for you guys," Tim offered. His eyes remained on Jessica just long enough to make Henry uncomfortable. Jessica told him earlier that the clerk had creeped her out, and now he could see why. He debated saying something, but then Tim spoke again, "It's a bit late in the season for swimming, but if you're looking for a place with ambiance, may I suggest Bird's Nest Campground? Even if you're not campers, many go there just to go on hikes through the beautiful trails."

Jessica flinched, pulling Henry's attention back to her. She didn't say anything, but her eyes opened wide and she blinked repeatedly as if trying to clear floating balls of light from her vision.

"You okay?"

She cleared her throat, then nodded. "It's nothing. Just a headache, is all. I need a nap."

Henry turned back to Tim. "Thanks for the suggestion, we may check it out. And please, let me know if anyone calls for us. Thank you again."

He put his arm around Jessica and guided her toward the exit, feeling Tim's eyes burning into her as they went. When he pushed the door open, the clerk spoke again, "I seriously hope you take me up on that.

It's a beautiful place, and I think you'll both like it quite a bit. But if you plan on being gone for the night again, please be sure to let me know ahead of time. Don't want my cleaning staff thinking you left all your belongings for them to rummage through!"

He said it in a playful manner, but Henry took it as anything but playful. He whirled around and took a step toward the desk. Jessica attempted to grip his arm, but he ignored it.

"Do you have a problem with us? We paid for the room. It doesn't matter what the hell we decide to do. As soon as we can leave this place, we'll be gone."

Henry held his stare, unwilling to blink first. Tim's eyes narrowed behind his thick lenses.

"I'm sorry, I didn't mean to offend you. Please accept my apology."

"Henry, let's go," Jessica pleaded.

Henry clenched his jaw, wanting to say more to this small-town freak. His fiancée's demand won out. He turned and burst through the door, marching to their room as Jessica followed.

"You weren't wrong to do that, Henry. But we need to be careful picking fights in such a small town like this. I appreciate you standing up for us, though," Jessica said, trying to catch up with his angry pace.

"Fucking creep. If we haven't heard from the realtor by tomorrow, I'll drive down to that office myself and demand they either let us move in or break the contract," he said, turning toward Jessica for the first time since the lobby. He couldn't help but see how scared she looked at the thought of having to move on again. "I'm sorry. Everything will be fine. He just pissed me off, is all. Let's go rest up for a bit, then we can go for a ride and grab dinner somewhere later."

They walked into their motel room, and Henry immediately scanned their belongings to make sure they weren't missing anything.

"I really would like to check out those trails. As weird as that man was, it's a good idea. We haven't been on a hike in a long time," Jessica said.

Henry wasn't so sure he agreed. Anywhere that man suggested was a place he wanted nothing to do with. The way his eyes lingered on Jessica and the tone he spoke in while recommending the campground, it was almost hypnotic in a way.

"I don't know if that's a good idea."

"It's not like he's going to be out there with us. Seems like he practically lives in that lobby. Besides, the less time we spend in this room, the better. Right?"

"I guess. After all those drinks last night, I suppose our bodies could use some exercise. Let's nap and shower, then we can head out later. Sound good?"

Jessica smiled. "Sounds perfect. I can't wait until we can shower together, and...you know."

For a moment, Henry forgot all about the creep in the lobby He walked up and kissed Jessica long and hard. When he pulled back, her eyes were glossed over like she was about to cry.

"What's wrong?" Henry asked.

"Nothing. Nothing's wrong. I just can't believe I found you. I don't want a big fancy wedding. Once we get in our house, can we just go to the town hall and elope?"

"If that's what you want, of course! The sooner I can call you 'my wife,' the better."

They hugged again, then Jessica went to shower while Henry lay on the bed. He heard the water blast on in the bathroom, then started to doze off.

His eyes jolted open when he heard movement behind the wall. He stared at the far corner. Something was *behind* the wood paneling. The shower still roared from the bathroom, so he couldn't have been asleep for more than a few minutes. He got to his feet and crept toward the faint scratching. Henry kneeled, sticking his head close to the wall.

SCRAAATCH!

He startled back, landing on his backside. With his heart pumping in his ears, he didn't hear the shower turn off or Jessica exiting the bathroom. He pulled back the edge of the wood paneling to reveal empty space. Where there should be support beams and a foundation with insulation, there was a dark nothingness. He sensed movement within, leaning in to get a better look.

A mouse skittered past him, and he yipped like a scared child.

"Henry Black. Are you scared of that same mouse you told me not to worry about?" Jessica asked with humor behind her words.

He turned to see her standing at the edge of the bed, wrapped in nothing but a towel. Her black hair dripped as her smile lit up the room.

"Hardy har har. I heard something behind the wall. Guess it was just your little friend. But come look at this, babe."

Jessica came to his side as he pulled back on the paneling again.

"I'm no contractor, but that sure as hell doesn't seem up to code, does it?"

She furrowed her brow, then asked, "Does anything about this place seem up to code?"

"True. Still, it's rather odd. I wonder how deep this goes. Care to check it out with me?"

"Absolutely not!" she exclaimed, stepping back. "Speaking of, where did that mouse run off to?"

Henry scanned the floor, finding it empty, and shrugged.

"Probably in your shoes somewhere."

She slapped him on the shoulder as he gave her a shit-eating grin.

"You saw what one of them did to me. If we found a whole nest, who knows what that would do to my soul?"

Henry chuckled, rubbing the back of his neck. "Fair point. I'll tell the clerk about it when we check out. Maybe he can send his cleaning crew in with a flashlight and broom."

"Have you seen this place? What cleaning crew?"

"Fair point again."

Jessica grabbed some clothes from her bag. "I say let it be their problem. But I swear, if I find one of those things in our bed, I'm burning this place to the ground."

Henry stood, still glancing at the strange hollow behind the wall. "Might not be such a bad idea to burn this place down."

As Jessica dressed, Henry went to look in the hole again.

The telephone blared from the nightstand.

"Christ!" Henry yelled.

"Someone's a bit jumpy," Jessica said in amusement. Henry stared at her. It was so odd to see her acting like herself again after seeming so dazed and distracted not too long ago.

The phone's persistent ringing tore him from his suspicions.

"Must be news from the realtor!" Henry said, jumping to his feet. He picked up the phone on the third ring. "Hello?"

Jessica watched him with an expectant expression.

"Mr. Black, it's Tim from the front desk. Just got a call from your realtor to come down to the office later today to sign the final paperwork and approve the requested improvements to the home."

"Praise the Lord! Thank you," Henry said, suddenly forgetting his anger toward the man.

"Happy to break the news to you. And Henry?"

"Yeah…"

"I'm really sorry about earlier. Didn't mean to upset you. I often forget that people don't always get my sense of humor."

"It is what it is. Thanks for letting me know, Tim."

He disconnected the call before the clerk could respond, feeling a sense of victory at getting the last word in.

"And?" Jessica asked.

"Babe, we got ourselves a livable home."

They embraced, but then Jessica pulled away.

"Henry?"

"Yeah?"

"Let's go to Bird's Nest tonight.

He frowned. "You sure?"

She hesitated. "I think…I need to."

Henry nodded, unsure what she meant but sensing the weight behind the words.

"Okay," he whispered. "After we pop in at the realtor's office, we'll go for a nice hike."

It was late afternoon by the time Henry and Jessica had finished signing paperwork. She couldn't believe they were officially homeowners, and she hadn't even seen the house yet. The home could wait, though. Henry offered to drive straight there so she could see it; in fact, he was *excited* for her to step foot inside. But she couldn't stop thinking about Bird's Nest Campground. Ever since the motel clerk mentioned it, there was a distant voice in the back of her mind demanding that she come.

"The realtor said it was just over the town line in Goshen, that we couldn't miss the big blue sign," Henry said.

But Jessica was only half paying attention. Something kept calling to her. In all of her years devoted to religion, God had *never* done that. They had only been in Newport for a short time and the signs were constant. She knew the next step in her self-discovery was waiting at the campground. More specifically, the pond. Tim didn't even mention the body of water, but the *voices* did.

"Yes...the pond is your salvation. Be one with us. With Vodyanoy. With Vorathor. With The Withered Tongues."

Up ahead, a blue sign appeared, the words standing out in freshly painted white.

BIRD'S NEST CAMPGROUND
NEXT RIGHT

"Here it is," Henry said.

Jessica's heart went into overdrive, ramping up with every passing second. Trees flanked them on each side as they drove down the narrow dirt road. After crossing a small bridge, they rounded a corner and came to a second sign for the campground. As Henry turned in, Jessica noticed a closed gate with a padlock on it, preventing them from continuing on. A sinking feeling came over her until she spotted a parking area for guests to check in located outside the gate. Henry parked and stared at her. She didn't look back, too focused on the surrounding forest.

"This is perfect, Henry. Can you feel it calling you too?"

He continued staring at her and finally, the uncomfortable silence pried her attention away from the foliage and to her fiancé. Henry was terrified. Jessica couldn't understand why.

"What do you mean, Jess? What's calling you?" A frown creased his brow, only highlighting the fear in his expression. "I'm getting worried about you."

That statement hurt. She knew he meant well by it, but he promised to be her rock as she tried to find what was missing, what was needed to fill the void in her empty heart.

"I told you I'd be honest with you through all of this, Henry. When Tim mentioned the campground, something happened inside me. Like something out there is giving me a sign that the campground would have answers for me. I know it all sounds crazy, but please trust me."

He closed his eyes and sighed. When he opened them, Jessica thought she saw a tear forming in the waning daylight.

"Of course I trust you. I'd do anything for you, Jess. You know that."

"I do. Let's go for this hike before it gets too late. Then let's go move into our new home," she said, leaning in to kiss him. His lips were stiff, not holding the usual softness behind each kiss. "Are *you* okay?"

Henry pulled away, nodding hesitantly. "I'll be fine. Let's go check this place out."

They followed a path through the campground, past the house that the front office resided in. The farther they went, the more Jessica knew it was the right choice. Tall grass crept to the edge of the path, which was just wide enough for a vehicle to drive through. There was an eerie silence around them. No birds. No rustling of animals in the brush. The trees leaned slightly inward toward the path, as if they were protecting it from the outside world.

And then she saw the clearing. In front of them, the trail cut sharply to the right, but the water was straight ahead, through the tall grass behind the tree line. Henry stopped, scanning the area, but Jessica walked forward with purpose. The grass tickled her bare skin between her boots and the bottom of her dress, welcoming her.

She continued, her boots damp with dew, until she stepped through the last barrier of trees into the clearing. The pond was beautiful. The surface was a flat mirror, not a single ripple.

Henry was now a few paces behind her, mumbling something about the low fog rolling in over parts of the water. But Jessica paid him no mind, instead allowing the pond to draw her closer, the silence wrapping around her like a cocoon.

And then, it spoke to her.

Not aloud, but in her head. Not even in words exactly, but in emotions. In *temperature*.

A radiant warmth swelled in her chest, as if the pond itself had whispered in her ear, telling her she was where she needed to be. She leaned forward, staring into the green-tinted water. Her reflection stared back at her—at first. But then it blinked, no longer in sync with her real face. The eyes in the pond narrowed just slightly, giving off a faint glow. Her reflection smiled back at her, with something dark behind the teeth.

"Join us. Be one with Vodyanoy."

Jessica gasped and stumbled back. The water remained still. Henry helped her up to her feet and asked if she was okay, but everything sounded muffled to her.

"Did you hear that?" she asked.

"Hear what?"

Jessica didn't answer. She stepped closer to the water again, slower this time. The warmth returned inside her chest. She felt...*seen*.

Somewhere below the surface, below the muddy floor of the pond, something stirred.

It was waiting.

And it had chosen her.

CHAPTER 14

2024

Derrick Patten pulled the black station wagon into the campground, wipers on full blast. Even in the downpour, the tire tracks from another vehicle stood out as water pooled in the indentations of the muddy path. Before he could question it, the green-eyed man, whom he now knew as Mr. Ruger, spoke from the back seat.

"No need for concern, Derrick. They've already been disposed of. They have officially joined our ranks."

Derrick learned quickly not to question Mr. Ruger. His new leader was more than just smart. He was always one step ahead of him, his thoughts exposed to the man like an open book. It wasn't like Derrick could speak anyway—his tongue had been torn out, leaving only a bloody stump. Just two days ago, he had woken up in the back of the station wagon, pain radiating through him. Outside, night had fallen, but a sickly green glow crept through the rear window.

Then Mr. Ruger opened the hatchback, introduced himself by name, and informed Derrick of how he would be of service. And over the last few days, he had been running errands and doing whatever his boss needed of him. It was simple to follow orders; easy to listen to the sibilant whispers coating his brain like algae.

As they approached the pond, he wondered what his next task would be. He would do everything Ruger required.

"Pull up to the end of the path. I have something I want to show you, Derrick."

Mr. Ruger was a man of few words, but every time he spoke, it was mesmerizing. It felt like thousands of tiny feathers tickling the inside of Derrick's head.

The rain continued to pelt off the windshield as they inched closer to the pond. Just like when he awoke in the cargo space, the green glow rolled through the trees in front of them with the fog holding the land hostage. Derrick pulled as close as possible and killed the engine. He watched the towering pines blur through the rain, accompanied only by his leader's slow breathing. Every now and then, something thudded in the back. He had no idea what.

"Do you know what we are here for, Derrick?"

He started to turn toward the back seat but remembered one of the rules. *"Don't look at me unless I tell you to," Mr. Ruger had hissed at him once.* His posture stiffened at the thought of disobeying his leader.

Derrick kept his eyes on the road and shook his head, unable to form words with his ruined mouth.

"I wouldn't expect you to know, so let me tell you. Twenty-five years ago, my father was taken from us. He was a very powerful man, a beloved father, and the leader of The Withered Tongues."

The mention of *tongues* sent a phantom pain through Derrick's butchered mouth.

"All those years, we never knew where he went, only that he was trapped, waiting for us to free him. Oh, we searched. But my twin and I were just young adults when he went missing, and the rest of the coven had been destroyed. We were smart, but without the proper knowledge of the coven and resources, it was impossible to come to a resolution."

Even after surviving the Halloween Homecoming Massacre, even with the power Mr. Ruger had over his mind and body, Derrick struggled to believe what he was hearing.

"Instead of wasting more years looking for him, we decided to spend that time learning the ways, going through all of his books, and mastering the dark arts of the coven and the hierarchy of the demons. It wasn't until a real estate agent and his family came to this very pond a few months ago and awoke the water demon, Vodyanoy, that we learned where our father was. After feeding on countless sacrifices, Vodyanoy and the pond gained the strength to reach out to us.

"They called to us and told us that Father was here, trapped in the pond, and that they could help us get him back. And he wasn't alone. The demon Vorathor had possessed him. Which, of course, our father invited in, but a group of miserable kids learned how to seal him in a concrete block with a ritual they had no business knowing. With strength, the pond's reach has expanded, which allowed Vodyanoy to communicate with us. But he and his army will always be confined to water. The demon needs more strength, and that's where you come in."

A knot of dread twisted in Derrick's gut. He wasn't ready to sacrifice himself to the water. While he would do anything Mr. Ruger asked of him, he wasn't ready to die. Not yet. Ruger seemed to sense his unease and snorted derisively.

"Not you, fool. You are here to serve me. You will do me no good dead. No, I don't want to feed you to the pond. I need you to *find* food. I need you to bring us sacrifices until Vodyanoy and his army have enough strength to erase the seal. Once that happens, Vodyanoy will help us free Vorathor and my father. Do you understand what I'm asking of you?"

Derrick nodded again, though he wasn't sure he could do this. He had never killed or abducted anyone.

I will do whatever Mr. Ruger asks me to do. I want to live. And he promised he could make me live forever with them.

"That's right. Do as I ask, and you'll have everything you could dream of, Derrick. I need to know you are all-in with us. I need you to prove it. Now, please open the hatchback."

Without hesitation, Derrick climbed out into the rain, his clothes instantly soaked and clinging to his body. He rounded the station wagon and pulled the latch to open the rear door, which slowly glided up. Derrick stared down at the squirming body of a teenage girl, her mouth stuffed with a rag to prevent her from screaming. She had been so quiet that Derrick never realized she was back here.

"I'm sure you're surprised to see her. Don't be. This will become second nature to you in the coming days. What I need you to do now is bring her to the water. Show me you're willing to sacrifice an innocent life for the greater good. Can you do that?"

His throat caught, as if choking on something dry despite the storm. The girl, who couldn't be more than sixteen years old, stared up at him with wide eyes. The fear was undeniable. She attempted to scream despite the cloth in her mouth, letting out a muffled plea. Her hands were tied behind her back, her clothes dry, indicating Ruger had abducted her before the storm.

He stared at her as water pounded off his shoulders and face. He was thankful for the rain disguising his tears, masking his anguish and pain.

Derrick groaned, trying to form words but only managed a garbled sound meant to form an apology to the girl.

It didn't matter whether he apologized to her or not, though. All this poor girl cared about was living, and he was about to deny her that.

"Do not be sorry. It must be done. You eat when you're hungry, don't you, Derrick? The pond does too. But its hunger is older than time. We must feed it," Ruger said from the back seat.

Derrick grabbed the girl by the arm and began to pull her from the back, when she surprised him with a kick to the jaw. It sent a jolt of pain through his already wounded mouth, the taste of blood absorbing into his remaining taste buds.

The girl fell onto the muddy surface behind the car, then attempted to get to her feet and make a run for it. The guilt Derrick felt just seconds prior vanished, replaced with an unequivocal rage. He kicked her in the ribs before she could get to her feet, sending her splashing into a puddle. Still, the girl was in survival mode, quickly rolling onto her stomach in an attempt to get up.

Derrick kicked her again, this time in the face. The rag dislodged from her mouth, but she was too disoriented to scream. Her eyes fluttered, filling with rain. The water splashed off her mouth, diluting the blood that now poured from swollen lips.

Her body's instinct to fight was stubborn, but her movements were slow and sluggish. She kicked at Derrick again but barely connected with his shin. It was just enough to piss him off even more. He grabbed her by the hair and lifted her in one quick motion, then dragged her toward the pond.

"Nooo, let me go!"

Derrick ignored her pleas and marched toward the dock that stretched to the center of the pond. As he closed in on the water, a voice whispered but sounded like it was coming from every direction.

"Yesss. Bring the girl. Sacrifice her to us."

The pond began to thrum to its own pulse, a green glow moving with the buzzing. The light coming from the water burned through the low-hanging fog, slowly allowing Derrick to see the surface. For the first time, he saw not just the pond, but what existed inside it. Inside the Devil's Nest.

Dark shadows moved below, creeping closer to the dock. The buzzing intensified, and the water started to bubble like a pot of boiling water. Derrick froze, unsure of what to do next. He turned, staring back toward where he entered and spotted the tall, intimidating figure of Mr. Ruger, watching his every move with green eyes that matched the luminescence of the water. The rain created a wall between them, distorting Ruger's features.

And then the shadows rose, breaking the surface. Derrick trembled as multiple sets of white, hazy eyes burrowed into him, waiting for their sacrifice. For their meal.

"Do it, Derrick. Make Vodyanoy *happy*!" Mr. Ruger yelled through the storm.

A snap of lightning was quickly followed by a cracking blast of thunder, and in that brief flash of light, Derrick couldn't help but see the genuine terror on the girl's face. She had given up fighting but forced one last cry, "Please...I didn't do anything."

Derrick considered it for a second, then remembered Ruger watching from the woods.

That was all he needed to shake off the momentary compassion. He narrowed his eyes, then shoved her off the dock. She flailed in the air before splashing into the pond, and they were on her like a school of piranhas.

The sounds coming from the poor girl were guttural, inhuman. Derrick didn't want to watch, but he couldn't take his eyes off the nightmare in front of him. Pale white hands, wrapped in strings of green algae, tore and clawed at her flesh. Even through the intense rain, Derrick still heard her skin shredding, her insides squirming. She screamed at the top of her lungs until one of the figures wrapped her in a bear hug from behind and pulled her beneath the surface. The others followed, disappearing below.

Just when he thought the horror was over, the girl's head bobbed up briefly, locking eyes with him one last time. She reached for Derrick, but instead of helping, he backed away, unable to stop himself from crying. Then a gnarled hand reached into her screaming mouth, digging jagged nails through her cheek, and tore out her tongue.

The girl was pulled below for the last time, returning the pond to the calming sound of a thunderstorm and nothing else. Derrick wiped the tears away. His clothes clung to his body like a second layer of skin.

He watched until the water settled after swallowing the girl whole. Then he watched until the crimson cloud faded and the water returned to its shimmering green.

The pond echoed in Derrick's mind. *"Thank you for your sacrifice."*

Mr. Ruger clapped a hand to his shoulder, watching the waters still and illuminate. Derrick's hands shook, and he felt more than saw Mr. Ruger's grin.

"Do not worry, Derrick. It gets easier."
And it did. It got much easier.

"Do not worry, Derrick. It gets easier."
And it did. It got much easier.

CHAPTER 15

The minute Howie sat down in the funeral home's back office, the nightmare returned. Not the memory, but the *feeling*. Part of him wished this, too, was a nightmare, and in a way, it was. But it was his reality. Today was the day his mother would finally be laid to rest. He knew he was supposed to be greeting all the people who came to pay their respects, yet he found it difficult to leave the office. The funeral home director, a nice old woman named Veronica Banks, told him to take his time and come out when he was ready.

Howie had no idea how many people were in the main room, but the murmuring of the crowd continued to grow, signaling a nice turnout. He liked to think that he knew this would happen, but the truth was that he didn't even know his own mother anymore leading up to her death. Pretending she didn't exist was easier than wondering what made her stay in Newport while he bled in some therapist's office hundreds of miles away.

That's not true and you know it, he thought, but the feeling stuck, whether it was fair or not.

No amount of therapy could change that, and now the one person he could make amends with to change that feeling was dead. Dead at the hands of some mysterious drug that nobody had answers for. Sure, the toxicology report that Shawn had requested as an addendum to the ME's findings hadn't come back yet, but Howie knew. Deep down, he knew all along that it was something beyond "natural causes."

The office door opened gently, and Veronica poked her head in.

"How you holding up, Howie?"

"Oh, you know. Could be better. How's the crowd size?"

She gave a sympathetic smile. "It's a big one. Your mother clearly had the respect and love of many people. Do you need a few more minutes? If so, I can stall them."

"No, thank you. I'll be right out."

Veronica smiled again and closed the door, leaving him in solitude. Thinking of how nice she was brought to mind the funerals Howie had attended for his friends after the massacre, which reminded him of the old funeral home director, Burt Rollins, who had been a member of the coven. He had also treated Howie and his family with respect, but it was all a front.

Was Veronica also linked to them?

The coven is dead, Howie. You know that, his father's voice commanded in his head.

"I don't know shit, Pops."

The truth, if he was being honest with himself, was that he never thought the coven would be dead. One of the main reasons he left town, beyond the soul-crushing heartbreak that hit him wherever he went, was that he had no idea who was connected and who wasn't. People he grew up trusting turned out to be monsters in hiding. Teachers, cops, the fucking town barber. Even though their leader was dead and gone, the odds were that some of the past members remained alive and well.

He shook the thought and got to his feet, catching a glimpse of himself in the office mirror. Graying temples, bloodshot eyes, and permanent dark circles beneath those eyes reminded Howie that although he was in his childhood town, he was closer to middle age than he was a teenager. And he felt every day of it physically, yet being in Newport brought back those childhood insecurities.

He sighed, then opened the door and was hit with a tightness in his chest at the sight of so many familiar yet strange faces. He scanned the crowd, recognizing some of his mom's old friends mixed in with townsfolk who likely came to every funeral in Newport to pay their respects. Or, more likely, to attend because they were nosy and had nothing better to do. Veronica greeted an older man who entered, and Howie recognized him as his old T-ball coach, Christopher Horne. He hadn't seen the guy since he was in middle school, assuming he either moved away or died.

Behind Veronica, Howie noticed Shawn standing by the door in full uniform, his hands on his hips. Shawn made eye contact with him and gave a two-finger wave. Then he nodded his head to the side, and Howie realized he wasn't waving but trying to get Howie to look at someone across the room. It took a moment for him to understand who he was supposed to be looking at. He scanned the crowd, and then he saw her.

Bethany Carver.

Howie's legs went weak, and he grabbed the wall to hold himself up. Bethany hadn't seen him yet, as her back was to him while she conversed with someone.

How is she here? I can't do this, not today, Howie thought.

While they had remained in contact until she found out Howie was writing the memoir, he hadn't actually seen her since a few months after the massacre. Twenty-five years later, yet he still felt that strange feeling come over him at the sight of her, just like it did in high school. She was battle-worn but beautiful as ever, her long blonde hair flowing down to the middle of her back.

Howie had a thought to sneak out the back door and never return. He wasn't sure he could face her after what he had put her through. There was also the fact that anytime she was in his presence, he was hit with an overwhelming sense of guilt. His best friend, who died trying to save them, had been in love with Bethany since second grade. And the more Howie hung out with her through high school, the more he shared similar feelings for her. In a way, he felt relieved that she avoided him all these years. She was one of his best childhood friends, but she was also the only girl he ever truly loved.

Again, he was a kid in a grown man's body, taken back to 1999 on the inside while his body fell apart on the outside. As he attempted to move to a different part of the crowd, Bethany turned and locked eyes with him. It was like everyone else in the room disappeared. Someone gave their condolences from Howie's side, but he drowned them out. Bethany smiled and gave a slow wave, then walked toward him.

His heart rate accelerated.

"Howie Burke. Give me a hug," she said.

He leaned in, his posture as stiff as a senior on prom night, and she wrapped her arms around him. She smelled wonderful, and he could have held the embrace forever.

When he pulled away, she was crying.

"Bethany, I'm so sorry. For everything."

She bit her lower lip and shook her head.

"Not now, Howie. Right now, we need to celebrate your mother. There will be time for this conversation later, okay?"

He nodded, relieved to change the subject—for now. Then a thought occurred to him.

"How did you even find out about her? I'm so happy you came, but to say I'm in shock right now would be an understatement."

"Shawn. He emailed me and said he thought I should know. Said he knew you would want me here but were too scared to ask after...everything that happened."

Howie shot a look to where Shawn had been standing, but he was gone. He made a mental note to rip him a new one when he found him.

"I just...I could never get over the guilt I felt. Once I was old enough to realize the pain I caused, it was too late."

"It's never too late, Howie," she said, her hypnotic hazel eyes staring into his. He didn't know how to respond, and he could feel his cheeks burning. Now that she was closer, he noticed how she'd aged. He had to remember that she had also been to hell and back. Watching her parents and sister be brutally murdered at the hands of the coven, seeing Cory fall to his death after they had just recently confessed their feelings to one another, and then being adopted in the prime years of her childhood and moving a few thousand miles south, away from her friends, away from the only people she ever knew. Howie was all she had left back then, and he fucked it up.

"Can we talk later? I really should greet other guests, then I'm supposed to say something about Mom. But it's so good to see you. You have no idea what this means to me, Bethany."

He found himself choking up, worried his voice was about to crack.

"Yes, I want to catch up. I'll be in town for a few days before we head back to Florida."

Howie's heart sank. *We?* He couldn't help feeling a twinge of jealousy at the thought of her with someone. It was selfish. Stupid. Unrealistic. But he had no control over it.

"Oh, you brought someone? I'd love to meet them," he lied.

It was Bethany's turn to blush. She turned and scanned the area she had just come from.

"Ryan! Come here! Howie wants to meet you," she said over the crowd.

Ryan... The name made him think of Ryan Star, another of his best friends who died that fatal night at the high school.

His eyes immediately flitted back and forth across the crowd to see which man would step forward, then was taken aback to discover a young child, a boy who had to be under the age of ten, trying to squeeze through the adults. The kid ran to Bethany's side and clung to her, looking like a deer in headlights. He buried his face in her side, hiding his features.

"This is my son, Ryan. The best thing that's ever happened to me," she said, kneeling to get eye level with him. "Ryan, this is my good friend, Howie. We grew up together. Can you say hi?"

Ryan buried his face deeper and shook his head. Bethany patted him on the hair and gave Howie a mock frown.

"I'm sorry, he's extra shy today. So many strangers. Plus, we had to take the red eye here. Only flight that had seats on short notice."

Howie laughed, catching one of the boy's eyes peering out from beneath Bethany's arm.

"Don't worry about it, bud. I'm an acquired taste. I like your name. One of my best friends was named Ryan," Howie said.

"That's who he's named after. I figured if my son grew up to be half the man Star would have been, I did something right."

The thought of Ryan always made Howie emotional. It was such a beautiful gesture, and it made him respect her more than he already did. She whispered something in Ryan's ear, and the boy separated from her and sped back to the corner of the room he had been hiding in.

"He's the spitting image of you. Although I don't ever remember Bethany Carver being shy," Howie said.

He expected her to laugh but instead, she glanced back at her son before speaking. "The poor kid has been through so much. His dad isn't even in his life."

"Sorry to hear that."

"He's strong, he'll be fine. So will I," she said, then placed her hand on Howie's shoulder. "What about you? How are you handling all this?"

"I don't think the shock has worn off yet, to be honest. Once she's buried and there's nothing left for me to do here, then I'll probably have no choice but to think about it more."

"We've done enough grieving for multiple lifetimes, haven't we? It's not fair."

An awkward silence followed, which was interrupted by Veronica, and Howie had never been so happy to see the old lady.

"I'm sorry, Howie. It's time to start the service."

Howie nodded, then turned back to Bethany.

"We're doing a small get-together after at Salt Hill Pub. I'd love to chat some more. Bring your kiddo," he said.

"Sounds good. It's great to see you, Howie."

And with that, she was lost in the crowd. Howie had gone years without seeing her, yet now that he had a small taste, he didn't want to let her go again.

Veronica cleared her throat to regain his attention.

"Sorry. I'm ready now," he said. As he approached the front of the room, he realized how untrue that was.

After his speech—more of an incoherent rambling, if he was being honest—Howie made his rounds to thank each person individually for coming. Bethany took off with Ryan, apologizing for her son's lack of patience, but promising she'd meet up with him later at Salt Hill.

When he was done, exhaustion set in and he lumbered out of the funeral home, loosened his tie, and sat on the curb. He grabbed a bottle of water that he had snagged from the welcome area and took a long sip. As he watched people leaving, going back to their normal lives, unlikely to have another passing thought of his mother, he noticed Zack King, the kid from the motel, pushing through the crowd toward him.

"Fuck me. Not right now," he muttered to himself.

He immediately felt bad when Zack got close, holding a bouquet of flowers. The boy hesitated, so Howie waved him over and forced a smile.

"Hey, kid, thanks for coming. You didn't need to do that."

"I'm sorry about your mom. I didn't know if I should come since I didn't know either of you well, but it felt like the right thing to do," he said, handing Howie the flowers.

"You're a good kid. Surprised you were given time off work to come here," Howie joked.

"School day. I work nights and weekends. Gramp has me working any free minute I have, though, that's for sure. It's okay, though. I got nothing better to do. Plus, it's how I found your book and had time to read it."

"Someone actually bought my book at the motel?"

"Yeah, I think it was my gramp. But the copy sat there for months untouched, so I took it. He hasn't said anything about it missing, so I'm claiming it as mine." He sounded rather proud of himself, much to Howie's somewhat conflicted amusement.

"Well, since I signed it to you, I guess he can't take it back now, right?" *Maybe it's a good thing he hasn't run into me yet, then.*

"He's pretty old now. Honestly, I'm okay with him staying away. He's kind of a grump."

They sat in silence for a few minutes, and Howie's thoughts shifted to the coven. About how so many long-term residents had ties to them, and he wondered if Zack's grandfather was part of it all. Then his mind came back to what he considered responsible for his mom's death.

"Hey…you told me a lot of kids you go to school with are mixed up in drugs. Have you run into anyone who has used needles at all?"

Zack's eyes narrowed in confusion. Howie understood the kid assumed he might be asking for himself.

"All kinds of drugs, really. Why you asking?"

"I'm not going to pretend to know the first thing about what kids do these days, but it was clear when I drove into town that this place wasn't the same. I've seen more junkies in Newport than I did on a Friday night in Vegas. I…" he trailed off, uncertain if he wanted to confess to a kid he hardly knew that his mom was a closet druggie who overdosed.

Fuck it, I need answers, Howie thought.

"I found a box in my mom's house. It contained a needle and some slimy green substance. Smelled like death. The reason I ask is because she was never into drugs, and she was a healthy lady, so her death doesn't sit right with me. I think that stuff had something to do with it."

Howie noticed Zack's Adam's apple bob up and down, his eyes cutting to the left to avoid eye contact.

"I don't really hang with that crowd, but I've heard of it. It's got a few names."

Howie arched his eyebrows. "Oh yeah? Like what?"

"Devil Juice, Swamp Sauce, but most people call it Thred."

"Those all sound so appealing," Howie said sarcastically. "Why would anyone put that shit in their body? I saw it. Looked like poison."

"It *is* poison. It's taken over the past few years. Before that it was just normal drugs, but it's gotten worse every year."

"Any idea who's responsible for distributing it?"

Zack coughed a nervous laugh. "Me? I wouldn't have a clue. Do I scream druggie to you?"

"No. But neither did my mom. And now she's dead."

Zack turned red. "I'm really sorry. That was a stupid thing to say—"

Howie held up a hand to stop him.

"Don't worry about it, I know you didn't mean anything bad. I'm just trying to figure out how my mom got it, and what on earth could have convinced her to try it in the first place."

"I can ask around for you. Least I can do," Zack said, sounding far too eager for Howie's comfort.

"You barely know me, kid. That's way too dangerous to get mixed up in. You seem like you got a good head on your shoulders. No need to mess that up."

Zack shrugged. "You're right, I barely know you. But you barely know *me*. I have no life outside of the motel, and you're the first person to show me any ounce of respect, maybe ever."

Howie was ashamed that he let himself even consider letting Zack get involved, but he felt like he was talking to himself. The parallels were eerie, to say the least. Only Howie had his group of friends growing up—a pack of kids who would do anything for each other, no matter how bad things got. Poor Zack didn't even have *that*.

A lot of good that did me. All my friends are dead because of me. Can't put this kid into the same danger, Howie thought.

"I appreciate it, I really do. But I'm going to have to pass. I shouldn't have even asked you about it." Howie smiled, his earlier annoyances with Zack dissolving. He was just an earnest kid wanting to help, just like Howie and his friends had been. "You're a good kid, and probably the only one in this town who actually *enjoyed* my book. That's more than enough support for a walking cancer like me. Promise me you won't get involved?"

Zack sighed deeply. "Fine. But if you change your mind, I'm your guy."

Howie got to his feet and shook the kid's hand.

"I'll see you at the motel. Thanks again for the flowers."

As Howie walked away, his mind wandered, too distracted by all the things he needed to do: go to the cemetery to watch his mom buried, set up the party at Salt Hill, and countless other errands that the day wasn't long enough to complete.

Had he not been so distracted, he might have noticed the figure in the alleyway watching them, listening to every word, hanging around like a vulture waiting for roadkill to take its last breath.

CHAPTER 16

1979

The trunk groaned under the weight of their final load as Henry slammed it shut, eager to leave behind the motel's mildew, mice, and unsettling atmosphere. He walked around to Jessica's side, where she smiled through the open window. The motel loomed behind her, still as bleak as ever. Henry ignored it for the moment, leaning in to kiss her on the forehead.

"We're finally leaving this place and on to our forever home, babe. I just have to check out, then we can go. I can't wait for you to see it!"

"And I can't wait to see it myself," she said with mounting excitement.

He kissed her again and headed toward the motel lobby. A blinding glare from the morning sun reflected off the window, forcing Henry to squint as he opened the door, setting off the bell hanging above. He blinked to erase the bright spots flashing through his vision, expecting to find Tim Ripple sitting in the chair where he seemed to spend most of his time.

There was no one manning the front desk.

"Hello? You in here, Tim?"

The clock ticked from the far wall in the otherwise silent lobby. Henry waited impatiently by the desk, wanting nothing more than to leave this place behind and never come back. After another minute of standing around, Henry tapped on the dust covered service bell sitting on the counter.

"Hello? Just looking to check out."

He considered just leaving, saying to hell with checking out. They paid in cash anyway, so he wasn't even sure if he technically needed to do anything. But he wanted to let the motel owner know about the hole in the wall and the rodents that had made the space their home.

Henry's curiosity got the better of him, so he walked around the small space, inspecting the framed photos and décor. He stopped at a black-and-white image. In it, a group of people in matching clothes faced the camera, not smiling, not laughing, just...*looking*. Their gazes were so intense and focused, Henry felt like they were looking directly at him. It sent a chill down his spine, and as if it wasn't creepy enough, he spotted Tim in the photo. The same bald head, the same Coke bottle glasses, but he was only a teen. He either lost his hair really young or shaved it his entire life.

If it was a family photo, it sure was a strange one. Henry leaned closer to get a better look to see if he recognized anyone else from town.

"Hi there!" Tim said from a few feet behind him.

Henry jumped with a start and turned around to find the motel owner smiling, his stained teeth fully exposed.

"You scared me. I rang the bell a few minutes ago, was about to give up and hit the road."

"Sorry about that, I was just out back taking care of some stuff. Must've been making too much noise to hear ya," Tim said.

Yeah, right. This place isn't that big, Henry thought.

"I'm just looking to check out. And again, I wanted to apologize for my actions the other night. It's been a stressful few weeks, to say the least."

"No apologies necessary. I made a joke that was out of line, and you called me on it." Tim made his way behind the desk and picked up a clipboard. "Not much you need to do for checking out. Just need the key and signature on the guest log."

Henry scribbled his name and the date, then set the room key on the counter.

"Oh, before I forget. Our room seems to be a breeding ground for a family of mice that live in the wall. We kept hearing them scurrying around at night. Found a hole they like to go in and out of."

Tim's lips thinned as he stared at Henry, his mood immediately shifting from happy-go-lucky to defensive.

"I'm so sorry you had to deal with that, Mr. Black. I'll be sure to get that taken care of as soon as possible."

"It's fine. I just thought you should know, that's all. We appreciate your hospitality."

Henry made for the exit when Tim spoke again before he had the door open, "We want newcomers in town to feel welcomed. Don't wanna be scaring them with rodents. I'll put some traps out." He then asked, in a lighter tone, "So, when's the big day?"

Confused, Henry turned around. "Excuse me?"

"Wedding day! When you two tying the knot?"

Henry didn't recall telling the clerk that he had proposed to Jessica the other night, but it must have come up in passing.

"Oh, uh, we haven't set a date yet. Sooner than later, though. I don't remember telling you about it."

Tim chuckled.

"When you've been in this industry as long as I have, you can tell. You two are ripe with young love. Just an educated guess on my end."

"Well maybe you should pick up a second job as a fortune teller. Because I proposed to her just the other day. We plan to elope once we get settled in the house. How long you been doing this?"

"Since high school. My parents ran it before me."

"You don't look that old," Henry said, thinking how depressing it must be to spend your entire life in a place like this.

"I'm forty. Still a kid inside, though. I still laugh at farts and blush when a beautiful lady looks at me."

You sure didn't have a problem keeping your eyes on my fiancée, Henry thought, but decided to keep it civil.

"Well, have a good one. And thanks again."

"Pleasure's all ours!" Tim said, as Henry walked out the door, triggering the bell again.

"Fucking weirdo," he muttered to himself.

When he reached the car, he opened the driver's side door and hopped in. Jessica was filing her nails, humming "Hotel California." Henry sniggered, thinking The Eagles wouldn't exactly picture a shoddy motel like this when writing that one.

"What's so funny?" Jessica asked.

"Oh, nothing. Just ready to get out of this dump."

"You and me both. Let's go see our home," she said, leaning in and kissing him on the cheek.

Henry backed out of his parking spot, taking one last glance toward the motel. The glare from the sun still blasted the front of the building, but he noticed one of the curtains move as he drove away. It wasn't until he got on the main road that he realized it wasn't the lobby window that the curtain moved in.

It was their motel room.

CHAPTER 17

Henry pulled up the driveway, simultaneously paying attention to where he was driving and trying to catch Jessica's reaction when she saw the house for the first time. He parked the car and turned to her, relieved to see a wide smile.

"What do you think?"

"It's perfect, Henry! We have our own place!"

"Let's go check it out, shall we?"

Jessica didn't answer, just opened her door and excitedly climbed out. Henry followed her to the porch. The home was a white split-level with a small overhang porch. Henry had hoped to find a place with a wraparound farmer's porch, but this was within their budget.

He handed Jessica the keys, gesturing for her to have the honor of being the first to enter.

"After you, madam," he said in a fake British accent.

Jessica giggled and excitedly turned the key, then burst through the front door.

"It's perfect, Henry!"

"You haven't even seen the place yet, love," he teased. But he knew it didn't even matter what the inside looked like. She had freedom. From her family. From her forced religion. The home wasn't just a place to live—it was a sign of her newfound independence.

"This will be our living room. I can picture a couch right there." She pointed to the far wall. "And a dining table here! The kitchen's a little small, but we can make it work," she said as she rounded the corner. She went from room to room, admiring it like a kid getting to visit the North Pole. Henry trailed behind, absorbing the happy moment.

When they reached the center of the main floor, they came to a small staircase going up and another going down. Jessica chose to check the lower level, speeding down the smooth wooden steps.

"Careful! Don't need you slipping and breaking your neck before we even move in," Henry joked.

The lower level had an open concept floor plan, revealing a space the realtor called the family room. The left wall had two doors, one which led to a small laundry room, the other to what the previous owners had used as an office.

"It's so big down here! Maybe we can use the living room upstairs as a large dining room and make this our living room?" Jessica asked.

"Whatever you want. 'Happy wife, happy life.' Isn't that the saying?"

Jessica hugged him again, then noticed the feature on the far wall and gasped.

"Oh, Henry, I've always wanted a fireplace!"

"It's propane, not wood, but I knew you'd love it. I'm sure we'll spend plenty of time right here in front of it with a drink and a book."

Jessica's elated expression became almost dreamy. "It sounds perfect."

They moved to the laundry room, which had its own toilet. And as a bonus, the previous owners left their old washer and dryer. Henry appreciated it, as their money would only last maybe six months if he didn't find a sufficient job to match what he made down south.

Next, they entered the small office, which had wood panels going halfway up the wall and bright red shag carpet.

"Yikes! We'll have to put new carpet in, but this will do for now."

Henry couldn't agree more. The room looked more like a seventies shrine to worship the Devil than it did an actual office, especially with the lights off. When he had toured the home and put in an offer, the light was on and the curtains open, so he hadn't noticed how damn creepy the room actually was.

"It will be an easy fix for sure. I figured you could use this space as your study. We can install some bookshelves along the wall and put a nice desk in here for you."

"Thank you, thank you, thank you!"

She wrapped her arms around him and locked lips, and for the thousandth time in the last few months, Henry had to keep his arousal at bay. The wedding couldn't come fast enough.

She grabbed his hand and pulled him out of the room and up the stairs to the second level, where the three bedrooms were located. It was a small hallway with four doors—two on each side. To the left were two smaller bedrooms, to the right the master and main bathroom.

"Two extra rooms for any little Henrys running around," he said.

"What makes you so sure we'll have boys, Mr. Black?"

"Who says I won't name a little girl after me?"

Jessica slapped his shoulder and entered the master bedroom, which had its own full bathroom. As far as master bedrooms went, it wasn't huge by any measure, but it was far bigger than what either of them had back home. The closet was also a nice size, but Henry assumed he'd still lose two-thirds of it to Jessica. But he was okay with that. This was the first step in their journey.

"I love it. How soon will the furniture be delivered?" Jessica asked excitedly.

"Perfect world, it would have been here for us already. But it should arrive within a few days. In the meantime, we can either go back to the motel or camp out on the floor with sleeping bags like a couple of squatters."

"I'd sleep in the trunk of the car before I went back to that place. We can make it comfy in here until the stuff comes," she said, then her eyes lit up. "Oh! We get to have our first meal here tonight! How exciting. Obviously, we won't be able to cook yet, but maybe get takeout from somewhere?"

Henry chuckled, her happiness contagious. "Sounds good to me. Bill said Plaza Pizza was a great spot. Just opened recently. Told me the pizza's to die for."

"Then it's settled. Now we should unpack some of our stuff from the car, huh?"

"Nonsense," Henry said, shaking his head. "I'll grab all the boxes while you relax, explore some more, and envision how you want the rest of this place to look."

She smiled and kissed him on the cheek. Henry turned and exited the house, feeling that the fresh start they were looking for was finally here.

Jessica lingered in the spare bedrooms, imagining a family, safe, growing, and *hers*. She pictured a new life here without ever needing to worry about the stress of her parents forcing her to live by their rules. They called them "God's rules," but she knew plenty of her friends growing up never had to deal with half as much as she did.

Satisfied with her exploration of the upstairs, Jessica made her way back down to the main floor, noticing a three-season porch with a sliding glass door. She stepped out to an amazing view. All three walls were lined with large windows overlooking the forest beyond. It was an ideal place to relax after a long day.

As she envisioned sitting out in a hammock with a cup of tea while reading a book, something caught her attention in the woods. The sun had yet to come over the front of the house, leaving the backyard and forest covered in shadow, so it was difficult to see with any clarity. But she sensed movement. And with it, the feeling that something was watching her. She froze in place, locking her eyes on the swaying branches. All of the excitement she felt seconds before, now put on pause.

Just the branches blowing in the wind, she thought.

In her heart, she didn't believe that, though. It was more than seeing something. It was *feeling* it. Before she even caught a glimpse of movement, she sensed eyes on her. After a few minutes of watching the forest, Jessica left the porch, entered the home, and locked the sliding door behind her.

Her biggest fear was discovering that her parents knew where she was and that they sent members of the church to retrieve her. She reminded herself that PTSD would never go away. Glancing over her shoulder was part of her normal life now, and she had to accept that. Still, it didn't make it any easier to live with. And she sure as hell couldn't tell Henry. Not when he put so much effort into securing her safety. Put his life on pause, leaving his job and home behind so they could start over together.

He was the perfect man, and she felt extremely grateful whenever she allowed herself to take it all in.

She decided to take a second tour of the house now that the initial surprise had worn off a bit. When she made it to the family room, she noticed a door they hadn't opened. She opened it, staring down into the darkness, choked by a sudden panic attack.

The basement.

Jessica did not like basements.

It was the place her parents often locked her in to teach her lessons; to confess her sins to the miniature statue of Jesus they'd displayed overlooking the basement floor. She was often forced to sleep multiple days at a time on the concrete floor with only minimal food and water.

They moved away so she could overcome her fears and start over. Entering the basement was part of that. She turned the light on, relieved that it worked, illuminating the space below. The stairs were wooden but sturdy, unlike the warped stairs that groaned every time she had faced punishment.

The air felt much heavier, like it hadn't been disturbed in decades. The basement was unfinished, with cold concrete floors and a looming oil tank in the corner beside the furnace. A large bench went from wall to wall on the opposite side of the room, and Jessica imagined Henry spending time down here, putting his carpentry skills to good use.

The space was very dusty, which wasn't surprising considering the ceiling wasn't finished, allowing all the dirt and grime from above to fall through the spaces in the plywood between the ceiling beams. She forced herself to step deeper into the basement, and that's when she noticed something on the back of the bench, hidden from the overhanging light.

She approached it with unease, somehow drawn to it by an invisible thread.

It was a book.

Not just any book, but one that resembled a Bible. Except rather than the words *Holy Bible*, there was a strange symbol on the front. She had never seen it before but knew immediately that it held religious significance. Instead of a cross, engraved on the center of the cover were the raised letters *WT* with what Jessica thought to be a serpent tongue wrapped around them. She slid her fingers over the symbol, noticing that while the table itself was covered in dust, the book was perfectly clean. It was as if it had just been placed there a few minutes before Jessica arrived.

The thought caused her to whirl around and make sure nobody was standing over her shoulder. The basement was empty. She turned back to the book and flipped to the first page. As the cover opened, a whisper came with it, but it was inside her head. Indistinguishable words, but she knew they were telling her to read on.

There were pictures, passages, and handwritten pages. Jessica realized what she was looking at, and it sent her heart rate into overdrive. It was a book that belonged to the coven; the same coven she had learned of at dinner with Sheila and Bill. The same coven she wanted to know more about, and here was their handbook, teasing her with their power.

How did they know she wanted to learn about them? Did they plant it here a while ago? Or just before she and Henry pulled into the driveway?

Jessica thought back to the sensation of being watched on the porch.

There was a sense of comfort, knowing they'd hand-delivered the book to her. She couldn't bring herself to think of the reasons they knew of her curiosity, or how they got into the house uninvited. That didn't matter right now. What did matter was that she had the answers to what she sought. Before she even read a single page, she knew this book would show her the way.

CHAPTER 18

2024

Zack King sat behind the desk at the motel, staring at the old wallpaper that peeled like dead skin, his mind racing. He had promised he wouldn't get involved, but his thoughts kept going back to what Howie said. How his mom never did drugs, that something didn't add up. Zack wasn't stupid. He heard stories of how easy it was to get hooked on the stuff.

But the biggest reason Zack knew his fair share about Thred was because his grandfather sold it. Zack wasn't allowed to question it, and anytime someone came to the motel to buy, he had to turn a blind eye while his gramp made a deal in whatever room the junkies were staying in.

The motel would easily have gone out of business a few years ago if not for Thred. It was a battle Zack faced internally every single day. Watch the people around him crumble as they filled their veins with poison, or see the family business shut down after generations of being a staple in Newport. It wasn't just pride—his family knew nothing else. The motel was their everything. And while Zack didn't know the specifics as to what led to his grandfather selling the stuff, he knew there was a higher power controlling it all. He heard whispers around town, and on a few occasions, had eavesdropped on his gramp talking with someone in the lobby at night after he thought Zack was sleeping in the back room.

Zack was only three when his parents died. His grandfather told him it was a car accident when Zack had been at the motel. He had next to no memories of them, and those that he did have, he realized were likely from repeatedly hearing the stories of them from his gramp growing up. His entire life revolved around his grandfather and the motel.

He had lied to Howie when he mentioned only working at the motel when he wasn't in school. The truth was that Zack had never attended public school. He was homeschooled by his grandfather, who only taught him what he considered necessary to live. There were no real academics outside of reading and writing. There was occasional math work, but he was allowed to use a calculator for that. Most of what Zack learned, he got from watching television or eavesdropping on customers.

When he discovered a copy of Howie Burke's memoir in the motel lobby, his life changed forever. He had only heard bits and pieces of the things that happened back in the seventies and nineties, and Howie's book helped fill in many of the gaps. Of course, Zack's grandfather would not have approved of him taking the memoir, let alone reading it. He used to wonder why his gramp even kept a copy of the book, then figured it out one night when he heard him talking with someone buying Thred. The customer asked about the book, and Grandpa told them he read it to make sure the motel wasn't painted in a negative light. Otherwise, Mr. Burke would have heard from his lawyer.

Zack spent so much time working at the front desk that he had nothing better to do than read, and what better to read than the horrifying past of his hometown? He obsessed over the book, reading it multiple times, so much so that he felt like he knew Howie and his friends. Then, when Howie magically showed up at the motel's doorstep, it felt like a sign.

While he said he'd stay out of the mess, he felt that if Howie really knew his connections to it all, he would reconsider that request. Zack just wasn't ready to admit that to him yet. He didn't want to risk his literary idol holding him responsible in any way for his mother's death.

Zack had put a lot of thought into how he would help; how he would gather information that Howie might find useful. The next time his gramp told him to go to the back so he could handle business, Zack would do just that, then slip out the back door and get a good look at who was bringing the supply to the motel.

Zack knew the motel was just one of the many outlets for Thred to be distributed. And while he didn't want to mess anything up for the motel, he knew it was his best chance at gathering enough intel. It was like clockwork. Twice a week, a black station wagon would pull into the parking lot, and Zack's grandfather would tell him to head to the back so he could attend to business.

Today happened to be one of those days.

So, while Howie mourned the loss of his mother with family and friends, Zack would get to work. As the sun set, he heard his grandfather shuffling around in the back office, then saw the headlights of a vehicle pulling into the parking lot cut through the lobby window, momentarily blinding Zack. His gramp exited the back office and stepped behind the front desk.

"Okay, kid, let me handle some business. You know the drill. Off you go."

Zack forced a smile but couldn't help noticing how old his grandfather looked. Tim Ripple had been part of the motel for decades, running it himself for the majority of that time. Zack knew that after the murders in the seventies, his gramp was forced to grow up fast, taking on more responsibilities than he otherwise would have needed to. The years of stress and worry had taken their toll on the old man. As much as Zack despised the situation, and as horrible as he felt for the residents of Newport who were dependent on Thred to numb the pain after so much loss in their lives, he understood why his grandfather did what he did. Zack wouldn't have done the same himself, but desperate people would go to desperate lengths to fix things.

And Tim Ripple was a desperate man.

"Okay, Gramp. I'll be in the back if you need me."

His grandfather motioned him away with a distracted wave, keeping his bifocals locked on the parking lot.

How dangerous are these people? Zack wondered as he slipped into the back office.

He shut the door, leaving it cracked enough to hopefully pick up more of the conversation. There was another door in the far corner of the office that led to the back of the motel where they stored the dumpster. Zack planned to listen to some of the conversation, then sneak through the back and around the side of the motel to get a better view of the dealer.

The motel bell chimed when the front door opened.

Zack leaned against the wall, close to the back office door.

"Good evening, gentlemen," Gramp said.

"It's a good evening indeed, but I don't think *gentleman* is the best way to describe my associate," a deeper voice responded. "How has distribution been this week?"

"A little slower, sir. But I'm moving it as quickly as I can."

Zack couldn't believe how nervous his grandfather sounded. Normally, he was the most confident old man Zack knew. He didn't take shit from anyone. But right now, Zack could hear the quiver in his voice.

"A little slower," the man repeated ominously. "You know I don't like excuses, Tim. We are doing important work here. Just like you used to help my father, you now help me. You believe in the cause, do you not?"

What cause? Who the hell is this man? Zack wondered.

"Y-yes, sir. It's just...after the Burke son came back to town, we've had to be extra careful. He's asking questions about his mother."

Zack felt like he'd been punched in the gut. Howie was right. Something happened to his mother, and Zack's grandfather knew about it.

"We knew this would happen, Tim. As a matter of fact, we *wanted* it to happen. Howie Burke coming back to Newport is part of our plan."

"What do you need him for? He was out of your hair for years. Now he's back snooping around."

"Mr. Burke simply being *out of our hair*, as you put it, isn't enough. Not that I need to explain this to you, but he is responsible for our father disappearing. We have spent two decades trying to bring him back, and now we know where he is. And we know what must be done to bring him back, stronger than ever. You play a big part in that, Tim. Do *not* let me down."

Zack thought he might throw up. He always had a feeling his grandfather was involved with the coven somehow, and he was just provided proof. They wanted something from Howie, and Thred was somehow involved.

He wanted to stay and listen more, but knew he only had a few minutes. If he wanted to get a look at the man speaking, he needed to get outside right now. Carefully, he snuck through the office, then slowly turned the knob on the back door and stepped out into the night.

The rotten stench of the dumpster hit him hard. The alleyway behind the motel wrapped around the building, hiding Zack from plain sight, yet he still felt completely exposed. He clung to the side of the building until he reached the corner, then peered out at the parking lot.

The station wagon idled in front of the lobby door, but it was too dark to see inside the car from his vantage point. Zack considered his options. Taking a gamble and running to the car to look for any possible clues was what his heart wanted him to do, but he knew that was a stupid idea and could get him killed. Still, after learning Howie might be in danger, Zack didn't care as much about his own safety. Howie was a hero in this town. Even if half of the remaining residents didn't see it that way anymore, *Zack* saw it that way.

Before he read the memoir, depression had been a constant, dark cloud over his head. The isolation through the years, being picked on whenever he showed his face in town, living the same routine every single day...it got to him. On more than one occasion, Zack had considered ending it. He knew exactly where Gramp kept his gun. But Howie's book had changed everything. It answered questions Zack never thought to ask or hoped to gain answers to. It showed him it was okay to be the weird kid, that it was still possible to make friends, that there was more out there beyond Newport. There was hope even for the most hopeless kid in a backwater town.

He made up his mind: it was worth the risk. Howie was worth the risk. He crouched and ran across the parking lot toward the car, quickly glancing back at the lobby window to make sure nobody saw him. The blinds hid him, but they also blocked out whoever was standing at the desk talking to his grandfather.

Zack moved around to the driver's side, the car now blocking him completely from the motel. His hands were sweaty and his heart rate accelerated as he reached out with shaking hands and quietly opened the driver's door. He had no idea what he was looking for, but he couldn't leave empty-handed. The front was empty, almost too clean. He leaned over and opened the glove box, which triggered the light in the cubby.

He quickly rummaged through the belongings, only to come away empty-handed. There was nothing of use here. As he prepared to exit the car, the back seat caught his attention. The space back there appeared more...lived in. Like maybe the man in charge sat back there. Zack didn't dare open another door, afraid to make too much noise. Instead, he climbed over the front seat into the back.

"Come on, give me something," he whispered.

A bottle of Thred sat in the cupholder, but it was different than the stuff Zack had pictured. There was no needle, nothing to shoot it with. Instead, it was in a tumbler, as though it was mixed in a shake. Did the leader drink this shit?

He didn't dare touch it, too afraid to even come in contact with the substance. Then his eyes landed on the pouch on the back of the driver's seat. He reached in and pulled out all the contents, mostly just papers and things that meant nothing to Zack.

This is taking too long, they'll be out any second, he thought. That fear made him take another glance at the lobby again. There was movement behind the blinds. He had to hurry.

As he shoved the contents back into the pouch, a small black book fell from the stack and landed on the floor. Zack quickly picked it up and flipped through the pages. His heart leaped and sank at the contents. It was some type of handbook for the coven. Symbols, spells, phrases; some in English, others in what he assumed to be Latin.

It felt important.

He shoved it into his pocket and started to climb back over the front seat to exit the vehicle.

The bell jingled on the lobby door.

Shit!

He had to not only escape, but somehow shut the door so that they wouldn't hear it en route to the vehicle. Zack quickly climbed back into the driver's seat, almost bumping the horn as he did. Two figures stood in the doorway of the lobby, their backs still facing him; the shorter man holding the door open while the tall dealer continued talking to his grandfather.

Zack took advantage of the distraction and climbed out of the car, crouching behind it. He gradually pushed the door until it was an inch from shutting, clenching his teeth so hard that his jaw hurt, and then he gave the door a quick shove, cringing as it clicked shut. The sound was quiet and muffled, but it might as well have been a gunshot going off in the quiet night.

He wouldn't be able to make it back behind the building without being seen, so he turned and ran to the ditch near the edge of the parking lot and climbed down in. Just as he readjusted himself to get a better look at the men leaving the motel, they were there, moving halfway across the parking lot toward the station wagon. Did they see him? It was too dark to tell.

As they got closer, he recognized the shorter figure.

He couldn't believe who he was looking at.

Derrick Patten.

Why would Derrick get involved with this stuff? Zack quickly realized it was a stupid question. While Derrick had been a hero in his own right back in the nineties, he had matured into a life of irrelevance. The stereotypical high school jock-turned-town drunk. It wasn't surprising to see him trying to gain back some of that power he lost from his youth.

Still, he was blindsided seeing someone who, up to this moment, Zack had no reason to believe was involved. And there was something about Derrick that wasn't right. Zack had only talked to him a few times over the years, but he just seemed...off. His posture was hunched, his facial expression numb, and the way his bottom jaw hung open like there was something inside his mouth trying to claw its way out. His eyes were dead to the world as he opened the back door for his boss, a man Zack did not recognize. Tall, intimidating, with eyes a piercing green that almost lit his face, his presence stifling. He wore black dress pants with a button-up shirt that fit him tightly, showing off his chiseled physique.

"Bring me to the office, Derrick," the leader said.

After the man climbed in, Derrick moved around to the driver's side and opened his own door. As he went to climb in, he paused, snapping his head toward the ditch.

Zack dropped out of sight, holding his breath.

He saw me. He's going to come over and kill me, right here at the motel.

But it never happened. Instead, Zack heard the door shut and risked lifting his head enough to see the car pulling out. It was too late to try and follow them.

It didn't matter. Zack had obtained far more information than he could have expected on his first night trying to help. He knew what he needed to do next, and he knew it was going to be dangerous. Zack decided it was time to pay Derrick Patten's home a visit. The tall man said he wanted to be driven to the office. That meant Derrick wouldn't be going straight home. It was now or never.

Zack's grandfather would expect him to be working in the back office until bedtime, which meant he needed to sneak out. He took one last glance in the window, finding his gramp behind the front desk reading through a newspaper like he was stuck in the nineties. Zack took advantage of the situation, climbing on his bike and speeding away from the motel.

Toward Derrick Patten's home.

CHAPTER 19

Howie entered the private function room of the Salt Hill Pub, wishing he were anywhere else but surrounded by sad looks and forced sympathy. He felt bad showing up late to something *he* set up, but he knew half the people here were likely just taking advantage of discounted drinks and hoping to hear any gossip. One of the many things he didn't miss about a small town was everyone's insistence on knowing everything about everyone.

Music played at a low volume, drowned out by the chatter of the crowd as they sipped their drinks. Howie scanned the wall, seeing Boston Red Sox, Celtics, and Bruins memorabilia scattered across in no particular order. He was thankful that everyone appeared too occupied to notice his entrance.

As he glanced across the bar, there were many faces he didn't recognize, but then his eyes landed on Bethany, making his heart flutter. It was like being in her presence turned back the clock, giving him the mentality of a lovestruck teen again.

She was tending to her son, who sat in a chair with his eyes glued to a tablet. She handed him a kid's drink from the bar, then allowed her attention to swing back to the crowd. She spotted Howie and smiled, waving him over. It reminded him of the night spent at Sunset Lanes as kids—the last fun night they ever had. Back then, Howie had walked in, just as disheveled as he was now, and Bethany had called him over to the lane they rented for glow bowling. That was the first time he admitted to himself that he, too, loved her, just like Cory did. It was also the night Cory killed his first victim, Larry Foreman, the owner of the bowling alley and a coven member.

He shook the memory and cut through the crowd to reach Bethany.

"You made it!" she joked.

"Suppose I didn't have a choice, huh? Sorry I'm late."

"No need to apologize, Howie. At least not to me. But Ryan over here..." she said, ruffling her son's hair, "he's running out of things to watch on his tablet."

A smile creased Howie's face. Hearing his friend's name had a way of doing that.

"Sorry, dude. You know, back when your mom and I were your age, we didn't even have tablets or cell phones. We had to make our own fun."

Ryan glanced up and arched a brow. "That sounds boring. I'm glad I'm not old like you guys," he said with a smirk. The kid had his mother's wit, that was for sure.

"Ryan Carver! We're not old. And maybe it'll do you some good to get off that screen for a few," Bethany said.

"Someone learned your sass," Howie joked.

"Yeah, well, what was it you used to say your dad always said? 'Do as I say, not as I do.'"

"Yep, that's the one. Along with many other sage words of wisdom."

An awkward silence followed, somehow amplified by the chatter surrounding them, as if they were the only two in the entire bar not talking.

Howie cleared his throat. "Thanks again for coming. Can't believe Shawn reached out to you."

"Why's that? Were you afraid to see me, Howie?" she asked flirtatiously.

"Honestly...I didn't think you'd ever talk to me again after the book. I—"

"I've forgiven you for it. It's okay, really. Yes, I hated you for years. I felt hurt, betrayed, and that the one person left in this world who I could trust had broken that trust. But as time went on, and I was able to take a levelheaded approach to it all, I understood why you did it. And I appreciate you leaving out many of the details about my family. I could tell that in your own way, you were trying to protect my privacy."

Howie's eyes stung with tears. He wanted to say something, but it took a moment for him to regain his composure.

"Thank you. It doesn't mean I don't regret it every single day. And then my mom moved back here, erasing the sole reason for me writing it. Not a day went by that I didn't want to call you and talk. After the last email I sent went unanswered, I forced myself to stop."

"Nothing you could have said would have helped when I had my blinders on. I needed time and space. I wish it didn't take something so horrible for us to cross paths again."

Someone approached from the corner of Howie's eye. All he wanted was for everyone else to leave. Now that he had Bethany back in his life, he didn't want to let her go.

It was an older man who interrupted their conversation, someone Howie didn't recognize at first. The man was hobbling up to Howie with a grimace, a worn Newport Tigers baseball cap covering his salt-and-pepper hair that hadn't been cut in a while.

"Howie Burke?" the man asked, his hands trembling.

The stench of cheap beer gave him the familiar scent of decades-old grief.

"That's me. I'm sorry, do I know you?"

"You probably don't remember me, but I'm Matt Kelly's dad. I'm sorry about your mom and all, but I just wanted to let you know that I didn't appreciate the way you portrayed my son in your book. He died that night, and all you did was make him sound like a dumb jock who bullied you all. You should be ashamed of yourself, trying to make a buck off our suffering."

Just lovely, Howie thought.

"Look...I'm sorry about a lot of the things I wrote. Not just about Matt, but all of it. You have every right to hate me. I don't blame you. But now's not the time for this. My mom just died, man."

"And I said I was sorry to hear that, but I wasn't going to let you slip away again—"

Bethany stepped forward, standing between them.

"Mr. Kelly, he already apologized. Have some decency and walk away."

"*Decency?* Maybe big shot here shoulda had some decency and—"

"And what? Not told the world how awful your son was to all of us growing up? Nobody deserved to die that night, but let's face it, your son was an asshole. A misogynistic jerk who treated everyone like they were beneath him. Howie and his friends *still* tried to save Matt that night, but your son was too focused on maintaining the high school pecking order. So I suggest you leave, maybe go downstairs and drink in the regular bar and not the private function for Howie's mom."

Mr. Kelly scowled. "Yeah...I'll be on my way. I hope it still haunts you like it does me."

"More than you know," Howie mumbled to himself.

With that, Mr. Kelly walked away and bumped past Howie on his way to the stairwell that led to the main bar.

"Wow. Reminds me of the time you told that dirtbag reporter off for me when we were kids. I should hire you as my bodyguard," Howie joked.

"You couldn't afford me," Bethany said with a wink.

"I'm sure you won't be in town long, but I'd love to hang out without...all of this," Howie said, gesturing to the crowd of people. "How long you sticking around?"

"I haven't figured that out yet. All these years, I never planned to come back to Newport. But now that I'm here, there is that sense of nostalgia under all the bad memories, you know?"

"Yep. One minute, I'm driving around doing the McDonald's 500 for old times' sake. The next, I'm passing the school and seeing the top of the ski jump towering over the town like a giant tombstone."

"Jesus. That's an image right there. No wonder you became a writer."

"Mommy, I'm really bored. Can we please go?"

They both turned to Ryan, who had set his tablet down and was just people watching.

"Soon, love. Just let me catch up with Howie some more, okay?" Bethany asked, prompting an impatient sigh from her son. "Unless you want to go mingle with others," she said to Howie.

"Please, I don't want to be here. You're the only one keeping me sane."

As Howie spoke, another person approached, this time a middle-aged woman. Again, someone Howie didn't recognize. She had short blonde hair, reminding him of something Sharon Stone would have rocked in her prime. Her skin was smooth, almost tricking Howie into thinking she was their peer until she got up close. Her hazel eyes represented someone with far too much wisdom to be anyone younger. She was at least a head taller than Bethany, who sensed Howie staring over her shoulder and turned to see who was approaching.

"Hi, guys. Sorry to interrupt. I just wanted to come over and give my condolences, Howie. You probably don't remember me, but your mom used to babysit me when I was a little girl."

"Thank you for coming. She would be grateful. I'm sorry, what's your name?"

"Oh, where are my manners? Tanya Pearce. I moved out of town when I graduated, but your mom left a lasting impression on me. I felt I needed to come pay my respects. You were lucky to have her as a mother."

Howie smiled sadly. "Thanks. And I agree. I just wish I had more time with her."

Howie realized he was bringing the mood of the conversation down, but he couldn't help it. If these people were coming up to him and expecting him to say something about his mom, they should have known things could get emotional. Tanya turned to Ryan, sitting in his chair and sipping on the straw in his drink.

"And who might this young man be? Your two's son?"

"My name's Ryan. But that's definitely not my daddy."

Howie let out a nervous laugh, and again, Bethany swooped in for the save.

"I'm Ryan's mom, Bethany. Howie and I were childhood friends. My son and I came up from Florida to be here for Howie."

"Aw, that's sweet of you. A pleasure to meet you and this handsome little man here," she said, kneeling to meet Ryan. "You must be pretty bored being the only kid here, huh?"

"Yes! But my mom promised me a new bike if I was good this week-end," he said, then resumed sucking on the straw. It started to slurp the bottom of the empty glass.

"And you're doing an admirable job, Ryan. I think that drink is gone, though. I'd be happy to grab you another, assuming it's okay with your mom," Tanya said.

Ryan shot a look at Bethany with desperate eyes.

"Oh, fine. But this is the *last* one. You know soda is a special treat," she said.

"Thank you! Can I have a Sprite?"

Bethany nodded. Tanya held out her hand for Ryan to grab, and the boy didn't think twice.

"Oh...um, I can get it for him. He isn't usually too comfortable around strangers," Bethany said.

Howie sensed her unease. After what they had been through, he understood all too well how hard it was to trust people you didn't know. Hell, even people you *did* know, especially in this damn town.

"Nonsense. Kids can sense good people. They're like dogs in that way. You can catch up with Howie, and I'll take Ryan over to grab a drink."

"Ryan, do you want Mommy to come with you?" Bethany asked, a last-ditch attempt to maintain control of the situation.

"No, it's okay," he said, leaning closer to his mom. "I like this lady," he whispered.

Bethany smiled and let go of her son. Tanya pulled him through the crowd toward the bar. Howie and Bethany didn't say anything at first, both too focused on Ryan and making sure he was safe.

"He's a good kid. And you're a good mom. I always knew you would be," Howie said.

Bethany turned to him, prying her eyes off Ryan just long enough to flash a smile.

"Oh, yeah? Based on all the times I had to look out for you boys back in high school?"

"Yeah, you could say that," Howie said with a chuckle. His expression quickly sobered. "Have you noticed how bad it's gotten here? Newport was never popping with life, but it's like a ghost town out there. And the drugs...Shawn said it's become a real problem over the past few years."

"It's sad to see. As bad as things got for us, this place was our home. It did have its good moments though, right?" Bethany sounded hopeful, but it was halfhearted at best.

"Yeah...it did. It brought all of us together. Something my therapist always tries to get me to focus on are the good memories of my childhood. I've done a lot of thinking on that lately. We really did have the best group of friends."

They sat silent, watching as Tanya flagged down the bartender and Ryan stood on his tiptoes to see his drink filled.

"My mom...she didn't die of natural causes, Bethany. I found a box in her closet that had some strange drug inside. The kid from the motel told me it's called Thred and that a lot of people in Newport have gotten hooked on it."

Bethany again took her eyes off her son and furrowed her brow.

"Your mom? She'd never do drugs."

"Exactly. I don't understand how it happened. But I need answers. I wish Shawn would get back to me. Last time we talked, he basically said to stay out of it and let him handle it. Unfortunately, the cops in this town don't have the best track record. But... he's Todd's family."

"Howie, I'm so sorry. I had no idea it was something like this," she said, then pulled him into a gentle embrace.

Howie closed his eyes, fighting back tears. "Death is death. But why can't there be a fucking normal death in this town?"

Bethany kissed the top of his head, and in that moment, Howie wanted to be nowhere else. But Tanya and Ryan had come back from the bar, forcing them to part. The boy had a huge grin on his face as he gulped down a large portion of his Sprite.

"You got a good kid here. So much innocence. To be young again, am I right?" Tanya asked.

"You can say that again," Bethany said.

Tanya shifted her attention to Howie. "I know you don't know me well, but I would have done just about anything for your mom, but if there's anything else you need, help packing her things or anything like that, please let me know. I'm happy to help."

"That's really nice of you. I don't think I'll need any help, but it's a kind gesture. Thank you."

"Well,"—Tanya grabbed a pen and cocktail napkin from the table— "here's my number, just in case. Same goes for you, Bethany."

She ripped the napkin in half and wrote the number a second time, then handed one to each of them.

"Thank you for being nice to my son. He doesn't usually take to people so easy," Bethany said.

"Anytime! Maybe I'll see you around before you head out of town." Tanya smiled, winking at Ryan. She gave a polite wave, then made her way through the crowd.

"She was nice," Bethany said.

Howie didn't hear her. He was too busy watching as Tanya left the bar, thinking how hard it was to trust anyone in this town.

"Earth to Howie?"

He blinked and turned his attention back to Bethany.

"Sorry, I was just thinking about how I don't recognize most of these people. Maybe that's a good thing." Howie rubbed the back of his neck awkwardly. "I should probably get out of here. I'm mentally exhausted after today, and tomorrow I need to go back to my mom's place and pack up more stuff."

"Care for some company tomorrow? Not sure how much Ryan can lift, but we're in town for at least another day or two. I'd be happy to help."

"You don't have to do that. I'm a depressed mess. Not too much fun to be around, especially there."

"I want to be there. There's been an emptiness without you in my life. Need to get in as much Howie time as I can. Even if you're bringing back the emo boy in you from the nineties."

"Hey! I wasn't emo. I was too cool for that. Cory was the emo boy. I liked awesome bands like Limp Bizkit and Godsmack." Howie laughed.

"Those sound *so* much better," Bethany drawled sarcastically. "You can't get rid of us so easy. What time should we meet you tomorrow?"

"I'll be there all day. Stop by whenever. I'll have some beer in the fridge waiting...and Sprite."

Ryan looked up from his drink with his eyes wide, and Howie smiled in return.

"Okay. See you tomorrow, Howie," Bethany said, then leaned in and kissed him on the cheek.

He watched them as they walked away, forgetting he was the one who intended to leave first. For the first time in days, he felt a sense of happiness he didn't think was possible. Maybe things would turn out okay, after all.

CHAPTER 20

1979

Jessica ran her hand over the pages, feeling more alive than she had in years. She'd read the book front to back, soaking in its knowledge, listening for its voice.

It spoke to her, helped her understand. And the more she read the book, the more she knew this was what she had been seeking this entire time. She wasn't even sure how long it had been since they moved into the house. A week? Longer? Henry had handled moving everything in and setting up their new home, allowing her to do what she needed to do. He had also reminded her countless times about their decision to elope, but she was far too distracted to make plans for that. Bill and Sheila visited a few times to check out the home and brought housewarming gifts, but Jessica only had a faint memory of talking with them. Her mind was in one place.

It comes from within.

That phrase meant something. It was in the book repeatedly, carving a way into her brain. When she lay down at night to sleep, the phrase slithered through her mind, a distant voice whispering to her.

Jessica knew, even before she practiced what she read in the book, that it was real. And she knew the magic within would work. So it wasn't surprising when the first spell showed her it was all worth it. It was a healing spell. Jessica had taken a sharp knife, carving a line down the center of her palm. There was a moment of panic when the blood started to pour over the bench, staining the wood crimson. But that fear quickly dissipated as she recited the healing spell, watching as the blood flow stopped and the wound slowly sealed. It hadn't been a small gash; in fact, she feared she'd cut too deep for the spell to work. And it wasn't just the wound that disappeared, but the pain as well.

This is what a true greater power could do for someone. The book regularly mentioned a greater power named Vorathor. It detailed sacrifices. All of this would terrify the unfaithful, but not the devout. Not Jessica.

Ever since she discovered the book, Jessica had a recurring sense of being watched. What once had her peeking out windows, locking every door, and clinging to Henry's presence had slowly converted into something else—an acceptance. A sense that whatever watched her now...was guiding her. Making sure she knew she wasn't alone in her discovery of faith.

It comes from within.

Jessica knew it was important. Far more important than any prayer or Scripture. She was ready to take the next step and meet the coven. How she would accomplish that, she wasn't sure. As she sat on the red carpet in her dimly lit study, she considered her options. Right now, Henry was running errands and searching for a job before their savings ran dry. They only had one vehicle, and even if they had another, Jessica had never driven a car. Her parents raised her to be terrified of all the horrible things that could happen to someone behind the wheel. Now that she understood they had been trying to fabricate risks so she would remain their religious puppet, she understood driving wasn't scary. But it was too late to change her ways. She could try and force the awful thoughts away, but her parents beat them into her until they were buried deep. So driving was out of the question.

She could walk, but she wasn't sure where to go yet. Although she thought someone or something would give her a sign along the way. Jessica wrapped the book in cloth and returned it to the desk drawer, then locked the drawer to keep it safe. She pulled back the curtain to find that the day had once again gotten away from her, the sky now a star-filled black canvas.

She left the study, feeling an odd sense of silence as she walked through the house. It wasn't just quiet, it was hollow. The voice that had followed her from room to room for days was suddenly gone. It left her feeling exposed.

The house was dark, and Jessica wondered how long Henry had been gone. She walked into the kitchen and opened the refrigerator, grabbing a pitcher of water. As she shut the door, she sensed movement in the far corner of the dining room.

"Hello? Henry? Is that you?"

"It's time. Join us."

The voice—no, *voices*—hummed all around her, as if the entire coven was hiding in the dark corners of her home. Jessica's pulse thrummed. She couldn't see anyone, but she knew she wasn't alone. Slowly, she reached out and flipped on the kitchen light. And almost screamed.

Someone in a black robe stood in the corner of the dining room, the hood hiding their facial features as the kitchen light didn't quite reach them.

"Who are you?"

"No need to be scared, Jessica. We have been watching you closely. We left you a housewarming gift, you could say. I'm here to introduce myself."

The voice was male and as the figure stepped forward, Jessica realized how tall the man was. She wanted to feel at ease, knowing it was someone from the coven here to greet her, but this man sent a chill down her spine.

"Why are you in my home? My fiancé will be back soon."

She knew it was an empty threat and understood that this man knew it too.

"I'm not here to threaten you or harm you, Jessica. My name is Brian White, and I am part of The Withered Tongues. Have you...*enjoyed* our book?"

Jessica hesitated. But almost against her will, her voice clawed up from her throat. "Y-yes. It has changed my life. How can I join? Tell me the way, *please*."

"Eager. We love to see that. You see, it's not often that we trust someone with the book. We've had eyes on you since you arrived in town. We knew that you were one of the chosen."

The chosen. It sounded so important.

Jessica thought back to the motel and how no matter where she went, it always felt as if someone was behind her. The movements in the walls. Was it possible someone had been observing her in the privacy of their room? The thought made her sick, but she didn't dare question it. She couldn't mess this up.

"What do I need to do? I'll do anything to join!"

"We take new members very seriously, Jessica. You have passed the first test. The next test will not be so easy. Tell me, do you have plans tonight?"

"Henry...he'll be here soon and would worry about me if I wasn't home."

"No, dear. Haven't you wondered why he's not back already? We... have our ways of taking care of problems."

Jessica's stomach dropped. "Don't you dare hurt him! He's the reason we even came to this town."

"We will not harm him. But we have taken him out of the equation tonight. He won't even know what happened. Tomorrow he will wake up comfortable in his own bed, a day wiser."

Jessica understood what he was telling her. They had put Henry under a spell—one she recalled reading about in the book. She tried to ignore the fact that they tricked Henry, doing something to him against his will. She could only hope it would have no lasting effect on him.

"So, what do you need me to do? I'll do anything for Vorathor."

"I want you to come with me, Jessica. I want you to meet the other members of the coven. And tonight will be your initiation. Where the Jessica you see in the mirror becomes a thing of the past. You will be stronger than ever before." Brian stepped closer, nearly looming over Jessica. "Does that sound good to you?"

Tears slid down her face. Everything she had sought would soon be hers.

"Yes. Please take me to them. Thank you. *Thank* you."

"We have a car waiting right out front. Come join me and be prepared to have your life changed forever."

Jessica followed the man outside, spotting a black station wagon idling in the driveway. Brian stopped, motioning her toward the car. The back door opened from the inside, and she saw the outline of two more coven members. She hesitated, suddenly unsure. Was this truly what she wanted? Something felt wrong, but she longed for a place to belong; the freedom to believe what she chose.

She was halfway to the car when something was drawn gently over her head. A hood soaked in an acrid sweet scent. She gasped, legs buckling. Maybe she couldn't trust these people. But then the mantra of The Withered Tongues repeated itself, and all was right again. She heard the voice one final time.

"It comes from within."

CHAPTER 21

Jessica awoke unaware of where she was. Her head pounded as she tried to sit up, a bout of nausea overwhelming her. She leaned over and threw up, noticing she was somewhere outside, in the pitch black. Her eyes were blurry, and she had to place both hands on the grass to hold herself up. As her senses came back to her, she heard a sound. Like a consistent hum in the distance.

As shapes came back into focus, Jessica realized she was in the forest. The last thing she remembered was...

The coven member, Brian White. He was taking me somewhere special. But then...they did something to me, she thought.

Where was she? It was far too dark to identify her location, especially with nothing but trees surrounding her on both sides. Then the volume of the humming increased, and she realized it wasn't humming at all. It was chanting.

The coven.

She forced herself to her feet, hit with a spiraling dizzy spell. She found herself in a field on the other side of a line of trees. Behind them, a throbbing green glow forced its way through, as if calling to her. Jessica wondered why they would have just left her alone like this to fend for herself.

As she got closer to the trees, the low chant became clearer. It was the four words she had come to hear for hours every day.

It comes from within.

She peered through an open space in the trees and spotted the pond. She had seen it in her dreams, had read about it in her book. But when she saw it on the hike with Henry, its true beauty hadn't presented itself. The water glistened in the moonlight, a sheen of bright green covering the surface.

Around the pond, dozens of robed figures stood at the water's edge holding hands, surrounding the entire perimeter, not a single break in their connection. In the middle of the dock, a tall man stood front and center leading the chant with raised arms

Is that Brian White? Is he the leader of The Withered Tongues? She stepped out into the open, closer to the dock.

Suddenly, the chanting stopped, and every single member of the coven turned to face her. Jessica felt paralyzed under their stares, made small and meek. Their faces were hidden by their hoods, but a hint of green shone from their eyes. Jessica froze, waiting for someone to speak. If the silence stretched any longer, she might turn and bolt into the woods, run all the way to her home, and tell Henry they must leave town immediately. But then she was reminded of two things: The coven had done something to Henry and she had no idea where he was. Additionally, she didn't know where this pond was in relation to her house.

Someone stepped out of the trees to her left, and Jessica backpedaled away from the figure. She recognized him instantly as Brian White. But if he was next to her, who was the tall man on the dock?

"Jessica...sorry if we scared you. We felt it was best that you woke up away from the ceremony so that you weren't startled as soon as your eyes opened. I was to be with you when you awoke, but I left your side for a moment when I shouldn't have."

"Wha-what did you do to me?" Her voice trembled with fear and elation.

"Simply a precaution, I assure you. We needed to be sure we got you to this location expediently. And now that you are here, we can proceed. Please, follow me."

Brian walked toward the dock. Up close like this, Jessica finally got a good look at his face. He wore thick glasses and had a brown beard with no mustache. He walked with an eerie confidence through the crowd of coven members. If he wasn't in charge, he at least had to be high in the hierarchy. Jessica felt every single set of eyes on her as she followed Brian to the dock where the tall man waited. The closer she got to the water, the brighter it became, as if it fed off her presence.

Brian walked up to the tall man and whispered something in his ear. Seeing them side by side made Jessica realize just how big this other man was. His face was covered by an all-black mask with no facial features. The three of them were alone on the dock as the rest of The Withered Tongues remained around the water's edge, watching. *Waiting.*

The tall man called the attention of the coven members, his voice bellowing out: "My people, join me in welcoming the vessel that we have been in search of. The missing piece brings us what we seek. Tonight's gathering is the most important in our history, as it will bridge us with Vorathor, making us whole. It will forge a relationship between Vorathor and Vodyanoy, two of the most powerful entities this universe has ever known," the man said, turning his attention to Jessica. His eyes were a hazy white, shifting behind the mask. She wanted to meld with the dock or jump into the water and never come back up. And yet...she found a cold strength under his gaze. She knew how important this was—how important *she* was.

"You are here because we chose you. *He* chose you. You must understand the importance of this. In a moment, we will bring forward a sacrifice. You will do as I say, following all the instructions, or it will not work as intended. Do you understand?"

Jessica nodded slowly.

The leader motioned toward the pond. Jessica turned to see two coven members, fully robed and wearing white masks that looked identical to the black mask worn by the tall man. They held something in their hands. As they got closer, she realized they were gripping large chalices tightly against their bodies, as if whatever each contained was extremely valuable.

"What I need you to do now is lie on the dock and face the sky. What we do next will not be comfortable for you, but understand that it will all be worth it, Jessica."

The two coven members stepped up to her side. Something splashed around within their chalices, giving off a shine that faintly lit their masks. Jessica had no idea what was inside, but she didn't want it anywhere near her body. Yet, she knew the substance would play a part in what came next.

As she tried to see inside one chalice, a commotion came from somewhere behind the dock. Jessica turned and saw two more coven members dragging a young girl toward the pond. She screamed and tried breaking free. The hooded members ignored and overpowered her.

"To obtain power, one must sacrifice. This offering is our sacrifice to the pond. To Vodyanoy. By us giving him something, he gives us something in return. Power. Connection. A link that binds every single one of us in The Withered Tongues."

The girl being dragged looked like an innocent teen who had been yanked out of bed in the middle of the night, her white gown torn and smeared with blood. The members of the coven had a firm grip beneath each armpit, but the girl wasn't giving up without a fight. She lifted her legs high and kicked one of her captors in the face, sending the white mask soaring into the pond.

Frozen, Jessica watched it float on the surface, a green glow emanating from the eye holes.

The water bubbled around it like a boiling pot.

More screams.

Jessica shifted her focus back to the girl, just as the coven member who lost his mask punched her in the face, cutting her cries short.

"Do you have it under control or not?" the leader snapped.

It was the first time Jessica noticed any lack of confidence in the coven.

"Yes. Sorry, sir."

"Don't be sorry to me. Be sorry to Jessica. And to Vodyanoy. Now, let's get on with it."

Without another word, the two coven members dragged the dazed girl to the edge of the dock, her blonde hair covering most of her face. They lifted her, forcing her into a standing position, then waited for their next order.

One of the members holding the chalices approached Jessica. Now up close, she smelled a strange odor coming from within. It stung her nostrils, and she again feared having the contents anywhere near her.

"The first chalice," the leader demanded.

The coven member held it out to Jessica, giving her a clear view. A bright green substance sloshed around inside, clinging to the wall of the chalice. It moved and writhed, as if searching for something.

Searching for me, she thought.

As she focused on its movements, a calmness overcame her unlike anything she had ever felt. The paralyzing shock and fear that had been choking her from the inside vanished.

This is what she was supposed to do. This is what she was here for. This is what belonging felt like.

Her hand trembled as it reached for the chalice. A flicker of Henry's voice in her head begged her to stop. But then came the chorus of whispers.

"It comes from within."

"Drink it," the leader said.

Jessica did as she was told. She raised the chalice toward her lips and could have sworn that the slimy substance reached for her, whispering into her mind—her soul— in an ancient tongue.

She didn't think, holding her breath as she poured the contents into her mouth. She tried to swallow, but the substance clung to her tongue, wanting to move at its own pace. Her mouth burned as the substance slithered down her throat; it was both intoxicating and excruciating. Jessica dropped the chalice onto the dock, clutching at her neck. She couldn't breathe, the slime suffocating her.

"It's okay, Jessica. Do not worry. This is how it's supposed to feel. Soon, the pain will be gone, and you will feel better than you ever have before. Now, lie on your back."

His voice was so calming. Jessica knew she would do anything for this man. For this coven. She slowly lowered her body onto the dock, gasping and shaking. Flashes of Henry attempted to vie for her attention, but she pushed them and the pain aside.

As she stared at the night sky, the coven began to chant around the pond. It was a language she wasn't familiar with, yet she knew the message.

It comes from within.

The leader's voice led the way, deeper, more powerful than the rest.

The girl they had dragged to the dock must have been coming to her senses, as her cries now mixed in with the chants. The water simmered, the brightness intensifying. Jessica no longer felt fear or pity for the girl.

With each sentence the coven chanted, the substance inside Jessica's body spread. To her limbs. Her organs. Her *mind*.

"Let me go!" the girl yelled.

Again, her cries were cut short by someone's fist.

As Jessica lay on the dock, she sensed movement in the water, beneath the surface.

"Exsurge, daemon edax carnis, et hanc hostiam accipe, quam tibi devoti offerimus. Ab intus be it!" the leader shouted.

The coven repeated the phrase in unison: *"Ab intus be it! Ab intus be it! Ab intus be it!"*

It comes from within.

The substance spread throughout her insides, tingling every nerve along the way.

Her vision blurred; the substance was blinding her. The coven leader stood over Jessica, his black mask staring down at her. He drew a long dagger from his robe, the moonlight glimmering off the blade.

She thought that he might lean closer and cut her, slit her throat and sacrifice her to the pond along with the girl they dragged here. But he stepped over Jessica, closing in on the offering being held up by two members of The Withered Tongues. One of them pulled back on her blonde locks, exposing her throat to the night sky.

"Thank you for your sacrifice," the leader said calmly—*too* calmly.

Then he raised the blade and slid it across her throat. Her eyes shot open, just long enough to see the blood pump from her throat onto the dock. The coven members pushed her over the edge, into the green water. There was no more screaming or struggling. No attempts to climb back onto land. The girl remained on the surface for a few seconds, then multiple sets of pale hands covered in green slime shot out of the water, wrapping around her body and pulling her below.

Jessica's vision continued to blur, but she wasn't alarmed. She heard the girl's skin being torn from bones, heard the faint moans of a dying person making one last weakened plea.

The blurred sky above Jessica darkened, and she soon realized it wasn't the sky, but the leader of the coven again standing over her. No longer holding the blade, he instead held the second chalice filled with the green substance. While her vision faded, Jessica's hearing intensified, so much so that she thought she could hear a pin drop. She heard the hands tearing the girl's body apart. She heard the coven chanting. She heard the heavy but calm breathing of the leader as he leaned close to her, his cold hand cradled the back of her neck.

"We need you to drink the second chalice, Jessica. This...will hurt. But pain for the greater power is pain most would be honored to endure. Close your eyes. Open your mouth. When you awaken, you will be a changed woman. *More* than a woman. You will officially be one of us."

Jessica's voice was so calm, so foreign to her own ears. "Yes...whatever must be done for Vorathor. For Vodyanoy. I'm ready to merge us with the water demon. Please, tell me your name. I must know the leader I am devoting myself to."

"Of course," the man said in a pleased tone. "I am Felix Ruger. I am the vessel in this world for Vorathor."

Jessica closed her eyes and opened her mouth wide.

The coven continued their chants.

"Ab intus be it! Ab intus be it! Ab intus be it!"

Then Ruger poured the liquid into her mouth. He was right—it was agonizing. The pain she felt before was nothing compared to the piercing daggers now coursing through her veins. She opened her eyes, and while she couldn't see more than a few feet, she noticed green lines branching beneath her skin, traveling through her entire body. Her back arched, snapping in multiple places as the substance wrapped around her bones, fusing with her nerves.

The Withered Tongues grew louder.

A burning sensation formed in the pit of her stomach, pulsating as it expanded into her chest. Ruger began to bellow a passage from the book. Something Jessica recalled reading just a few days prior.

Like her vision, she knew the rest of her body was fading as well. Before she lost consciousness, she had one last thought upon realizing what the leader of the coven chanted.

He is conjuring the demon.

As darkness claimed her, something else opened its eyes inside her skin, inside her soul.

CHAPTER 22

2024

Zack approached Laurel Street on his bike with only the occasional streetlight to guide him along the way. He knew he might not have long to search Derrick Patten's home before he showed up and also knew he might not even find anything useful. He was just lucky he remembered where Derrick lived. When the school had its homecoming parade a few years back, Zack rode his bike into town to watch it. He had picked a spot on the side of the street where the parade route would travel through, which just so happened to be across the street from Derrick's house. He wouldn't have known had Derrick not come out hungover, yelling at the sirens on all the cop cars and fire trucks to "Shut the fuck up!"

The home came into view up ahead. Zack felt his stomach drop just before he stopped pedaling fifty feet from the house.

Derrick's truck sat in the driveway.

Scattered thoughts bounced around inside his head, but then he remembered that Derrick was driving the black station wagon, so he wouldn't have his truck. He slowly approached the driveway, making sure no neighbors were watching from their windows. Why would they be? It was the middle of the night. Most sane people would be sleeping peacefully in their beds, not snooping around some drug dealer's home.

He hopped off his bike, pushing it the rest of the way until he reached the driveway, then hid the bike out of sight of the road in front of Derrick's truck. His nerves were a jangled mess, but he forced himself to continue. There were no streetlights in this neighborhood, and while Zack hated the fact that anyone or anything could be waiting around the corner, he appreciated the extra cover that nightfall provided.

Derrick's house was a modest, single-level ranch, so Zack hoped it wouldn't take too long to search. At least he knew a home like this, in small-town Newport, wouldn't have any top-notch security.

Just to be sure, Zack checked the front door, finding it locked as expected. Many people in town felt it was safe enough to leave the front doors unlocked, the keys in the ignition of their cars...until Thred became an issue. And given the fact that Derrick was somehow involved in the distribution of the drug, it was no wonder he'd lock up.

Zack moved around the side of the house, creeping through the wet grass that reached his shins. Clearly, Derrick had let his normal day-to-day responsibilities slip. Around the rear of the home, Zack tried the back door, surprised and relieved to find it unlocked. That was one less problem to worry about.

The door led to the kitchen, which had an odor of rotting food and spoiled milk to it. Zack gagged, covering his nose with his shirt. He pulled out his flashlight from his backpack and turned it on. The beam revealed a counter cluttered with dirty dishes and trash. Sure enough, an open carton of milk sat near the sink.

Flies buzzed around, having a feast on all the crumbs and aging fruit. It seemed like nobody had been in the home for weeks.

Maybe since he got involved with Thred. Maybe this is a waste of time, Zack thought.

He left the kitchen, happy to distance himself from the disgusting stench trying to suffocate him. Not that the rest of the place smelled much better. The living room had a large sectional couch, far too big for the space it occupied, and a giant flat-screen television mounted on the wall between two windows. On the coffee table in front of the couch, more food wrappers and empty beer bottles were hogging the space.

"What a slob," Zack whispered.

He kicked some trash out of the way and opened the drawer on the coffee table. Inside, he found the television remote, a used syringe, and a bunch of past due bills. He grabbed a crumpled piece of paper next to the drug paraphernalia. On it was a strange sketch of what looked like a body of water with multiple sets of eyes watching from the trees in the background. Written beneath the drawing, he saw four words.

It comes from within.

On the back of the page, there were odd symbols he didn't recognize. And on the bottom, scribbled in barely legible writing were scattered thoughts that sent a chill down his spine.

They *are watching me.*
We must obey.
We will spread.
It comes from within.
We are watching **them**.

"What the hell?"

As disturbing as all of this was, it was the last sentence that really made Zack's skin crawl.

Who was "*We*," and who were they watching?

He balled the paper back up, returned it to the drawer, then wiped his hands on his pants as if that cleaned him of some deadly bacteria. Zack got to his feet and decided it was time to check elsewhere. He entered a hallway with a few doors on each side. The first one he checked was Derrick's bedroom, but all Zack found in there were dirty clothes and an unmade bed. The space smelled like body odor, reminding him of a room at the motel after a guest who had long overstayed their welcome finally departed.

As he trekked through the messy house, he thought maybe the notebook would be his only discovery. As he rummaged through a small office, something clattered in the distance.

Zack froze.

It sounded like it came from the other end of the house, maybe the kitchen.

Or below?

He turned slowly, ears straining. Another sound. A *thump*, faint but undeniable.

Making his way back to the kitchen, Zack spotted a door he hadn't noticed before that blended into the wall's color.

His pulse quickened. Yet he found himself approaching the door, needing to know. Derrick wasn't home, so something or someone had to make that sound. He reached out and turned the doorknob, expecting it to groan open and alert whoever was on the other side. Luckily, it opened silently, revealing a flight of stairs that led into darkness.

A basement. Of course it was a basement.

This is a mistake. Turn around and leave, he thought.

But he didn't listen to his inner voice. He took one step at a time, slowly descending. The air grew colder, thick with mildew and...something else. It wasn't a familiar scent, but it smelled almost chemical.

At the bottom was a wide, concrete basement with old rusted tools, unused gym equipment covered in dust, a washing machine with the door partially open and dirty clothes stuffed to the brim. Zack aimed the flashlight toward the washer–and felt his heart lurch into his throat. The shirt hanging out was covered in dried blood, making the machine look like a giant mouth chewing up some poor victim.

He shook the thought and aimed the beam at the far wall, seeing a second door, slightly ajar. Before he could convince himself to leave, he pressed forward, the smell intensifying the closer he got.

This is how people die in movies, you idiot...

Behind the second door was another, smaller room; shelves lined the walls with glass bottles and vials stacked like some underground apothecary. There were dozens of them. Most were filled with a slightly glowing green liquid.

Thred.

This wasn't just Derrick's private stash. It was a damn distribution center.

He stepped closer, reaching for one of the vials.

"Yessss. Join us. Take it."

Zack paused.

The substance talked to him.

He felt it calling him. Not only in his ears but something buried deep in his brain, whispering promises he couldn't comprehend.

As he reached out again, a soft moan came from behind the wall. He whipped his head toward the sound, aiming the flashlight and discovering another door. This one was made of solid steel, bolted on the outside.

He approached it slowly, the moaning becoming clearer.

Someone was behind the door, and it sounded like they were in a great deal of pain. Hands shaking, Zack undid the latch and pushed the door open. The door groaned loudly, the weight of it wearing down the rusty hinges.

Revealed was a room that smelled of piss and shit, causing Zack to let out an audible gag. It didn't take long to see the source of the smell.

In the far corner, a young girl maybe fifteen or sixteen years old sat curled up in a ball, hugging her grimy legs. She was rail-thin, mud-caked skin sagging from her bones. He aimed the light at her, triggering a scream, and she immediately shielded her eyes.

"Jesus! I'm sorry, are you okay?"

Dumb question, Sherlock, he thought.

The girl couldn't respond; she had a gag wrapped tightly around her face, pressing into her mouth. The fabric was soaked with blood. Her hands and ankles were tied up with thick zip ties. Based on her disheveled appearance, Zack figured she must have been kept in here for days.

He tried to hold his breath as he walked in. The girl crawled backward, keeping a safe distance between them.

"I'm not going to hurt you. I can help you escape. Okay?"

She whimpered, tears pooling in her eyes and flooding her face. He proceeded with caution, aware that any wrong movements might scare the girl more. The room was windowless, making Zack's flashlight the only source of visibility. As she continued to shield her eyes from the beam, he noticed bruising on her face. Her damp hair clung to her cheeks, hiding more bruises.

Zack pulled off his backpack, slowly unzipping it. His heart was racing.

"I'm pulling out a pocketknife. I promise I won't hurt you. I'm just going to cut the zip ties."

She looked up at him, eyes wide with pleading hope.

He took another step forward, careful to avoid the feces on the floor. This time, she didn't try to back away.

"Let me take that rag out of your mouth. I'm going to reach around and untie it, okay?"

More tears slid down her dirty cheeks. She nodded, hesitant, as though she wasn't sure she wanted him to touch her. He could only imagine what that monster was doing with her down here. He reached behind her head, her greasy hair sliding across his forearms made him instantly itchy all over. She couldn't help her appearance or smell, but that didn't stop Zack from feeling disgusted while being in the same room.

The knot on the back of the rag was tight, so he carefully raised the knife and placed the tip of the blade facing outward so it wouldn't stab her. He worked it until the fabric started to rip, then grabbed hold and tore it with his hands. It dropped to her lap, and Zack couldn't peel his eyes away. It was sopping wet with blood.

When he raised his gaze back to the girl, it took everything within him not to shout at the sight. Her mouth was ravaged, her lips cut, dry, and peeling. But it was what was *inside* her mouth that floored him. Behind her chipped teeth, a bloody nub sat where a tongue was supposed to be.

"Oh, my God."

Derrick had cut out her fucking tongue.

Suddenly, Zack didn't care about the drug anymore. He needed to go to the police as soon as he freed this girl and tell them how he found her.

"I'm going to do your hands next, then your feet. We're getting out of here."

He got to work on the zip tie, slicing back and forth. It was a thick plastic that wasn't easy to cut. As he worked, he felt the girl's body stiffen. The poor thing was terrified of the knife.

"It's okay, I won't hurt—"

He took his eyes off the zip tie mid-sentence to look at her and froze. Her eyes were wide, but they weren't staring at Zack.

They were looking over his shoulder.

She shook her head frantically, but Zack was no longer focused on her. He slowly turned, the hair on his neck standing on end.

Derrick Patten stood in the doorway, shirtless, his skin covered in grime and bruises. Bulging green veins branched across his upper body, wrapping around his waist and traveling up his torso to his arms. His appearance, the way he stood...it wasn't human. Not anymore. His limbs hung loosely, as if something inside was controlling him. His face was expressionless. His breathing was heavy and wet. A rusty tire iron hung from one hand.

He didn't speak. He didn't have to.

Derrick stepped all the way into the room, slamming the steel door shut with a finality that stole Zack's breath.

He was stuck in a hellhole with a monster.

The monster didn't wait. It came in swinging.

CHAPTER 23

Howie opened his eyes to a blinding light coming in through the front window. He numbly felt around for his phone, finding it tucked beneath his pillow on the couch. Instead of returning to the motel after he left Salt Hill, he decided to drive back to his childhood home. Maybe it was talking about memories with Bethany, maybe it was the liquor-infused confidence, but after vowing that he'd never sleep another night in the house, he somehow convinced himself it was a good idea.

An idea he now regretted.

He forced himself to sit up, attempting to ignore the familiar splitting headache behind his skull. Howie understood what he was subconsciously trying to do. He knew his mind wanted to forget this place and the things that happened. Living out of town helped to a degree, but booze helped more. Now that he was back in Newport—specifically the house his mother died in—the alcohol didn't quite take care of business. Instead, it just left him in a state of irritable fogginess.

Sluggishly, he shuffled to the kitchen for a drink. After taking a few sips of his water, he checked his phone and saw that he had a few missed calls and texts. The most recent text was from Bethany, saying she had a good time catching up last night and would stop by with Ryan sometime before lunch to help. But all he wanted to do was curl up on the couch and sleep the hangover away.

It was already past ten a.m., which didn't leave him much time to shower and clean up before they arrived. Howie scanned the living room, embarrassed to discover countless empty beer bottles littering the floor between all the half-packed boxes. He got to his feet and stepped over the trash and junk, making his way toward the kitchen. The medicine bucket that held all the painkillers and cold remedies was located under the sink exactly where it had been his entire childhood.

Howie pulled out three Advil and swallowed them down with a glass of tap water. He then grabbed a trash bag and walked around gathering all the bottles and food wrappers until the place looked presentable. The scent of bachelor slob still clung to the home, so he opened a few windows to let in some fresh air.

After taking a five-minute shower, Howie felt somewhat refreshed. He went back to the kitchen and opened the fridge to see if there was anything quick to eat. He smiled at the sight of Sprite, remembering that he promised Ryan he'd grab some. He didn't remember stopping at the store, which made him realize he hadn't been very responsible driving back to the house from the bar.

There wasn't much in the fridge, but Howie found some apples that hadn't gone bad yet and grabbed one. He packed a few more boxes in the kitchen after eating, then retreated to his childhood bedroom. The first time he came back in there, he had been too distracted by his mother's death to really take it in.

It was a time capsule of the best years of his life. Stepping foot inside brought him back to the nineties in all the best ways. Beyond all the movie posters, CDs, and VHS tapes, it was the pictures of his friends that hit a spot he didn't think could be reached anymore. It was something Howie pushed to the back of his memories—both intentionally and unintentionally—due to how much pain it brought on.

He walked up to his desk and scanned the collage he made back in his sophomore year of high school. There was one picture of Cory filming a scene in one of their awful horror movies, with Todd and Ryan the focus of the scene. Howie remembered all the little details about taking that picture out in the woods. The smells of the forest, the sounds of the birds chirping, and of course, Ryan complaining that they had to walk so far to film it.

The next photo was a group picture at a school dance. All the guys with their arms around one another's shoulders, and in the center of them was Bethany, smiling that heart-melting smile that was customary for her. Howie remembered the exact song playing when the picture was taken—"MMMBop," the earworm by Hanson. He remembered because every time the band said "bop," Todd, who stood behind Howie in the picture, thrust his genitalia against Howie's back and whispered the word in his ear.

"Fucking Todd. I miss you, man," Howie said. His bloodshot eyes burned, and he had to forcibly shake himself from his memories of his friends. Now wasn't the time for tears. Just as he left his room, the doorbell rang.

Howie glanced at himself in the hallway mirror on the way to the front door and almost jumped at his reflection. He looked like a walking corpse. He threw a baseball cap on and did a breath test, winced, and wished he had the toothbrush he left at the motel.

He opened the door and saw Bethany holding a large pizza, the aroma sending Howie's stomach into a fit of hunger.

"Oh, you know your way to a hungry man's heart."

"Don't give me too much credit. I know you and the guys worshipped Plaza Pizza, but I grabbed Village Pizza at the other end of town. Hope you don't mind."

Howie laughed. "Right now, I'd devour a frozen pizza. I ended up sleeping here last night and most of the food is stale or expired." His smile faded as he realized why the food was old. His mom died. She hadn't bought groceries in weeks. "Please, come on in. Don't mind the mess."

Bethany walked past him through the door, then Ryan hesitantly followed. He gave Howie a hint of a smirk on the way past.

"Hey, buddy. I got that Sprite I promised."

"You didn't have to do that, but thank you for thinking of Ryan," Bethany said.

"Of course. Let me clear off the table and we can eat lunch and catch up without all the people around, for once."

Howie entered the kitchen, embarrassed at the mess, even though he had every excuse in the world for it looking this way. He quickly slid some empty bottles and junk mail into the trash and grabbed the pizza box from Bethany.

Bethany's smile on him was sympathetic. "Howie, I can see it in your eyes. Don't worry about the mess. I live with a young boy, I'm used to messes."

He knew she was just being nice, but that was Bethany. Always trying to make people feel better. He grabbed some paper plates from the cupboard and the promised Sprite for Ryan from the refrigerator. After the night he had, Howie didn't feel like having a beer, so he grabbed two waters and brought everything to the table. Ryan immediately grabbed the can of soda and popped the tab.

"Easy, killer. Don't chug that thing. Only one today," Bethany said.

"Have you heard from Shawn? Last I saw him was briefly at my mom's funeral, but he hasn't answered my calls or texts since."

"No. I actually didn't even see him there. Only interaction I had with him was the email exchange," Bethany said.

He wasn't ready to explain everything going on to Bethany. Like Howie, she stayed away from Newport to avoid the problems. He couldn't tell her that Shawn was supposed to be looking into how and why his mother had Thred in her possession. Or how the kid from the motel was acting just like Howie and his friends growing up, sticking his nose into trouble to find answers he'd regret. Howie was worried about both Shawn and Zack.

"He must just be busy," he said.

"Really? In this town? What could he possibly be busy doing? There's nothing left here..." Bethany trailed off, her eyes trying to mask the pain of the troubles that used to exist in Newport.

Howie decided to change the subject. "I want to hear more about you guys. What have you been up to all these years? What's Little Man here into?" Howie asked, forcing a cheerful tone to lighten the mood.

"Ryan's life is far more interesting than mine. Guess what he wants to be when he grows up?" Bethany asked.

Out of the corner of his eye, Howie noticed Ryan glancing at him. "Hmm...a wrestler!"

Ryan giggled and shook his head.

"Tell him, buddy," Bethany said, ruffling her son's hair.

"I want to make movies. I make some with my toys at home and Mom says they're pretty good."

"No way! That's so cool. I need to see them. Think you can mail me a copy when you get home?"

Ryan looked at his mom and laughed.

"What? What's so funny?" Howie asked.

"He picks on me all the time for my lack of knowledge with technology. All his stuff is on his YouTube channel. You can watch it anywhere in the world. Isn't that cool?"

"Get out of here! We would have killed to have something like that as kids," Howie said, grabbing two slices of pepperoni pizza from the box. "What type of movies do you want to make?"

Bethany smiled. "That's the part you'll like the most."

"Scary movies!" Ryan exclaimed.

"A man after my own heart. Not sure how much your mother told you about our group of friends growing up, but we used to make scary movies too. Your mom even starred in a few of them."

Bethany kicked Howie under the table and gave him an exaggerated stare.

"Really? Can I watch them, Mom?"

Howie realized too late just what he'd mindlessly stepped in. Obviously, Bethany kept these things from her son for a reason. Maybe because all their friends in the movies were now dead, and she didn't want to have that heavy a discussion with him yet. Or, more likely, it was the foul language the guys always used while making the films.

"Well, those tapes aren't around anymore, which is probably a good thing. Wouldn't want you thinking we were less cool than you already do," Howie joked.

He bit into his first slice of pizza and savored the flavor. Clearly, he had missed out by being loyal to Plaza Pizza all those years.

"What about you, Howie? I know we talked briefly about life yesterday, but how have you been? I know that's a dumb question when your mother just passed away. I meant over the last decade that we haven't really talked," Bethany said.

"Boring. But that was by design. I needed a boring life after the craziness we dealt with. Working in finance was *not* something I ever expected to make my career. Hell, the thought of going back home and back to work after this bereavement leave is over is the last thing I want to do." Howie shrugged, the weight of his mediocre life pressing down on his shoulders. But that had been what he wanted. No adventures, no excitement, no cults or demons or nightmares. "I can't complain, though. After coming back here and seeing how much this place has decayed over the years, seeing so many people look sick or unwell, I feel like we dodged a bullet getting out of here."

"Yeah, when you look at it that way—" Bethany paused, glancing at her phone now vibrating on the table. "Ugh. Speaking of the real world, I need to take this. It's my boss. You cool hanging with Ryan for a few?"

"Sure. I'll tell him some more of his mother's dark secrets." Howie smirked.

Bethany rolled her eyes as she sped out of the kitchen and headed to the front porch.

Howie turned back to Ryan, who was slowly eating a slice of pizza while staring at the table. Howie felt that the kid liked him, or at least tolerated him. But without his mom here, it must have been a little intimidating.

"Hey," Howie said, leaning back in his chair. "Can I see one of those movies?"

Ryan's eyes lit up with excitement, and he was grabbing his tablet from his backpack before he even responded.

"Sure! Right now, I only have two uploaded. Do you wanna see the zombie one or the creepy doll one?" Ryan asked with a huge grin.

"Oh man, both sound awesome. Let's go with the zombie one."

Ryan swiped his finger across the screen, but Howie couldn't see what he was doing.

"Okay. Tap the play button," Ryan said, turning the screen so Howie could see.

Howie pressed play, immediately impressed with the display. The kid was a natural. The video started with a cardboard set that had been hand-painted to look like a downtown area, the camera moving slowly just above the ground level. Creepy music played in the background, edited in professionally, unlike the music Cory used to dub in by playing a CD in the background while filming.

"You did all this yourself?" Howie asked, impressed.

"Yup. Even the voices."

On the screen, a toy soldier walked through the town, momentarily pausing just in front of the camera for a dramatic shot.

"It's too quiet here," said the soldier in a child's voice imitating a grown man.

The camera panned out, and Howie caught a brief glimpse of Ryan's hand in the frame holding the figure. He held his smile in check. The whole thing was cuteness overload.

"How does it spread? This disease?" the soldier asked.

The creepy music paused as a zombie toy came into the far end of the shot. Howie furrowed his brow, the features of the zombie reminding him of something. The corpse was covered in green slime as it staggered forward.

"It's too late to stop it...it comes from within."

Howie stopped chewing his pizza. He stared at the screen; his words caught in his throat. He must have misheard the toy.

"Ryan, what did he just say?" Howie tried to ask calmly, but his voice trembled.

Ryan rewound the video, tapping the screen again to play.

The figure repeated the line, "It's too late to stop it...it comes from within."

A chill swept down Howie's arms.

"Where'd you hear that line? Who said that to you?"

Ryan shrugged. "I don't know. I just made it up."

But Howie wasn't listening. Not really. His heart was thudding. The pizza sat like a concrete slab in his stomach. His eyes drifted to the kitchen window, a sudden sense of being watched. Only his tired expression stared back at him with sunken eyes.

Did something just plant that in Howie's head? Did the video really say it? He thought back to his nightmare, of his mother jumping out of her casket covered in green sludge, of the crowd chanting behind him: *It comes from within. It comes from within. It comes from within.*

He looked back at Ryan, now staring at him in growing terror.

"I'm sorry, buddy. It just reminded me of something, is all. This is really good. Keep up the great work."

Ryan smiled, and Howie brought his attention back to the window. Back to his reflection. Behind his reflection, for a brief second, he swore he saw someone else looking in at him.

The front door swung open, and Howie spun around, startled.

Bethany walked in, sliding her cell into her pocket. Her expression became concerned when she caught sight of Howie's face.

"Everything okay?" she asked.

"Y-yeah. Ryan's video just scared me, is all. The kid's got talent," Howie said.

He felt horrible lying to Bethany, but he couldn't scare Ryan. And he had to be sure he wasn't losing his mind before alarming her.

"Well, good news...my job just gave me an extra few days. So you can't get rid of me yet, Howie Burke. You ready to get to packing?" She jerked a thumb to the piles of boxes and junk.

Howie smiled and nodded, happy to have her here longer, but unease churned in his gut. He was scared; scared because he sensed something happening that he couldn't identify. The last time he felt this way, half the town died in a massacre.

CHAPTER 24

1979

Jessica lurched up in bed, her clothes clinging to her skin. She immediately reached for her mouth at the thought of the writhing, green substance slithering down her throat. But there was nothing there. The phantom pain of a horrible nightmare, nothing more. She looked over and saw Henry sound asleep, snoring comfortably.

It was just a terrible dream, she thought.

It all felt so real though. Flashes of the nightmare blasted through her mind like a slideshow. The pond. Chanting. A girl—a *sacrifice*—screaming for her life. The taste of the liquid pouring down her throat. But most of all, she remembered the sensation of something spreading inside her, absorbing into every inch of her body.

Henry rolled over in bed and yawned.

"Everything okay?" he asked blearily.

"I-I think I had a bad dream," she said. Her hands wouldn't stop shaking, then she noticed something and squinted to focus. Her fingers were covered in dirt, caked under her fingernails.

Jessica climbed out of bed and went into the bathroom. She heard Henry snoring again as she shut the door and turned the light on. The first thing she noticed was the dark, sunken craters beneath her bloodshot eyes. She looked horrible, like she hadn't slept in days..

Then she glanced back down at her hands and gasped at the sight. It wasn't dirt covering her fingers. It was dried blood. And there weren't any wounds that she could see as being the source.

Is this someone else's blood? The girl? Maybe they made me do something to her? Jessica wondered with growing anxiety.

It wasn't just the blood or her reflection that scared her. The more alert she became, the stronger the feeling that she wasn't alone. It didn't feel like it was just her and Henry in the house, it felt like there was...something else. She turned on the tap and scrubbed her hands, watching the pinkish water spiral down the drain. Her dream wasn't a dream at all. The last thing she recalled was suffocating on the substance as it forced its way through her.

The man in charge of the coven, what was his name?

The name clawed its way to the surface of her memory. *Felix Ruger.* That was it. The leader. The voice behind the dagger. The one who fed the girl to those things in the pond.

He had told her they did something to Henry. Everything seemed fine with him when he woke up. They had kept their word that they wouldn't hurt him. Of course they had. Why would they break her trust? She was devoted to the coven.

But that poor girl. They threw her to the wolves. Whatever crept beneath the surface of the pond devoured her.

"It was for you. They sacrificed her for you, and the ceremony brought you closer to them," a voice whispered.

She suddenly felt lightheaded as a burning bolt of pain shot up through her stomach. Jessica clutched the vanity to hold herself up, trying to remain quiet so she wouldn't wake Henry again. She bit her bottom lip, groaning as the sensation continued traveling through her insides. The taste of blood filled her mouth. As she stared down at the sink, she noticed movement out of the corner of her eye.

Jessica locked her gaze on one forearm and choked on her breath.

Something was moving beneath her skin. Swimming around in her veins as they bulged out, forcing the skin to become taut. She was about to yell for Henry when she heard something foreign. A sound that at first, she thought was her own beating heart. But it was someone else's heart beating.

TH-THUMP. TH-THUMP. TH-THUMP.

She recognized the sound—not her heartbeat but Henry's. Steady. Slow. So vulnerable. It made her chest ache. But underneath that, something else brewed. Something sharp. Something...*hungry.*

Jessica shifted her focus back to the mirror, back to her reflection. Only the face staring at her was not her own. It held her features, but it was an expression she had never seen before. A disturbing smile stared back at her, blood dripping down from her cut lip. She stood that way for an indeterminable amount of time, only coming out of her trance when she heard Henry stir from the bed.

She turned around and exited the bathroom in silence. The closer she got to the bed, the faster her heartbeat raced. Jessica stood over Henry's sleeping body, watching him. A violent urge came over her, one that she tried to force away. As he slept, she wanted to hurt him. She wanted to rip his body apart. He wouldn't even notice. She'd make it quick.

No! What is wrong with me? I love him. I can't hurt him.

She resisted the other voice inside her telling her it was okay. It was okay to take a life if it meant becoming stronger. Jessica pried her feet from the floor and exited the bedroom. She slipped into the dark hallway. Though the house was pitch black, she could see everything clearly. As if the night worked for her, showing her the way. Her bare feet slapped on the cold floor as she moved through the house, and before she knew what she was doing, she was back out into the night. The trees surrounding their home swayed in the evening breeze as if they sensed what she'd become. The temperature was below freezing, but Jessica didn't even notice. Her bare arms were fully exposed as her nightgown flapped against her body.

She stepped off the porch onto the thick grass that was covered by evening dew. There was no destination in mind, only the drive to find...something. She entered the woods, her naked feet crunched over the top of fallen branches, breaking the skin, but she didn't care. Instead, the smell of blood only made her more focused. She needed to feed.

Whatever now resided in her, it was hungry. The deeper she went, the less of herself remained. The other thing took control. And that's what it was. A thing. It wasn't a ghost or a spirit. It wasn't a split personality. A thing was growing inside her, using her entire body to do so.

A branch snapped in the distance, drawing her attention. Jessica paused, crouching low to get a better look beneath the overhanging foliage. Something moved between the trees, unidentifiable from her location. She dropped even lower, bending her knees and placing her open palms on the forest floor.

A bushy tail passed her line of sight.

She slowly crawled on all fours, her limbs bending at odd angles. Jessica moved that way for a few minutes until eventually, she spotted it. No, she *heard* it. Heard its heart's rapid-fire thumping. Unlike Henry, this thing wasn't calm and relaxed; it knew something was hunting it. She peered around a wide tree to find a raccoon sniffing the air, just out of her reach. It turned its head to the side, locking one black, beady eye on Jessica. Everything afterwards happened too fast for her to recall.

The critter attempted to sprint away, but at the same time, Jessica lunged, farther and faster than her body had ever moved before. She grabbed hold of the raccoon's tail and squeezed tightly. The animal whirled around and hissed, swiping at her hand. Its sharp claws slid down the top of her hand, instantly drawing blood. Her grip remained tight, and the raccoon thrashed around as if it knew it had little chance of surviving. She pulled it toward her, baring her teeth.

Jessica had no control over her body, watching on in horror behind her own eyes as her hands ripped the animal apart. She wasn't sure why this thing inside her felt the need to do something so horrible. Until she recalled the sound of its heartbeat. Then her hand shot forward, digging into the cavity of the raccoon, clawing for its heart. She tore the organ free, then threw its limp body against a tree with a sickening *splat*.

Her body tingled, her limbs numb. She locked her eyes on the bloody heart in her hand, disgusted by the gore.

Then her hand moved toward her mouth.

Before she could stop herself, she bit into it and swallowed a chunk, blood sliding down her chin. She wanted to throw up. Not because of how repulsive it was, but because it satisfied her. Worse, she wanted more.

CHAPTER 25

Henry woke up, his brain feeling like complete mush. It reminded him of a brutal hangover, but he hadn't even had any drinks the night before. He thought maybe he was coming down with something, or that he was simply exhausted from the move and carrying most of the weight around while Jessica spent countless hours in her study.

Henry blinked in the morning light. Jessica's side of the bed was ice-cold. He sat up, rubbing the back of his neck.

"Jess?"

His voice came out phlegmy, and he realized his throat was sore. That explained the fogginess. But he couldn't get sick right now. Not with so much to do around the house still. Not with the elopement that they had yet to set a date for.

Henry got out of bed, stumbling slightly from leftover sleep, and double-checked their bathroom, finding it empty. He moved to the hall, still no signs of his fiancée. When he made it to the kitchen, he noticed a half-full glass of water, its rim lined with blood. Not lipstick. Not juice. Blood. *Fresh* blood. His stomach turned.

"Jessica! Honey, where are you?"

After checking every room on the main floor, he made his way down to the lower level. The door to her study was shut. He breathed a sigh of relief, giving a polite knock before opening the door. He expected to find her sitting on the floor reading through her countless books. But the room was empty. The only object in sight was a large book lying open in the middle of the floor. It wasn't uncommon for Jessica to sit there and read for hours on end, so discovering a book there wasn't out of the ordinary. What was strange was the page it was opened to.

The text was handwritten and difficult to read, but there were images to go along with the words. A picture of a girl tied to a dock and hands coming out of the water to hold her down took up half the page. Of the words Henry could read clearly, the one that stood out in bold was ***SACRIFICE***.

He stared at the image for a minute, a ball of dread forming in the pit of his stomach. Why was she reading about a damn sacrifice? Henry turned to the next page, which was far more legible. At the top, ***DEMON HIERARCHY***. Below it, a list of strange names in an apparent order.

DEMON HIERARCHY

VORATHOR

The almighty. Vessel to The Withered Tongues. We die for this entity. Sacrifice for it. Everything we do, everything we believe, is for VORATHOR.

VODYANOY

The water demon. Confined to bodies of water where the veil between our world and theirs is thinnest. Provides us with the power to stay connected as one, working with VORATHOR to rid Hell of ATAHSAIA. We sacrifice to VODYANOY to maintain that power and keep the relationship between VORATHOR and VODYANOY strong.

ATAHSAIA

The cannibal demon. Feeds on both demon and human flesh. Singles out the victim's heart as the strongest source of power.

"What are you doing in here?"

Henry jolted up, his heart lurching into his throat.

There stood Jessica in the doorway. No footsteps, no warning. Just the unexpected, ice-cold presence of her voice.

"Jessica, where have you been? I've been looking everywhere for you."

She looked sick. Sunken eyes. Pale skin. And then he saw a set of three claw marks across the back of her hand.

"You weren't looking for me. You were reading what wasn't meant for your eyes. You shouldn't be here."

Her voice sent Henry's nerves on edge. It wasn't just the words she said; she spoke in a monotone that was completely out of character for her, as if she was focused on something else entirely while speaking.

"I-I came in looking for you, then saw this book open. What is this, Jessica?"

"I said it's not for you, Henry. I'd like you to leave my study, please."

Henry stared at her in silence, her eyes burning into his soul. He had an overwhelming sense that he was losing her. Everything he worked so hard to give her—the space to find her true self—felt as though it was backfiring. Jessica was getting lost in her search. Obsessed. But the look in her eyes right now was beyond all of that.

"Honey. Are you okay? You look ill," he said.

Jessica lifted her upper lip in an unnatural smile. "I'm fine. Just didn't sleep well, is all. Are *you* okay?"

Her tone was like ice trickling down Henry's spine. Moving slowly, as if afraid of spooking her, he pulled her into an embrace, noting her stiff posture. *It's the pressure of it all. It's getting to her, and I need to do my part to ease that,* he thought.

"Let's go. I'll make us breakfast, and you can relax on the porch. It's a nice morning for this time of year."

She didn't say anything, just turned around and walked stoically through the downstairs and out the sliding glass door to the back patio. Henry followed, kissing her on top of the head as she sat in one of the outdoor chairs. He reached just inside the door and pulled a blanket from the bin they kept in the family room, then draped it over her shoulders. Jessica zoned in on the trees, not acknowledging the blanket. As much as Henry wanted to press her right now, he left her alone. Before he made them breakfast, he made a few calls and pulled a few favors. He was going to get Jessica out of her funk.

Henry was both excited and anxious as they drove through town. He didn't tell Jessica where they were going, only that it was a surprise. At first, she fought it. She wanted to stay home and study. She had only eaten a few bites of breakfast before she said she was full, which only added to his concern. Eventually, he convinced her to leave, and they were now entering downtown Newport.

"Where are we going?" Jessica asked, staring out the window.

"You'll see. I promise it will be great. We've been sitting in the house doing nothing, it's time we take the next steps."

He glanced over at her, wondering if she was catching on. They passed the town hall and Henry slowed the car down, turning into the church parking lot. Jessica recoiled in her seat at the sight of it, and Henry realized too late that he may have screwed up. All of Jessica's trauma from her parents, her church upbringing, all rushed to the forefront of his mind. He had been so focused on surprising her with eloping that he had practically forgotten Jessica's trauma.

Off to a great start, asshole, he thought.

"W-why are we here, Henry?!"

"Babe, it's okay. I called in a few favors for today. We're getting married!"

She didn't even look at him, just kept her eyes glued to the church, specifically the enlarged cross at the roof's peak that towered above them.

"I'm not going in there. Y-you should know better. I can't do it, Henry. Why didn't you set it up at the town hall? They do elopements."

Henry sighed.

"They're closed today, but don't worry. There won't be any religious significance to this, Jess. Just because it's in the church doesn't mean we need to have a religious ceremony."

"That doesn't matter. It's the *thought* of being inside there." Jessica's voice cracked, her entire body shaking. "I'm sorry. I know you wanted to surprise me, but...I can't. It hurts too much even just looking at the place."

A car pulled up next to them on the driver's side, and Henry was relieved to see Bill and Sheila smiling over at them. He called the couple to be their only guests. He made eye contact with Sheila, who had opened the passenger door. She saw the concern in Henry's eyes and mouthed, "Is she okay?". Henry shrugged.

Jessica finally turned and noticed their friends approaching the car.

"Henry...please don't make me go in there, I'll be sick."

As she said it, Jessica held her hand with the claw marks on it over her stomach. Before he could respond, Sheila walked around the front of their car toward Jessica.

"Hey, girl! I'm so happy for you! You okay? Nerves getting to you?"

Henry sensed Jessica's annoyance at the number of questions. But she held it together, at least for now.

"Henry planned this surprise, but I'm just not feeling well. I should have told him before we left the house."

"Oh, dear. I'm sorry. We can be quick here. The main thing is making sure you two become husband and wife. I'll help you inside."

Jessica sighed, bringing her eyes back to the massive cross. Henry reached over and set his hand on her lap, feeling her tense beneath his touch.

"Okay. Let's do this," she said. Her tone was depressingly resigned.

Henry's eyes lit up. He was starting to worry that this wouldn't happen.

They all headed into the church, with Jessica moving reluctantly. It wasn't how he pictured their wedding day, but he hoped the ceremony would get her out of this funk. When Henry called the church, he made sure they knew Jessica grew up in an extremist religious home and asked that the priest, Father Grimes, acting as justice of the peace keep the ceremony secular.

He expected her to flinch at the sight of the church, but he underestimated just how bad her reaction would be. Jessica's body trembled as they moved between the pews. Henry wondered if they should just call the whole thing off and wait for the town hall to open on Monday.

No. You're losing her to this obsession with finding a new faith. It has to happen now.

Part of Henry felt selfish for thinking that way. Like he was only doing this to make sure it happened before Jessica had a full mental breakdown. But he also truly believed that the act of marriage, the sacred bond that was about to be forged, would be the first step in fixing these problems.

Jessica whispered something under her breath as they approached the sanctuary at the front of the room. Bill leaned in toward Henry. "She okay, man? Doesn't look so hot."

"Yes. She's been having a rough go of it. Everything will be okay."

Bill nodded, almost nervous. After a beat, he said, "Sheila is going to ask her directly, and I wanted to tell you myself. We want you guys to be the godparents of our baby. I don't believe much in that stuff, but she does. And I told her if we had to do it, I wanted it to be you guys."

Henry pried his eyes from Jessica and looked at Bill. He was a number of years younger than him and rough around the edges, but he was a good man and Sheila was an amazing woman. Tears gathered in the corner of Henry's eyes.

"Thank you. We'd be honored, Bill."

"Ah, come on, man. Don't get all teary-eyed on me. I don't do well with that shit."

Henry chuckled, then gave Bill a tight embrace.

"Someday, you'll get it. The world can be a horrible place. When something like this happens, it's a big deal. I'm glad we met you guys."

"Welcome!" the priest called from the sanctuary.

They all climbed the steps until they were front and center. Jessica's eyes flitted wildly from side to side, above and below. It was like she expected to see her parents leering from every corner or dark space.

Henry softly took her hand. "Jessica, we're safe. Your family won't find us here," Henry whispered.

She furrowed her brow and looked at him. "That's the *least* of my worries, Henry."

Before he had a chance to ask a follow-up question, the priest greeted them, "Henry told me you don't have much time, so I'm honored to unite the two of you in marriage today. I've prepared a speech that I think will suit the occasion. If you will, please stand over here. As you know, the state requires two witnesses over the age of eighteen for elopements. Do you have any witnesses?"

Bill and Sheila stepped forward.

"We're not here for show, preacher man."

"Oh, leave him alone, Bill. He's just doing his job," Sheila said.

Father Grimes smiled and gave a nod. He stepped up to the podium, with Henry and Jessica standing on each side of him. He spoke clearly and with practiced ease.

"Welcome. Today, we gather not in the name of any one tradition or doctrine, but in celebration of something that transcends all boundaries—*love*. Jessica and Henry have chosen to join their lives in partnership, choosing each other not because they must, but because they wish to walk this path side by side. This is a choice rooted in love, trust, and deep respect."

Henry closed his eyes and let the words wash over him. No mentions of God or faith or sins. Just honest, mortal words that didn't need any higher power's blessings.

"To marry is to invite another soul into your private world. It is to say, 'I see you. And even when you're not at your best, I choose you.' There is risk in that. Vulnerability. But also, *power*. Because strength, too, it comes from within."

Jessica flinched at the sound of those four words, digging her nails into Henry's palms. He opened his eyes to see her mouth trembling, eyes locked on the priest.

"Now is the time when you both commit to one another with vows, with honesty and solidarity." Father Grimes raised a hand, signaling for Henry to go first.

Henry cleared his throat, trying to keep his emotions in check.

"Jessica...we have been through so much together. Good times. Bad times. But no matter what, we were there for each other. I made it clear very early on that I wanted to spend the rest of my life with you, no matter what stood in our way. I'm here today to tell you that nothing has changed. There will be more good times. There will be more bad times. I am your rock through all of it. I want to grow old with you. Share my soul with you. Most of all, I want to raise a family with you. You are the strongest woman I know, and I don't doubt for a second that you will be the strongest mother I know. Everything out there"—Henry gestured toward the stained-glass window—"is noise. It's me and you, through thick and thin. I'm so grateful you chose me to go on this journey with you, Jessica. I love you."

Sheila sniffled behind Jessica, wiping away a tear. She mouthed, "Good job," and Henry couldn't help but smile, relieved he didn't make a fool of himself.

"Jessica," the priest said, prompting her to say her vows.

Jessica didn't speak at first. Her eyes were glossed over, but Henry noticed something else there for the first time. Not just fear, but a slight orange tint to her irises. He squeezed her hand, and she nodded.

"Henry Black, you mean the world to me. So much so that I come here after all I've been through with my family. Because *you* are now my family. I can't let my past get in the way of *our* future. There is nobody else I could imagine spending the rest of my life with. The world is far bigger than just you and me, but I know that you will be at my side as I explore that big world. As—" Jessica paused, clutching her stomach.

Henry could have sworn he saw something move beneath her skin. Something pressing against it between the throat and chest.

"Are you okay?" Henry asked.

"Y-yes. Sorry. I don't feel well. I want to marry you, Henry. I want to become Jessica Black."

"Henry, do you take Jessica to be your partner—your home in the storm, your calm in the noise, your companion through all unknowns?" Father Grimes asked.

"I do."

"And will you protect the bond you share not because it is demanded of you, but because you feel it deep down, where love stirs quietly and fiercely?"

"I will."

Father Grimes turned to Jessica next, and Henry saw the concern on the priest's face at the sight of her. She was pale, sweat giving her white skin a sickly sheen. Her breaths were coming in short, desperate bursts.

"Jessica, do you take Henry as your partner—your mirror, your memory, your witness?

"I do," she said, barely audible.

"And will you honor the life you build together, knowing that all love, all devotion... it comes from within?"

Jessica swallowed. She flinched again, as if the priest's final words struck her across the face.

"I-I will."

"Rings, please," Father Grimes said, and Bill stepped forward, handing them to the priest.

"These rings are not binding. They are reminders. Of what is chosen freely. Of the fire we carry inside us. The heart may falter, the body may weaken...but what truly matters cannot be taken, because it is already inside us."

The exchanging of rings came next, and Henry couldn't help but feel that it was drawn out. Like a ticking time bomb waiting to go off. The longer they stood in the church, the worse Jessica looked. Guilt gnawed at his chest for springing this all on her. This was supposed to be the happiest day of their lives, but it was tainted with something he couldn't quite name.

When Father Grimes put the ring on Jessica's hand, her entire arm trembled as if the priest's touch was hurting her.

"Jessica and Henry, by the words spoken here and the bond declared before us, I now pronounce you husband and wife. May you carry each other through the days to come. May your union flourish, because it is not rooted in place or even in time, but in something deeper. Henry, you may kiss your bride."

Bill and Sheila encouraged them, and Henry leaned in, kissing Jessica's icy lips. Her body was drenched in sweat, but her lips felt so cold. She forced a smile, one of relief. Henry embraced her, crying because they were officially husband and wife now.

"You and me, lady, we did it."

"Jessica Black. It's official, huh?"

"It is."

Sheila hugged them both, and Bill shook Henry's hand.

Behind them, the church doors opened, sending a thunderous echo through the nave. Everyone turned around, staring at the tall figure who entered. Henry didn't recognize him, but Jessica clearly did. She let out an audible gasp and took a step back behind Henry. If this asshole was dangerous, Henry didn't care how big the man was, he'd kick his ass right here in the church.

"Hello there. You're more than welcome to come in, but this is a private ceremony," Grimes said.

The man walked forward slowly, his long feet slapping on the hard floor.

"Good day, Father. I just thought it would be great to introduce myself to the new residents. And congratulate them."

"Who are you?" Henry asked.

"I'm Brian White. I am the principal of Newport High."

"Not to sound rude, but this is between just us and our friends. I appreciate the gesture, but we would like you to leave," Henry said.

"Oh, screw the politeness, Henry. I know Brian. Always sticking his nose in town business. Piss off, Brian," Bill said. He stood in front of Sheila protectively, anger clear in his expression.

The church went silent, and nobody moved. The man stood his ground with a smile spreading across his face. Father Grimes walked to the edge of the sanctuary and peered down at Brian.

"I normally say all are welcome in the house of God, but I'm asking you to leave."

As if Henry needed any more reasons to be confused. It seemed that everyone but him knew this man, and none of them were going out of their way to be nice to him.

"I just wanted to introduce myself to Jessica's husband, is all," Brian said, turning to look at Henry. "Now that the two of you are married... well, we will be seeing a lot more of each other. Good day, sir. And Jessica, good to see you again."

With that, the tall man turned and walked out of the church, leaving everyone in stunned silence. When the doors slammed shut, Henry turned to see Jessica hunched, sweating profusely.

"How do you know that man, Jess?"

"Please...not now. Can we leave? I'm going to be sick, Henry," Jessica said, each word coming forth as a painful plea.

He didn't hesitate. Questions could come later, but for now, he needed to make her comfortable. Henry guided her toward the stairs of the sanctuary.

"Thank you so much, Father. We really appreciate you taking the time out of your day for this," Henry said over his shoulder.

"Of course. May your marriage shine bright." He gave a beaming smile and waved as the quartet left the church.

Bill and Sheila followed them out of the church and back to their vehicles. Once Henry had Jessica in the passenger seat of his car, he walked over to Bill and Sheila.

"Who was that man?"

"Brian White is one of the people I mentioned who has ties to the coven. Did Jessica meet with him or something?"

"I...I don't know. I'm not sure when she could have. She's been cooped up inside since we moved into the house."

Henry's heart raced at the implications. His worst fear was coming true; Jessica had somehow made contact with the coven, and he had been completely oblivious. Henry thought back to the odd feeling he had when he woke up, almost like he was hungover. It was also the first morning that Jessica really started acting strange. His gut told him something had happened to him, but he shook it off.

Bill patted a firm hand on Henry's shoulder. "The way he talked...like he knew Jessica well. Be careful, Henry. These aren't people you want to fuck with."

With that, Bill got in his Escort and they backed out of their parking space, leaving Henry to his own disturbing thoughts. Which were cut short when something slammed the car window.

CRACK!

Henry spun around just as Jessica rammed the side of her head into the passenger window, creating a web of cracked glass. He ran to the car, opening the door.

"Jessica! What are you doing? Stop it!"

She snapped her head to the side, locking eyes with him. Her pupils had grown to the point that they filled the majority of her eyes, and behind them, the orange Henry had seen earlier now burned bright.

"It comes from within! We are bound together now, you pathetic scum!"

Henry felt a strange sensation spin through his head, and he had to grab hold of the door to catch himself.

"Wha-what's happening to me?" he asked.

"Get me away from this fucking shithole," Jessica snapped, but it wasn't her voice, not entirely. There was a second voice behind it, a much lower octave.

Henry found himself obeying. Something had reached inside and taken the wheel of his mind, and he was only allowed so much control. Numbly, he climbed into the car, unable to look at his newlywed wife. But he didn't need to. She was controlling his every move.

CHAPTER 26

2024

After Bethany and Ryan left, Howie spent the next few hours packing up more of his mother's stuff. But he did so in a daze. His mind kept going back to that YouTube video and what Ryan said. Could it really be a coincidence that he heard the same exact phrase in his nightmare? Maybe he imagined Ryan saying it, the exhaustion finally getting to him and planting twisted thoughts in his head.

He checked the time and realized the day had gotten away from him. Glancing around the house, Howie sighed. Hours spent packing and it hardly looked like he'd made a dent. He decided to take a break and sat on the couch, pulling out his phone. Still no response from Shawn, which was worrisome. Howie wanted to touch base with him about the drug. *Thred.* Such a stupid name, yet lethal.

After checking for messages from Shawn, he noticed that he had forgotten to read some missed texts. Zack had texted him.

> **Zack:** *Hey Howie! I know you told me not to get involved, but I think I'll have some answers for you tomorrow. I'll come knock on your room to chat!*

"Ah, Christ, kid."

Howie noticed the message was from the night before, when he had clearly been too drunk to notice it come through. Which meant Zack would want to talk with him today. The selfish part of Howie was glad the kid wanted to help. At least this way, someone else could slog through the dredges of Newport and get him the information he wanted. But this was far too dangerous for a kid to get mixed up in. Howie knew firsthand how dangerous it could get. That's why he entrusted the job to the one cop he actually believed in.

Howie decided to shoot Zack a quick text back.

Howie: *Zack, I told you it's dangerous. Listen, I'll be back to the motel in a bit. I'll come looking for you. But DON'T get into any more trouble. Please.*

He waited for a response, but one never came. Zack seemed to work every waking hour besides the few times Howie saw him in town, so he probably wasn't allowed to use his phone while on the clock. As he was about to set the phone down and get back to work, his thoughts went back to Ryan's video again. He pulled up a search browser and went to YouTube, trying to remember what Ryan's channel was called. *Ryan Carver* brought up many results, but not Bethany's son. Howie was relieved knowing Bethany wouldn't be careless enough to let her kid use his real name.

Then he remembered some keywords in the title of the movie and searched for those: *Sergeant Zombie.*

Not the cleverest name, but it still had a good ring to it, and that was enough to find it. Howie's palms were sweating as he tapped on the video, which started after an ad.

It was all in your head, Howie. He didn't really say it.

But when the video reached the point where that line was spoken, it was exactly as he remembered. *It comes from within.* Sure, it could be meaningless, but little kids don't talk that way. Howie forced himself to watch more of the movie this time, paying attention for any signs. The line dropped, hollow and cheerful, from the little soldier's voice. A chill trickled down Howie's spine. His scalp tightened. He paused the video, staring into the frozen frame like it might blink back at him.

"What the hell am I doing watching a damn kid's movie with toys and freaking myself out?"

He forced himself to keep going, feeling stupid the entire time. His therapist had diagnosed him with severe PTSD after what he went through as a child, and had warned him that he'd still have episodes from time to time. Being back in Newport would only increase the likelihood of it happening.

The movie continued playing, with Ryan attempting many voices in a rather straightforward plot about a sergeant in the Army who finds himself stranded in a city of the undead, trying to get through to find a fellow soldier who had radioed him from the underbelly of the deserted town. If it wasn't for that single line of dialogue, Howie would have found himself enjoying the fun little film. But then some of the zombies showed up—regular action figures that were either broken or scuffed up. There was something about the zombies that again filled Howie's stomach with a ball of dread. Ryan had colored green lines across their skin, as if their veins were filled with poison. It was another coincidence that was hard to ignore, reminding him again of the nightmare of his mother's corpse bursting from the casket with green trails spreading across her skin.

Howie finished the movie in a trance, numb to everything around him. When it ended, he scrolled down to the comment section, finding mostly Ryan's friends and classmates praising his work. As he scrolled farther down, one comment caught his eye and he stopped, reading it multiple times. It wasn't just the comment, but the username that caused his hand to shake, making it difficult to hold on to the phone.

Liveinthedarkness101: *great work, Ryan. You are beyond your years. It does come from within!*

Howie dropped his cell.

That username. He hadn't seen it in decades, but he knew it. It was the one that threatened Bethany on Instant Messenger before her family was slaughtered.

He checked the timestamp. Posted a week ago.

Howie snapped a screenshot and pulled up his text thread with Bethany. He hovered over the image, thumb twitching. Something about sending it in a text felt wrong. Too cold. Too dangerous.

He texted a short message instead.

Howie: *We need to talk. ASAP.*

Then he grabbed his keys and bolted for the door. He needed to talk with Zack before it was too late.

Howie sped into the motel lot, parking in front of his room. He double-checked his phone, disappointed to find no new texts from Shawn, Bethany, or Zack. Before he did anything, he forced himself to take some deep breaths, practicing the meditation techniques his therapist had taught him to help with his anxiety. Howie knew he couldn't keep himself busy to avoid the stressful situations anymore. It was all too much. His mother's death, specifically what led to it; the strange things that had been happening since he returned to Newport; and now the lack of response from the only people in town he trusted.

After his heart rate settled, he got out of the car and decided to stop by his room before finding Zack. He located his room key and slid it into the lock, thinking this must be the only motel in America that still used actual keys. When he opened the door, he was met with a space that looked like a tornado had ravaged through just minutes before he arrived. The room was trashed. Bedsheets torn from the mattress and all the drawers opened, with Howie's belongings strewn across the floor.

"What. The. Fuck."

He stepped inside, first scanning to make sure nobody else was in the room. Whoever was responsible couldn't have gone far. It wasn't until he got closer to the mess that he realized his stuff wasn't just scattered about... it was *searched*. Everything was opened, bags unzipped. His higher-valued belongings, however, all appeared to be present.

Howie's first thought was that maybe it was one of the strung-out drug addicts he had seen meandering around town. Desperately seeking out something that could bring them the money they needed to buy more Thred. But they had left all of his valuables behind.

He had another, far more disturbing thought.

They were searching for something specific. They knew it was *his* room and were looking for something they were sent to find.

Howie pulled his phone out and dialed Shawn. He couldn't trust the entire police force, not after half of them proved to be under the influence of the coven when he was a kid.

The phone rang numerous times, eventually going to voicemail.

"For fuck's sake, Shawn. Where are you? Someone broke into my motel room, and I don't know what to do. Call me back. *Please.*"

He ended the call and sighed.

Zack.

He needed to talk to Zack.

Howie stormed out of his room and slammed the door shut behind him, heading straight for the lobby. He pushed through the door hard enough that the bell jingled wildly and almost fell off. There was no one there.

"Hello! Who's working in this shithole?"

When nobody responded, Howie slammed his fist on the front desk, causing a bunch of papers to fall to the floor.

"Hey! I need some help here."

Finally, there was a shuffling in the back office. The old man who owned the place slowly walked into the lobby.

"I'm sorry. I was out back and just heard yelling in here. Can I help you?"

"Yeah, I think you *can.* Who the hell had access to my room?"

The old man, Tim Ripple, furrowed his brow behind his Coke bottle glasses.

"I'm sorry? You're the only guest staying here, sir. Nobody else has a key. Matter of fact, I keep meaning to make extras because I only got one master key to each room! Thanks for the reminder," he said with an odd smile.

"Someone was in my room. They went through my stuff."

Tim stared at Howie without speaking for an uncomfortable minute. "Mighta been the cleaning crew. Only thing I can think of."

Howie realized he was grinding his teeth. Some of his dad's old anger issues coming to the surface. He didn't have time for this bullshit.

"You just said there was only one key to my room. How could the cleaning crew get in there?"

Tim shrugged, his lips thinning.

"Well, you've got a lot on your plate. Suppose maybe you coulda left the door unlocked? This town isn't as safe as it was when you were a kid here, Howie. How long were you gone anyway?"

"What does that have to do with anything? I don't care if I was gone a week, my stuff should've been safe. And of course I locked the damn door."

"Hey, hey. No need for hostility. I only asked so we could try and narrow down a time that someone coulda been in there. Is anything missing?"

"I haven't gone through it all yet. I was a bit distracted by the fucking mess I walked into. And if I didn't lock it, why would it be locked when I got back? Someone breaks in, trashes the damn place, then decides to be polite and lock the door behind them on the way out? None of this makes sense."

"I'm sorry, Mr. Burke. Nobody has been here that I've seen. Course, in the middle of the night when I'm sleeping, who knows? I'll have to ask Zack if he saw anyone."

"Where is Zack? I need to talk with him."

Tim chuckled. "Why on earth do you need to talk with my grandson? Kid's dumber than a box of rocks."

The comment reminded Howie of something his dad would have said to him. Always belittling him, making him feel stupid. Howie was already pissed off enough as it was, and hearing an asshole talk down about a good kid always set him off.

"Zack's a smart kid. A good kid too. You should feel lucky to have him working his ass off for you, probably getting paid pennies, while you sleep the day away."

"Mr. Burke, I've been patient with you and your accusations. But I won't sit here and listen to you judge how I run my business. Like I said, I'll talk with Zack when he comes in. He's already late and he knows I don't deal well with tardiness. I'll be sure to inform you after I talk with him."

Howie stared at the motel owner, baffled.

"So...that's it? I just have to accept that someone broke into my room and the owner of the place tells me I must have left the door unlocked?"

The clock ticked loudly overhead as they locked eyes in silence. The way Tim was staring at him, Howie wouldn't have been shocked if the old man pulled a gun from beneath the counter and shot him dead. But then Tim forced a smile.

"I'll tell you what. I will file a report and call the authorities. Then I'll speak with my grandson, if he ever shows up to work. Once I have an update, I'll contact you. That's all I can really offer."

"Fine. Whatever. I'll be checking out today as soon as I pack up all my shit," Howie said, then turned and left.

As he exited, Tim called after him: "Stay safe, Mr. Burke."

CHAPTER 27

"This is where I grew up," Bethany said, staring at the house where she spent most of her childhood.

"Can we go inside?" Ryan asked, starting to unbuckle his seat belt.

"No, honey. Someone else lives here now. I just wanted to show you my old neighborhood."

And she had no desire to step foot in that hellscape again.

She wouldn't have even come to the neighborhood, but Ryan asked to see it. Bethany should have been prepared for the pain it would bring back to the surface, but she wasn't. Simply driving down the street felt like she was heading directly into the eye of a deadly storm waiting to suck them up and spit out their bones.

"It's a cool house. I like ours better, though," Ryan said.

"Me, too, sweetie." *Because it's where we started our family.* "I love you, ya know that?"

"Yes. You tell me all the time!"

Bethany ruffled his hair and laughed.

"Get used to it because I won't stop saying it every single day."

She decided to pull away before the current homeowner peeked out the window and thought someone was stalking them. Bethany could relate to that all too well. She'd seen the coven coming from the woods.

Heard them stab her father in the hallway. Watched them kill her mother and sister after finding the family cat hanging from her sister's ceiling fan.

A car horn blared from her side, breaking her from the horrible memories. Bethany slammed on the brakes, her head snapping forward. She had been so distracted by her thoughts that she blew through a stop sign, almost getting T-boned.

"Oh, my God. I'm so sorry, Ryan. Are you okay?"

Bethany's heart pounded, her hands shaking as she gripped the steering wheel. Ryan nodded, but she knew her son. He was attempting to hide how scared he was to make her feel better. The car that almost hit her swerved around her, with the guy driving it flipping her off as he sped by.

I don't know what's gotten into me. That was careless.

"Let's go get you some ice cream at my favorite spot growing up. It's called Fabulous 50's. It's where I had my first job in high school. They give really big servings too."

The distraction worked, as Ryan flashed a smile so wide it took up most of his face.

"Yes! But that's a weird name for an ice cream place."

"Well, it's been there since the fifties. Waitresses used to come to your car on roller skates to take your order. Pretty sure they don't do that anymore, though."

"Sounds cool."

They rode the rest of the way in silence until the ice cream shop came into view. It looked just like Bethany remembered. The parking lot was almost full, with only one vacant space underneath the oversized carport roof not taken. Bethany parked in the last spot, happy that Ryan would get the full experience of being served in the car.

"We wait right here, and they come to us. Pretty cool, huh?"

"Yeah! I want to get chocolate peanut butter cup in a cone."

"You got it."

A teenage girl walked up to the driver's side window with a small notepad.

"Good afternoon, welcome to Fabulous 50's! My name's Courtney. Do you need a food menu or just here for some ice cream?"

"Just ice cream, thanks. I'll get a small mint chocolate chip in a dish, please. This little man wants a small chocolate peanut butter cup in a cone."

"A small? Ah, come on," Ryan griped.

"I promise, a small at this place is really big," Bethany assured.

"Yep! I bet you can't even eat it all," the waitress said.

"Sounds like a challenge," Bethany joked.

"Okay, I'll be right back with that," Courtney said, then tucked the notepad into her pouch and went back to the front counter to place the order.

As Bethany turned back to face Ryan, she noticed the car parked diagonally in front of them.

The angry driver from a few minutes ago.

He stared at Bethany as though he was just waiting for her to make the first move, ready to pick a fight. She stiffened in her seat. The man refused to look away, his sunglasses perched just low enough on his nose that she could see the challenge in his eyes.

"Mom? Why's that guy staring at us?" Ryan asked, his voice timid.

"It's okay—"

A tap on her window cut her short, sending her heart into her throat.

She turned to see Courtney holding their ice cream. Bethany lowered the window all the way, letting out an embarrassed laugh.

"I'm so sorry! I didn't mean to startle you. Here you go. I'll leave the slip with you so you can pay whenever you're ready."

"Thank you," Bethany said, taking the treats.

The waitress left them, and Bethany handed Ryan his cone. He immediately started licking along the edge to prevent the ice cream from melting down his hand. She rolled up the window and took a deep breath.

Bethany gave him a forced smile, then looked back at the man who still watched her. He mouthed something she couldn't make out, but his expression told her it wasn't friendly.

His car door opened, and Bethany's breath caught in her chest. He stepped out slowly as if making a show of it. He kept his eyes on her with each deliberate step.

"You got a death wish, lady? You could have killed me back there," he said loud enough for nearby cars to hear.

Bethany cracked the window just a smidge.

"I'm really sorry. I was distracted. It's been a rough few days."

He stepped closer.

"We all got problems. It doesn't work that way. You drive around with a kid in the car and nearly slam into someone because you're *distracted*. You don't get to just brush that off!"

Bethany flinched, wanting to roll the window back up and leave. The way this guy was acting, though, he'd get in his car and follow her, and then she wouldn't have the added security blanket of bystanders.

Ryan's small voice piped up from the passenger seat: "Leave my mom alone."

The man laughed. "Smart mouth, kid. Your mom teach you to run people off the road too?"

Bethany's fists clenched and she set her ice cream dish on the dashboard.

Before she could respond, a woman behind the man did instead.

"You feel tough picking a fight with a mom and her little kid?" she asked. Calm. Confident. Icy.

He turned around, and Bethany got her first look at the lady.

Tanya stood at the edge of the carport, the man's scowl reflecting off her mirrored sunglasses. Her black leather jacket hung loosely off one shoulder as she crossed her arms and took a few steps forward.

"Mind your business. This chick almost killed me with her reckless driving."

"They *are* my business. You're scaring the kid, and I happen to be very fond of him. So I suggest you go back to your car, or ice cream will be the only thing you can eat from now on."

"Hey, screw you," he said, already backing away.

Tanya cocked her head. "No thanks, you're not my type. I prefer people who don't threaten women or children."

Ryan snorted from the passenger seat. Bethany watched on in stunned silence. The man muttered a curse under his breath, then turned and walked back to his car. He slammed the door shut, started the car, and sped out of the parking lot.

"Looks like he's the one not driving safe now, huh?" Tanya turned back to Bethany, kneeling low enough to get eye level with Ryan. "You okay, soldier?"

Ryan nodded, wide-eyed. "That was so cool! He won't be messing with us anymore, right, Mom?"

Bethany chuckled. "Nope. People like that don't stick around when they get a taste of their own medicine." She smiled at her son, then looked out her window at Tanya. "Thank you. You really didn't have to do that."

Tanya shrugged. "This town's full of bad seeds and ghosts. Some of them like to walk around during the day. Just gotta remind them they aren't as scary as they think they are."

Bethany paused. That comment hit a nerve she didn't expect. It was something her dad said to her as a little girl when she was scared of a bully. Her phone buzzed in her purse, but she ignored it, not wanting to be rude in front of the woman who just shooed off her potential attacker. Bethany hadn't trusted anyone new in years. But there was something about Tanya. Something strong. Steady. She felt safe around her.

"Please, sit with us and have some ice cream. What do you say, Ryan?"

"Yeah! Please, Ms. Tanya?"

Tanya grinned. "I thought you'd never ask."

CHAPTER 28

Zack wasn't sure how long he had been held captive in the dark room. He was surprised he was still alive; all but sure that when Derrick had discovered him, he would make him his next victim. Instead, Derrick drove the tire iron into Zack's ribs, dropping him to his knees. It was clear as soon as the metal struck that he had cracked a few ribs. Every time he inhaled, he was met with an agonizing, sharp pain shooting through his core.

At one point in the night, Derrick had returned and grabbed the girl, dragging her out of the room by her hair. She hardly let out a whimper, too drugged up on Thred to realize what was going on. Now, Zack was alone with his thoughts, wondering why Derrick hadn't come back for him yet and why he was still being kept alive.

Zack's neck hurt, but not as much as his broken ribs. Sleep came in brief, miserable stretches, never offering peace. On top of that, he was so damn hungry. He had been so distracted trying to play investigator that he forgot to eat lunch and dinner before he broke into Derrick's house.

His eyes had adjusted slightly to the darkness, but that didn't help in his effort to find a way out. Derrick had put zip ties around his wrists and ankles, so walking around wasn't possible.

Howie would be pissed at him. But he didn't understand how much he meant to Zack. He didn't know that his book saved Zack in more ways than one.

After years of monotony, bullying, and being treated by his gramp as a lackluster employee rather than family, Zack had nearly ended his life. Twice. The last time, he'd been inches away from pulling the trigger, until a copy of Howie's memoir beneath a stack of old magazines caught his eye. That book changed everything.

Instead of grabbing the gun, he grabbed the book. He found himself sitting behind the desk, planning to only read a few pages out of curiosity before setting out to finish his plan. It was Howie's words that saved him. One line specifically was embedded in Zack's mind and recalled anytime he felt that depression coming back. And right now, tied up in the dark, likely to die, those words came back to him.

They took everything from me, but they never took who I was.

It was more than a motto to Zack. It was a credo. This town, these people, they tried to take everything from the residents. They wanted everyone to suffer. Thred was just a part of a bigger plan.

Footsteps approached from the other side of the wall. Muffled voices. If it was Derrick returning, he wasn't alone this time. Zack felt his chest tighten as the voices got louder. And then the door rattled. The lock disengaged. When the door opened, a blast of light forced Zack to cover his eyes.

"What do we have here?"

It was a man's voice, one Zack recognized from the motel—the guy who talked with his grandfather in the lobby. Zack squinted, forcing his eyes to adjust. The tall man towered over him, with Derrick standing behind him. It was the first time that Zack had gotten a good look at this man's face. His eyes were like daggers laced with disgust. He viewed the kid the same way he would a stray cat who had broken into his house and pissed all over his floor.

"Derrick tells me you were snooping around where you don't belong," the man said. "Well, he can't speak, but he still *communicates* with me. Why are you here?"

Zack averted his gaze from the man, unable to answer. Those eyes drained any ounce of confidence he had. There wasn't anything he could say that would justify breaking into someone's home.

"It's okay. Whether you speak or not, I know. But you're making me work harder than I want to for answers. Zack...I know exactly what you're thinking. Just like I do with Derrick. Call it a gift that I got from my father. So, are you going to tell me or make me get in your head for answers?"

"Why are you doing this? To the town?" Zack asked, his voice cracking.

"Ah. One of those. I see." The man seemed amused. "The short answer is that everyone here deserves what is coming. There is no amount of suffering Newport can endure that is enough for what was taken from *us*. Every time one of you self-righteous types pop up seeking answers, all that does is get in our way. Why do you need answers for your inevitable demise, Zack? Isn't that enough?"

Zack had no idea what this man was talking about, and the vagueness of it all was somehow worse than the answer itself.

"Why are you making people take Thred?"

"There it is! The million-dollar question. Isn't that a fun name for it? It has meaning, you know, beyond just the catchy word. Thred does exactly what its name implies. It binds us. Makes us one. It's the first step in our bigger plan."

This man was crazy. Why would he want to create a connection with a bunch of junkies? Junkies he was guilty of getting hooked.

"I assure you, I'm far from crazy, Zack. This connection, it is *everything*," he said, his lips raising in a disturbing smile. "You look shocked. Soon, Zack, you will join the rest. And when I need you, when I call, you will come."

He took another step inside, and Zack pressed against the wall to keep as much distance between them as possible. The man's presence was suffocating.

"Why, though? Why do you *need* to do this?" Zack managed to ask between fearful breaths.

"My father was a powerful man. One who demanded respect. But he had his weaknesses, and that's what led to him being taken from us. We've spent years trying to find him, and now we know where he is. In order to bring him back, we needed a plan that could bring The Withered Tongues the strength we had all those years ago. And unlike my dad, we are patient. *Methodical*. This has been twenty-five years in the making."

Zack had no idea what he was talking about, yet he had every reason to believe him. It sounded like Thred was being used to not just weaken the residents of Newport, but to link them together mentally, and they were all connected to this man.

"Very observant of you. I still haven't decided how you will fit into all of this, Zack. I know your connection to Howie Burke can be of great use to us. While I don't fear any normal man, I won't make the same mistake my father did. He let his guard down, which allowed Howie Burke and his pathetic little clan to trap him." The man's smile became a furious grimace. "When we are done, Felix Ruger, leader of The Withered Tongues, will not only be freed, but Newport will never be the same. The residents will suffer greatly. Slow, agonizing deaths for what they did to us."

Zack felt sick, his stomach twisting into a ball of panic. In Howie's book, he mentioned Felix Ruger as the leader of the coven. Suddenly, it clicked. Howie's mom hadn't overdosed on Thred. The coven had poisoned her, forced her to take it, which got Howie back to Newport—his return being an integral part of their revenge plan for what he did to their leader. This was far more than just a single act of revenge. But what did Ruger's son mean when he said the whole town would suffer?

He shuddered as the man chuckled. "Precisely. You're too smart to just kill. Isn't that neat how I can read your every thought?" Ruger smiled. "So, what to do with you? Too valuable to feed to the pond, at least for now. Derrick, step forward."

Derrick entered the room, now standing side by side with Ruger. Derrick was a large man, but he looked puny next to his leader. Derrick's eyes burned into Zack, begging for the chance to make him suffer.

"I could always give you the same treatment I gave Derrick. Care to see?"

No, I really don't, Zack thought.

Ruger nodded to Derrick, who then slowly opened his mouth, revealing a bloody, disgusting mess where a tongue used to be. Zack swallowed back the urge to vomit. It looked like someone had stuffed the bottom end of a blender inside his mouth and turned it on, letting the blades spin until the tongue was torn off in tiny bits. Derrick closed his mouth in an angry grimace.

"The thing is, I only like to have one silent helper. Too many of them, and it forces me to do more talking than I'd prefer to do. And your words carry value to me, Zack. Howie Burke trusts you. I have a plan, and you are going to be a key part of it. Be thankful you get to live to see another day. Anyone else dumb enough to get in my way would have been killed."

Zack took a deep breath and slouched, allowing himself to release some of the tension tightening around every muscle. Tears slid down his cheeks. He wasn't sure what Ruger had in store, but at least he still had a chance to live.

"That does not mean you will get away with no punishment, however. Derrick?" Ruger nodded toward Zack.

Derrick charged at Zack, kicking him in his already broken ribs. A stabbing pain shot through his entire upper body; the wind knocked completely out of him. Before Zack had a chance to inhale, Derrick grabbed him by the throat and lifted him off the ground. Ruger stepped forward, taking something from a pouch that Zack hadn't even realized he held.

A vial filled with a glowing green fluid was presented to him.

Thred.

Zack's heart plummeted to his feet, and he began to weakly struggle. "No, no. Please! It will kill me!"

"It will only kill you if you let it, Zack. But you won't. I'm going to give you just enough to connect to us."

Zack attempted to break free, but it was pointless. He was in too much pain, and even if he wasn't, Derrick was far stronger than him. The hand around his throat tightened, blocking his airway.

From the pouch, Ruger removed a syringe and filled it with the bright green substance, idly tapping the glass to dislodge the air bubbles.

Zack felt tears well in his eyes. "Please, don't. I'll do anything else. Don't make me take it."

Zack felt disgusted with himself. He sounded desperate—because he *was* desperate. One of his biggest fears was becoming infected with the drug that he witnessed kill so many. And that's exactly what this was. An infection.

Ruger slid his index finger along Zack's exposed neck, sending a tingling sensation through Zack's body.

"Here we go. When you wake up, you will be one of us, Zack. We'll see you on the other side."

And with that, Ruger jabbed the needle into Zack's neck, causing his eyes to go wide. A burning pain swam through his bloodstream, traveling down his entire body. His heart went into overdrive, rattling against his broken ribs, but he no longer felt that pain.

Something was happening to his vision. At first, it blurred as the green substance filled every cavity of his body. Then, everything went dark, yet he was still alert. Still conscious. Images flashed before him.

A body of green water illuminating in the night.

Pale, white hands covered in green sludge, breaking the surface. Ripping and tearing at the flesh of a screaming victim.

Then he was traveling *beneath* the surface.. He sank deeper, deeper, until the glow faded and was replaced with a suffocating darkness.

Zack tasted the pond water, felt it cool his insides. Just when he thought the darkness would consume him, something else lit up below. The image moved around a large concrete slab, sinking deeper until a set of glowing red eyes appeared.

Vodyanoy. The water demon.

He moved closer to the eyes until the outlines of the demon's facial features appeared. The red eyes were glimmering just enough to display a mouth full of jagged fangs stained green from years of living below.

The mouth opened wide—too wide—stretching the skin.

Before Zack had a chance to scream, the mouth lunged forward.

This time, the darkness took him.

CHAPTER 29

1979

Henry was relieved that the strange feeling in his head had subsided once they made it home from the church. After parking and entering their house, Jessica had retreated to her study, leaving Henry confused but relieved. The closer he got to Jessica, the worse the sensation of her having some kind of control over him became. Now alone, he was able to relax and think.

He'd known something was wrong for a while, but convinced himself he was just being dramatic. He couldn't push it away any longer. It wasn't just the look in her eyes or the fading color of her skin. It wasn't just the strange voice she used to spit commands at him.

How had she infiltrated his mind?

Henry knew she had researched forms of mind control with her witchcraft studies, but it had never been anything beyond curiosity. It shouldn't even be possible. The idea of mind control seemed like comic book bullshit.

Once he was sure she'd stay in her study, he went to the landline. He dialed Bill, not sure what he expected his friend to do, but he needed to voice his concern to *someone*. On the third ring, Bill picked up.

"Hello?"

"Bill, it's Henry. I wanted to call and apologize for how that all went down earlier. I... I'm not sure what's going on with Jessica," he said in a low voice.

"Henry...those people are fucking dangerous, man. The way Brian talked to her, it sounds like she's already involved with those freaks. I suggest you put a damn leash on her from now on."

It wasn't just the words that caught Henry by surprise, but the tone of Bill's delivery. Up until this point, he had been pleasant in all their conversations. Sure, he lacked certain people skills, but he had never given any sort of attitude. Which meant the man was scared.

"Excuse me? I don't appreciate that, Bill."

"I'm sorry for the bluntness. But this isn't some relationship she can just brush aside. They don't do what they did to her to just anyone, Henry. They have a purpose for her, and she's not one of them. Not really. It's worse."

"What does that mean, exactly? 'Not one of *them*.'" He talked as though she was the piece to some puzzle. "What am I dealing with here?" Henry asked, trying as hard as possible to keep his voice down. The last thing he wanted right now was Jessica, in her aggressive state, overhearing him voice his concerns about her.

"It means exactly what I said. She's not a member of the coven. Even if for some reason she thinks she is, she's not. They have a blood oath. Which means if she's not a member, they have another use for her." Bill paused, the sound of a door squeaking closed coming over the line. "Brian White isn't just some low man in the pecking order. He's one of the highest-ranking members. For him to show his face, in a fucking *church* of all places? It can't be good."

"I...I can't believe any of this. Why didn't you say something to me at the church? Jessica has been acting really strange even *before* the incident today. Something's been off. Like she's stuck in this constant state of mental paralysis. And then when we were leaving the church, she got in my damn head, Bill. I thought I was going crazy."

The phone line remained silent, and for a second, Henry thought his friend had ended the call. But then Bill spoke, "If I were you? I'd go back to that church, alone. Talk with Father Grimes about what you're dealing with. I'm no religious man, Henry, but I sure as hell know what a possession sounds like when I hear it."

"Possession? What? I—"

The call was interrupted by a blast of static blaring in Henry's ear. He lost his hold on the phone, which dropped until the line went taut, the handset swaying like a corpse in a noose. Even with the phone dangling near his ankles, Henry still heard the unbearable sound. He started to lean over to grab it, but a shift in the air stopped him cold. He wasn't alone.

Jessica stood in the doorway, hunched in a painful posture. She was breathing heavy, forced breaths, but her eyes looked anything but hurt or scared. They were glued to Henry, a fiery rage crackling behind obsidian pupils.

"Jessica..."

"No phone calls. You do what I say, or I'll rip your heart from your chest and squash it into a pulpy mess. Do you hear me, husband?"

Henry covered his ears, a sudden, unbearable pain shooting through his head. Her real voice was right there, escaping between her beautiful lips. But inside his head, the deeper, sinister tone tore through his skull.

"Jessica, what is happening? Please..."

He expected her to scream again, but instead, he heard sobs. He hadn't realized he'd shut his eyes and when he opened them, Jessica was leaning against the doorframe, sobbing.

"I'm sorry, Henry. They did something to me. They put something inside me. I can't stop it...I can feel it spreading like a disease."

That was Jessica. That was his wife. That blank monotone was gone, and her eyes had returned to normal during a brief, torturous respite. He wanted to hold her, to promise her it would all be okay. He stepped toward her, but she backed away.

"No! It's not safe. Don't come near me. It's...*hungry*."

Henry froze, unsure what to do. His wife was suffering, and he was helpless.

"What can I do? How can I help? I'll do anything to make you better."

Jessica stopped sobbing, lifting her gaze to meet his. The fire in her eyes had returned, and she exposed her teeth, which now had sharp tips on the ends as if she had filed them into daggers. Green veins rippled beneath her skin, traveling along her forehead and down her neck, beneath the dress that clung to her sweat-soaked body.

"If she won't let me have you, then you *can help me feed."*

The words sent a chill down Henry's spine. It was the first time that whatever was inside Jessica acknowledged her as a separate thing.

"Who are you?"

"I am Atahsaia. And your cunt wife is just a hollow host for me in this world. Although, I must say, she has some...useful skills," the deeper voice said. The words sounded like they were digging their way out of Jessica's throat.

Hearing her reduced like that, her voice twisted and accompanied by that foul sneer, made Henry want to vomit. But he stood still, afraid any weakness would trigger the thing inside her.

And then it was in his head again, seizing control of his thoughts and his body.

"Bring me something. It must be living. I need to feed."

Flashes of red pulsated through his field of vision with every word. It hurt so damn bad.

"What? What do you want?" Henry rasped. His voice strained, chest tight with a mixture of defeat and a single thought: Protect Jessica. And yet...

The thought of bringing anything living to her, whether it be animal or human, terrified Henry. What did this demon have planned?

"I feast on the hearts of the living. I am eternal, and you are simply my source of food. Now BRING me something! I must feed!"

Henry dropped to one knee, clutching his head. Tears spilled as the pain exploded behind his eyes like dynamite. He took deep breaths, trying to calm himself. When he looked back toward the door, Jessica was gone.

The next few hours were miserable for Henry. While Jessica had left his mind, the headache stuck around like a stubborn bitch. He found himself getting irritable, yet unable to move from the couch. He knew if he didn't get out soon and find something for the demon, it would come back with a vengeance, and that thought alone was enough to finally force him to his feet.

When Jessica disappeared, Henry worried that she'd left the house altogether, out hunting for something to feed the demon. But as he moved through the home, he noticed the study door was shut once again. And as he got closer, her sharp whispers itched inside his ears. She was reading to herself. It sounded like it was from the spell book she had been studying. The words were so quiet yet filled with such venom.

Henry moved quietly past the door and upstairs to the main level. He shoved his boots on and exited through the front door. It was early evening, the sun barely creeping above the tops of the trees. He didn't know what he was looking for, just that the demon wanted something alive. Henry wasn't a killer. He rubbed his hands on his jacket as if he could wipe away the thought. A person? No, absolutely not. He couldn't.

He scanned the surrounding forest, hoping maybe he would discover a wounded animal that needed its suffering to end. Then it would be a mercy killing, a good deed, right? As he walked along the trail heading deeper into the forest, a sinking feeling came over him that he was about to be responsible for ending a life. Back home in the South, he had plenty of friends who hunted, and he didn't judge them for it. Hell, he even enjoyed eating some of the meat they'd brought home. But this was different. He didn't even own a gun, let alone know how to shoot one.

So how would he catch something? With his bare hands? That seemed highly unlikely. The deeper he walked, the darker it got. Suddenly, he wished he had worn a thicker jacket, as the late fall evenings in New Hampshire tended to be chilly. With it being late November, the leaves had passed their peak colors weeks ago; all were now a dark brown as they slowly died. His feet crunched over those that had already fallen, which wasn't helping his hunt.

Hunt. Ha! Says the confused idiot getting lost in the woods, he thought.

Just when he contemplated turning around, the trees thinned up ahead. The closest neighbor's house came into view.

Henry stopped and waited.

The lights were on inside. They had yet to introduce themselves to this family, too preoccupied with the move, eloping, and now Jessica's problematic "house guest." Henry had no idea what sort of folks lived there. He observed the window that he assumed looked into the dining room. A woman in her late thirties walked past the window with a plate full of food. She smiled, and her mouth moved as she talked to someone out of sight.

Henry took a step back to make sure he wasn't visible. The sun was now completely set, so he imagined the darkness hid him, but he wanted to be sure. The lady sat at the table, and a man about the same age came into view. He sat across from her with the back of his head visible. Then a little boy, no more than five or six years old, flew by the window with a smile spreading from ear to ear. They all laughed at something the man—the father—had said. Henry's mind immediately went to the boy. He would put up the least fight.

What the hell is wrong with me? A damn kid? I can't do that!

Henry watched the trio eat their meal, envisioning a family of his own someday. Would he ever get that chance now? He hoped so. But in order to achieve that dream, he would need to figure out a way to free Jessica from this monster.

His thought was cut short as the back door opened and the little boy stepped outside. It wasn't clear what he was doing standing at the door and holding it open.

"Come on, I see you," he said.

Henry stiffened. How could the kid see him from that far? Henry didn't dare move. His breaths came in rapid succession.

"Get out from under there, Whiskers. Go on. Now, outside!"

A fluffy, black cat sprinted past him out onto the lawn, heading straight for the woods. The boy went back into the house and shut the door, then turned the light off, sending the forest into absolute nightfall. The cat's collar jingled as it entered the woods a few feet from Henry. It turned and spotted him, its eyes shining bright as it turned its head.

It was a perfect opportunity, one that cast bitter relief over Henry. A cat, not a kid, to bring to a hungry monster. His knees trembled as he knelt to be more level with the cat.

"Here, kitty. Come on, Whiskers," Henry whispered, then clicked his tongue to call the cat.

Whiskers watched him, not trusting this stranger hanging out in the woods. Henry called to it again. This time, the cat approached slowly, curious of the new human. Then it rubbed along his leg and purred. One of its teeth poked out, scraping along Henry's pants.

"Good kitty. Come here..."

Henry scratched Whiskers along the back, bringing on another bout of purring. His arms moved before his brain caught up, gently scooping and cradling the cat.

The purring gutted him. He continued petting it as it rubbed its face along his shirt.

And then Henry was walking back through the forest with the cat in hand. Whiskers didn't fight it. The poor animal thought it had just made a new friend, trusting him enough to be held, and perhaps expecting a treat from him. After a few minutes, his house came into view. He knew this was the end of the line for Whiskers. A single tear slipped down his cheek.

"I'm so sorry."

Before he reached the house, the horrible voice came back.

"Yes. Bring it to me. I can hear its beating heart."

CHAPTER 30

Henry doubled over the toilet, bile splashing as he retched again. He flushed quickly. He couldn't stand the color, or what it reminded him of. When he returned with the cat, he cracked the door open to the study, expecting to find Jessica there. But the room was empty. He feared she'd grown too impatient, gone out to hunt for herself, and still not returned. But then the demon's voice boomed in his head, demanding that he bring the sacrifice to the basement. As he approached the door, the cat—which up until that point seemed to love his attention—went ballistic, clawing at his wrist, trying to break free. Henry held firm, opening the basement door to reveal a blanket of darkness. The knob burned his palm. The demon groaned in his ears, almost orgasmic.

A disgusting sulfuric odor blasted his nostrils, forcing him to gag.

In the darkness, the piercing orange eyes appeared, staring up the stairs at their next meal. The cat bit and clawed, hissing in Henry's face with mounting fear, anger and—Henry would swear to his dying breath—betrayal.

No way in hell was he going down those stairs. Instead, he had gently tossed Whiskers down, then he slammed the door shut and locked it from the outside.

Within seconds, the cat's screams split the air—shrill, raw, and desperate. Henry pressed his hands to his ears, but the sound burrowed through him anyway, as though it came from inside his skull.

That was almost an hour ago, and Henry still couldn't get the horrible sounds out of his head. The only time he didn't hear them was when the demon teased him.

"Thanks for the meal, sweetie pie. That was delicious."

Henry stood frozen. His legs trembled, ready to bolt from whatever still fed below. But he couldn't leave Jessica. This demon had control of her, and if it didn't get what it wanted, *she* would suffer.

He couldn't believe what it had come to in such a short time. Newport was supposed to be their escape from the nightmare Jessica grew up with. A fresh start. And now an evil far worse than her mother ever could have been had ruined their lives.

Out of the frying pan and into the fire, as they say. But Henry wasn't about to give up without a fight.

Bill had suggested he go back to Father Grimes and ask for help, and that's exactly what he planned to do now. With Jessica locked in the basement, Henry hoped she would stay down there until he was back with some answers. He quickly grabbed his keys from the counter and left.

When he made it to town and parked in front of the church, he realized just how late it was. What were the odds that the priest would even be awake at this hour of the night? Still, he had to try. He ran up the steps, hoping to find the door unlocked. He pulled on the handle and was met with resistance.

"Come on…"

Henry ran around the side of the building to the back entrance but found the door there also locked. Father Grimes was not inside. The lights were off. He sat on the back steps, face buried in his palms, and wept. With every passing second, he felt Jessica slipping further away from him. There was nobody else to go to. He knew if he waited until morning, it would be too late.

As if God spoke to him directly, a light snapped on in the building across from the church. Henry glanced up at the window that had previously been dark and spotted a figure looking down at him. It was Father Grimes.

Of course, the rectory! He wouldn't be sleeping in the church, Henry realized.

The light switched off again, and for a moment, Henry thought the priest was ignoring him and going back to bed. But shortly after, the outside light shot on, almost blinding him. The front door opened, and Father Grimes leaned out. His expression seemed unsurprised, as if he'd been expecting Henry all along.

"Please. Come in," he said, holding the door open.

"Thank you. Thank you so much, Father."

They entered and immediately came upon a dark set of stairs. Henry followed the priest up to the second floor.

"I heard something out my window. Lucky for you, I was reading and not asleep yet. Once I'm out, a train blasting by wouldn't wake me," Grimes said, opening the door to his apartment. "Come. Have a seat on the couch."

Henry did as he was told, and Grimes sat across from him. The priest was fairly young, and Henry wondered if this man had enough experience to even know what to do in a situation like this.

"Thanks for letting me in. I didn't know who else to go to."

"I know. I saw it in your eyes when you were here for the wedding. I saw it in *hers* too. Tell me what's going on, Henry."

Henry hesitated, head bowed and still trying to make sense of all he had just witnessed.

"It all sounds so crazy to say out loud. The coven, they did something to her, Father. She's got something evil inside her now, and it's hungry. But it's not her, I swear."

Grimes's lips thinned as he flashed a look of compassion.

"This coven has been around Newport for decades. They are still shrouded in mystery, but something has changed with them in recent years. I don't know whether it was a shift in the power dynamic or something sinister influencing them. I suspect it's a bit of both."

"What do they want with Jessica? And how can I stop it from happening? She's deteriorating by the hour."

"When you say she's *hungry*…tell me more about that."

Henry clenched his jaw. His shoulders shifted as if they wanted to pull the words back in before he could say them. "It demands to eat something living. It wants their hearts. And…it gets in my head, forces me to do things. I think it's using Jessica's witchcraft knowledge against me and reading my thoughts."

"Atahsaia," Grimes whispered.

Henry stared at Father Grimes in shock. "Yes! How do you know that?"

" the cannibal demon. *That* is who possesses your wife, Henry."

The words seemed to validate and damn in equal measures. Henry wasn't crazy. There really was something wrong, and it was because of that damn coven. But that begged the question...

"How do we get it out of her? Please, help me save Jessica," Henry begged, sobbing between words.

"First, we need to know *why*. Why did the coven want this demon inside Jessica? Then we can seek a way to exorcise it from her. Did you know she was involved with them?"

"I had no idea. Just that she had a book she'd been studying." Henry wilted, tired and heartsick. "When I asked you to marry us, I know I mentioned on the phone that she grew up in an extremist household. Religion wasn't just something they practiced, it was something they forced on her. Physically and mentally. The reason we came here was to get away from her parents. But she wanted *something* to believe in. I gave her space, and I regret not trying harder to intervene, but I didn't want to be like her parents."

Would it have mattered anyway? The book had a hold on her long before I knew it existed, Henry thought.

Father Grimes reached across and patted Henry's knee. "Do not be too hard on yourself, Henry. You were showing her mercy. Giving her the tools to make her own decisions is all we can do. Do I wish everyone who walked into the church believed every word I speak? Of course. But that's not what we do. We educate and hope those who are willing to listen make the right decisions."

Henry leaned back, rubbing the tears from his eyes.

"So, what now? You said we need to know why this demon is inside her."

"Yes. But it's important you know up front that I cannot perform an exorcism without the church's approval. But if I can talk with her, I can speak with Atahsaia. We must do this before the coven gets control of her again. Where is she now?"

"She's in our basement. I locked the door when I left. She was...feeding. Oh, God, I helped her, Father. She killed an innocent cat."

"The demon's influence is almost impossible to resist without proper training. Let me gather some supplies, and we can go speak with her tonight. Time is of the utmost importance."

"Thank you. I can't lose her. She means everything to me," Henry said.

As Father Grimes moved through his apartment packing supplies, Henry just hoped they weren't too late. An uneasy feeling sat in the pit of his stomach, but he had to cling to the hope that Father Grimes could help his wife. He had to believe she could be saved, because the alternative was too terrifying to think about.

CHAPTER 31

2024

Howie had spent the rest of the day packing things at his mom's house, regularly glancing at his phone for any response from Shawn, Zack, or Bethany. When her name finally lit up his screen, apologizing for the delay as she gave Ryan a tour of Newport, Howie's shoulders relaxed. He hadn't realized how tense he'd been until that moment. She had agreed to come back and talk. He kept his messages light, no need to worry her yet. There was still a chance he was overreacting, and that all of these things could be chalked up to coincidence.

Bullshit. I know this is all connected. Something is going on again in this town, he thought.

As Howie contemplated how to explain it all to Bethany, the sound of tires rolling over the crushed gravel in the driveway snapped him out of his thoughts. He got to his feet and peered out the front window to see Bethany pulling in.

She opened the back door and leaned in. When she stood, she was cradling Ryan's limp body. Howie's thoughts immediately turned morbid; he worried something had happened to the boy. That the coven or whoever the hell was fucking with Howie had gotten to Bethany before he had a chance to warn her. But then she gently reached out and kicked the door shut and saw Howie staring out at her. She smiled back at him; her expression wasn't one of concern but quiet happiness.

Howie opened the door and Bethany shushed him to be quiet. It took a moment for Howie to realize that Ryan was simply sleeping, and he had allowed his mind to assume he was hurt, or *worse*. Bethany motioned to the couch, so Howie ran over and cleared everything off, then propped up a throw pillow for her to rest the boy's head on. When she laid him on the couch, he briefly opened his eyes and mumbled: "Where arrre wee?"

"*Shhh*. We're at Howie's place. Go back to sleep, buddy," Bethany whispered.

Ryan didn't fight it. He closed his eyes and within a minute, he was sleeping calmly again. Howie pointed toward the kitchen and Bethany nodded. It was far enough away from the living room that they wouldn't have to whisper, yet close enough that they could hear if Ryan woke up.

Howie opened the fridge, grabbed two beers, and brought them to the table.

"Thanks for coming back."

"You can't get enough of me, huh?" Bethany asked.

"So, what did you show Ryan? Whip through the McDonald's 500 for old times' sake?"

"Ha! No, that was you boys who always felt the need to show off your bass with nineties rap blasting through town. I showed him my childhood home, then treated him to some Fabulous 50's ice cream before bringing him to Meadow Park and the library."

"Ohh, I didn't even think of Fabulous 50's! Do they still serve massive portions?"

Bethany grinned. "Yes. You should have seen Ryan's face when the waitress brought his cone to him."

They both glanced toward the living room, where the back of the couch hid Ryan from view. Howie couldn't help but smile.

"He's such a good kid," he said, the smile fading at what he had to reveal next. "After you guys left, I watched the zombie movie he made again."

"Yeah? That much of a fan?"

"You could say that. But...I need to show you a few things, Bethany," he said, fidgeting with his beer.

"I know your nervous tics, Howie. What's wrong?" she asked, taking a long sip of her beer in preparation for some bad news.

"I've had quite a day since you guys left. The reason I went back and watched the video was because of a line Ryan said as one of the characters. At first, I wanted to believe it was a coincidence, but when I replayed it, I just don't see how that's possible."

Bethany furrowed her brow. "What do you mean? It was just a kid's homemade zombie movie."

"Yeah. But he had a character say a line, 'It comes from within,' that I've been hearing in my dreams since I've been back in town. Before I even watched that movie. And the people in those dreams—those *nightmares*—all had disgusting green veins spreading across their skin just like he drew on the zombies. I know it seems ridiculous, but how can that be a coincidence?"

Bethany snorted as she drank from her beer.

"Come on, Howie. That's creepy, sure. But you think Ryan somehow tapped into your nightmares? Think about it: He's never been to Newport before this. Our past would have no influence on his films, and even if it did, that phrase isn't something we ever heard from *them*."

"That was my first thought as well. But it ate at me. I couldn't get it out of my head, so I went back and rewatched it. Look here," Howie said, opening up the picture he'd screenshotted of the comment section earlier. He handed Bethany his phone. The same username that once promised her death now stared back from her own son's video. Her face drained of color.

> **Liveinthedarkness101:** *Great work, Ryan. You are beyond your years. It does come from within!*

"How...how did I not see this? I'm so strict about what he does and who he communicates with online. There's no way anyone from the coven would know who my son is. I don't even let him use his real name!"

"There's more, though. I went back to the motel after packing some more stuff, and when I got to my room, it was ransacked. Bags opened, all my shit dumped across the floor. My first thought was that one of the junkies hanging around the motel broke in to take some valuables to pawn. But *nothing* was missing. It was like whoever broke in was searching for something specific that they didn't find."

Howie felt awful breaking all this news to her at once, but it needed to be done.

Bethany stared at him with glossy eyes. "Do you think they're back? Are we— Is Ryan in danger?"

"I don't know what to think right now. But I won't let anything happen to Ryan. You have my word."

"Howie, you have no way of knowing if you can keep that promise. We've seen what they can do."

Howie knew she was right, but he wanted to try. "I think you and Ryan should stay here tonight. And then I think you both should leave tomorrow, get out of here before anything bad happens."

"If they were in contact with him online, who's to say we're safe back home?"

Howie sighed. Bethany was clearly shaken and scared—not for herself, but for her son. And she was right too, he had no way of knowing if the coven wouldn't try to hurt or manipulate Ryan from a distance. At least here, she had the support of a select few who knew the history of Newport. Back in Florida, nobody would know the first thing about covens or demonic possessions. But Howie felt like he was going into this blind. He needed answers.

"The other thing really bothering me is that I still can't get a hold of Shawn or Zack. Neither of them has responded to my texts or calls, and I'm starting to get worried."

"Who is Zack?"

"Oh, right. You don't know him. He works at the motel. Really good kid, reminds me a lot of us growing up. When he saw that I was staying there, he fanboyed over my book. At first, I was annoyed, but he grew on me, and we got to talking about how my mom died. About the substance I found in her closet. This thick, green sludge that these people are shooting up. It's called 'Thred'. That's what all these folks limping around town are on. They act like...holy shit." Howie paused in disbelief.

"What?"

"They act like *zombies*...like the monsters in Ryan's movie." To anyone else, his conclusion would sound absolutely insane. But Bethany knew Howie, and she had been through the same hell as him. The proof was in front of her, and for the first time in their conversation, Bethany began to believe it all. There was a connection.

"How is any of this possible? My son has never..."

And then it clicked for both of them at the same time.

"The commenter on the video. We need to ask Ryan if that username has been in contact with him before. They could have been planting things in his head, influencing him," Howie said.

Bethany started to get up, but Howie held on to her hand, getting to his feet as well.

"Where are you going?" he asked.

"To wake him up and ask him. We need to know what's going on, Howie."

"No, that will just scare him. He'd be half asleep and delusional. Let's wait until morning. We'll sit him down then and talk calmly with him."

Bethany leaned her forehead against Howie's chest and sobbed.

"I'm such a terrible mother. How could I not have paid better attention? After what we went through? What our families went through?"

Howie gently placed a hand under her chin and raised her face to meet his gaze.

"You are *not* a terrible mother." He tucked a strand of hair behind her ear. "You raised a great kid, all on your own. You put a few thousand miles between him and this place. He's lucky to have you—"

Bethany kissed him. Howie was caught off guard but quickly let himself relax and kissed back. He hadn't felt this sort of sensation from a simple kiss in his entire life. Bethany leaned back against the fridge, allowing Howie to kiss along her neck as he caressed her body. Her breath hit his ear, and a shiver ran down his spine.

And then he had her up, lifting her off the floor, carrying her through the house and into the spare bedroom, where all that remained was a mattress and a comforter with no bedsheets. Their lips remained locked as they blindly undressed one another in the dark. Bethany spun around to be on top of Howie. She leaned in and kissed him, gently sliding her tongue in his mouth.

Howie noticed the door was still open and pulled away.

"Should we shut the door?"

"No. I need to know he's okay. Just be quiet, Howie Burke."

They made love into the night, until they were panting and exhausted, then embraced and fell asleep in each other's arms.

For now, the fear was gone, buried beneath years of longing.

CHAPTER 32

A knock at the door startled Howie awake. Bethany jumped up as well, both of them glancing at the couch to make sure Ryan was okay. Daylight bled in from behind the curtains, letting Howie know they had slept through the night. It was the first time he had slept peacefully in months.

The knock came again, which woke Ryan. The boy sat up on the couch, rubbing his eyes.

"Wait here," Howie said, scrambling out of bed to get dressed.

He passed Ryan on his way to the door, taking in the kid's wild bed head. He reached the front door and peeked out the window just to the left. A sense of relief overcame him, and he opened the door.

"Zack. Jesus. Where the hell have you been?"

"Sorry. Can I come in?" Zack's eyes were sunken, as though he hadn't slept in days. Even with the cool morning air, his skin glistened with sweat. His posture was hunched like he was in a great deal of pain.

"Sure. Are you okay? You look like shit." Howie moved to the side so Zack could enter. As he walked by, Howie picked up a strange odor wafting off him—familiar, but he couldn't put a finger on what it reminded him of.

Zack stopped when he saw Ryan sitting on the couch and Bethany coming out of the bedroom. His Adam's apple bobbed. His hands twitched constantly.

"I'll be fine. Just haven't slept much these past few days. Sorry I wasn't responding to your texts. My gramp took my phone away, saying I was slacking on the job. He was really mad at me, so he didn't give it back."

Howie furrowed his brow. The last he knew, Zack hadn't shown up for his shift at the motel. There was a chance he arrived right after Howie checked out, but that didn't explain why he hadn't been responding before that.

"Your last text said you were getting information for me. I told you not to do that. It's dangerous. But what did you find out?"

Zack's eyes darted from Ryan to Bethany, then back to Howie.

"It's okay, they're fine. This is Bethany and her son, Ryan," Howie said. Something was off about the kid, but he couldn't put his finger on what it was. He looked seriously sick.

Zack nodded awkwardly.

"Actually, Bethany, maybe grab Ryan some breakfast while I talk with Zack? Ask him about what we discussed last night? I found some cereal in the pantry. No milk, though, sorry."

Bethany picked up the hint; this was no conversation for a young kid to be part of.

"Let's go, buddy. You hungry?"

"Starving! How did I end up on Howie's couch?"

Bethany laughed. "You were sleeping when we got here. I carried you in, you woke up, then you passed right out."

The confusion on Ryan's young face would normally make Howie smile, but he was too concerned about what Zack had to say. Bethany and

Ryan disappeared into the kitchen, and Howie returned his attention to Zack, who had deteriorated before his eyes. In only a few minutes, he looked half-dead.

"Have a seat, kid. You sure you're okay?"

Zack shuffled in and sat on the love seat opposite the couch. He inhaled deep, laboring breaths. Howie couldn't help but think he looked like the residents he had seen hooked on Thred. It had only been a few days, had Zack already gotten in that deep?

"I'll be fine. Really. I wanted to make sure I had enough information before talking with you," he said, wrapping his arms around himself as if he had the chills. "I found out what Thred is."

Howie sat across from him, every muscle now alert. "Go on."

"They say it's a drug, but it's not really. I mean, it works like one at first. Once it gets in your system, it hooks you. It's all you can think about. But it's not just about getting high. It *connects* people."

Howie frowned. "Like some sort of hivemind?"

Zack squirmed, wincing at something. "Yeah. Something like that."

Howie stared searchingly at Zack. "Are you on it now, Zack? Is that what's going on?"

Zack ignored him and reached into his hoodie pocket, pulling out a small black notebook. He slid it across the coffee table. The notebook was worn, the edges frayed.

"What is this?" Howie asked.

"I found that before Derrick caught me snooping."

"Derrick? He's part of this? Wait, you snooped through his things? What the *hell* were you thinking?"

Zack looked up at him, eyes distant. "I broke into his house after I saw him distribute Thred. But that's not important. What's in that notebook *is.* It's notes, about Thred and how it works. Someone's been testing this stuff for years. They write like it's a science experiment, all these weird formulas and stuff. There's other stuff in there about the coven and demon connection."

Howie bit back the urge to chew Zack out for being so stupid. He opened the notebook, flipping through some of the pages, which were filled with sketches and old symbols. Some of the writing was in English, some was foreign. Ancient.

"What does this all mean?"

Zack shrugged. "Before it was Thred, before it was distributed around town, the coven used to use it. But they weren't just users. They were *receivers.*"

"Receivers of what exactly?"

Zack looked as if he might puke across the coffee table.

"That's what I was trying to figure out."

Howie watched him closely. "Zack, why didn't you *really* answer my calls and texts?"

"I told you why," the kid said, moving around uncomfortably.

"I stopped by the motel. You weren't there and your gramp said you hadn't shown up to work."

Zack's jaw clenched. "Maybe he didn't want me talking with you. He's weird like that."

He's hiding something, Howie realized. But why Zack would be keeping secrets from him now of all times eluded him. Maybe it was the Thred in his system, maybe it was shame. Whatever the case, Howie needed answers.

"Any idea why my room would have been broken into and searched? Your grandfather said he'd ask you about it, but I didn't think you would have any idea."

There was a slight stiffness in Zack at that statement.

"No. Why would they break into your room? I would have seen anyone coming or going. I saw nobody...at least while I was there."

Howie nodded slowly, but something in his gut twisted. It was in how the kid was avoiding eye contact, his posture, his subdued tone; he was dodging something.

Zack suddenly started to get up, then stopped.

"There's someone else. Higher up than Derrick. I've seen him behind the motel, always at night, handing people vials. You might find him there."

Howie's pulse quickened. "Are you sure? "

Zack nodded. "He's a really tall man, has a lot of tattoos. I don't know who he is," he said.

"Holy shit."

Howie suddenly recalled Felix Ruger, the leader of the coven when he was a kid. But...he was dead.

I don't know that. The last time I saw him, he was trapped in a concrete slab with Cory's body. Patrick Ellis said he would make sure nobody ever found it. But who's to say someone didn't find it and free the demon?

"I can take you there tonight, if you want. I...I just need sleep first. I'm burning up," Zack said.

Howie rubbed a hand tiredly over his face. "Goddamn it, Zack. Why would you shoot that shit into your arm?" He couldn't keep the disappointment out of his voice. As little as he knew about Zack, he cared about the kid, and he had been the last person Howie would ever think of shooting up Thred, or any drugs for that matter.

Zack stared at the floor, chewing the inside of his cheek. His voice was barely audible.

"When Derrick found me, I had to think fast. I couldn't risk him finding that book on me, so I told him I saw him at the motel with the tall man and that I wanted to get some Thred for myself, figured he could hook me up. He didn't trust me and demanded I take it right there in front of him or he'd know I was lying. He threatened me." Zack scratched the back of his head, remembering the pain, the creeping sensation in his blood, the *presence* invading his mind. "He shoved the needle into my hand and said I had five seconds to prove myself. I didn't even think. I just did it."

"Fuck, kid. I told you to stay away from it. You're too young to be getting mixed up in this. You have a whole future ahead of you." Howie studied Zack, brows creased in worry. "How are you feeling now?"

"Pretty sure I'm the walking definition of needing a fix. I'm sick. All I want is to get my hands on more of it. I could hear them, you know. It was like being tuned in to a radio station that never turned off. Voices everywhere. Sometimes they whispered, other times they screamed. But it felt...amazing."

Howie put his face in his palms and sighed. He should have expected nothing less from this town, but everything was unraveling so quickly. He felt like a helpless teenager all over again.

"You've done enough, Zack. Please, just take care of yourself and let me deal with this stuff from here on out."

Zack swayed as he stood, barely steady. He opened the door and stepped out into the morning sun, his gait slightly off, like he wasn't used to his own body. He paused in the doorway, unable to look at Howie.

"Your book got me out of some dark times. I just want you to know that." His words were spoken like a quiet confession. There was a resignation in his voice that made Howie's chest tighten. "I need to rest. Meet me behind the motel tonight at ten. After that, I'll go back to my miserable life. And Howie, be careful."

Howie watched him walk away, struggling with each step. He wanted to at least offer him a ride, but he was too stunned by what just happened. Instead, he shut the door and went back to the couch, picking up the little book. He opened to a page covered in looping symbols and ancient text scattered beneath. At the very bottom of the page, there were three sentences in English, and they made him feel sick.

The thread pulls tighter. It comes from within us all. We will all be connected.

CHAPTER 33

1979

Henry sped down the dark road toward his home. It didn't feel like a home, though. It felt like he was driving to Hell. He wasn't sure what to expect when he opened the basement door, or what Jessica would do when she spotted Father Grimes with him.

"Henry...I know you're scared, but please, slow down. We won't be able to save her if we're dead." Grimes's voice was calm in spite of his warning.

"That doesn't sound like a man with a lot of faith, Father. Let me do the driving."

They rode in silence; Henry focused on the road and those awful sounds he heard coming from the basement while Father Grimes went through his supplies to make sure he had what he needed. Every passing minute felt closer to losing Jessica forever.

"What is all that stuff? I thought you said you couldn't perform an exorcism?"

"I can't. This is just stuff to help ward off the demon. Yes, we want to get Atahsaia extracted from her, but if we don't protect ourselves, there's no stopping it from taking one of us. Holy water, crosses, the Bible—these things will only defend against the demon, not eliminate it. The plan right now is to get more information about why it's in her."

Father Grimes glanced at Henry with a severe expression he couldn't see while focused on the road.

"You need to let me do the talking, understand? It will try to goad you, use Jessica to mock you, but you must not give in to its games."

Henry hesitated with his response, and Grimes didn't wait long for an answer.

"I am serious, Henry. The demon will say things that will make you want to listen to it. Hurtful things. It will attempt to trick you into thinking it's Jessica communicating with you."

Henry's knuckles turned white as he squeezed the steering wheel.

"I know my wife. That evil bastard can try to trick me all it wants."

Their driveway came into view, and Henry slowed to turn.

"Your biggest mistake, Henry, is assuming you can match a demon without proper training. This isn't some schoolyard bully. It's not of this world, and it knows exactly what each of us wants and will use that to its advantage."

Henry considered the warning as he turned off the car and got out. Grimes followed him up the porch. Henry's hands shook so much that he nearly missed the lock. When he got it open, a thick, smothering air rolled out into the night.

"Be careful," Grimes whispered.

The house was completely dark, and when Henry reached out to turn the light on, it clicked, but nothing happened. Father Grimes was already pulling out a flashlight from his bag and handing it to Henry.

"Is this common? They kill the power?" Henry couldn't help but be curious in spite of the situation.

"Demons live in the darkness. Not just to hide but to *watch*. And wait."

Henry's spine tingled with a chill at the ominous words. The thought of walking into a demon's trap never even occurred to him. It made him realize just how unprepared he was. He entered the kitchen and froze. The shine of the flashlight caught a gleam off something metal on the ceiling. Henry aimed the light up to see multiple steak knives hanging in the air, blades pointed down.

"Do you see that, Father?" he whispered.

"Go around them. If you so much as step within a foot of those blades, they will fall and rip you to shreds."

Henry changed direction, going through the dining area instead. As they reached the stairs to head down to the family room, loud clangs of metal on the tile floor exploded from the kitchen, causing Henry to almost drop the flashlight. He forced himself not to think about those knives landing on him instead of the floor.

The closer they got to the basement, the warmer and thicker the air became. Henry was sweating profusely, wiping away the moisture from his eyes with the back of his trembling hand.

"You should let me lead the way, Henry. This isn't safe."

"She's my wife, Father. I want to see her first."

"Oh, honey. Let the priest go first, then bash his fucking skull in with the flashlight."

"No!" Henry yelled.

Grimes paused and stared at Henry in apprehension.

"What is it? Is the demon communicating with you?"

Henry nodded, closing his eyes to clear the command from his mind.

"You must not listen. Fight it," Grimes whispered.

Henry wasn't so sure the priest would sound so confident if he knew what the demon was commanding. Remembering how hot the knob was earlier, Henry pulled his sleeve over his hand and quickly opened the door. A cloud of dense smoke rolled out, bringing with it a sulfuric stench that stung Henry's nostrils. The basement was dark, but the miasma made it even darker.

"Dear God," Grimes said.

The space was suffocating, but Henry forced himself down the first few steps as Father Grimes followed.

"Jessica? Can you hear me?" Henry asked.

"Husband. Help me. It's so hungry."

It didn't sound like Jessica as much as it sounded like someone *imitating* her. Henry aimed the light toward the voice, but it was like turning on high beams in a snowstorm, making it even more difficult to see. But through the smoke, through the darkness, he spotted a set of glowing orange eyes watching them from the far corner. There were no other visible features, but he could hear her heavy breathing rattling inside her chest. And with each exhale, the demon released a decaying rot into the room.

"Jessica... Demon! Get out of my wife!"

Atahsaia let out a deep, bellowing laughter.

"You are not the one to give commands, you weak scum. I am. Now bring me that young priest so I can savor his insides."

Father Grimes pushed past Henry, who was too numb to react.

"Atahsaia!" Grimes tightened his grip on the cross. "Why her? Why take this form?"

"I was summoned, you dumb fuck. Why else? And there's nothing I love more than a virgin soul to corrupt. To rape from the inside out." The demon let out a deep laugh again, then its orange eyes shifted back to Henry. *"Oh, husband, don't you wanna pop my cherry? Isn't that why you*

married me? Come split me open, lover. Spill your seed while we chew the priest's heart together."

Henry knew better; he knew this wasn't Jessica. But her voice, her scent, her face was right there. And beneath his disgust, his body betrayed him—a sensation in his pants that made him want to vomit. How was the demon doing this to him?

"Why would the coven summon you? They worship another demon, Vorathor. You don't belong here, and they are planning something for you, demon!" Grimes barked.

Henry recalled seeing the demon hierarchy in Jessica's book he found lying open on the floor. Vorathor was the highest-ranking demon.

"You think I don't realize that? I'm steps ahead of you pathetic humans. Vorathor wants to trap me on Earth. He's too weak to admit it, but he fears me. The cannibal demon is too strong for him, too dangerous. I don't only like your hearts, your flesh, but I loooove my own kind. And he can plan his little rituals. While he's drawing circles, I'm carving kingdoms. This world will be mine, just like my own world will. One bloody heart at a time."

"Get out of my wife and leave her alone! Your problem is with the coven, not Jessica!" Henry snapped.

The demon laughed but behind it, Jessica's cries were faint, buried deep. She was still in there, fighting to break free.

"I'll tell you how this is going to play out, lover boy. I'm going to make you my bitch while I spread my seed inside your wife. You'll obey. She'll rot and watch. Jessica has quite the talent, doesn't she? And I'm not talking about how good of a blow job she used to give her old priest..."

It took everything within Henry not to charge at this monster. This was exactly what Father Grimes had warned him about. It was trying to get a reaction out of him, to trick him into moving first. He had grossly overestimated his ability to ignore the demon. He forced himself to remain where he was, clenching his jaw so tight that his teeth hurt. He knew exactly what the demon was referring to: Jessica's cult studies had led her to gaining the ability to read minds.

Grimes held his crucifix tight and stepped past Henry on the stairs, casting a large shadow over the cloud of smoke. He held the cross high and began to recite a verse that Henry couldn't understand, praying under his breath.

"Exorcizo te, immundissime spiritus..."

The words cut through the smoke like finely sharpened blades.

He moved the flashlight beam to the side of Grimes to get a better look, and in doing so, the cone of light struck the crucifix. A giant shadow, broad and defiant, flared behind Grimes. It fell upon the demon's form like a brand.

A scream followed—a sound like metal dragged across bone.

"Keep the light there, Henry!" Grimes yelled.

The demon's flesh was sizzling, and then Henry noticed the shadow of the cross wrapped around Jessica's body. Her skin smoked, sounding like bacon in a frying pan.

"Henry! Make it stop! It hurts so bad!" Henry felt ice in his veins. That was Jessica speaking, not the demon.

Father Grimes was hurting his wife. That was her voice, her pain. The smell of cooked flesh was real, and so was the agony. What if the priest was wrong? What if this was burning her alive?

"Stop it! You're killing her!" Henry yelled, then aimed the light at the side wall, allowing the demon to return to the shadows.

"Henry! Don't listen to her! It's not your wife speaking. Atahsaia is attempting to trick you!"

It was too late. Before Henry could make another move, Jessica burst from the shadows like a rabid animal, limbs cracking, eyes glowing, mouth smeared with blood and viscera. Henry braced for her to pounce on him but instead, she forced between them, swatting her hands in each direction and sending them flying against opposite walls. Henry slammed against the concrete foundation with a loud *crack* and dropped in a heap.

He heard the priest groaning, then heard Jessica speeding up the stairs on all fours, followed by glass shattering from somewhere on the main floor.

The house returned to silence.

Jessica had escaped.

CHAPTER 34

Jessica tore through the forest, ignoring the sharp branches slapping her skin like whips. She didn't have time to worry about her pain right now. Not when she was so close to causing it on the one person she cared for the most. The monster inside her wanted her to hurt Henry. It wanted her to *kill* the priest. Somehow, she had fought it long enough to get away from the house and into the woods.

Eventually, she slowed to a stop, her body demanding a break. The temperature had dropped well below freezing, but Jessica hadn't noticed. Her body felt like it was on fire, skin blistering as if it was covered in third-degree burns.

"It was that fucking priest and his cross. You should have bitten out his jugular," the demon snapped.

"I won't give in to you. Leave my body, *now!*"

A deep, sinister laugh filled her head, forcing blood out of her ears.

"Bitch, I'll leave your body when I decide your corpse is useless to me. Until then, you're coming along for the ride."

Jessica leaned against a tree and cried. She glanced up at the night sky, taking in all the stars. Her breath created a cloud of steam that blurred her view. A light snapped on up ahead, and that's when she realized there were neighbors through this portion of the woods. She clung to the tree, waiting to see if anyone appeared.

A little boy opened the back door, and the backyard light turned on. He looked to be no more than five or six years old.

"Whiskers! Here, kitty kitty. Come on, kitty!"

A woman came up behind him and kissed him on the head.

"Honey, we need to get to bed, okay? We'll try to find him again in the morning. He'll come back."

"No! I want to find him tonight. He never leaves for this long, Mommy. Please..."

The woman sighed. She had a blanket wrapped around her, and even from where Jessica stood, she noticed the woman shivering. She said something too quiet for Jessica to hear, then stepped out and shut the door behind her.

The boy ran across the lawn, straight toward where Jessica hid in the woods.

"Just along the edge of the lawn, okay, Joshua? There could be bears out there."

The kid stopped and turned to her. "Do you think they could have got Whiskers? Would they eat him?"

"No, honey. Bears don't eat cats. Just be careful."

The mother walked slowly behind him, wanting to be anywhere but out here in the cold searching for a dead cat in the middle of the night.

"Do you hear that little heart beating? Oh, it sounds so delicious."

"No, no. You won't force me to hurt a child," Jessica whispered.

"Mom? Did you hear that?" the boy asked, now standing right at the forest entrance.

The whites of his eyes lit up with terror as he peered in Jessica's direction.

Please, go back inside, she pushed the thought into the boy's mind. There was an odd moment of confusion where she swore that he locked eyes with her, and then he turned and went back to his mother. She wrapped her arm around her son, and together they entered the house. The mom briefly poked her head out, glancing at the trees as if she could feel that she was being watched, and then shut the door. The outside light went off, sending the backyard into darkness again.

Jessica breathed a sigh of relief. She closed her eyes, trying to calm herself. But when she did, she saw horrible things. Teeth as sharp as knives piercing into flesh. The thrusts of multiple mangled bodies wrapped in a ball of limbs during some twisted orgy. And then she envisioned herself in this home, taking the heart of each family member one at a time. It was only when she found herself peering in the window at an empty room that she realized it wasn't a vision anymore. She blinked. Her putrid breath fogged the glass. Her reflection, although dark and blurred, stared back at her. Her eyes glowed a fiery orange, her teeth were no longer her own; sharp fangs in rot blackened gums stood in their place.

She blinked, and the world shifted. The cold night vanished. She was moving...then she was *inside* the house. Hardwood flooring creaked beneath her feet. No sense of time passing.

She watched on in terror as the demon took complete control of her body, shifting through the dark house in eerie silence.

I told you, I won't harm a child, she thought.

But the boy's bedroom door was creaking. Her hands—no, not her hands, the *demon's* hands—pushed the door open. The skin beneath the fingernails had turned the darkest shade of black, the nails themselves extending to sharpened talons.

The boy didn't hear her enter, already sound asleep. His face looked so peaceful with the blanket pulled up to his chin.

Jessica felt a warm tear sizzle down her cheek.

"It's time to feast."

Amber tossed and turned in bed, unable to fall asleep. Something Joshua said after they came back inside stuck with her. *Who was that lady in the woods staring at me?*

She told him he must have been seeing things. A trick of the light, shapes in the trees; nothing more than a tree branch swaying in the breeze. But then he told her the lady got in his head and told him to go back inside. She convinced him that was simply his subconscious telling him it was bedtime. But what she didn't tell him was that she sensed something out there too. Watching them.

She glanced over at her husband snoring obnoxiously. Amber was worried about his health. Worried that he wouldn't be around to see Joshua grow up and go off to college.

I'm just full of cheerful thoughts tonight, huh?

Amber rolled onto her side and looked at the clock. Had it already been an hour since she put Joshua to bed? It felt like it was minutes ago. She practiced her breathing exercises to calm her anxieties, avoiding the thought of morning creeping closer. That would just lead to more hours of tossing and turning.

She closed her eyes, listening to the snoring of her husband, which sounded like a chainsaw refusing to start. *Goddamn it, Rick.*

There was another sound, muffled by the snores, but Amber knew she heard it. She opened her eyes, but that was useless thanks to the blackout curtains she insisted on. Since she had to listen to the snoring all night, she at least wanted a nice, dark room to influence her mind that it was time to sleep. But right now, she wanted to see. She heard movement brushing past her, close, deliberate. She rolled over to face Rick, trying to shake him awake to no avail. All that did was pause his sputtering engine in his chest.

As her eyes adjusted, Amber noticed the shape of a person standing on Rick's side of the bed. Too tall to be their son. Plus, Joshua knew his dad wouldn't wake up if he tried to rouse him, so he always went to Amber's side when he was scared.

She blinked a few times, hoping her eyes just needed more time to adjust.

The figure was still there, and above Rick's snoring, she heard it breathing. Amber froze, holding her breath as if that would keep her hidden. Then the figure lowered out of sight, down past the mattress.

The next few minutes crept by. Amber considered reaching over and stuffing the bedsheet in her husband's mouth so she could listen for other sounds. He lay sprawled out, hogging the bed as usual, his arm dangling over the side of the bed. She resented his ability to sleep through anything and everything.

Another noise came, a slurping sound. At first, she thought Rick was licking his lips in his sleep, but it sounded too *sloppy*. And then he began to moan. Squirmed.

"Not now, Amber...too tired," he mumbled.

As she prepared to get out of bed and turn the light on, the figure rose slightly from the floor next to Rick, only the head visible. This time, its eyes burned orange, giving off a few inches of light. It was the face of a sickly woman staring directly at her. She was sucking on Rick's index finger like a child with a lollipop. Then came the *crunch*, wet and sharp, as bone split between her teeth. Rick roared in agony.

Amber recoiled in the corner of the bed with a shout, ready to bolt out of the room.

Rick opened his mouth to scream again, but the disgusting woman leaned over him as if she was going to kiss him, then opened her mouth wide—too wide—and chomped down on his bottom jaw, before ripping her head to the side and breaking it free.

A horrifying sound erupted from the hole where his mouth used to be, like his soul trying to crawl out of the wound and escape. The woman climbed onto the bed, mounting Amber's screaming husband. He turned and looked at her, his eyes wide in shock and pleading for help.

But Amber only had one thought.

Joshua...I have to save him!

Amber jumped out of bed and ran to the hall, taking one last look back at her husband. She wished she hadn't. The woman drove her clawed hands into his chest, pulling it apart in the center. The sound of skin ripping followed Amber all the way down the hall. She was so distracted by it that she didn't realize her son's door was already open. She slammed the door shut, again finding herself in a darkness so black she was hit with vertigo, as if flying through space.

Something's wrong. Where is Joshua's night-light?

After locking the door, Amber turned around to face her son's bed. He should have woken up from all the commotion. The silence hit her harder than any scream. Amber wouldn't let her mind go there. She wouldn't allow herself to come up with reasons why her beautiful boy was silent.

"Joshie? Buddy, you need to wake up. We have to leave," she whispered through tears, her voice and body trembling.

She inched closer to his bed, in too much of a daze to turn the light on. She was about to reach out and pull his blanket off when a loud rapping slammed on the other side of his door.

KNOCK! KNOCK! KNOCK!

Amber let out a brief scream before stifling the rest of it. She faced the door, waiting for the pounding to return. She sensed someone standing silently on the other side. It had to be the feral woman.

But then Rick spoke. "*Amber...open the door. She's out here. She's not human.*"

Amber reached for the door but stopped herself. Rick's chest had been ripped open. His jaw torn from his face. How the hell was he out there talking to her right now?

"It's not you, you're not real," she choked out through tears.

"*Of course it is, baby. How else would I know that you fucked my best friend? How else would I know that our little boy is really a bastard child and not really mine?*"

The words stabbed her like a knife. The one-night mistake—that's what it was, not an affair—was a secret she planned to take to her grave. Not a day went by that she didn't regret it, but it brought her Joshua. She couldn't taint that blessing by letting Rick know he wasn't the father.

So how does he know? And why did he never say anything about it? And why is he bringing it up now, when there's a psychotic bitch tweaking on acid, trying to eat him?!

"What's wrong? Thought you could keep those secrets from me? I can smell the fear leaking from your whorish cunt!"

"Please...stop, Rick." Amber cried so hard that she felt a headache coming on.

"Turn the light on. Show him Daddy's home. Let him see what a real father looks like."

It was Rick's voice, but something was wrong with it. One word deep, the next in a higher pitch, distorted. She moved slowly toward the wall, feeling for the switch. Hearing heavy breathing on the other side of the door.

She flicked the light on, then turned around.

And screamed until her throat went raw.

Joshua's body was unidentifiable. She had a brief thought, thankful his head was facing the wall, so she didn't have to see his dead eyes staring back at her. From his throat to his waist, there was nothing but gore. Amber wanted to turn away, to throw up, but she couldn't take her eyes off him. His heart was missing.

Torn from his little chest.

The light flickered, then went out, blanketing the room in darkness once more.

Amber was numb, no longer caring about what happened to her. Her drive to live had been drained. But that didn't stop her from screaming again when the bedroom door splintered off the hinges. Didn't stop her from turning and struggling to hold herself upright as she stared at the monster who brutally murdered her husband and son.

The woman had hands with piercing claws and bare feet turned a deathly black, just like the hair that clung to her cheeks, matted with blood and grime. She opened her mouth to show off her grotesque teeth, locking her orange gaze on Amber, who closed her eyes so she didn't have to see the horrible face with blood dripping down her chin. As the woman entered the room, Amber felt a strange sensation in her stomach, followed by the most excruciating pain she'd ever experienced. She forced her eyes to remain shut, knowing they would never open again. Knowing she would be with her son soon.

CHAPTER 35

2024

Howie hadn't stopped reading the little black book all day. Even when Bethany tried speaking with him, his face remained buried in the pages, trying to figure out what it all meant. What any of this meant. He'd confronted Derrick Patten at Salt Hill Pub just a few nights ago. Could he really be dealing Thred? And if so, was it connected to the coven?

The book was filled with riddles, most of which he assumed were useless.

"Give it a break, Howie. You're going to drive yourself insane," Bethany said, leaning her head on his shoulder.

"I just can't figure out how this all connects. These shapes. The drug. I know it's related to my mom's death. I believe they forced her to take Thred, and it killed her."

Bethany peeked at Ryan, who was playing a game on his tablet, wearing his noise-canceling headphones.

"Why would they do that?"

"I think they forced others to do it too. Think about how many strung-out people we saw in town. About how Zack looked when he got here. I'm telling you, I had just talked with that kid a few days before and he was stone-cold sober, never tried a drug in his life. But the question is: why force them all? Revenge?"

"Why wait twenty-five years for that, though? You and I weren't even here—" Bethany paused, a sudden realization hitting her. "Unless they found a way to get us back here. Forcing your mother's overdose so you had no choice but to return to Newport."

Howie shook his head. It made sense, but there were still missing pieces.

"Shawn reached out to you, not the coven."

"Yeah, but could he be linked to them? We've seen dirty cops here before."

Howie vehemently shook his head. "No way. Todd was his cousin. They were like brothers, Bethany. And he was the one who gave me information about the drug in the first place."

"To gain your trust."

Howie didn't want to believe it. Couldn't believe it. The reason Shawn joined the PD was to honor Todd. But Shawn hadn't responded to him since the funeral.

Why is he ignoring me after I told him my room had been broken into?

"I have to go to the motel tonight. I know it's dangerous, but I have no choice."

Bethany pulled away from him and bit her bottom lip. She clearly didn't want him to go but didn't resist. Instead, she glanced at Ryan on the couch and sighed.

"Then I'm coming with you."

"No. Absolutely not. I've already put your life on the line more than once. Now you have a damn kid to think about. Besides, I wouldn't want Ryan in that kind of danger."

Bethany got up and crossed the room to where her purse sat on the counter, rummaged through the contents, then grabbed her phone.

"What are you doing?" Howie asked.

"Texting Tanya. She'll watch Ryan while we're gone."

"Are you crazy? You don't even know that lady. What if *she's* connected to the coven?"

"She's from here, Howie. Your mom babysat her. That has to count for something. Plus, the coven didn't have female members anymore, remember? They sacrificed them all when we were kids."

She had a point. Still, after years of building an invisible fortress around him and those he cared about, Howie found it difficult to let his guard down. An idea popped into his head, so he got up and went to his mother's room. Wanting to get the pain out of the way early, her room was the first he'd packed up.

He found the box he was searching for and pulled out a yearbook.

"I don't think a trip down memory lane is what we need right now," Bethany said from the doorway.

"If my mother babysat Tanya, then she should be in this book. It was my mom's senior year. Tanya would have been at least a few grades below her."

They sat on the bare mattress, and Howie tried to ignore the fact that his mom had died in that very spot. He started with the senior class with the intention of working his way down through the grades. The class of 1985, the year Howie was born. His mother was seven months pregnant at graduation.

As he turned the pages, Bethany put her hand over his to stop him.

"Look at your mom... She was beautiful. You look just like her."

"Are you calling me beautiful?" Howie joked, trying to deflect the emotions he felt brewing inside.

"That's one word for you."

When he reached the sixth-grade class, he searched alphabetically and stopped at the *P*'s.

"Pearce. There she is. Can't say she aged too well," Howie said.

She looked so young. It was strange seeing Tanya as a kid. He had to force himself to see the resemblance. Bethany gave him a light slap on the arm.

"Be nice. I told you, I trust her. She's one of the only people I've ever seen Ryan open up to the way he has. He won't stop asking about seeing her again."

Howie sighed. Yes, they seemed to have a safe person for Ryan to be with, but that didn't change the fact that Bethany was putting *herself* in danger if she went. If anything happened to her, and Ryan was left alone, Howie couldn't live with himself. He had seen enough families torn apart by this town, including Bethany's as a child.

"I really don't like the idea of you going. Is there any way I can convince you otherwise?"

She smiled. "I asked you and Cory that same question the night of the massacre, when you sent me into town to get help. My answer is the same as yours that night. Whether you like it or not, I'm part of this."

"Well okay, then. Guess that's settled. If you trust her, so do I. But we need a plan. Zack was high as shit when he came here, but he gave us a lot of helpful information. I just want to make sure we aren't running into an ambush."

"What exactly are we hoping to find there? You said he knows who's distributing the drug, but why do we need to confront them?"

"Because they're responsible for killing my mom. And whoever's in charge, it's becoming more and more clear that they wanted me here. And they think I have something they want."

"Like what?"

Howie shrugged, expression tight with his own confusion and frustration. "I wish I knew. I don't have a damn thing. But why else would they search my motel room and not take anything?" Howie nervously rapped his fingers on the table. "Why don't you reach out to Tanya? I'll try Shawn again before I text Zack."

Bethany nodded, then got up to go tell Ryan. Howie couldn't believe he was going through with this, but he needed answers. He needed to know why his mother died, why they wanted him back in Newport. And if the coven was still active... His mind couldn't go there. Vorathor was living inside Felix Ruger's corpse, sealed in a concrete slab somewhere. Atahsaia was trapped in Cory's teenage body in the same slab. There was no other higher power that controlled the coven, at least that Howie knew of.

He dialed Shawn, half paying attention as he expected it to go straight to voicemail like the past few attempts. But this time it didn't. It rang.

Once.

Twice.

Click.

"Howie?"

"Shawn? What the hell? Where have you been?! Why weren't you responding?"

"Listen, man. I told you too much when we talked. Call it nostalgia, loose lips, whatever you wanna call it. But I let you get too close to this investigation. If I really want to take this down from the inside out, I can't be worrying about someone whose emotions put us both in danger."

"What? That's bullshit, and you know it. This involves me and my family. What we went through when I was a kid—"

"Which is *exactly* why you shouldn't be getting involved, Howie," Shawn interrupted. "Please, look at it from my perspective. If I let you know information that could help lead to an arrest, and you mess that up for us... Not only is my job on the line, but a drug dealer is still out there spreading this shit."

"*I'm* in danger, Shawn. Did you not listen to my fucking voicemails? Someone broke into my motel room and left my shit all over the floor. They were trying to find something. And I know, and so do *you*, that my mom wouldn't have done this voluntarily. They wanted me back here."

"This is what I'm talking about, Howie. Listen to you. You had me legit thinking the coven was back. It's been gone for over fucking twenty years, man. It's in the past. Whatever this is, it's not them."

Howie got up to pace, agitated and frustrated. "What about everything you told me? About Ellis. About avenging Todd."

There was an audible sigh on the other end. Then silence. Howie thought Shawn had disconnected, but then he spoke again, "Howie, I'm begging you to let it rest. Let me do my job, and you take care of your mother's affairs. This is just unnecessary stress for you."

The defeat in Shawn's voice was the hardest part to believe. He was so motivated, so driven to get answers just a few days ago, and now he seemed like a completely different person. Howie was about to throw in the towel on expecting any sort of help from the one cop in Newport he trusted.

"I'm going back to the motel tonight. I received information that whoever's in charge of spreading this disease distributes there a few nights a week," Howie said, feeling the anger boil in the pit of his stomach. "Pretty sad that I've been in town only a few days and have more answers about Thred than a cop who has lived here for decades. Todd would be disappointed." Howie ended the call before Shawn could respond.

Good. Let that fester inside him and make him feel like shit, Howie thought.

The brief satisfaction vanished when he turned and saw Ryan staring at him from the couch, his headphones now off.

"Hey, buddy. Sorry if you heard some of that."

"Where's my mommy?"

Shit. Now the kid's scared of me.

Bethany walked back into the room to save the day, finishing up her call.

"Hey, Ryan, I got a surprise for you."

His eyes lit up. "What is it?"

"How would you like to hang out with Tanya for a few hours tonight while I go do something with Howie?"

"Really? Yes!"

"She's excited to hang out with you," she said, then glanced at Howie. "She's going to come here, is that okay?"

"Of course. As long as she doesn't mind the mess. My mom's cable goes till the end of the month, so they can watch a movie or something."

"Perfect. I'll text her your address."

Howie knew she was putting on a front to convince Ryan everything was all right, but he wasn't sure how she pulled it off so convincingly. He was a nervous wreck on the inside. The motel break-in, Zack's health, his mom's death, Shawn no longer acting like himself... That was just the stuff he knew of. In a few hours, he expected to know a lot more. And deep down, he feared he already had the answers inside him.

CHAPTER 36

"She's here!" Ryan yelled, his face glued to the window.

Howie had just finished packing some supplies to bring to the motel. As Tanya climbed the porch steps, he thought to quickly hide the little black book between the mattress and bed frame, then entered the living room just as Ryan swung the door open and greeted her with a big hug.

"Hey, little buddy! You excited to hang?"

"Yeah. Howie said we could watch a movie. Can I choose?"

"Well, of course, silly. I brought some popcorn to make. Assuming the microwave is still here."

"Yeah, it's above the stove. Thanks again for doing this." Howie nodded once to Tanya in greeting.

"You bet! We've become pretty tight the past few days, haven't we, Ryan?"

The boy nodded. Bethany was right. Tanya was great with him. He allowed himself to let his guard down—just slightly.

Bethany gave Tanya a hug and then leaned down to Ryan.

"Be good for her, okay? I love you."

"Love you, too," he said, then leaned closer to Bethany's ear and whispered something while looking at Howie with a smile.

Bethany hugged him and kissed him on the cheek before standing to face Howie.

"Okay, you ready?" she asked.

Howie didn't want to answer. He wasn't ready. Not even close.

As they neared the motel, Howie began to have second thoughts; the doubt infected him worse than Thred infected the residents of Newport. What was he going to do once he confronted this mysterious drug dealer? Tell them to "Say no to drugs" like he was some D.A.R.E. instructor? Threaten them with law enforcement? Clearly, the law wasn't something these people feared around here. Yes, he wanted answers. And *yes*, he wanted to confront the person responsible for his mother's death. But then what? He wasn't some rogue bounty hunter seeking justice.

Up ahead, the cheap motel sign was lit by a flickering spotlight on the ground. The smaller vacancy sign swayed beneath it. As if the sign needed to be there for people to know there were rooms available. The parking lot was empty, not a person in sight.

Howie parked across the street in the parking lot of a low-income apartment complex and killed the engine.

"So, what's the plan?" Bethany asked.

"I think first, we wait to see who pulls in. I'll text Zack and ask what the situation is. When they get here, I'll confront them. I want to know how and why my mother got involved with them. Once I know who's in charge, I'll report it all to Shawn."

"Howie...this all sounds so dangerous. Drug dealers aren't people to mess with. You don't even have anything to defend yourself. And don't you think if Shawn really wanted to know who was in charge, he would have figured that out by now? You didn't exactly train to become some undercover sleuth to get this information."

"I know that. I just...I don't have anyone else to go to. The feds? If I mention some mutated drug that a kid told me links anyone who uses it, and I think a coven that vanished years ago because we trapped their demon leader in concrete is back and distributing a mind control drug..." He shook his head with a grim chuckle. "They'd look at my record and think I'm just some guy that suffered trauma here as a kid and chalk it up to small-town crazy."

Bethany smiled and Howie couldn't help but smile back. He understood how ridiculous it all sounded. And then she leaned over and kissed him, and he felt revitalized.

"What was that for?" he asked.

"Just for you being you. You're the same guy you were back in high school. Just a bit more guarded these days, but that goofball is still in there. It's good to see it show once in a while."

"Speaking of, what did Ryan whisper to you about me?" Howie asked.

Bethany's cheeks darkened. "He said he really likes you and asked if you could come back home with us when we leave. I told him, 'We'll see'. I didn't have the heart to tell him that you have a life of your own."

"Yeah, well, don't give me too much credit. It isn't much of a life at all."

"Then maybe a change of scenery could do you some good," she offered.

He looked her in the eyes, trying to determine if she was joking. He would drop everything in a second to be with her. Hell, his company had offices all over the country. They were bound to have one in Florida he could relocate to—

A light turned on in the lobby of the motel, breaking up their conversation.

"Let's see who this is. If it's Zack, he'll text. If it's his grandfather, we'll wait to see who he's meeting," Howie said.

They waited for half an hour, then the light turned off. Zack never responded to his text, which meant it had to be Tim Ripple working that night. But no vehicle had shown up. Howie was beginning to feel that the kid had given him misinformation.

"I'm going to check around the back of the motel, see if anyone's there. This isn't what Zack said would happen."

"What is with you and making stupid decisions, Howie? That sounds like a death trap."

"Either nobody's back there, or the person I'm looking for is. I'll have an answer regardless," he said, then opened his door to get out. Bethany put a hand on his arm to stop him.

"What if there's a delusional tweaker back there? They might attack you."

He hated himself for not even considering the possibility of someone waiting to get their fix hiding by the dumpsters.

"Good call. But I'll be alert."

"What if something happens to us? What will happen with Ryan?"

"I know this may sound like an empty promise, but nothing will happen to either of you. I won't let it."

He stepped out of the car and shut the door, and Bethany followed. He didn't want her to but knew she wouldn't listen. They crossed the street together quietly.

When they reached the side of the motel, Howie felt like his heart might burst from his chest. It was one thing to run around playing hero when you were young and spry—and *stupid*—but he was going to be forty soon. Adrenaline hit differently now. He leaned against the brick and peered around the back. There was no light on behind the building, so he snuck around the side, trying to make sure his feet were as silent as possible on the packed dirt. Halfway down, a door was cracked open.

Must lead to the back office, he thought.

He walked tightly along the building with Bethany right behind, eventually making it to the open door. They paused, listening for any sounds from inside, but it was silent. Howie double-checked his phone, hoping Zack had texted him, only to see a missed call from Shawn. He didn't have time to call him back right now. That could wait.

Before he could talk himself out of it, Howie entered the back of the motel. The stale scent of snubbed cigarettes and cheap air fresheners he'd become familiar with during his stay greeted him. Again, he paused to listen. The ticking clock that drove him crazy while arguing with Tim was still there, muffled by the wall, but it was otherwise silent. He aimed his phone at the floor and turned the flashlight on. Sure enough, he appeared to be in the back office. He saw the door that led to the lobby.

There was a desk in the corner with a laptop, the surface otherwise covered in mail and notebooks. On the opposite wall, there was an old twin-sized bed with messy sheets hanging over the side like they were trying to crawl away. In the center of the mattress was a circular stain, and Howie pictured the old man pissing himself. This must be where Tim slept when he was working overnight.

There was no sign of Zack, no sign of *anyone*. So who the hell flipped the light on and off? He turned to Bethany, who looked equally confused and terrified, and motioned toward the door that went to the lobby. Whoever was here had to be on the other side waiting for them. He inched closer, ready to open it.

His light caught something on the far wall.

Howie paused, aiming the beam toward it, confused by what he was seeing. It was like an optical illusion. No, there were lines traveling in the center of the wall, in the shape of a door.

A hidden door.

"Look," he whispered.

They hesitantly moved toward the wall, and Howie found himself instinctively shielding Bethany the closer they got. There was no door handle, just a section of wall that matched the rest, except it was a few inches deeper. Howie tried to push the space, but it just rattled and remained in place. Then he slid his hand across it, and the wall went with his hand, revealing a dark space beyond.

He pointed the light inside and was surprised to see that the space was narrow, maybe a few feet wide. Insulation covered the wall inside and farther in, Howie noticed a sliver of light.

"What the hell?"

He stepped inside, and Bethany grabbed his arm.

"What are you doing?" she whispered.

"I have to see where this goes."

She sighed but didn't argue. His claustrophobia kicked in, his body barely fitting between the two walls. Insulation rubbed against his nose, and all he wanted to do was scratch it, but he couldn't lift his hands enough to do it. He squeezed forward, the insulation brushing his cheeks like cobwebs, each breath tighter than the last. Bethany remained at the opening, watching him and occasionally glancing back into the lobby to make sure they were alone.

Howie wasn't sure what he expected, but when he reached the space emitting the small beam of light, a chill went down his spine. A hole had been cut into the wall at some point, letting in a trickle of light. But it wasn't the hole that spooked him, but what was on the other side of it.

It was the motel room Howie had stayed in. Tim had been watching his room from inside the walls.

The tight space felt as if it was closing in on him, his breathing becoming more difficult.

Why would he be watching guests?

Howie peered out the hole into his former motel room, but everything looked normal. He couldn't believe he missed a hole in the wall, but it was tiny. Easy to miss if you weren't looking for it.

Is this just a peephole? Or...

Howie stuck his finger in the hole and pulled to the side, just like he did with the secret door.

The space moved.

It opened into the motel room he had slept in. Whoever had gone through his stuff had entered his room from the back office.

Howie's phone screen lit up. A text from Zack.

"About time," Howie muttered.

He read the text.

Zack: *I'm so sorry. I tried.*

Bethany screamed.

What the h—

Howie turned just as she was snatched from the opening and pulled back into the lobby, where he couldn't see her. He pushed through the narrow space, moving as quickly as possible.

Howie no longer worried about his own safety. He couldn't let anything happen to Bethany.

When he reached the opening, he expected to see coven members holding Bethany with a knife to her throat. But the lobby was empty. How were they already gone?

But then he heard a muffled cry on the other side of the wall, out in the lobby. He noticed the back office door leading to the lobby cracked open. Then the jingle of the entrance bell sounded, and the muffled cries came to an abrupt stop. Howie entered the lobby and had just enough time to see a large man dragging Bethany across the parking lot with her legs flailing, trying to kick him. It was Derrick Patten, forcing her toward a black station wagon.

Howie bolted into the parking lot after them.

"Hey! Let her go!"

Derrick stopped, turned slowly, his grip tight in her hair. There was twenty feet between them, but even in the dark, Howie saw Derrick smile and open his mouth to reveal a mangled mess. He leaned in close to Bethany's face and she screamed, fighting to break free. He was too strong for her. Derrick moaned, then kissed along her neck with his filthy mouth.

Howie charged but came to a sudden stop when Derrick revealed a blade in his other hand.

"Derrick, what the hell? I know you don't like me, but what the fuck are you doing? Let her go before you do something you'll regret! She's got a kid!"

Howie realized all he was doing was buying time. Why was Derrick only taking Bethany? They didn't even know she was coming with him. He should be the target.

"Behind you, Howie!" Bethany screamed before Derrick struck her to the ground.

Howie spun around and stared up at a massive figure. He wore a black suit and had tattoos covering his hands and neck. The bald man towered over him. His face... *Ruger?* He realized he saw this man in the bar the same night Derrick got in his face. He must have been there watching Howie.

"I see the confusion in your eyes, Howie. But if you really think about it, really look in my eyes, you will know who I am."

"How—?"

And then it clicked. It wasn't Felix Ruger he was looking at. Was it his son?

The man smirked. "Ah, light bulb go off? You and Ms. Carver were responsible for taking our father from us. I have waited for this moment for twenty-five years. But we won't simply just kill you like we did your mother. That would be too easy. Instead, you are going to be the first thing he sees when we summon him. He will take great pleasure in tearing you to shreds."

Howie heard Bethany gasping for air behind him. He heard Derrick making odd, urgent noises from his horrible mouth. But then he heard something else, in the trees. Out of the corner of his eye, he sensed movement, then realized Derrick wasn't just grunting, but trying to communicate with Ruger's son.

"Your dad was evil. He killed countless people in this town. He deserved what he got."

The tall man took a step forward, lifting his upper lip in a snarl. He ignored Derrick's plea, too focused on Howie.

"My father didn't kill. He *sacrificed*. There are greater powers than any of us. The Withered Tongues knew that, and we sacrificed to Vorathor, to Vodyanoy. You wouldn't know the first thing about the greater powers—"

A gun clicked from the woods.

"Put your fucking hands up! Now!"

Shawn exited the woods, keeping his firearm locked on Ruger's son, who turned and spotted the cop. For a moment, no one spoke. Derrick grinned. Ruger's son didn't even flinch.

"Really? You know it's too late, right? Things are already in motion. This town will die. All of you will *die*."

Shawn fired, but Howie couldn't see where it hit. Then Ruger spun around, clutching his shoulder. He bared his teeth and Howie saw his chance. He lunged at the tall man, but Ruger was too quick. He backhanded Howie in the face with a closed fist, dropping him to the ground. He was in too much pain to lift his head, but more gunshots echoed in the night.

Then car doors slammed shut.

Tires peeled, kicking up dirt.

He lifted his head just as the black station wagon sped out of the motel parking lot. Shawn ran to his side.

"Are you okay?"

"I'll be fine. What about Bethany?"

"She's here. Let's get you two somewhere safe before they come back."

Howie stood, shaking with terror and anger. "What's going on, Shawn? You know more than you're letting on. Why didn't you tell me Ruger had a kid?"

"I'm sorry. There were certain things I couldn't tell you. But it's too late for that now. We need all the help we can get."

"We?"

"We're going to talk with Ellis."

And just like that, the nightmare from his childhood came full circle.

CHAPTER 37

1979

Henry and the priest searched well into the night for Jessica. After coming up empty-handed, Grimes promised to return in the morning. Henry drove home alone, the house as dark as ever. Father Grimes said the longer the demon resided inside her, the more control it would gain. Eventually, her thoughts would be completely overshadowed by the cannibal, and she'd be unable to resist the urge to kill. Henry knew if he could get her back, he could help her until Grimes assisted in an exorcism. He told himself that he would bring her any animal she wanted just to keep her in the house. It broke his heart, but not nearly as much as watching her deteriorate before his eyes.

Henry wiped at his eyes again. He entered the home that was supposed to offer a fresh start for them. Instead, it brought them a life of misery. It was quiet inside. Uncomfortably so. He walked around turning on all the lights, which worked again since the demon was no longer present to mess with them. As he sat at the kitchen table, debating what he could possibly do, the lights flickered.

He raised his head and stared at the overhead lamp in the kitchen. Part of him prayed for the power to go out. It would mean she was back, but he realized it also meant the demon would be with her. Henry saw the sorrow in her eyes when she'd fled earlier. She was still in there.

"*Hennnry*. I don't know how long I'll have control to communicate with you this way. The demon is eating away at my body. I can't stop it."

He looked around, but she wasn't anywhere in sight.

"Jessica. Where are you? Let me help."

The lights flickered again. A warm gust of putrid air washed into the kitchen.

Still, there were no visible signs of Jessica anywhere. Henry decided to check every room in the house, just to be safe. While he had no way of knowing for sure, he assumed she could only communicate this way if she was nearby. Maybe she was hiding in another room.

He checked the study first, finding it empty. The sulfur smell from earlier still poisoned the room. Next, he moved downstairs to the basement. He flipped the light on, immediately regretting it. The floor was stained with dried blood and leftover viscera, all that remained of the poor feline.

Those awful sounds... The cat's screams from behind the closed door would haunt Henry for the rest of his life.

With no sign of her in the basement, he was headed back toward the stairs when the light bulb above shattered, sending sharp, tiny fragments across the floor, blanketing the room in darkness. The door slammed shut at the top of the steps.

Something tickled along his neck. He swiped at it, but there was nothing there. Then the same sensation moved up both of his arms, like hundreds of tiny spiders crawling across his flesh. Henry shouted out as he clawed at his exposed skin, but then the sensation vanished, replaced by a sound overhead.

He looked up and saw the outline of Jessica, crouched low on the top step.

"Hi, man of my dreams. Ready to eat my slit?"

The voice wasn't Jessica's. Henry froze, searching for a way out.

"You won't get past me unless I let you," the demon hissed. *"Now that I've fed on human flesh, I feel oh so wonderful. So, here's the deal, lover boy. You will bring me sacrifices to feed on, and I won't leave your wife's body in pieces when I move on. Sound good?"*

Henry couldn't respond. The ultimatum allowed no way of winning either way. *I must bring human sacrifices to my wife—No, that's not her, it's Atahsaia!—or the demon will drain her of any life she has left in there. Who's to say he wouldn't do that anyway?*

"Demon...I'll do whatever I need to do for my wife. Just tell me what to do."

The orange eyes shimmered from the stairs, as if Henry admitting defeat somehow aroused the demon. A sinister cackle escaped from Jessica's chest, then she tilted her head to the side, her neck cracking like dry twigs.

"How about you start with a young, virgin teen. My favorite flavor. Bring me some breakfast in bed, sweetie."

He wanted to ask why. Why kids? But he knew better. This thing, this *monster*, was vile. It thrived on the suffering of others. He loved his wife; he would die for her. But Henry wasn't sure he could go through with this. His thoughts went back to the confusion in the cat's eyes when he tossed it into the basement and slammed the door shut. Henry couldn't envision that same expression in the eyes of an innocent child while sending it to slaughter.

There was a sudden thumping overhead. At first, Henry thought it was Jessica moving across the ceiling. But then he realized it was footsteps on the first floor. The demon snapped its head toward the sounds, sniffing like a rabid dog.

If it's you, Father Grimes, please turn and run. Get far away from this thing!

The thumping was coming from more than one place, though. If it was Grimes, he brought backup. The demon crawled down a few of the stairs and turned around to face the closed door, waiting for whoever had entered the home to open it.

Henry could hear voices on the other side of the door.

The demon growled, then leaped to the ceiling, clinging to the support beam above the stairs.

The door opened, and a hooded figure appeared in the doorway. Jessica dropped from above, tackling the intruder down the stairs. His skull smacked against the concrete with a sickening *CRACK*. She tore at his flesh. He didn't respond, and she didn't stop, clawing and biting until there was nothing left but a ruin of skin and bone.

"She's down here!" another voice shouted.

Three hooded men appeared in the doorway, one of them spotting what the demon was doing to their fellow member. The man let out a gasp but quickly grabbed something from a pouch he carried. He started chanting something in Latin, grabbing the attention of Jessica, who stopped feasting on the dead man beneath her. Her orange eyes snapped up, her mouth opening wide to reveal a set of daggers dripping with blood and chunks of flesh. She hissed, a deep, guttural growl rumbling from her chest.

Scorching air rushed from her mouth, suffocating the tightly spaced basement with her sulfurous stench. The coven member ignored it, continuing his chant, holding up an item in front of him. At first, Henry thought it was a crucifix, but then realized it was a sigil—one that the demon feared.

Jessica crawled off the corpse, her palms slapping in the puddle of blood beneath her. Henry felt bile forming in his throat at the combination of copper and sulfur in the air. Jessica's orange eyes flitted wildly, looking for a way out. She briefly locked eyes with Henry, the orange glow momentarily fading to display her natural color.

"Help me, Henry. *Please* stop this thing."

The pain in her voice broke his heart. But he didn't have long to feel that sorrow as both eyes reverted to a blazing orange and her snarl returned. The coven member leading the chant increased the volume of his voice. Jessica crawled to the far corner like an insect trying to sneak back into a small crack in the wall.

As she retreated, the coven members descended the stairs, one of them holding a flashlight that lit up the bloody mess between them. What were they planning to do with Jessica? He had to save her. They wanted to hurt her. He couldn't let that happen.

Henry ran at the member chanting, wrapping both arms around his torso in an attempt to tackle him to the floor. The man paused briefly, then continued his mission of subduing the demon. When the second member stepped up, Henry felt an icy sensation in his stomach. He looked down in shock to discover a dagger firmly buried in his abdomen. He dropped to the floor as Jessica—it *was* her this time—screamed, watching him collapse.

He tried to crawl toward her, his hand outstretched. Everything was now displayed behind a blurry lens. Through it, the coven descended on Jessica. She thrashed as the demon returned, but it was too late. One of the members wrapped her wrists in something that made Jessica's skin sizzle and blister instantly. She bellowed in agony, but it was cut short by something thrown over her head, muffling the screams.

Henry wanted to stop them, but he was fading. He clung to consciousness long enough to see them dragging Jessica up the basement stairs, disappearing above. And then he was lost, swimming in a sea of darkness.

CHAPTER 38

Jessica wasn't sure how many days had passed. Enough that snow began to fall. On occasion, someone from the coven would bring her food—roadkill starting to rot—to keep Atahsaia at bay. They had found a way to neutralize its powers: something on the rope they used to tie her up. And now, they kept her trapped in a small, dark room guarded by obsidian stones.

She was thankful for the little window in the corner that kept her from total darkness and from slipping into madness. With the demon weakened, Jessica had control of most of her thoughts for the first time since the possession. She tried communicating with Henry through her thoughts, but either the distance was too far, or he was dead.

He is dead. I watched them stab him as he bled out, she thought.

It wasn't something she could allow herself to believe. After all they had been through, it couldn't end this way. He had saved her from the horror back home. She needed to return the favor, even if it meant sacrificing herself to the demon.

She looked to the window. The snow fell in heavy sheets of white across the night sky. To Atahsaia, beauty wasn't snowfall, it was tearing apart flesh, ripping out organs, making victims suffer before devouring their hearts. And right now, the hunger was returning, which meant the demon was as well, weakened or not.

"As soon as I get out of this shithole, your body is mine again, bitch. I'll lick your intestines dry before eating away at them. I'll plant rot inside you and spread it through your bones. Your body will be nothing but a husk I chew from the inside out."

"I won't let you. I'll die before I allow you to take everything from me."

The demon laughed, sending a sharp pain through Jessica's stomach. She curled into a ball, crying as her body failed to fight the disease taking hold.

A lock clanged, then the door opened inward, revealing a few coven members in their black robes. One of them held the sigil that weakened the demon during capture, another held a long pole with a noose-like loop at the end of it.

"It is time. Stand up," the member with the sigil said. Jessica recognized him as Brian White, the one who had coaxed her into believing she belonged to the coven. Not just as a pawn, but something more. A vessel.

Jessica hesitated, so Brian stepped closer, holding up the sigil inches from her face. The demon thrashed around inside her, causing so much pain she had no choice but to obey. She stumbled to her feet, and Brian White nodded for the other member to enter.

"Stand still while we get this on you."

"What is it? Will it hurt?" she asked.

"Compared to what you'll feel later, this is minor, Jessica. Now shut up, and don't move," Brian said.

The second member raised the pole so the loop hung over her head, then they lowered the rope over her, pulling it snug against her throat. The material instantly burned, singeing into her flesh. Jessica refused to scream, refused to give them that satisfaction. They forced her out of the room, down a narrow hallway, and into the parking lot, where she was met with a blizzard.

With the demon burning away at her core, the fresh air felt nice. The coven members shivered as the wind whipped a wall of snow into their faces, but Jessica inhaled the fresh air deeply. She saw multiple vehicles lined up in a row, all idling as if they were about to take off. They pushed her toward them, specifically a van that said *NEWPORT POLICE DEPARTMENT* on the side of it.

"Bronson, you sit in the back with her, hold the sigil close," Brian White ordered. "As long as the restraints are on her, she can't hurt you."

"Ah, hell. Can't we make one of the recruits do it? She's fucking crazy." The man was overweight with long brown hair and a beard that covered his entire face. Jessica figured that if she tried to escape, she wouldn't be able to break free from him.

"But he will satisfy my hunger perfectly."

"Who is the highest in command here?" Brian asked.

"Y-you. Sorry, Brian, sir. Won't happen again."

This man was scared of Brian. Terrified. Was this how all of the members acted around him?

"Open the door, Miller," Brian ordered.

A young cop in uniform stood at the back door of the van and nodded. He opened the door and the two members at Jessica's side shoved her into the back. Her knee slammed on the metal floor, sending a jolt of pain down her leg.

"I'll gouge your fucking eyes out and eat them, you little prick!"

The threat came with no warning, clawing through Jessica's vocal cords like shards of glass. But even as the demon said it, she could sense it getting weaker with the restraints burning into her flesh.

She snapped her head back toward the door and burned her eyes into the cop. Unlike the other man, he didn't seem too threatened by her.

"We can change that real *quick. Make some bacon out of big piggy."*

Miller scowled, then the overweight Bronson climbed in next to her, and the officer slammed the door shut. After a moment, the van pulled onto the road, driving slowly through the suffocating storm. Bronson sat across from Jessica, keeping his eyes locked on her and his hand tightly wrapped around the sigil. Just the sight of it pained Jessica.

The ride was mostly silent, with only the sound of the windshield wipers aggressively moving back and forth in a failed attempt to clear the snow. Through the back window, the dark sky was impenetrable through the violent storm. The headlights of other vehicles highlighted just how severe the blizzard truly was.

"Where are we going?" Jessica asked.

"Shut up. I don't answer to you."

"No, but you sure answer to Brian. Why are you so scared of him?"

Bronson's upper lip trembled. Not in fear, but rage. She struck a nerve, just as intended. If she couldn't beat him physically, she'd try mentally.

"Bitch, what part of shut up don't you understand? There's a hierarchy in this coven, one you begged to be part of. Only we never intended to let you in. You're a damn pawn, is all."

"Bronson, *enough,*" the driver said, glancing over his shoulder.

Jessica itched to dig deeper but bit back any further comments. One wrong word and she'd never leave the van.

"What's the matter, Bronson? Afraid you'll never move up from babysitting duty? You know the demon inside me—that *you* people put there—wants to rip out your insides, right?"

This time, the lip tremble *was* fear, and Jessica knew she was now living in his head.

"Winter solstice is upon us. Soon, you will see exactly what we used you for. Enjoy your last night."

The van slowed carefully, the roads slick with ice. They turned onto a narrow road where the branches had already begun to sag beneath the weight of the snow. Bronson said it was winter solstice. Could it possibly be late December already? She realized that since the possession had occurred in November, the demon had been inside her for over a month already.

"Time flies when you're having fun, doesn't it?"

Atahsaia still had enough strength to intercept her thoughts, but his voice was weak, barely audible in her mind. As they moved along the bumpy road, Jessica tried to look for landmarks that she could remember if she somehow escaped the coven. But to do so, she would need the demon's help.

"We're here," the driver said as the van came to a stop.

"Don't try any funny business. I'll shove this sigil in your fucking mouth if you even think about it," Bronson said, raising the sigil threateningly.

The back door swung open, and Jessica was blinded by a set of headlights from the vehicle behind them. Brian White stepped forward, blocking the beams, but Jessica could hardly see him through the snow falling.

Her neck burned, and she realized it was because Bronson had tightened the loop around her throat. He dragged her out of the van into the snow, which was already ankle-deep. Jessica was barefoot, her skin so hot it melted the snow around her feet.

"Bring her through on the trail. The ritual grounds are half a mile in. Ruger is already there with the others," Brian said.

She remembered Ruger from the summoning at the pond. While Jessica felt betrayed by the coven, she couldn't help but feel anticipation overwhelm her at the thought of seeing the leader again. His power was intoxicating.

They trudged through the snow, branches clawing at her cheeks. Just when she thought they would never make it to their destination, she spotted a clearing up ahead. A group of coven members were all congregated in the center of a wide circle with wooden torches sticking out of the ground to light the area.

Inside the circle of flames, a Devil's star was displayed using smaller candles on the ground. In the center of the star was a wooden plank with bindings where her hands and feet would go.

A ritual in the making.

Questions filled the Rolodex of her mind. *What are they doing to me? The demon is already inside. What could they possibly need with me?*

When the coven members saw her being led toward the plank, they spread to the outside of the circle, all dressed in their black hooded robes.

"Bring her to the plank. It is time," Ruger's voice boomed over them.

She only knew it was Ruger because of his height, standing at least a foot taller than everyone else. He too was in a black robe, but he also wore a black, featureless mask. Bronson forced her toward the circle. Jessica stopped cold. The demon was resisting the circle. With its strength weakened, it wasn't enough to completely overpower the coven member, but enough to cause resistance. All that did was dig the collar into her neck even more.

"Move it," Bronson said, kicking her in the back. The force of his meaty leg almost sent her toppling over, but she kept her balance. Again, the rage of the demon resurfaced. She found herself wanting to tear Bronson's body apart, limb by limb.

As soon as they entered the circle, the demon gathered enough strength to growl, exposing teeth she knew were not her own. That was the one thing she found most difficult to adjust to. Trumping the pain inside and the sense of no longer being in control, was the change in her appearance. Long nails, as thick as talons and sharp as knives, had grown from her fingers and toes. Every single warped limb on her body pulsed in excruciating pain. Her mouth hurt just as much; the fangs pushing through her blackened gums had forced many of her regular teeth to fall out, while others remained pressed tightly beyond her new mouth.

Bronson pushed her down on the plank, then twisted the pole so it forced her to turn onto her back and face the gathering crowd. Two more coven members approached from each side, securing her limbs to the plank with the same material that burned into her throat. She was displayed in a crucifix position, similar to how she had been at the pond.

That was all Atahsaia needed to be fully awakened.

"You fucking scum! Set me free and let's see how powerful you really are!"

"Atahsaia, you know that isn't going to happen. You see, you are here for a very important reason. Do you know what today is?" Ruger asked.

Jessica flashed her teeth, fantasizing of chewing out his throat.

"Today is the day you take your last breath. Did I get it right?"

"Oh, no. Quite the contrary," Ruger said in a calm, confident tone. "Today is the winter solstice, demon. The day when you take *your* last breath. We will summon the great demon, Vorathor, and he will bestow upon me and my children otherworldly powers. Powers that will take this coven to where it needs to be. In return, we will condemn you to this body for all of eternity. No longer will you be able to return to Hell and devour your own kind."

Jessica was still alert, still listening. The thought of being forever bound with the demon sent her heart into a frenzy. The only thought worse than dying was being forced to live forever while something else had possession of her body and mind.

"You are all far too weak to stop me. Vorathor gave you a fool's errand."

"No. We took extra precautions with you. It has been months in the making. Waited for the perfect virgin host to lure you in. Waited for the solstice when the veil between your kind and ours is thinnest. When you are at your weakest." Even with a dark mask hiding his face, Jessica could feel Ruger's smile.

"My weakest is still far superior to your strongest. Vorathor thinks trapping me on Earth will stop me? You shitstains underestimate my abilities. I will kill every last one of you!" Jessica felt the rage consuming her, drool leaking down her face.

Yet, Ruger remained composed. "Bring my children," he ordered.

Jessica squinted through the snow as a robed figure stepped from the trees wearing a white mask instead of black, cradling an infant in each hand. They cried loudly, and Jessica thought they sounded like they couldn't be more than a year old. The babies were wrapped in white blankets, tightly swaddled to protect them from the bitter temperature.

"Ohh, appetizers? I love the taste of infant hearts."

Ruger snapped his head at Jessica. The fact that she couldn't see his face somehow made his piercing gaze far worse. But his posture, his tone, told her he was enraged.

"If you threaten my bloodline again, I'll make you suffer for hours before proceeding. I'll burn a fucking cross into your forehead!"

The member holding the babies reached the perimeter of the Devil's circle and stopped. Jessica got a good look at the crying children. They were wailing, their faces turning bright red.

"Set the twins at their designated places," Ruger ordered.

He didn't even care that his own children were suffering greatly in the frigid cold. The member kneeled in the snow and placed them carefully on the ground. The rest of the coven closed in around the outside of the circle, holding hands. The demon thrashed around, trying to break free, but the restraints were too powerful. Jessica felt a jolt of pain every time the demon pressed against the material.

"We shall begin," Ruger said. "Tonight, we bond my blood with the power of Vorathor to keep the coven strong for generations to come. We bind Atahsaia within the body of Jessica Black, where the demon will forever suffer. And then we will transport the demon to its sacrificial grave for eternity."

The coven members nodded in agreement, enthusiastic yet focused.

Ruger raised his arms, his voice ringing clear through the storm. "Almighty Vorathor, we ask you to grace my children with the power you promised upon completion of this sacrifice. I ask that you take my twins, Elias and Rachel, and grant them strength and intelligence."

The demon had stopped thrashing, but Jessica didn't think it was giving up. It was planning something, she could feel it. If it harmed these babies, she wasn't sure she could live with herself. Although if this ritual proved successful, she wouldn't be living at all.

"First, we bind the demon with the vessel. Let's begin," Ruger ordered.

The wind was fierce, with strong gusts blowing snow squalls across the open space between the trees. A few of the torches flickered, close to going out, then the flames returned.

"Now, join hands and recite with me," Ruger said.

They all began to chant in unison. Some of it Jessica understood, other parts she didn't but the *demon* did.

"Liga corpus, animam, et cor cum dæmone. Fac ut unum fiant."

Something stirred inside Jessica. The demon, who had been previously growing stronger within, content on draining her body slowly, now wanted out. If it escaped, she worried the coven would kill her, leaving no chance to see Henry again. She wanted it gone, but not yet. She needed its strength.

Stay inside me. We must work together to survive, she thought, hoping the demon got the message.

The coven continued their chants. Atahsaia slithered through her. Something needed to happen soon, or there would be no chance of getting the demon out safely. Up until tonight, Jessica hadn't had her own thoughts long enough to consider the options of being free. The demon controlled her, fed off her. The idea of working together to take down the coven wasn't something that seemed realistic. But now, it was a necessity. While The Withered Tongues continued chanting, one of the members broke through the circle, holding a branding iron. Anxiety clawed at

Jessica's throat as the member approached, understanding exactly what the plan was now. She had seen it in the book. Binding symbols. If they marked her with the rod, there was no turning back.

Come on, demon. Where's your strength now?

The babies cried, drowning out some of the chant. The snow came down sideways, clinging to their black robes. Jessica noticed a puddle forming around her as her body temperature continued to increase. Her eyes burned, sending tears down her cheeks. The demon was attempting to gain control. For the first time since her body was infiltrated, Jessica let it. She submitted to it, *asked* for it to take control. One last thought scraped through her mind: if she let it in, she might never come back, never kiss Henry again, never get to say goodbye.

Ruger didn't notice, continuing his chant. One of the other members, a short, older man with a white mustache, glanced at her face, spotting the intensifying glow. He didn't dare interrupt his leader, but the fear was etched into his face.

The breeze blew through the land again and this time, a few of the torches did snuff out. Ruger paused, realizing the Devil's star was no longer complete. He turned to one of the members and ordered, "Quickly, light the torches!"

But it was too late.

Atahsaia had control, ripping her hands free from the restraints, followed by her legs. Coven members screamed. Some scurried away, others stood their ground, not wanting to upset Ruger.

"Stop her! Grab the sigil!" Ruger barked.

Jessica launched off the plank, sailing past the perimeter of the torches, and drove the short man with the white mustache to the ground. He cried out, but it was cut short as Jessica swiped across his face with her curled claws, snapping his head to the side and breaking his neck in the process.

The demon wanted the heart, but she forced herself off the corpse and scanned the area, wondering what the best escape might be. She saw members of The Withered Tongues running in every direction, lost in the snowstorm. Then her eyes landed on a coven member who stopped her cold.

Bronson.

Her muscles tensed, her teeth grinding. He turned and saw her leering at him. That false sense of confidence he had in the van was washed away. Abject horror replaced it. The demon didn't waste another second. Jessica sprinted toward him, clawing at other coven members as she passed, then lunged through the air, colliding with the overweight brute.

They hit the ground hard, rolling a few feet before coming to a stop with Jessica mounting him.

"I told you I'd tear you apart piece by piece!"

He started to beg, but Jessica didn't allow it. She drove her claws into his open mouth, hooking them on the back of his throat. His gag reflex kicked in just as she tore downward, pulling his bottom jaw and throat from his body. Blood and vomit spouted out of the hole, his tongue now hanging by a thread. His eyes bugged out as an animalistic *squeal* blasted from his chest.

Jessica felt herself smile, the sharp teeth poking into the inside of her lips. She drove three fingers into the meat surrounding his sternum and raked down, tearing open his belly like a wet canvas. Blood pooled on the snow around him as his eyes rolled into the back of his head. He was still alive, still suffering. Just like she wanted him to. And then she pried the skin from his chest, opening it enough to see his insides glistening in the torch light.

"Get her, now!" Ruger yelled.

His babies, little Elias and Rachel, continued to cry. One of the coven members lifted them and ran in the opposite direction. Jessica knew she didn't have much time, but she was *hungry*. She drove her hand deeper, finally latching on to Bronson's beating heart, then tore it completely free, sending a splash of scarlet across the snow.

Before she had a chance to bite into the ripe organ, a gunshot blasted through the air. The bullet connected with her shoulder, and she hissed.

"Don't kill her! Just subdue her!"

Jessica jumped off Bronson's shredded remains and bolted for the forest. Behind her, the mob of coven members yelled, screamed, and cried. She heard Ruger barking orders. But she was free. The storm ate her up, and she vanished into the trees.

CHAPTER 39

2024

Howie and Bethany sat in the back seat of Shawn's cruiser as they sped through town. He told them Patrick Ellis now lived one town over in Claremont, and that he was your typical retired police officer—full of regret, depression, and alcoholism. Howie recalled Ellis saving their asses that fateful night at the factory. A night when Vorathor killed so many, including Howie's dad. A night when they trapped two demons in one concrete slab, which Ellis promised to take care of.

Howie often wondered what exactly Ellis did with that slab. How he could guarantee the demons wouldn't escape. But he was always able to push it to the back of his mind, his specialty in life. By keeping himself busy, Howie was able to avoid many of the horrible memories of his childhood. Instead of meeting it head-on like his therapist insisted he do, he usually took the easy way out and allowed his thoughts to go elsewhere.

They passed the Claremont town line before Shawn decided to speak up. "I know you have a lot of questions. I don't blame you. I have to get this off my chest, though. What you said about Todd being disappointed in me...that hurt, man. All I ever wanted was to honor him after he passed."

Howie felt like an asshole. He'd inherited his dad's temper; words that felt good in the moment always came back to haunt him.

"I'm sorry, Shawn. I didn't mean it. I was pissed off and scared, but you didn't deserve that."

"Yeah, I did. You were right, Howie. I set out on this big mission years ago to make sure this town never again faced anything like we did in the past. I lost more than just a cousin with Todd. I lost a best friend. A brother," Shawn said, then paused as he tried to hold back tears. "And then when something bad *does* come along, I let the town politics hold me back. Newport doesn't want any big news breaking. If word got around of a deadly drug making its way through town, killing many and putting others out on the streets...that would cripple any last ounce of life we have here."

"So what? What has this place done for you, Shawn? Newport is forever cursed. Maybe bringing the whole town down isn't such a bad thing," Howie said.

Bethany was silent, texting Tanya to make sure Ryan was okay.

"Any luck?" Howie asked.

"Yes, she just responded. Said they are having a blast, watching a movie and eating candy."

"We talk with Ellis, get some answers—*hopefully*—then get you back to your boy," Howie said, rubbing her shoulder. "Shawn, are we almost there?"

"Turning onto his road now."

Howie couldn't help but feel a sense of déjà vu as the anticipation of seeing Ellis finally hit home. Back when they were trying to end Felix Ruger's reign of terror, he went with his dad and Father Grimes to visit Henry Black, who had been living off the grid for years. The only difference then was that everyone thought Henry was dead. And he was crazy.

Shawn slowed his cruiser and turned into the driveway of a normal-looking home. Howie wasn't sure what he expected, but Henry had been hiding in a run-down shack that was owned by the church for years when they found him. At least on the outside, Ellis seemed to be much better off. Maybe retirement suited him.

"He knows we're coming?" Howie asked.

"Yeah. I called him earlier. He's expecting us. Just be prepared, he's a retired old grump."

That wasn't the image Howie had in his mind for Patrick Ellis, but he assumed spending decades stuck in Newport would make even the nicest of people a bit jaded. The porch light popped on, followed by the front door opening and Ellis walking out to greet them. Age hadn't done him any favors, but he was still recognizable behind the receding hair and liver-spotted skin.

"Howie! Bethany! How the hell have you been?" he asked, raising his arms for a hug.

Shawn looked confused. "Where's this warm welcome when you see me?"

"Oh, please. You worked for me," Ellis said, embracing Bethany. "These two were just kids when I met them. I reserve my attitude for my replacement as chief. Comes with the territory, Seymour. Now come on inside and let's chat."

Up close, the wrinkles really added to Ellis's age. Stress had a way of doing that. Howie knew he probably looked years older than he actually was as well. They followed Ellis inside and walked into a cozy living room that had a blueberry scented candle lit. It was the home of a retired bachelor, but it was clear Ellis at least made an attempt to tidy up the place.

"Please, sit. I'm sorry to hear about your mom, Howie. She was a good woman," Ellis said sympathetically.

"Thank you," Howie replied as he sat on the couch beside Bethany. Shawn stood next to them with his arms crossed, as if he was still on edge around his former chief.

"How have you been, Bethany?" Ellis asked.

"Staying busy. My son keeps me on my toes, that's for sure."

Ellis grinned proudly. "A son? Congrats! I'm happy for you." He looked over Bethany and Howie, and something like bittersweet nostalgia fell over his face. "I'm happy to see you both, it's been too long. Shawn told me why you guys were coming. I'll help as best I can."

"After the night at the factory, what happened?" Howie asked, getting right to the point.

Ellis scratched his cheek and squinted.

"I only remember pieces of it. Everything immediately after you left, the following days, and then... it went blank. I remember driving through the woods to a place I'd never been before. I kept hearing whispers, real quiet, telling me I was doing the right thing. There was water, strange-looking. That's it, though."

If Ellis didn't remember what he did with the demons, he might not have any answers about Ruger.

"What do you know about Thred?" Howie asked.

"Not much. It wasn't really around until after I retired. I still listen to my scanner out of boredom and from time to time, I talk to this dipshit who couldn't hold my jockstrap as chief," Ellis said, gesturing toward Shawn.

"You would wear a jockstrap on the job, Ellis," Shawn said.

"I'm still Chief to you, Seymour."

Both of them laughed, and as good as this friendly cop banter was to see between two old colleagues, Howie was getting impatient.

"Tonight I went to the motel in town to look for answers. The kid who works there told me a distributor would be making a run with Thred. I wanted to see how my mom got hooked on the stuff. But it was a setup. They attacked me and tried to take Bethany. I know it's the coven; it's back again."

Ellis nodded and bit his lip. He didn't seem nearly as surprised or concerned as Howie expected him to be.

"Yeah. I always suspected they weren't done for good. The question is: why now? From the night we got rid of Ruger, all the way through my retirement, they never showed their ugly faces. The moment you two are back in town, shit gets thrown upside down again. Almost like they wanted you here."

"That's the thing. I think they poisoned my mom with Thred to get me back here. But Bethany only came because Shawn reached out to her—"

"What?" Shawn interrupted. "I didn't reach out to anyone. You told me Bethany hated your guts."

Bethany frowned in confusion. "You emailed me. Told me Howie's mom died, and he needed all the support he could get."

Slowly, Shawn shook his head, looking unnerved. "No. I didn't do that, Bethany."

"Then who the hell did?"

"Can you pull up the email, Bethany?" Howie asked.

She scrolled through her phone and found it. Shawn read it, shaking his head.

"That's my email address, but I did not send that. What the fuck is going on here?"

"Exactly what Howie suspected. What else do we know?" Ellis asked.

"When we were at the motel, they ambushed us. Derrick Patten was involved."

"That moron isn't smart enough to orchestrate a plan like this," Shawn said.

Howie continued. "He was just a lackey. But the one in charge…I swore it was Ruger. The resemblance was uncanny—"

"His kid. Fuck," Ellis interrupted.

"Yeah, he told me Ruger was his father. Am I the only one who didn't know he had a kid?" Howie snapped.

"After Felix died, we were told he had twin sons. But something didn't add up."

"Christ, he had *twins*? There's another fucking brother out there?" Howie asked.

"That's what I was told, but it's not true."

"What does that mean?" A knot was forming in the pit of Howie's stomach.

"After searching and searching, digging into medical files, I finally located the doctor who delivered the twins, long retired. Someone messed with the files, forged the birth certificate."

The riddles were maddening.

"How? Like wiping them off the grid to hide them?" Howie asked.

"Only one was a boy. The other was a girl. Elias has a twin sister. Her name is Rachel."

"Why go through all that effort to hide the gender of your child?" Shawn asked.

Howie got to his feet, a realization hitting him.

"Because the coven sacrificed all their female members after the failed Jessica possession. Ruger must have been trying to protect his daughter."

"Exactly. But I was never able to determine if she was still alive. For all we know, she could be out there helping her brother," Ellis said.

"Oh, my God," Bethany whispered.

Howie was about to ask what was wrong, but then he realized what she was thinking, and he felt his legs weaken.

"Tanya."

"Who?" Ellis asked.

Bethany's eyes widened. She was already dialing Tanya's number. It rang once, then went to voicemail. "No, no, no. Please pick up." Her hands shook.

"We left Bethany's son with a woman named Tanya. She introduced herself at the funeral, said my mom used to babysit her. Ryan instantly became attached to her, and it felt safe—"

"We need to go, now!" Bethany snapped. She was understandably panicking. "She's not answering my texts. Please, we need to go to my son."

"I'll throw the lights on and get there as quick as we fucking can. Let's go," Shawn said.

CHAPTER 40

Howie held Bethany's hand tight as Shawn sped toward Newport with his blue lights flashing. Bethany continued her attempts to reach Tanya to no avail. Ellis sat shotgun, the odd man out with Shawn focused on the road and Howie consoling Bethany. They crossed the Claremont/Newport town line at eighty miles per hour, but that still didn't feel fast enough. Howie wanted to help Bethany. He wanted to do everything possible to ease any of her concerns. An idea came to him that could either make her feel better or send her further into the whirlwind of panic.

"Shawn, can you run a name for us to see if Tanya is real?"

"Let him focus on the road. I can run the search," Ellis said. "What's the name again?"

"Tanya Pearce. P-E-A-R-C-E."

Ellis typed into the MDT system on Shawn's laptop.

"Will it be easy to find her without other information?" Bethany asked.

"Well, just be thankful her last name isn't Smith. Shouldn't take too long to narrow it down. This will search any warrants, criminal records, missing person alerts, and more," Ellis said, scrolling through text too small for Howie to read from the back seat.

The glow from the screen lit Ellis's features as he squinted with concentration. A list popped up within seconds, and he paused.

"Bingo."

"What? What is it?" Bethany asked.

"Tanya Pearce. Missing person case, twenty years ago. Never found. Suspected abduction. Cold case ever since."

Tears poured down Bethany's face. Howie pulled her close and kissed the top of her head.

"We're almost back. He's a smart boy, Bethany."

She said nothing, and as they whipped around the corner toward Howie's driveway, their worst fears became a reality.

Tanya's car was gone.

Not Tanya. It's Rachel Ruger. They have been planning this whole thing to get us right where they want us, Howie thought.

Shawn didn't even have the cruiser in park before Bethany was out and running toward the house, yelling her son's name. Howie caught up to her as she was opening the front door, and the emptiness inside swallowed them up. On the coffee table sat a bowl of popcorn, half-full. The movie's end credits played on loop.

Howie already knew Ryan was gone. Still, they searched the house anyway, calling his name, hoping for a miracle. Bethany was a mess, but she was the strongest person Howie knew, and she forced herself to maintain a certain level of composure, knowing she needed to think with a clear head.

They all regrouped in the living room.

"They've been planning this for years," Bethany said, her trembling words matching Howie's thoughts.

"Why do you say that?" Shawn asked.

"That same screen name—the one who messaged me when I was a kid—commented on Ryan's video. It was them. The coven."

"What did the comment say?" Ellis asked.

Howie and Bethany looked at each other and spoke in unison: "It comes from within."

Ellis stumbled, the color draining from his skin as he grabbed hold of the couch to hold himself up. Howie thought he was suffering a heart attack and ran to his side.

"Are you okay?"

"That phrase...the voices said it to me when I was trying to hide the concrete slab," Ellis said, rubbing his temples. "A pond. They told me to bring the slab to a pond and dump it in."

"Devil's Nest," Shawn muttered.

"You know where it is?" Ellis asked.

"Yes. It's in Goshen."

Howie recalled the conversation he had with Shawn about it back when they got lunch together. He remembered the horrible stories about the campground and the cult rumors.

"That's where she took him. They are planning something big," Howie reasoned.

"Please. Don't let them take him. He's all I have left," Bethany sobbed, her frame trembling.

"Then let's go save your boy," Ellis said.

"We can't head in empty-handed. We need weapons," Howie said.

"Do you still carry?" Shawn asked Ellis.

"Of course I do. Let's go."

And with that, they left the house and got back in Shawn's cruiser.

En route to Goshen. To face whatever waited inside the Devil's Nest.

CHAPTER 41

1979

Jessica sprinted through the forest, her black robe—stolen from a dead coven member—swallowed by the night behind her. Free of the circle and the restraints, the demon's strength quickly recharged. She was afraid there wasn't much left of her true self, only worsened by her pact with Atahsaia, which allowed the demon to take her body without a fight to help them escape.

She had no choice.

Branches cracked and snapped behind her as coven members spread out through the forest to hunt her down. The only reason she was able to escape was because she caught them off guard. Had they grabbed the sigil and cornered her, they would have simply been able to force her back into the circle long enough to light the torches and trap her.

Her stomach growled, and she knew it was the demon's hunger. There wasn't time to stop right now; she needed to find a place to lie low. As she moved through the forest, she wondered where she was, exactly. They weren't near the pond, which is where she assumed they would bring her. The land looked foreign. Not that she could tell where she was in the middle of a snowstorm with the sky a black hole above.

Up ahead, the trees began to thin, and a clearing came into view beyond. Jessica spotted a red log truck and skidder parked in the clearing.

She paused. Her first thought was to hide in the truck, but that thought was quickly discarded. Not only would the coven members check there, but what if someone was out working? She wasn't sure she could live with herself if she killed another innocent person right now.

"You don't live here anymore, bitch. I've turned your guts into a playground."

She ignored the demon, forcing herself to think. She needed to make a choice. Either exit the woods and risk killing someone, or change direction and risk the coven finding her.

"Or...hunt them. Pick them off. One. By. One."

Jessica hated agreeing with the monster, but it was right. She couldn't take them down all at once, but they *feared* her. She could use that to her advantage. While she had no desire to harm someone innocent, the coven could rot in Hell.

She looked up at the sky, the heavy snow sizzling off her fiery skin. An overhanging branch reminded her of a tangled arm reaching for her, and she got an idea. Instead of going backward or forward, go *up*. She scaled the bark like a spider, claws sinking deep, until she sat perched above the trail.

And then she waited.

She could smell them before she heard them. Two coven members who had broken off from the group. Too rattled to follow her tracks, they wandered aimlessly through the forest. But then she sensed their hearts pounding aggressively. They were scared. Terrified. Finally, Jessica heard the crunching of their steps.

"Let's get out of here. They can hunt her. I'm not ready to die for this, are you?" a man asked.

"No. I say we make a run for it, then tell the others who weren't here. Warn them that she escaped," the second man said.

"Where the hell did Al go?"

"He was supposed to be right behind us. We can't wait for him. Let's go."

The two robed men were now right below Jessica.

"Gut them. Bathe in their fucking blood."

Again, she ignored the demon. Her stomach rumbled with hunger. She wouldn't be able to resist the urge much longer. But she didn't want to take on two at once. She let them pass, watched them crouch and approach the clearing. And then they left the forest. Their mumbling voices diminished, but the sound of their pumping hearts did not.

It didn't take long before a third coven member appeared, constantly glancing over his shoulder. She could hear his panicked breathing.

He was alone.

No other heartbeats. No other members. When the man stopped just below her tree, it was as if he were asking for death.

"So let's give it to him."

The urge came on strong, and this time Jessica couldn't stop it. She dropped from the tree, almost gliding down like a bat. Silent. Deadly.

The man looked up just in time to see her arched figure reaching for him. He let out a garbled scream, but then she was on him. They fell into the snow with a heavy *thud*. Jessica clawed at his face, ripping a hole in his cheek. The man she assumed was Al screamed again, but she quickly drove her hand upward under his chin, slamming his mouth shut. His teeth cracked on impact and his eyes went wide.

Jessica leaned forward, opening her mouth to tear his throat out, then savor his heart. He groaned at the sight of her teeth, but she was so focused on his fear that she didn't see his hand reaching into his robe. Before she could react, Al held a sigil up to her face, and a sharp pain pulsed through her insides. Jessica fell back into the snow.

"Leave me alone, demon!" Al ordered, brandishing the sigil.

She growled at him, wanting nothing more than to crush his hand so it could never hold anything again. Al turned and ran toward the clearing. The farther away the sigil got, the more the power returned to the demon. Al was a good twenty yards ahead of her, about to reach the tree line, by the time she got back to her feet.

The demon spread through her body like a poison, tired of her doubts, tired of her humanity. She felt her bones cracking and bending beneath the surface, and then she was down on all fours, speeding across the snowy terrain. She did it with the silence of a falling leaf, closing in on the unsuspecting coven member.

As he took his first step into the clearing, Jessica was right behind him. He started to shout to his fellow members just as her claws punched through his back, through skin and bone, and out through his chest.

The other coven members hollered his name as Al stared back at them in confusion. He looked down and discovered a crimson hand sticking through his robe, blood pouring down his chest and onto the snow. His friends didn't wait around to see if he survived. Instead, they turned and ran down a path toward the main road. She pulled her claw out, and Al collapsed into the snow with a heavy thud.

Jessica stood over the dying man, panting heavily. Her hood hid her face, but her eyes glowed orange, burning through the night. She flipped him over, then mounted his chest. He spat blood as he attempted to talk, the words unable to escape. He locked eyes with her, and she felt warmth beneath her as the man pissed himself.

She raised her clawed hand high, relishing the fear in Al's dying eyes. Then she drove them into his chest, hooking them inside and tearing apart the flesh and bone. The body spasmed and twitched beneath her, no longer trying to break free, simply trying to live. She twisted her hand around his beating heart, then tore it from his chest. Blood sprayed across the white canvas of the snow. Al stopped moving. Jessica raised the heart, observing it glistening in the moonlight.

She moved her hood out of the way and bit into the organ, feeling a sense of euphoria at the taste as warm blood traveled down her throat.

Something thumped nearby. In the log truck. Someone was watching her.

Before she could act, a set of headlights appeared at the end of the trail. Their bright beams sliced through the storm, aiming right at the trees Jessica stood in front of. She leaped off the corpse and retreated into the forest, making sure to enter on the opposite side the coven was coming from.

The vehicle crept forward toward the jobsite before coming to a stop. Was the coven sending reinforcements to capture her?

"Let them come. I'll kill them all!"

The demon had far more confidence than Jessica did. The headlights blinded Jessica, so she didn't get a good look at the vehicle. She decided to wait and see who approached before making her next move. The driver's side door opened, and a figure stepped out. Their features were hidden behind the glare and the storm, but Jessica knew it was a woman. Only she heard—*sensed*—multiple heartbeats. The woman and whoever was in the truck. But there was a third, fainter beat somewhere. Inside the woman.

She's pregnant, Jessica realized.

"Two meals for the price of one. Feed me, bitch!"

"No, please don't make me do it," Jessica whispered, but as she said it, she was exiting the woods, moving toward the unsuspecting victim.

"Bill! Bill, where are you?" the woman yelled.

That voice. Jessica recognized it.

Sensing the movement in the woods, the woman took another step toward the front of the log truck, allowing her features to display in the headlights.

"Bill! Is that you?"

Sheila. No, please no...

Sheila shielded her eyes, trying to get a better look at whatever it was she heard. Jessica felt her body, of which she was losing control over, pick up speed while sprinting toward her friend. Sheila spotted her, staring in confusion.

"Jessica? What are you doing out here?" she asked, taking a few steps back.

"Why are *you* here, Sheila? You shouldn't have come."

"I'm looking for Bill. He's usually home by now but—" Sheila stopped when she looked down at the snow and spotted the excessive amount of blood. "What..."

"You shouldn't be here. I can't stop it," Jessica hissed, straining to fight the demon down.

The demon clawed into her conscience, unwilling to let this meal slip away. Jessica flinched, her eyes blazing orange. Inside, she screamed, *Run!*

Sheila took a step back.

"Jess, what are you doing? Who's that man? Where's Bill?"

"I haven't seen Bill. I..."

"Fucking kill her! Rip that baby out and devour it!"

"No! She's my friend!" Jessica yelled, her voice turning into a deep growl.

"Are you okay, Jess?" Sheila asked, fear gripping her words.

"You should go. Go before I can't stop it, Sheila, *please*. Save yourself and the baby."

"Wha-what are you talking about?"

Jessica felt something ripple beneath her face. An odd sensation of something living under her skin.

She tried to stop herself, but there was no more controlling the demon. She lunged at Sheila, driving her to the ground. Jessica heard movement from the truck, the door opening, but it didn't stop her. Atahsaia controlled everything except for a small fraction of her mind, leaving just enough to make her aware of what it was doing to her close friend.

Sheila tried to pry her off, but it was no use. Jessica ripped and clawed, first breaking through the winter gear, then exposing her friend's pregnant belly.

"Delicious."

"Bill!" Sheila shouted.

Jessica forced her hooked fingers through Sheila's flesh, overtaken by a ravenous hunger. She dug. And dug. Eventually getting deep enough to find the organs and everything else inside Sheila's body. Including her unborn child.

She forced herself to pause, feeling boiling tears escaping her glowing eyes.

And then something struck her on the back of the head, sending her falling off Sheila's body.

Her vision faded as snow fell on her exposed face, but she heard *everything*.

"No!" Bill yelled, crawling to his fiancée. Shock and terror clung to his every movement.

Clinging to life, Sheila gasped and gripped Bill's arm. Her voice came out weak and desperate.

"Bill...s-s-save the baby."

"Sheila..."

Bill did exactly what a panicked fiancé would do: tried to stop the bleeding. It was pointless, as Sheila was already dead.

Distant shouting came from the forest. Jessica was in a daze, but Atahsaia sensed the threat of the coven, forcing her to stir.

"Get her, now!" She heard Felix Ruger order.

A burning hatred rose in Jessica's chest as she raised her head and saw members of the coven charging at her. She screamed in their direction, the force shaking the branches in the surrounding trees. The members covered their ears, and Jessica climbed to her feet, observing the situation. There were too many of them, and they were armed. She ran for the woods, hearing the *crack* of a gunshot behind her as she disappeared into the trees.

Behind all the shouts of the coven, one sound stuck with Jessica as she fled.

Bill Burke sobbing.

Holding his dead wife and unborn child.

CHAPTER 42

Henry opened his eyes, immediately wanting to jump to his feet, but his body refused to move. His muscles were battered and beaten, his head throbbing like someone had taken a hammer to it. The last thing he remembered before he lost consciousness was a knife being driven into his flesh, and a group of the coven members somehow dragging Jessica away.

He was supposed to be dead right now, his body rotting on the basement floor in a pool of his own blood. Instead, Henry found himself on a small cot, his head propped up on a stack of pillows with a tight bandage wrapped around his midsection where the knife had entered. He didn't recognize where he was, only that there was daylight creeping through the curtains.

Did the coven take him too? Some sadistic plan to keep him alive only to hold him prisoner?

No. He wasn't restrained. He wasn't in some dungeon being held against his will. As his eyes adjusted, he scanned the room and noticed the religious paraphernalia it displayed. A large crucifix hung on the far wall, a painting of the Virgin Mary holding an infant Jesus beneath it.

The door gently opened, and Father Grimes appeared holding a small tray with food and a glass of water.

"I thought I heard you stirring in here. How are you feeling, Henry?"

"Where am I?" Henry rasped, trying to sit up. The room spun.

"I hadn't heard from you after you dropped me off the other night. So I stopped by your home to check on you and found you alone, unconscious and injured. I brought you back to my place and used my limited medical skills to fix you up."

Henry's hands clenched into fists. "They took her again. But this time, they had some restraints on her that weakened the demon." His head throbbed as he turned it to look at Father Grimes. "How long have I been here? I need to save her, Father."

Grimes looked away, unwilling to make eye contact.

"It's been two days. I thought we were going to lose you at first. I couldn't risk bringing you to the hospital because they'd know you were still alive."

"Two days? Are you kidding me? I need to go, now. It's already been too long!" Henry attempted to sit up, sending a sharp pain through his abdomen.

"Henry, you're not ready. What good would it do for a man who can hardly speak without wincing in pain to go after a whole coven? You would be dead by nightfall. And that's *if* the wound didn't kill you first."

The words sunk in slowly, painfully. Grimes was right, and it killed Henry to admit it. He was seriously hurt, what was he going to do if he did find Jessica? "It might already be too late, Father. I don't have the luxury of healing first. Whatever they have planned for her, it's going to be the end. I need to stop it," Henry insisted, trying to get out of bed. He was met with resistance from his limbs. Whether he wanted to get up or not, his body wouldn't allow it. Father Grimes put a hand on his shoulder and sighed. He set the tray of food and water on a nearby table, then took a seat on the edge of Henry's bed.

"I want to be honest and transparent, Henry. Some demons go beyond possession. They become the host. Body, mind, soul. That's what Atahsaia wants—"

"What are you talking about? What the hell is 'beyond possession'?"

"Some demons are far more powerful than others. If they have control of a host for too long, it can transition to a perfect possession. Don't let the word fool you, there is nothing perfect about it. And perfect possession, I'm sorry to say, would be the endgame."

"What do you mean, exactly?"

"She won't be possessed, Henry. She'll *become* it. Even an official exorcism would prove useless."

"It can't be too late. I can't allow that..." Henry trailed off. Even as he said it, he knew it to be a lie. He had no control over such things. Jessica was strong. She would fight it off as long as she could. But Father Grimes was adamant that this wasn't some simple demon. Atahsaia was far more powerful than that.

"If it gets to that point, there are only two possible outcomes," Grimes said.

"Please. Tell me. I told her I'd protect her. I promised. And now...I don't even know if there's anything left of her to save."

Grimes sighed.

"I've prayed on this, Henry. More than I've ever prayed for anything. But I fear we're past the point of mercy. Only an outside force, or death, could sever the bond. The odds of that are slim. The other option is to trap the demon inside her for eternity. Keep Atahsaia isolated and at bay."

Henry squeezed his fists, feeling a tightness in his chest he knew was a crushing sadness.

"Trapping a cannibalistic demon inside her? How does that save Jessica?" Henry asked, his voice cracking.

Grimes squeezed his shoulder and locked eyes with him.

"It doesn't save her, Henry. It saves everyone else."

Henry couldn't believe what Grimes was saying. What good was a priest if he couldn't help with extracting a demon?

"You want me to give up, just like that? To send Jessica to Hell with that–that *monster*?"

"Of course I don't want that." Grimes almost sounded insulted, but he remained patient. "Are you familiar with Genesis 22?"

Henry furrowed his brow, shaking his head.

"God commanded Abraham to sacrifice his son, Isaac, as a test of faith."

"My faith was lost long ago, Father. I'm not about to sacrifice my wife to show God I believe."

"Abraham was willing to do it, to show his faith. That was what God wanted to see. He stopped Abraham at the last minute. It was a test of faith. Do you see?"

"I can't fake it. How am I supposed to prove something that isn't there?"

"You need to find a way to get that faith back, Henry. Show the Lord you're willing to sacrifice, and maybe, just maybe, there's hope for Jessica."

Rage burned inside Henry. Religion had ruined Jessica's life once already. It almost ended their relationship and it *had* ended her relationship with her parents. Now it was trying to do it again. Henry forced himself out of bed, ignoring the pain.

"I'd rather go to Hell myself before sacrificing the only woman I've ever loved. And if you won't help me, I'll figure it out myself." Henry pushed past Grimes, leaving the priest's apartment.

He could only hope he wasn't too late.

CHAPTER 43

2024

Shawn turned off the blues—a futile attempt to calm the anxious passengers—when they spotted the sign for Bird's Nest Campground. They turned onto Coon Brook Road, a winding dirt path full of ruts and potholes. They crossed a small bridge with rusty guardrails on each side, the river flowing aggressively below. The headlights shone off something ahead.

Shawn slowed, pulling up to the front gate that had already been opened. Faded blue paint was the backdrop to large white letters.

WELCOME TO BIRD'S NEST CAMPGROUND

Except the word **BIRD'S** had been crossed out with black spray paint and replaced with the word **DEVIL'S**.

"So inviting," Ellis mumbled.

Shawn slowly pulled through the gate.

The dirt path descended down a steep hill where an old farmhouse lay in shambles. The porch had collapsed into a pile of rubble around the home, the police tape now sagging loosely around the perimeter.

"It doesn't look like anyone's inside." Shawn pointed out.

"Pull in. We should still check to be sure," Ellis said.

Bethany stared out the window, unblinking. Her grip on Howie's hand was ironclad.

They parked in front of the house, but before anyone got out, Shawn cleared his throat.

"Be careful. Some of them might be hiding in here waiting for us."

Howie and Bethany nodded, and the four of them exited the cruiser, moving toward the deserted home. Shawn and Ellis led the way up the front steps, careful to avoid the debris from the collapsed porch. One hand on his gun, Shawn reached out and opened the front door, revealing a dark and empty house.

They progressed through the house, finding nothing but old paperwork and dusty furniture. Howie glanced at a sheet on a desk in what looked to be the front office of the once flourishing campground, seeing names that meant nothing to him. *Alister Black. Rebecca. Cole Springer.* As they moved through the kitchen and out the back door, it all felt like a giant waste of time.

Then the whispers came.

They all heard it. Like a swarm of locusts slipping through the trees.

"Come. Come join ussss. The water is soooo nice."

"What the hell is that?!" Bethany yelled.

Howie barely heard her through the persistent buzzing. It was enough to drive someone mad.

"It comes from within. Let us show you."

Before any of them could say another word, there was movement coming from the trees. Coming from every direction. Figures, hunched low, stalking toward them in the backyard. None of their features were obvious, none except their glowing white eyes. Howie felt as if the forest was closing in, suffocating them.

"Back to the cruiser!" Shawn yelled.

They made their way back through the house and ran to the car. More figures exited the woods at the front of the house. Once everyone was piled in, Shawn shifted into drive and sped down the driveway, then headed along the trail that led deeper into the campground. A single figure limped to the center of the road in front of them. As the person entered the path of the headlights, Howie's heart sank.

It was Zack, fully converted to whatever Thred turned users into. Howie could have sworn Zack saw him in the back seat as the cruiser closed in on him.

"Watch out!" Ellis snapped, but it was too late.

The police cruiser crushed Zack's body beneath its weight, the tires going up and over him like a human speed bump.

Not Zack! That poor fucking kid, Howie thought. "Fuck! They're everywhere!" Shawn said.

"Take a breath. We make mistakes when we're panicked," Ellis said, though he hardly looked calm.

The Thred junkies were everywhere. Some of them Howie recognized from town, others he'd never seen before. It was now clear what the Ruger twins were doing with Thred. They had created an army beyond the coven. Beyond some Renfield-helper like Derrick Patten. It was far bigger than any of them could have imagined. Shawn weaved through the bodies as if they were a horde of zombies. Which, in a way, was exactly what they were.

"I recognize this," Ellis muttered.

"What? It's coming back to you?" Howie asked.

"Yes. Keep going. The path will end at the trees, and the pond will be just beyond them."

It didn't take long for them to reach the end of the trail, which turned sharply to the right, and straight ahead was a copse of trees thick enough to hide the pond, but not enough to block out the glow. Shawn slowed to a stop, parking in the tall grass. In the rearview, Howie spotted a few of the Thred tweakers making their way back toward the water. As they went to get out of the cruiser, Bethany put her hand on Howie's shoulder to stop him.

"Wait. This might be a trap to get us down there. They'll think I'm just some desperate mother going in blind for her son."

"So, what do you suggest?" Ellis asked.

"That I play the part. Let me go ahead of you guys instead of going in guns blazing."

Howie sighed. "I don't like it. That puts you in far too much danger."

"Howie...my son is down there. I don't care how much danger it puts me in. But we can try to outsmart them. There are too many of them to take head-on."

"She's right," Shawn said.

Howie wanted to argue, but he knew it was true. He also knew Bethany would jump into the mouth of a volcano and swim through scalding hot lava to get to Ryan. He gave a hesitant nod, and they all exited the car, lightly shutting the doors and making their way through the grass.

"It comes from within. Let us show you the way."

The voices returned, and Howie realized it was because the army on Thred was closing in behind them.

Through the trees, the pond came into view. The surface was bright green, a dull glow pulsing across the surface. Around the edge, multiple robed figures locked hands, chanting in a foreign tongue. In the center of the dock, Ryan sat strapped to a chair with duct tape over his mouth. He thrashed around, trying to break free. While most of the coven surrounded the pond, there were two robed members standing on each side of Ryan. One wore an all-black mask and on the other, an all-white one.

Bethany spotted Ryan, and all thoughts of a well-oiled plan went out the window. She charged forward into the trees, bursting through on the other side to the pond. All of the coven members stopped chanting, then turned their heads simultaneously toward Bethany. Their eyes all glowed a hazy white.

"Welcome, Ms. Carver. We've been expecting you all," Elias Ruger said.

"Let him go! I'm coming, honey!" Bethany said, stepping forward.

"We are too far along to simply *let him go*. The horse has left the barn."

"Please. Take me. It's me, isn't it? I was the one who slipped through your dad's fingers."

Elias lifted his black mask and the look in his eyes sent a chill down Howie's spine. If Elias decided to make a move right now, Howie was too far away to stop him. Bethany was a good thirty feet in front of the group.

"The mistake you've made, Bethany, is that you seem to think it's one or the other. You are right about one thing. We do want you. But we want—*need*—both of you for this. So, I thank you for making it so easy for us. My sister can be very persuasive, can't she?"

The second robed figure stepped forward, coming to Elias's side, then removed their white mask. Sure enough, Tanya–no, *Rachel*—stared back at Bethany with just a hint of sorrow attached to a disgusting smile.

"Hey, darling, if it makes you feel any better, Ryan and I had a great time tonight, didn't we, Sport?" Rachel asked, rubbing the top of Ryan's head. The poor boy recoiled, groaning beneath the duct tape.

"I trusted you with my son. How could you be so awful?" Bethany hissed, her voice tinged with disgust and betrayal.

"Hon, you buried our father in concrete and dumped him into the bottom of a swamp. I don't think a long-lasting friendship was in the cards for us."

"Why do you need both of us? Ryan has nothing to do with this. Please..."

Howie and the others were hanging on every word, waiting for the right time to come forward. And the Thred tweakers were almost to the end of the trail. Something had to happen soon.

"It's a generational thing. To bond us with our father again, we need to sacrifice a bloodline to Vorathor, then feed your souls to Vodyanoy and your bodies to his disciples at the bottom of the pond. I'd say it's nothing personal, but, well, it very much is," Rachel said.

Howie felt a tightness in his chest. He needed to act now or both Bethany and Ryan would be dead. Shawn nudged him, prying his attention from the dock. The tweakers were now entering the woods.

"We need to do something, *now*," Shawn whispered.

Both he and Ellis raised their firearms and kept them trained on the approaching threats. Howie turned back to the pond as Elias and Rachel pulled their masks back down.

"It's time we begin," Elias said.

Derrick Patten and another member surrounded Bethany and pushed her toward the dock.

"Tonight, we conjure Vorathor. We bring him an offering that will return our leader, our father, to The Withered Tongues. Now, lock hands, my disciples. It is time!" Elias announced.

Bethany screamed and twisted, her heels digging into the sand as Derrick yanked her forward. The twins' voices cut through her cries, chanting louder, drowning out everything else.

As Howie stepped out onto the sand, he heard the sound of branches cracking behind him. He turned just in time to see Shawn pull the trigger, a deafening blast that echoed through the trees. And then Ellis followed, past and present chiefs opening fire on the approaching throng.

Elias didn't miss a step. Instead, he just raised his voice over the commotion as if he expected this to happen. The Thred junkies were just a distraction; here simply to slow them down so the Ruger twins had time to complete the ritual. The coven remained locked in a complete circle as their leaders chanted.

"Omnipotens Vorathor, te advocamus. Te precamur ut patrem nostrum ad nos reducas. Totam stirpem tibi offerimus quae pro te in saxum vinciendo responsalis fuit!"

The pond pulsated, the mild green glow intensifying to light the area around the water. Then the surface started to bubble. The coven members moaned in ecstasy, all of their eyes now glowing green like the water.

"Howie! We need to move!" Shawn yelled before firing off another shot.

The bullet connected, lodging in the forehead of the closest tweaker. Howie recognized the man from the motel alley. His head jolted back from the force of the bullet, then he dropped to the ground. Ellis fired next, his shot tearing through the neck of a woman whose face had sunken in, the skin taut around her cheekbones and jaw. Green veins traveled up her neck to her forehead where they bulged, pulsating to match the water.

She jerked to the side but kept moving. Ellis fired again, this time blowing a hole where the right eye had been.

Howie, Shawn, and Ellis backpedaled toward the dock with nowhere else to go. The pond was now boiling, the surface popping and bubbling. Elias continued the ritual, Ryan yelled beneath the duct tape, and Bethany struggled to break free of Derrick's grip.

"What the fuck is happening to the water?" Shawn asked.

"They're summoning the demon from the pond. We can't let them complete the ritual!" Howie said.

An angry howl came from the dock, and Howie risked a glance just as Bethany bit down on Derrick's arm. She broke free, charging toward Ryan, whose eyes went wide. She broke the circle of coven members and made it to the dock, yet the Ruger twins didn't seem fazed in the slightest. They continued chanting, the water still boiling, then an arm covered in green sludge pushed up from the pond, gripping Bethany's ankle.

There was a sudden *pop*, followed by an excruciating shriek from Bethany. She fell onto the dock, trying to crawl toward her son, but the hand squeezed tighter around her ankle, rupturing her Achilles.

Ryan screamed for his mother behind his gag, tears pouring down his face.

"Fucking shoot them!" Howie yelled.

Shawn and Ellis took their attention off the remaining Thred junkies and aimed at the coven. But before either of them could get a shot off, the ground beneath them rumbled, low and steady at first, then intensified until they had to hold on to a tree to stay upright.

Something appeared just beneath the surface of the pond in the shape of a rectangle, where the water was now rupturing like the ocean during a tropical storm. Pond water thrust against the dock, going up and over it, soaking Bethany as the gnarled hand held her firmly. The power of the water knocked Ryan's chair over backward, his head smacking off the dock.

Howie's legs moved before he could think. Every part of him screamed to run the other way, get far away from the nightmare. But Bethany was screaming, Ryan was in danger, and the damn rectangle was cracking open like some rotten egg.

The pond split. The concrete slab emerged, glistening, lifted by dozens of slime-covered green arms.

Cracks formed.

Then silence.

CRACK.

The concrete slab, the demons' casket, split open.

"He has risen!" Elias shouted.

"Our father! Our leader! Has returned!" Rachel added.

Howie's heart slammed in his eardrums.

"It comes from within," Elias and Rachel said in unison.

The slab plunged back below the water.

It didn't work. The binding was too strong for them, Howie thought. He *hoped.*

"It comes from within!" Elias repeated.

Another sudden *CRACK* exploded beneath the surface.

And then a massive figure shot out of the water, levitating at least ten feet above the pond.

The Ruger twins dropped to their knees. The coven followed.

Felix Ruger—Vorathor—hovered over the pond, bloated and half-rotted, but still crackling with dark power. His mask split with a long, wet *snap*. Beneath it, a mouth of blackened teeth infected with death. But the rot hadn't killed him. It had *preserved* him.

"No..." Howie whispered.

Vorathor ignored him. The demon descended on Devil's Nest.

CHAPTER 44

1979

Months had passed since Henry stormed out of Father Grimes's apartment, the bitter cold replaced with the gloomy browns and grays of early spring. Henry hadn't heard from the priest since that night. He was okay with that because it wasn't Grimes that he answered to. He answered to Jessica. To his wife. And when he returned home and heard her whispers in his head, he knew he had made the right choice by ignoring Father Grimes. The whispers started low and distant at first. By the second night, they were more frequent and urgent.

Jessica told him she was still there, inside her body. She said that she gave herself to the demon to help escape the coven, and that it was now the primary host of her body. She told him she loved him and couldn't wait to see him again.

On the third night, Henry woke to a faint scratching at his window. Jessica stood on the other side, her orange eyes burning through the glass. She pressed her clawed hand to his, blood dripping down her chin. Her mouth never moved, but he heard her anyway.

I miss you.

"Then come home. Be with me. I'll take care of you."

It's not safe. Not yet. They will be back for me. Soon, my love.

And that had been it. He pressed his hand against hers on the other side of the glass, then she was gone. Henry thought of her every waking moment. Hell, every sleeping moment as well. Every dream. Every nightmare.

On the fourth night, the coven *did* come back. They forced their way into the home, a few of them holding him down while they searched the house. He wanted to kill every last one of them. They tore the house apart, and when they didn't find her, Brian White threatened to burn it down. Henry was unmoved.

The coven left.

A few weeks passed, and they eventually came back around. Henry prepared for the worst, but after another sweep of the home, he saw the look of defeat in Brian's eyes.

"If we find out you're hiding her from us, your fate will be far worse than hers, Henry Black."

"I want to see her just as much as you all do."

That night, Jessica came to him. The demon was present, in total control, but just seeing her in the flesh was enough to give Henry hope.

Henry let his guard down, and Atahsaia took advantage. That was the night of the first victim. A woman in her mid-thirties, loading her laundry into the back of her minivan with wood paneling and stick figure family stickers on the back window. It was sloppy, the woman nearly escaped; screaming at the top of her lungs as he tried to wrestle her to the ground and tie her up. She screamed, kicked, almost slipped free. Thankfully, there had been nobody else there at that time of night, and an elbow to the back of her head knocked her unconscious. Silence followed, outside and inside Henry. He lost a piece of himself that day.

The part he hadn't been prepared for was the aftermath. The cleanup.

When Jessica was done with the body, the victim had been left unrecognizable. Her chest torn completely open, an empty hole where her heart used to beat. Henry placed a tarp on the floor of his car trunk, then carried the corpse from the basement to his car, dropping the dead girl in like she was no more than the bag of laundry she had been loading when Henry attacked her. He drove to the cemetery, then proceeded to drag the body into the woods as far as he could, leaving her in the soggy spring wilderness.

This became their marriage. Henry fed her, Jessica feasted, he cleaned up. With each victim, Henry knew a piece of his wife was lost forever. But so was a piece of him. And now, as he dragged an unconscious girl to the top of the basement stairs, he sensed the demon getting stronger. Hungrier.

"Bring my food, you useless scum!"

"Jessica...is there anything left of you in there?" Henry rasped. He wiped tears from his eyes before opening the basement door. He looked and felt like he had aged a decade.

"There will always be a part of her in here. I'll make sure of it. That way I can taste her misery."

Henry leaned his forehead against the basement door and wept. He stared down at the girl he had bound and gagged, wondering what her life was like before he abducted her. She was a pretty girl; at least she had been before he caved in part of her face with a tire iron.

There had to be another way. He could feel his sanity slipping away. He thought back to Father Grimes and the warning he had given before Henry stormed out. The warning he had chosen to ignore.

"Stop pouting like a bitch and bring her to me."

Henry sighed, then unlatched the locks he'd installed on the off-chance Jessica broke free of the Devil's circle he had drawn in the basement. His initial thought was that if he could keep her confined—which he did by tricking her while she ate the heart of a victim—he could maintain some level of control. Every time Atahsaia hurt Jessica, Henry knew he was losing the tug-of-war for his wife's soul.

The girl on the floor groaned as she slowly came to. Henry hated when they woke up before he left. As if by avoiding it, he was somehow less of a monster. The girl opened her eyes, wincing in obvious pain. Henry averted eye contact, then pushed her down the stairs with his foot, listening to the snapping of bones as her body tumbled into the darkness below.

"Oh, Henry. There might be hope for you yet. That was pretty cold. This poor girl has no idea where she is, and that's how you greet her when she wakes? Naughty, naughty."

"Stop! I'm giving you what you want, demon. Please stop hurting my wife. *Please...*" he trailed off, listening to the girl fight for breath. It was dark in the basement, but Henry still saw her body writhing, trying to crawl away from the monster in the corner.

"Come, join us. I insist."

"N-no. I can't watch."

"Don't question me. This is a demand, not a choice. I have a proposition for you, Henry."

He told himself not to fall for it, yet he was slowly descending the stairs. The girl was attempting to crawl away, but she had nowhere to go. The circle took up most of the basement, and he was behind her. A small part of him wanted to help the girl escape, but he stopped himself.

"Mind giving her a little push for me, honey?" the demon asked, attempting to sound as much like Jessica as possible. But there was a heaviness behind the angelic voice that didn't belong.

Henry pushed the girl into the circle, knowing he had no choice. Before he could turn away, Jessica was on her, tearing away the clothes first, then the flesh. When the demon's claws dug into her skin, the girl was fully alert, screaming through her busted mouth. The corner of the basement was darker than the rest, displaying only the silhouette and glowing orange irises of the demon.

The girl's eyes flickered frantically around the room, and she kicked at Jessica in a last-ditch attempt to break free.

"I love it when they put up a fight. It gets the heart pumping. Fills it with juicy blood."

Henry pried his eyes away from the scene and stared at the far wall. He heard everything, including the sound of the demon's sharp teeth biting into the heart. Blood sprayed across the space on the wall that Henry focused on. There was no escaping the nightmare.

Jessica slurped up the blood, and he swore he heard her licking her fingers. Henry did all he could not to vomit.

"What do you want? Why am I down here?"

"I know you want more of your wife back. I've been selfish, haven't I?"

Henry didn't answer. He knew the demon didn't have true compassion.

"Fine, fine. Don't play along. Here's the offer, lover boy. If you bring me a child, as I've so politely asked of you many times, I'll give you one whole day, uninterrupted, with your wife. Do we have a deal?"

The vomit Henry had been able to hold down earlier forced its way up, and this time he couldn't stop it. It splashed across the floor, mixing with the dead girl's blood. Setting eyes on her ravaged corpse brought on a second episode, and while his insides clenched, the demon laughed. A mixture of Jessica's sweet laugh and an octave designed only for nightmares.

"Don't be such a pussy. What difference is it to you whether they are young or old? You've already aided me in killing countless victims. Kids are easier to catch. And so much tastier. I've been thinking of it ever since the boy in the woods."

"I...I can't."

"I-I-I can't. Put your big boy pants on. Don't you want to spend more time with your wife? Fuck her for the first time before her snatch is full of maggots?"

"Stop talking about her that way! How do I know you'll hold up your end of it? Who's to say that if I bring you a kid that you won't laugh in my face and just demand another?"

"It's a risk you'll have to take, huh? I can't stay hidden down here forever. Eventually, I'll want to kill that entire coven. Every single one of them. I need to speed up this process."

"There has to be another way," Henry said, more to himself than the demon.

"Don't you want to be with me, Henry? Don't you want to hold me? Kiss me?" Jessica asked. It was her voice, sounding as innocent as ever, and it broke Henry when he didn't think it was possible to break any further.

"I'll do it."

The words tore from him. The demon laughed. As Henry dragged the dead girl over to the tarp in the corner opposite Jessica, out of her reach, he realized Father Grimes was right. It was too late to save his wife.

He couldn't really abduct a child, could he? Jessica would never want him to do such a thing. The demon was only prolonging his and Jessica's suffering. Henry wrapped the tarp around what was left of the girl and dragged her back up the stairs, stopping to shut and lock the basement door behind him.

He waited a moment, catching his breath after the laborious process of pulling dead weight up the stairs. His eyes caught a picture on the wall, the first one Jessica framed when they'd moved here. In it, she had her arm wrapped around Henry, kissing his cheek while his smile lit up the whole picture.

What was down in the basement was no longer the woman kissing him in the image. He sat on the floor and wept, hugging his knees.

He couldn't do this anymore. He had to stop Atahsaia.

He had to sacrifice Jessica.

CHAPTER 45

2024

Felix Ruger crashed onto the dock, almost knocking Ryan into the pond. Insects spilled from his rotting skin, squirming into the cracks of the wood. Elias and Rachel cried, holding hands as their father—their *leader*—rose before them.

But it wasn't really Felix anymore. It was Vorathor. And if they saw that, they didn't care.

Vorathor stepped toward Ryan, and Bethany screamed.

"Get away from him! It's me you want!"

Vorathor tilted his head curiously and looked at her. His eyes were a mix of glowing green light—powered by the demon that still remained *beneath* the surface—and a hazy white, like a poisonous cloud.

"*You will have your time, bitch,*" he said in a raspy voice full of fluid and sludge. He leaned down and grabbed the boy by the shirt, lifting him with ease. Ryan squealed beneath the duct tape, moving violently to try and break free. Vorathor simply laughed at him.

A gunshot rang out, sending a shock wave through Howie's eardrums.

Ellis stepped to his left and fired again. Shawn did the same on his right. Their bullets connected with Vorathor, his body jerking back with each shot, and they were lucky not to hit Ryan. Howie ran to Bethany, expecting someone from the coven to stop him but they continued holding hands, as if breaking the circle would stop the ritual from completing.

Felix Ruger's deformed body tensed, then he opened his mouth wide and bellowed a thunderous blast, sending a gust of sulfuric stench toward them. Howie fell to one knee. Shawn let off a wild shot, which connected with one of the coven members holding hands. They staggered before falling face-first into the pond, breaking the circle.

Vorathor tossed Ryan onto the ground and launched through the air, covering twenty feet in one move. He landed in front of Shawn, who tried to aim and fire again, but Vorathor swiped at his arm with a clawed hand, severing the cop's limb at the elbow. Shawn let out an inhuman cry as the jagged end of his humerus poked out, looking like a crooked tooth.

The demon leader grabbed Shawn by the throat and lifted him off the ground. Ellis fired two close-range shots into Vorathor's chest, allowing Shawn to break free and drop to his knees. As Vorathor turned his attention to the old chief, the coven members around the pond started hollering.

They started to back away in a panic, trying to escape from something. The water began to swirl in the center, a bright red color mixing with the glowing green. A shrill, piercing sound, like nails on a chalkboard, filled the air around the water.

All of the coven members surrounding the outside of the pond dropped to the ground, as if touching the water triggered intense seizures. Howie covered his ears, momentarily pulling a hand away to see blood. What the hell was doing this? The crimson trail spread across the surface, almost making the pond look like a pool of blood simmering above a fire.

Vorathor snapped his head back toward the water to see what was happening. Bethany finally made it to her son after crawling across the dock with her shredded Achilles, her leg dangling uselessly behind. Most of the coven members were now on the ground, clutching their throats as though their lungs had ceased to function.

A moon-white hand shot up out of the water, clutching the dock, followed by a second hand. Then a head rose above, eyes shimmering like the embers of a scorching fire.

Cory.

"Oh, my God!" Bethany gasped.

Howie's breath caught in his throat. The last time he saw Cory, he was a teenager fighting to save his best friend. Seeing him brought back some fond memories: Playing Nintendo 64 while listening to Linkin Park. Sneaking into horror movies after buying tickets to whatever Disney movie was showing.

Howie's best friend, long ago possessed by Atahsaia before being trapped in the concrete with Vorathor, climbed onto the dock a few feet from Bethany. His pale skin was covered with black veins that branched across his entire body, his clothes full of ragged holes. Now, he was just a demon hiding behind familiar eyes.

Vorathor launched through the air and landed a few feet from the cannibal demon. Everyone watched, too terrified to make any sudden movements as the two came face-to-face. Vorathor's body flexed, his claws twitched as if they were desperate for blood. Cory—Atahsaia—didn't move. He just stared, calm as death, the fire in his eyes flickering like the inside of a cremation chamber.

"Atahsaia...you are an insect to me. Below me. I will grind you beneath my foot and rip you to pieces," Vorathor vowed.

Instead of a verbal response, Atahsaia pounced, latching on to Vorathor's side and chomping down on his neck. Vorathor swiped, removing Atahsaia's much smaller frame, and black sludge sprayed from the wound like motor oil, only enraging the demon more. His body cracked and popped, increasing in size as his arms and legs stretched. Atahsaia crouched low on the dock, staying out of the monster's reach, then dove for its ankles and again bit into the rotten flesh. Vorathor reached for him but lost his balance. Both demons fell over the side of the dock, plunging below the surface.

Elias and Rachel called for their father, but nobody could see the struggle below. Bethany hugged her son, sobbing as she pulled the duct tape off his mouth. As the monsters fought, their bodies thrashed around in the water, jagged limbs quickly appearing above, then thrusting back down, splashing the dock.

Rachel turned to Bethany and Ryan, removing her mask.

"You...*you* are the sacrifices. We must give you to Vodyanoy now, so that our father regains the strength he needs to defeat Atahsaia! Brother, help me get them to the water!"

Elias shifted his focus from the demon fight to his sister and nodded. Bethany tried to get to her feet and pull her son with her, but she couldn't move quickly enough with her injury. Howie ran to her side and helped her move. Rachel picked up speed, closing the distance between them.

"Don't move! One more step and I'll blow your fucking head off!" Ellis yelled from the beach. He held a steady aim on the twins, who froze in place at the sight of the gun.

"This is far bigger than you. *Any* of you. We are all tiny specks in a much bigger plan. Don't you see that?" Rachel asked.

"Fuck you!" Bethany snapped.

Howie guarded Ryan and Bethany, ready to fight to the death to protect them if need be. But then Rachel and Elias smiled, staring toward Ellis. Howie risked a glance back just in time to see Derrick Patten, tongueless pawn of the coven, approaching Patrick Ellis from behind.

"Ellis, look out!" Howie warned.

Before Ellis could turn around, a long blade shot through his chest, stunning the old chief. He coughed up blood, dropping his gun to stare down at the dagger protruding from his body. He tried to speak, but no words came out. Only blood. Derrick dropped Ellis onto the ground, letting him die in the mud.

Farther beyond, near the tree line, Shawn crawled to his gun, clutching what remained of his arm to his chest. He grabbed the weapon, trying to hold steady.

Shawn raised the gun one-handed, shaking, bleeding, barely conscious.

"Hey, Derrick!"

Derrick turned. A shot rang out. The bullet blew through Derrick's open mouth, exiting out the back of his head. His knees wobbled, then he collapsed at the edge of the water, like a puppet with its strings cut.

Behind Howie, the water splashed violently and the two demons, wrapped around one another in a fierce fight to the death, came flying out of the pond, barreling across the land. They swiped and clawed, tearing at one another. Atahsaia bit into Vorathor, breaking free of his grasp, then glided above, landing on the dock behind the twins.

Elias went to grab his sigil, trying to deflect the demon away, but Atahsaia was on him before he could. He bit his blackened teeth into Elias, ripping his head violently to the side and tearing the Ruger son's throat free all the way up to his bottom jaw. Elias reached for his sister, who screamed for her twin incoherently. Atahsaia crouched over Elias, letting out a low growl. Rachel charged at him, and the demon backhanded her, sending her flying into the water. Then he focused his attention back on Elias, driving his disgusting claws into his chest, ripping the heart free in one fluid motion.

As Atahsaia savored the heart, Vorathor roared furiously, saliva spewing from his bloated maw. His body stretched further, the piercing tips of bones breaking through his skin and clothing. He charged at the dock.

Howie grabbed Bethany and Ryan and dove off the side, landing in the pond. Immediately sensing the algae wrapping around his limbs, he ripped it away and pushed Bethany and Ryan to the shore, then up onto the land. They huddled together as Vorathor collided with Atahsaia.

Vorathor's claws extended and curled, expanding to a few feet long as he raised both hands overhead. Atahsaia lunged, jaws open for one last strike, but Vorathor was ready. His claws ripped at a diagonal angle from the cannibal's left shoulder to his right hip, splitting his body in two. Rotting intestines and organs released from the upper half as it plopped down onto the dock. Howie's stomach churned. His best friend, the kid he did everything with, was a heap of ruin. Vorathor was covered in blood and viscera, standing over the remains of Atahsaia.

The orange in Atahsaia's eyes faded, revealing their natural color one last time before going completely dead.

Vorathor panted wildly, then looked to Rachel, who was holding her dead brother in her arms. *"Get the mother and son. Now."*

Rachel got up without hesitation and stomped toward Bethany and Ryan.

"You'll pay for what you did to him! Both of you!" Rachel growled, storming forward with blood on her face and madness in her eyes. Howie had to do something. Bethany was hurt. Ryan was just a boy. It was time to implement his plan. The plan he hoped all along he wouldn't need to move forward with.

Rachel was now only a few feet from them.

Howie stood in front of Bethany and Ryan.

"Wait!"

CHAPTER 46

1979

Henry stared at the basement door, his heart cranking so hard he thought he might have a heart attack. His plan had to work. Otherwise, there would be no stopping her. Jessica would suffer forever while the demon used her body like a warm blanket. He stared over at the sleeping victim, hoping it would be enough to complete the sacrifice. He knew the demon could hear the tiny heartbeat. He knew it was down there licking Jessica's chops with its foreign tongue.

"Yesss. Bring the child to me. You have done well, Henry."

For his plan to work, he couldn't bring the demon its meal. The demon needed to come to him.

Henry lifted a trembling hand and disengaged the locks, swallowing a mouthful of dry air. He didn't want to show weakness. He didn't want the demon to know he was doing something out of their routine. The demon had grown lax in constantly checking Henry's mind for any signs of rebellion. But Henry didn't need to keep his fears quiet; it would expect him to be scared and hesitant to bring a child.

He opened the basement door, and no matter how many times he was hit with the stench, he never got used to it. Granted, with each passing corpse that bled out down there, with all of the bodily fluids seeping into the floor, it was no surprise it smelled so disgusting. Henry made his way down the first few steps and sat, staring into the dark corner where the demon lay in wait. The orange eyes watched him intently.

"Demon...how do I know that if I do this, you will let me have my wife back for a day?"

"Life's biggest mystery, Henry. I'll promise you this, though: if you don't bring me a child, you will never see that fucking cunt again."

Henry seethed at the vulgarity of the demon. He wanted to cut the beast into pieces, then throw it in a fire and watch it burn. But it was his wife—still alive inside her body, even if only slightly—who stopped him from doing anything like that. He also knew he had to let her go. He prayed on it, thought of any possible way to avoid it.

"I can't...I can't bring the child to you," he said. The fire burned bright in the demon's eyes, and he knew this would work. "I brought the sacrifice. Upstairs. But I cannot bring myself to drag a child to you. I've done my part. You will have to get it yourself."

"You weak fool. You know I am trapped down here because of your cute circle. You think you're so clever, don't you? Now that our little Jessie girl is out of my way, why don't you free me so I can handle this myself?"

"Yes, I will free you. And then I'll leave. I can't bear to see a child suffer."

"I can hear its heart thumping wildly up there. It sounds wonderful. FREE me!"

Henry pulled out a cross and held it at eye level. The demon bared Jessica's deformed teeth and hissed, more like a venomous snake than a cat.

"Relax, demon. This is for my protection. So you can't harm me when I break the circle."

"I'll shove that cross up your ass, lover boy. Make one mistake for me, I beg you."

He ignored the demon, holding the cross up as he went down the rest of the stairs. He had drawn the circle in chalk, thick enough so that when he dragged the bodies over it, the entrapment spell wasn't broken. He pulled a facecloth from his pocket and dropped it onto the floor. The demon watched in silence with curious eyes.

Henry kept his mind on the floor, trying to avoid thinking too loudly of his plan in case the demon was listening for his thoughts. He scrubbed at the circle using his foot to grind the cloth back and forth. As soon as the circle and the Devil's star were no longer whole, the demon exhaled as if having an intense orgasm. Henry slowly backed away, holding the cross in front of him, careful not to trip on the stairs while going up.

"My Jessica is gone. I know this. After you're done, please leave, and never come back. I'm not the one you want to make suffer. It's them. The coven."

"Your mistake is thinking I don't want all of you to suffer. You will all die at my hands. And I'll save you for last," the demon said, then changed voices in an instant. *"I love you, Henry."*

Henry ignored Jessica's voice, knowing it couldn't be her any longer, then reached the top of the steps and waited.

He heard the demon crawling across the floor, the pitter-patter of bare feet and hands slapping slowly in the direction of the stairs. Henry glanced toward the corner at the poor, helpless victim. The bait. He grabbed the club he'd set against the wall and gripped it tightly.

The steps groaned as the demon moved up them, taking its time.

And then Jessica's head poked out of the basement as Atahsaia crawled forward. Henry caught just a glimpse of the demon's confused eyes as it stared not at a child, but at a rabbit in a cage, scurrying around frantically when it spotted the monster. Then he brought the weighted club down on the back of Jessica's head, cringing at the loud *crack* it made.

Jessica dropped to the floor, and Henry swung again, connecting harder the second time. For a second, he feared that he'd killed her, but then he noticed her body was still breathing. He couldn't dawdle. Next to the rabbit, Henry had set his supplies for the next part of his plan. Rope soaked in holy water that he used to tie tightly around her wrists and ankles. A sharp dagger, the one that the coven member had previously stabbed him with, which he used to carve the symbol that would trap the demon in her body. He carved it into her forehead, sobbing as he defiled his beautiful wife.

It's not her anymore. It's not her.

With that done, he had to treat this like he did all of the victims: convince himself they weren't people, wrap the body in a tarp, and load it in the trunk. So that's what he did. He avoided looking at her above the shoulders as he wrapped her up, unable to stomach her cut-up face. He didn't have much nightfall left, and he wanted to make sure he took her to the woods before anyone saw her.

Unlike the victims, he knew he had to bring her deep into the forest, then bury her where nobody would ever discover the body and risk letting the demon free.

"I love you, Jessica. I'm sorry. Sorry I couldn't protect you. Sorry I betrayed you. I hope you forgive me."

He shut the trunk, climbed into the car, and drove to Newport Cemetery, where he dragged his wife deep into the forest and buried her where nobody could ever find her.

CHAPTER 47

2024

Rachel stopped pursuing as Howie stood his ground. Vorathor, covered in thornlike markings and now at least ten feet tall, stood to his fullest height.

"I wait for no one. Get the girl and child!"

"You want a bloodline? Take me. I'm the one who survived the first time. I'm the one who freed Atahsaia. I'm the one who ruined your plan. They don't matter. *I* do. I offer myself for the ritual," Howie said.

Bethany reached for him instinctively, her voice a cracked whisper, "What? Howie..."

She had no idea what the bloodline ritual was. Howie had taken the time to read the black notebook Zack left him. Only after finding the ritual in the book did Howie realize that the kid had been trying to help him, even while lying to his face.

"Father, what is he talking about?" Rachel asked.

"He's a fool. Do you understand what this act means? What you're going to endure?"

Howie nodded, tears silently rolling down his cheeks. He thought of everything he'd lost because of this demon, because of the coven. And now, he was about to lose himself. But this time, his loss would benefit those he loved most.

"By blood and breath, I offer myself to The Withered Tongues, to seal the pact and grant power eternal."

Vorathor laughed, knowing those binding words locked it in. Knowing after all these years, Howie Burke was his. Bethany tugged at Howie, trying to stop him from doing anything. But it was too late. The words had been spoken. Forever binding. As soon as the last word left his lips, a burning sensation spread through Howie's body. He felt like he was melting from the inside. Every movement pained him. He turned to Bethany, allowing the tears to flow freely.

"I love you, Bethany Carver. I always have."

"Howie. Please, there has to be a way to stop it. *Please.*"

He shook his head, ignoring the flames spreading inside of him.

"This is the only way. To s-stop them forever—"

His sentence was cut short as he dropped to one knee, wincing in pain.

"You think this is going to stop us, you fucking imbecile? Nothing will stop us. We are eternal," Vorathor growled. He reached Howie in two large steps, grabbing him by the back of the neck and dragging him to the center of the dock. Bethany and Ryan clung to one another while Rachel watched on in stunned silence.

"I accept this new host, this sacrifice. And in turn, I will let the boy and mother live."

The demon latched on to Howie's arms, its claws wrapping around his wrists and fusing into the skin. The pond began to swirl, glowing bright green once more. The sound of distant thunder cracked through the night as a strong gust of wind blew through the campground. The glow moved across the water, climbing up the dock like marina mist and wrapping around both Howie and Vorathor.

"Howie!" Bethany yelled. Nearby, Rachel stood motionless with shock and awe.

He wanted to respond, to tell her she was safe now, but his last bit of energy needed to focus on the next part of his plan. His skin began to radiate. Vorathor inhaled, pulling some of the sacrificial life force. Howie waited. He waited until the demon had taken almost all he had left, and then it realized something was wrong.

"What...what did you do?"

Vorathor stared down at Howie's arm where the sleeve had burned away as they merged, revealing blistered skin. Revealing the symbol Howie had carved into his forearm before they left for the pond.

"And let this host be your tomb. Sealed not in stone, but in my soul. Where we will rot in Hell for eternity."

The symbol that he'd pulled from the notebook—a swirling circle with the tip pointed like an arrow—alone, it was useless. But with the words spoken and with the demon agreeing, it guaranteed a return to where the demon belonged.

Behind them, the glowing green water continued to churn, changing to a blood red color. The pond swelled and then collapsed, creating a funnel in the center that began to drain the water. The surrounding land rumbled; trees snapped and fell over. A few of the bodies of coven members were sucked into the watery vortex. Bethany hobbled with Ryan arm in arm, away from the water, keeping her eyes locked on Howie the entire time. Rachel remained paralyzed.

Howie screamed as he and Vorathor melded together, and from the symbol, Howie's blood trailed down his arm and wrapped around the body of Felix Ruger. Vorathor roared in agony as the funnel whipped around violently, picking up speed and force. And then Howie felt its pull. There was no stopping it. The demon tried to fight it, digging his clawed feet into the dock, which scraped along the wood as they were pulled to the edge.

"What have you done?! This is not the ritual!"

"You wanted my bloodline, now you're stuck with it," Howie said through gritted teeth.

"Howie!" Bethany yelled, and Howie forced his head to turn, fighting the pull of the pond. He made eye contact with her one last time. "I love you too."

He had just enough time to see a single tear slide down her cheek, then he was yanked into the water. Into the hole forming in the center—a portal directly to Hell. Howie's chest caved inward, his bones cracking and snapping throughout his body as he and Vorathor were pulled into the portal, the pond draining entirely into Hell. As soon as they vanished, the fiery pit closed around them.

The remaining Thred tweakers collapsed.

Then everything went quiet.

The curse was no more.

Bethany stared at the empty space where the pond used to be, now just a giant muddy circle with a hole in the center.

"Mom...where did he go? Will he come back?" Ryan asked quietly.

It was the first thing he'd said since they had arrived to save him.

Her voice trembled. "No, baby. He's gone. He saved us."

They cried together, and Ryan, seeing his mother unable to walk on her own, tried his best to help hold her up. Shawn lay at the edge of the grass, still clutching his partially severed arm. His skin was pale and glistening as dawn emerged from behind the trees.

"Shawn, can you call for help?"

"When we get back to my car. Can you help me up?"

In that moment, they had forgotten one last loose end. Behind them, Rachel snapped out of her devastated shock.

"You fucking ruined it! The ritual must be completed!" Rachel yelled as she charged from the dock. She ran right for Ryan, who pulled away from Bethany, accidentally sending his mom to the ground. Bethany attempted to get to her feet, but Rachel pulled Ryan toward the hole in the pond, dead set on throwing the boy to the demons.

"Ryan!" Bethany shouted.

"Vodyanoy, where are you? You did nothing to stop this! You're the fucking water demon!" Rachel screamed.

Ryan cried out as she squeezed his wrist tightly and pulled.

Bethany attempted to hobble toward them but was no match for the crazed coven member.

Rachel reached the center of the pond, ankle-deep in sludge. She brought Ryan to the edge of the hole.

"Let me go, Tanya! Please!"

"I'm not Tanya, you little brat! Now shut the fuck up while I finish the ritual."

Bethany worried that she wouldn't make it to them in time on one leg. Then she heard a *click*, and Shawn yelled, "Bethany, duck!"

She dropped to the ground, giving Shawn a clear shot. Rachel chanted in Latin and the hole pulsed green.

"You can't kill the bloodline! The Rugers are etern—"

Shawn fired.

Rachel's head snapped to the side as the bullet lodged in her skull, and she stopped chanting. She released her grip on Ryan, then fell face-first into the hole, disappearing within the void.

Ryan stared in shock at the black hole, then looked back at Bethany and ran through the mud to get to her. He wrapped his arms around her and cried. Next to them, Shawn also sobbed in relief, in agony, in grief. Bethany knew in her heart that it was really over this time. Howie had saved them. When there were no more tears to shed, the three of them made it back through the woods, leaving the coven behind for good.

EPILOGUE
Excerpt

**From *We Were Always Cursed:*
*The Howie Burke Memoir***

If I could go back to 1999 and stop us from digging up that grave, I would. Every day since has been full of darkness. As I drive through Newport, a carcass of its former self, I'd do anything to step into a time machine and go back to before this all started, even for just one last day with my friends. We live like life lasts forever, as if we are invincible, when the fact is: we all meet our demise someday.

Just one more day with the guys, to tell them how much I love them. Tell them how much they still mean to me a few decades later. There was nothing as magical as being out in those woods filming our horror movies with Cory, Todd, and Ryan. We were that cliché "kids on bikes" group of the nineties. Nerds obsessed with video games and horror movies. Laughing at offensive mom jokes without a care in the world.

We lived like we had forever when we should have lived like it was the last time we'd see each other.

We never said aloud how important we were to one another. And speaking for myself, those guys meant *everything* to me.

Ryan, with his ridiculous charm and obsession with shooting games. His standard camouflage attire, even though he never served a single day in the military. I like to think he lived each day like he thought he was an action hero, a single scene away from saving the world. And in a way? That's exactly what he did. He died fighting Jessica Black, trying to avenge his dad and protect the people he loved. If you're reading from heaven, big guy, I love you.

Todd, what can I say about you? You were always there when we needed a good laugh. Never taking life too seriously, and while sometimes that drove us crazy, it was the levity we didn't know we needed. I can't hear a dick joke without thinking of you. Todd died trying to protect us, too, and the world is duller without him in it.

Which brings me to Cory, my best friend in the world. The one I told my darkest secrets to. We met in third grade out on the playground, where we compared our *Teenage Mutant Ninja Turtle* action figures. The rest is history. We bonded over everything from sports to WWF, to movies, and music. When you saw my dad hurt me and I begged you to keep it a secret, you did it, no questions asked. And when I asked you and the guys to keep secret what we found out in the woods, you all did it.

This is my biggest regret in life. I know we all would have done the same for any of us if the roles were reversed, but by me forcing you all to keep that secret, it allowed the horrific events to unfold. It allowed for so many people to die. And I understand that while I was the one responsible, the curse was here generations before any of us. The coven held a grasp on Newport for decades, and all we did was stir up their dirty little secrets.

Knowing that doesn't make me feel any better. I lost my best friends. I lost my dad. And I lost my home. So, while my first choice would be to go back before we ever discovered Jessica Black's grave, my second choice with a time machine would be to go back and protect all those who protected me. I'd sacrifice myself for those I loved. Put them first. I've lived my life as an empty shell of myself ever since 1999.

I still want to believe there's hope. I want to believe that the next generation won't have to suffer the way we did, and that the world will be a better place without the coven or their monsters. If there is one thing that you readers take away from this book, I hope it's that you never take life for granted. Tell the people you love how much they mean to you. Call friends you haven't heard from in a while and ask how they're doing. We might not be able to change the curse we were dealt, but we can rise above it.

Acknowledgements

What a wild ride. This series has come straight from my heart, and I have a lot of thanks to give for it coming to fruition. First, as always, thank you to my wife, Danielle, and my kids, Will and Ellie, as you all cheered me on to chase the writing dream, and for a (brief) minute, my kids even thought I was cool. Thank you to Crystal Lake Publishing for giving the series a home after I self-published the first book as my debut novel. Those amazing covers you see in this series? Matt Seff Barnes is responsible for all of them, and they absolutely catch the attention of the reader. This book has been through many edits, but the editor I always use for myself on self-published work, as well as books through publishers, is Danielle Yeager. I highly recommend her (as long as I still have slots open for my edits!). My Patreon people have a dedicated thank-you page in this book, but I will thank them here as well, because they believe enough in me to keep coming back for more. My author friends who have become some of my best friends over the last three to four years, Nick Roberts, Felix Blackwell, Gage Greenwood, Jay Bower, John Lynch, Sammy Scott. I talk with these guys almost every single day, and it has made this writing journey so much more fun. They are all phenomenal writers that I'm lucky to have as friends. Thank you to all of my beta readers and ARC readers, for without you this book would have looked a little different. I can't go without thanking the town of Newport, New Hampshire, the real-life place that inspired this book. I can assure you—the real town doesn't have any covens or demonic witches lurking in the woods (or does it?), but it has a lovely small-town vibe and just so happens to be the place where I grew up and let my imagination run wild. Lastly, thank you all of you readers for continuing to read my books, follow me on social media, and connect with me at events. I love every second of it!

John Durgin
December 2025

About the Author

John Durgin is an award-nominated author. Growing up in New Hampshire, he discovered Stephen King much younger than most probably should have, reading *IT* before he reached high school—and knew from that moment on he wanted to write horror. His debut novel, *The Cursed Among Us*, released in June 2022 and went on to become an Amazon bestseller. Next up, his sophomore novel, *Inside The Devil's Nest*, released in January 2023, followed by his debut collection, *Sleeping In The Fire*, in June 2023. In 2024, he released two more novels, starting with *Kosa*, which released to stellar reviews, and *Consumed by Evil* through Crystal Lake Publishing. His most recent novels are *The Devil's In The Next Room* and *The Envelope*.

johndurginauthor.com
Twitter/X: @jdurgin1084
Instagram: @durginpencildrawings
TikTok: @johndurgin_author
Facebook: John Durgin author
Big Cartel (signed books): johndurginauthor.bigcartel.com

A Special Thanks to John Durgin's Patreon Members

Alicia Toothman, Crystal Evans, Janeth Acevedo, Julia Terry, Mary Trujillo, Megan Stevens, Meredith Livingston, Paige French, Sophia McIntyre, Aaron Masters, Gage Greenwood, Molly Mix, Stephanie Winegeart, Jay Bower, Megan Stockton, Tyler Shields, Carisa Kyle, Jim Donohue, Tim Feely, Shanda Langley, Michael Livingston, Andrew Nicolle, Stefanie Silvestri, Nicole Sonnenburg, Kayla Bullock, Stephanie Montelione, Mike Hughes, Jae Mazer.

THE END?

Not if you want to dive into more of Crystal Lake Publishing's Tales from the Darkest Depths!

Check out our amazing website and online store or download our latest catalog here.

We always have great new projects and content on the website to dive into, as well as a newsletter, behind the scenes options, social media platforms, our own dark fiction shared-world series and our very own webstore. Our webstore even has categories specifically for KU books, non-fiction, anthologies, and of course more novels and novellas.

Readers...

Thank you for reading *Conjuring the Demon*. We hope you enjoyed this novel. If you have a moment, please review *Conjuring the Demon* at the store where you bought it.

Help other readers by telling them why you enjoyed this book. No need to write an in-depth discussion. Even a single sentence will be greatly appreciated. Reviews go a long way to helping a book sell, and is great for an author's career. It'll also help us to continue publishing quality books.

Thank you again for taking the time to journey with Crystal Lake Publishing.

You will find links to all our social media platforms on our Linktree page. https://linktr.ee/CrystalLakePublishing

Follow us on Amazon:

MISSION STATEMENT

Since its founding in August 2012, Crystal Lake has quickly become one of the world's leading publishers of Dark Fiction and Horror books. In 2023, Crystal Lake officially transitioned into an entertainment company, joining several other divisions, genres, and imprints, including Torrid Waters, Sinister Smile Press, Crystal Lake Comics, Crystal Lake Games, Crystal Cove Press, Crystal Lake Kids, Memento Mori Ink, and The House of Shadows & Ink on YouTube.

While we strive to present only the highest quality fiction and entertainment, we also endeavor to support authors along their writing journey. We offer our time and experience in non-fiction projects, as well as author mentoring and services, at competitive prices.

With several Bram Stoker Award wins and many other wins and nominations (including the HWA's Specialty Press Award), Crystal Lake puts integrity, honor, and respect at the forefront of our publishing operations.

We strive for each book and outreach program we spearhead to not only entertain and touch or comment on issues that affect our readers, but also to strengthen and support the Dark Fiction field and its authors.

Not only do we find and publish authors we believe are destined for greatness, but we strive to work with men and women who endeavor to be decent human beings who care more for others than themselves, while still being hard-working, driven, and passionate artists and storytellers.

Crystal Lake is and will always be a beacon of what passion and dedication, combined with overwhelming teamwork and respect, can accomplish. We endeavor to know each and every one of our readers, while building personal relationships with our authors, reviewers, bloggers, podcasters, bookstores, and libraries.

We will be as trustworthy, forthright, and transparent as any business can be, while also keeping most of the headaches away from our authors, since it's our job to solve the problems so they can stay in a creative mind. Which of course also means paying our authors.

We do not just publish books, we present to you worlds within your world, doors within your mind, from talented authors who sacrifice so much for a moment of your time.

There are some amazing small presses out there, and through collaboration and open forums we will continue to support other presses in the goal of helping authors and showing the world what quality small presses are capable of accomplishing. No one wins when a small press goes down, so we will always be there to support hardworking, legitimate presses and their authors. We don't see Crystal Lake as the best press out there, but we will always strive to be the best, strive to be the most interactive and grateful, and even blessed press around. No matter what happens over time, we will also take our mission very seriously while appreciating where we are and enjoying the journey.

What do we offer our authors that they can't do for themselves through self-publishing?

We are big supporters of self-publishing (especially hybrid publishing), if done with care, patience, and planning. However, not every author has the time or inclination to do market research, advertise, and set up book launch strategies. Although a lot of authors are successful in doing it all, strong small presses will always be there for the authors who just want to do what they do best: write.

What we offer is experience, industry knowledge, contacts and trust built up over years. And due to our strong brand and trusting fanbase, every Crystal Lake book comes with weight of respect. In time our fans begin to trust our judgment and will try a new author purely based on our support of said author.

To date we've published around 300 books, and with each launch we strive to fine-tune our approach, learn from our mistakes, and increase our reach. We continue to assure our authors that we're here for them and that we'll carry the weight of the launch and deal with third parties while they focus on their strengths—be it writing, interviews, blogs, signings, etc.

We also offer several mentoring packages to authors that include knowledge and skills they can use in both traditional and self-publishing endeavors. This includes Shadows & Ink Creators on our The House of Shadows & Ink YouTube channel and our Crystal Lake Academy.

We look forward to launching many new careers.

This is what we believe in. What we stand for. This will be our legacy.

Welcome to Crystal Lake Publishing—Where Stories Come Alive!